# Interlude

## Books by Lin Stepp

Novels:
*The Foster Girls*
*Tell Me About Orchard Hollow*
*For Six Good Reasons*
*Delia's Place*
*Second Hand Rose*
*Down by the River*
*Makin' Miracles*
*Saving Laurel Springs*
*Welcome Back*
*Daddy's Girl*
*Lost Inheritance*

The Edisto Trilogy:
*Claire at Edisto*

Christmas Novella:
*A Smoky Mountain Gift*
In *When the Snow Falls*

Regional Guidebooks
Co-Authored with J.L. Stepp:
*The Afternoon Hiker*
*Discovering Tennessee State Parks*

# The Interlude

## A SMOKY MOUNTAIN NOVEL

## LIN STEPP

MOUNTAIN HILL PRESS

The Interlude
Copyright © 2019 by Lin Stepp
Published by Mountain Hill Press
Email contact: steppcom@aol.com

This is a work of fiction. Although numerous elements of historical and geographic
accuracy are utilized in this and other novels in the Smoky Mountain series, many other
specific environs, place names, characters, and incidents are the product of the author's
imagination or used fictitiously.

Scripture used in this book, whether quoted or paraphrased by the characters, is taken
from the King James Version of the Bible.

Cover design: Katherine E. Stepp
Interior design: J. L. Stepp, Mountain Hill Press
Editor: Elizabeth S. James
Cover photo and map design: Lin M. Stepp

Library of Congress Cataloging-in-Publication Data

Stepp, Lin
The Interlude: A Smoky Mountain novel / Lin Stepp
        p. cm – (The Smoky Mountain series)
ISBN: 978-0-9985063-6-4
First Mountain Hill Press Trade Paperback Printing: April 2019

eISBN: 978-0-9985063-8-8
First Mountain Hill Press Electronic Edition: April 2019

1. Women—Southern States—Fiction    2. Mountain life—Great Smoky Mountains
Region (NC and TN)—Fiction.   3. Contemporary Romance—Inspirational—Fiction.
I. Title

Library of Congress Control Number: 2019931135

This book—set in the Pittman Center and Greenbrier Cove area—is dedicated to the memory of Glenn Cardwell (1930-2016). A former Great Smoky Mountains Park Naturalist for thirty-four years and beloved long-time mayor of Pittman Center for almost eighteen years, Glenn touched many lives and left a beautiful legacy. Glenn was dedicated to preserving the culture and natural beauty of his community, wrote two books documenting the history of the area, and freely shared his knowledge through talks and hikes. The Glenn Cardwell Heritage Museum at the Pittman Center Elementary School celebrates Glenn Cardwell's memory and Pittman Center's rich history. ... I was privileged to know Glenn and his wife Faye.

# ACKNOWLEDGMENTS

Special thanks go to all the individuals and organizations that contributed to this book, each in their own special ways ...

Thanks to the Dr. Robert F. Thomas Foundation, Dolly Parton, and Dollywood for continuing to honor the memory of Dr. Robert Thomas (1891–1980), physician and Methodist minister. Dr. Thomas served as Pittman Center's first doctor in the area's early years with love and devotion, providing spiritual comfort and medical care regardless of ability to pay.

Thanks also to the many actual organizations that inspired the "fictitious" groups who met in Nonnie Wingate's Butterfly Tea Room in this book ...
    (1) a Red Hat Group
    (2) a DAR (Daughters of the American Revolution) Group
    (3) an FCA (Family and Community Education) Group
    (4) a local Book Club
    (5) and a weekly women's group

Thanks to Elizabeth Ruffing and Max Bailey of Raleigh, NC, developers of the Ruffing's cat art dolls mentioned in this book—prized possessions of five-year-old Suzannah James. See all the Ruffing's beautiful art at: *ruffings.com*

Thanks, also, to those who work to make these books their best:
    ____ Elizabeth S. James, copyeditor and editorial advisor
    ____ J.L. Stepp, production design and proofing
    ____ Katherine Stepp, cover design and graphics

Continuing gratitude, also, to all my wonderful fans for loving and reading my books And special thanks to all who take the time to write book reviews to encourage others to enjoy my work. I so appreciate you.

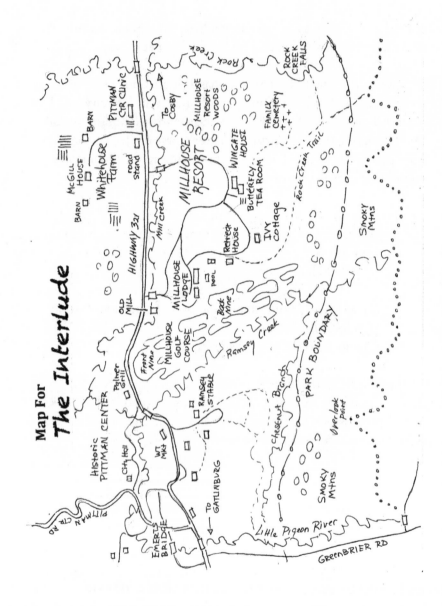

Map For
The Interlude

Historic PITTMAN CENTER

PITTMAN CTR RD

Cty Hall

Palmer Grill

WT Mkt

EMERTS BRIDGE

To GATLINBURG

Little Pigeon River

GREENBRIER RD

McGILL HOUSE

BARN

BARN

Whitehouse Farm

road stand

Highway 321

OLD MILL

PITTMAN CTR CLINIC

To COSBY

Mill Creek

MILLHOUSE LODGE

Front Nine

MILLHOUSE GOLF COURSE

Back Nine

RAMSEY STABLE

pool

MILLHOUSE RESORT

MILLHOUSE RESORT WOODS

WINGATE HOUSE

BUTTERFLY TEA ROOM

IVY COTTAGE

Retreat House

Ramsey Creek

Chestnut Branch

PARK BOUNDARY

Rock Creek

ROCK CREEK FALLS

FAMILY CEMETERY
+ + +

Rock Creek Trail

Smoky Mtns

Overlook Point

Smoky Mtns

# CHAPTER 1

**M**allory stood in line at the airport security checkpoint in Savannah, Georgia, waiting to pass through into the waiting area. The cackling laughter of the two women behind her and the whining of a small child in front of her made her head ache again. Putting a hand to her forehead, she almost stumbled as she reached the checkpoint.

"Are you all right, ma'am?" the security officer asked as she piled her briefcase, duffle bag, phone, and other items onto the conveyer belt for X-ray.

"I'm fine, simply a little tired," she answered, mustering up a smile as she offered the officer her ID and boarding pass.

Tired was a total understatement. She felt exhausted—and from only packing, riding to the airport with Nancy, and walking through the airport to her departure gate.

Earlier, when Nancy dropped her off at the terminal, she'd asked, "Will you be all right? I can go in and wait with you."

"No, go on home. I'll be fine." She'd offered her friend another of those practiced smiles she'd learned to give. When had smiling become so difficult?

Mallory sighed. Everything had demanded so much effort these last weeks since her collapse and stay at the hospital. Worse was having people tiptoe around her, acting so sweet and solicitous, always reminding her she'd been ill.

"You take it easy," Nancy told her earlier as Mallory got out of the car. "Get some rest at your grandparents' place. You've accumulated enough sick leave to sink a ship and we'll be fine without you, so don't worry."

She'd patted Mallory's arm. "David and I should have realized sooner you were under too much stress with your mother's illness, the ongoing care-giving, your heavy work load, and that unpleasant business with Ethan. Then the funeral arrangements hit and you caught that awful flu. It was enough to shred anyone's emotions and cause a little breakdown. You'll be yourself again before you know it after a good rest, exactly like Dr. Henry said."

Mallory sent another plastic smile Nancy's way, while wincing to hear the word *breakdown* again. She hated that word. She was never sick. She couldn't even remember the last time she took a sick day before this.

Moving to the waiting area, Mallory slumped into a seat, leaving her sunglasses on and closing her eyes behind them. *I just want my life back,* she thought.

She'd tried arguing with Dr. Henry about the idea of leaving town for a month or two of quiet but, admittedly, even her townhouse felt oppressive now—so full of memories that haunted her in the night hours, robbing her of sleep. Deep down, she knew it would be good to take a break.

When she tried to return to the office, shaky and rundown after she got out of the hospital, David shook a finger in her face. "What are you doing back in this office? You need a work break and a rest like your doctor recommended. In fact, when have you taken a vacation in the last few years anyway?"

"I went to New York, to LA, and to San Antonio last year."

David waved a hand dismissively. "Those were work trips to conferences. They don't count." Leaning over her desk, he gave her a stern look. "Nancy already made your plane reservation, Mallory. It's settled. Go and rest. Enjoy yourself. Sleep late. Get some fresh air, and don't come back until those dark circles under your eyes are gone and you feel like yourself again."

At the door, he paused, his voice dropping to a softer tone. "We care about you, M.T. Rest and get well. You've been under a lot of strain and you internalize. I'm not surprised your body finally said that's enough."

Mallory repeated his last words in her mind, remembering them. Perhaps that's what her body had shouted at last: *That's enough.*

With the priority seating of premium economy Nancy booked for her, Mallory soon made her way into the Delta jet, stored her duffle overhead, and settled into her seat by the window. She kept her briefcase with her, stuffed with personal items, her laptop and a few magazines for entertainment. The flight wouldn't be a long one, with only one stopover in Atlanta, and Nancy had arranged a rental car on the destination end.

Mallory glanced at the empty seat beside her, saying a prayer under her breath that its occupant wouldn't be someone difficult, someone prying. She watched as the other passengers boarded, glad to see the whining child and the talkative women pass her seat and head further down the aisle. Three businessmen took the seats across from her, and finally another tall man came down the aisle, pausing at the seat beside hers, and then settled into it after stowing his bag overhead. He carried a briefcase and laptop like the other men. *Good.* She hoped he would work during the flight and leave her to rest in peace and quiet. To Mallory's relief, he popped open his computer and began to check and send email.

After takeoff, Mallory closed her eyes for a short time and then opened them with a jerk, glancing out the window, as a rumble of thunder sounded.

"We're heading into a little bad weather, with worse coming," the man beside her said.

She glanced at him.

"Lucas here." He held out a hand.

"M.T." She replied, accepting the handshake.

"Which stands for?"

"M.T. is enough."

Unaffected, he looked across her and out the window. "This is an MD-80 jet airliner, a McConnell Douglas twin engine."

Mallory tried not to make a comment. Surely he wasn't one of those engineers to next launch into a technical explanation of airplane composition.

"Do you know how planes fly?" he asked.

She shook her head, wary now.

"Lift, weight, thrust, drag." He sailed a hand upward. "An airplane flies when all four forces work together."

She waited.

"I looked it up once." He grinned. "I had to read four Internet sites before I found one that made sense to me."

"So you're not an engineer?" She asked before she thought.

"No." He laughed, the kind of infectious laugh that makes you want to laugh simply hearing it. "I'm a golfer—or I was. I'm a golf pro now. I've been to a Pro-Am event in Savannah. Heading home. And you?"

"I'm an editor for a publishing company, taking a vacation to visit relatives."

He studied her, letting his eyes scan over her thoughtfully. "I've never met an editor."

"I've never met a golfer."

His eyes twinkled. "That's one of the things I like about flying on airplanes. You get to meet new and interesting people in a limited time capsule." He framed a small square with his hands. "You swap names, maybe only first names, chat a little about this or that. You might even say what you wouldn't say to someone you know well. You don't have an image to maintain or any expectations to fulfill, and you'll probably never see the person again. So it's like an interlude."

"An interlude." Mallory repeated the words. She liked words.

He leaned back in his seat and then turned to smile at her. "Tell me your first impressions of me, besides the fact that you thought I might be an engineer ready to launch into a technical explanation of aerodynamics."

"Why does it matter what I think?"

He cocked his head. "It's instructive to occasionally get feedback about first impressions."

"Why?"

He steepled his fingers as he considered her question. "People you know usually tell you what they *think* you want to hear or tell you information colored by what they already know about you."

"I see." He interested her, this man, and she liked the way his conversation pulled her away from thoughts of her own problems.

He spread his hands with a question in his eyes. "So? Tell me your first impressions."

"All right." She conceded, deciding it was harmless to play along. "My first impression was that you were a businessman, like the three across the aisle."

His eyes shifted in their direction. "Even with my tan corduroy jacket versus their neat three-piece suits?"

"I missed that." She smiled. "But you carried the comfortable, professional bearing of a confident, well-traveled man—easy with himself."

"I like that," he said, considering her words. "And in looks, what was your first impression?"

She studied him more carefully. "Tall, dark, and relatively handsome. Interesting eyes. A strong face. You should like that impression."

He grinned at her, obviously pleased.

"I'd say you're used to mastering people and situations," Mallory added, wanting to move the subject away from his looks. "Used to winning and to having things go your way."

"Not always." A frown crossed his face. "Life surprises you with more complications than you expect sometimes. Things you can't control. Things you can't fix."

"Yes, you're right," she said, realizing he held depths she wouldn't tap into during this short flight.

He smiled at her, a wide flash of teeth, and a charismatic smile you'd always notice. "As for my first impressions of you, I'd say you're more of an introvert than an extrovert like me."

"What makes you say that?"

"I watched you drop your eyes when I sat down, not initiate

conversation, then close your eyes to rest, shutting me out."

She crossed her arms. "Perhaps I was tired."

"Perhaps you are and maybe you really need this vacation." His eyes moved over her face. "But I think you worried I'd talk too much and pry."

"Just as you do."

He flashed a grin again. "But it's an interlude."

There was that word again. Mallory pulled a definition from her memory. "An interlude is an intervening space in time, an episode in a larger whole. In music, it's a composition inserted between the parts of a larger piece."

"Exactly. You're a thinker and smart, too. I saw that."

She raised an eyebrow in question.

He closed his laptop. "You dress like a woman who thinks and you have wise eyes."

"I hope that's a positive impression." She glanced down at her simple brown slacks outfit.

"Sure it is." His eyes roved over her, a little more intimately than she liked. "You're beautiful, too—tall, blond, leggy, with a good build. Pretty gray-blue eyes and smooth olive skin."

He leaned towards her—too close suddenly—startling her. Then he leaned back again. "You smell of a musky scent I like, too. What's it called?"

"White Musk." She hesitated before she answered, realizing he might be flirting. "You smell of Polo." He had leaned close enough for her to know and she wanted to shift the conversation away from herself.

"You recognized it." He shrugged. "I'm not very original in that."

"It suits you."

"What do you like to do for fun, M.T.?"

"Not talk this much." She opened her briefcase to take out a magazine and a pencil, flipping the pages open to a crossword puzzle. "Find something to occupy yourself, Lucas."

The stewardess stopped by then to offer colas, and Lucas

weaseled peanuts from her as well. He ate them in quiet, looking across her out the window, watching the rain.

When she paused, stumped in her puzzle a little later, he said, "Let me help you. I'm good at crossword puzzles and games."

She couldn't help a twitch of a smile at his persistence. He was like a charming child—appealing, eager, and difficult to say no to.

"All right." Mallory glanced down at her crossword puzzle. "What's a seven letter word for *objection* ending with a t?"

He looked over her shoulder. "Try *protest*." He tapped the page. "Then the word across, starting with a p, should be *piccolo*."

"Ah, yes, a small flute." She penciled in both words.

"You're good," she acknowledged. "What about this one?" Mallory pointed to another word she hadn't figured out yet, and they went to work together on the rest of the puzzle. Except that Lucas made her laugh throughout.

"You're fun," she admitted to him.

"And I was right that you're smart. I like that."

A crack of lightning startled them both, and the captain's voice came on telling them they would be passing through a little turbulence as they approached Atlanta.

"Where are you headed next?" Lucas asked as the jet started its descent.

"Changing planes to fly to Knoxville, Tennessee," she said, tucking her magazine back into her briefcase.

He beamed at her. "Well, it looks like our interlude is taking us a little further together. I'm heading to Knoxville, too, and then picking up my car to drive to a nearby town." He packed up his computer while he talked. "Atlanta is a killer of an airport if you don't know your way around it. Stay with me and I'll zip you through the crowds faster. We can grab a bite to eat at the Café Intermezzo during our layover. We have time."

"The Café what?"

He feigned shock. "I can't believe you haven't discovered the Café Intermezzo, you being an editor. It's practically inside a bookstore."

"Sounds interesting." She gathered up her things. "But you don't need to entertain me."

He flashed another wide, dazzling smile her way, which she imagined the cameras on the golf tour loved.

"It's an interlude, M.T. Why should we battle through the Atlanta airport alone and eat by ourselves when we can enjoy each other's company?" He sent her a questioning look. "Unless you're trying to get rid of me."

"It's not that …"

"Good." He interrupted, smiling at her as he unbuckled his seat belt to stand up. "I'll see if I can get our seats together on the next flight, too. With both of us in premium economy, it shouldn't be too hard."

Mallory, following him out of the plane, imagined Lucas could get whatever favors he wanted with his natural charm and charisma.

He whistled as he exited, even with the sound of rain still pelting outside. Nobody whistled anymore, but he made it sound as natural as anything, and Mallory caught several people smiling their way.

*Oh, well*, she thought, following along behind him. He was a happy interlude at least. She could use that sort of distraction right now.

The Café Intermezzo proved cozy and charming, set amid a calm oasis of books, with crisp white cloths covering the tables. No televisions blared around them, and only classical music played quietly in the background, even in the midst of the hectic terminal. Mallory loved it.

Seemingly at home from the minute he walked in the restaurant's door, Lucas greeted two of the waiters by name. They appeared to know him, and both began to talk to him about golf and updates on their lives, like old friends.

Mallory opened her menu to study it.

"The Italian Gnocchi and the Tuna Melt they serve here are great," Lucas told her, reading off the menu. "The French Dip on Garlic Toast is excellent, too, and, if you're into salads, the Almond Avocado Salad is fantastic."

She almost smirked at his enthusiasm. "What are you ordering?"

"Breakfast America." He laid down his menu. "I like breakfast late in the evening like this when I'm flying. Comes with eggs, sausage or bacon, good skillet potatoes, wheat toast or raisin bread."

"Plus great coffee," the waiter added, coming back to their table to bring water and take their order.

"Then I'll have the same." Mallory closed her menu. "Eggs lightly scrambled, bacon crisp, raisin bread with butter and honey. Cream for the coffee."

"You won't be sorry for ordering the breakfast," Lucas said when the waiter left. "It's easier on the stomach when you're flying, especially in storms. I checked several TVs passing by and listened to the talk around us. The whole area is in for some bad weather. Some flights are already delayed coming in."

"I hope ours isn't."

"Not the last I saw." He rearranged the salt-and-pepper shakers on the table as he talked, drumming his fingers in an erratic rhythm afterward.

Mallory shifted the shakers back to the right spot.

"Orderly," he said, his eyes lifting to hers. "Another impression. You like everything in its place."

She shook her head at his comment. "Obviously you don't, and you possess a lot of restless energy."

"No, just a high energy level." He popped his knuckles. "It's not a bad attribute, especially in my field."

"I guess not."

The waiter brought coffee and then their food. She and Lucas talked about mundane things over their meal—foods they liked, places they'd traveled.

"Have you been abroad?" he asked.

"No, but I've visited a number of cities in the States. I guess you've traveled overseas often."

"Yeah." He nodded. "Golfers travel a lot on tour but now I mainly do tournaments in the U.S."

She looked up from finishing the last bite of her toast. "Do you miss it? Being on tour?"

He lifted serious eyes to hers now. "Sometimes, but there were aspects of the pro life I don't miss. Fame changes you. You say it won't, but it does."

Lucas glanced at his watch before she could ask more about his remarks. "We need to leave in order to make our connection."

He paid the bill, overruling her objections to go Dutch, and then hustled them efficiently through the terminal and to their gate, managing to rearrange their seats so they could sit together again. Handing her a new boarding pass, he moved them through the crowd into the security check line.

Mallory usually disliked people handling her affairs, but at this particular time it felt nice to be coddled.

"We're still in the section where we get the extra legroom. I need it, being six foot two." Lucas glanced at her as he spoke. "You're tall, too," he said. "Five nine? Five ten?"

"I'm five ten, and I am tall." When younger, Mallory had disliked her height, especially in her early teens when she towered over the boys. Even now she stood taller than most men, but she'd grown comfortable with her height over time.

"I like tall women." Lucas's eyes moved over her. "They can keep pace with me better walking through crowded airports." He grinned. "And I don't have to lean down to kiss them and wrench my back."

Mallory saw the lady beside them smirk, and she gave Lucas a warning look. He only shrugged.

Rain streaked against the windows and lightning cracked the sky as they waited for their flight, but they boarded on time. As the plane taxied toward the runway, however, the captain came on to tell them they would be pulling over to the right side of the tarmac to wait for clearance, announcing a slight delay in takeoff.

Mallory heard the heavyset man across the aisle groan. He glanced her way, catching her eye. "Last flight when this happened, my plane sat delayed for two dang hours on the tarmac."

As he turned back to his companion, Mallory asked Lucas,

"What's happened? Why are we delayed?"

"It's the storm," he answered. "It probably delayed the takeoff or landing of some other flights and now the air controller has to coordinate traffic carefully. It's rare that a plane is stranded on the tarmac for more than a short time though."

Mallory glanced out the window. It had grown dark now and the wind howled, the rain lashing against the plane. It felt especially quiet and still with the engine shut down to conserve fuel, even though an auxiliary power unit kept some lighting on and the air moving inside. Mallory felt her still shaky anxiety levels rise with her thoughts. She knew her grandparents would worry if she was late and that they'd be watching for her.

"Your relatives picking you up in Knoxville?" Lucas asked, seeming to read her mind.

She shook her head. "No. They live out in the country. I didn't want them driving to the airport late. I rented a car. I only need to pick up the rental when I arrive."

"I doubt we'll get in now at 9:30 as scheduled, but we shouldn't be much later."

Mallory flipped the pages of one of her magazines to pass the time. It felt too quiet and dim in the plane. The man directly across from them fell asleep. She could hear him snoring softly in the quiet. Every minute seemed to crawl by at a snail's pace, the wind and rain whipping the outside of the airplane. Mallory fidgeted with her seatbelt, picked at some lint on her slacks, and studied her nails—hating the delay, hating the way it played with her emotions, already thin.

"Have you ever been delayed on an airplane before?" Lucas asked.

"No." She swallowed, uncomfortable.

"I've experienced tons of delays—some in the airport terminal, some on the tarmac like this. The only ones that rattle me are the delays involving problems with the airplane's mechanics." He drummed his fingers on the armrest. "I'll take weather issues any day over wondering if the ground crew got my plane fixed before they let it take off again."

Mallory felt herself tense more at the vision this played in her mind. She clenched her fists in her lap.

"Stop that." Lucas reached over to put a hand on her clenched fists. "You need to relax. I was trying to make you laugh with that last story."

"Well, it didn't work." A crash of thunder outside made her jerk in her seat. Mallory felt her heart began to race, her breathing quicken. She hated that her emotions were so ragged. Was she starting to have a panic attack?

Lucas offered some more casual conversation, but Mallory couldn't concentrate on his words. She found herself growing increasingly anxious as the minutes ticked by, the quiet and dark of the plane seeming to envelope her.

"You need to get your mind off this," she heard Lucas say, but her eyes only flew to the window to watch the next streak of lightning slash across the sky.

"Here, let's try this," he said.

And before she realized what he was doing, he leaned over, took her face in his hands and kissed her.

Mallory felt so shocked at first that she froze, but as his lips brushed over hers and his hands moved under her hair to gently rub the skin on her neck, she found herself, with surprise, relaxing and responding. He did this well, kissing, like he seemed to do everything else well.

"Don't think about the plane," he murmured against her ear, his lips soft against her neck. "Think about kissing. Remember it's only an interlude, entertainment in a short space of time. For a moment."

An interlude, Mallory thought, and I'll never see this man again after tonight. Almost giggling at the idea, she let herself relax a little.

Sensing the change, Lucas moved his lips back to hers, kissing her with sweetness and expertise.

Mallory smiled against his lips. This was nice, this odd interlude, especially after all she'd been through recently. She kissed Lucas back, threading her hands into his hair, enjoying the thick texture of it and liking the warm male feel of him. He'd become a bit of a friend on this flight, she reasoned to herself, and even more familiar over dinner.

"It's like a kiss goodnight." She whispered the words without thinking, and Lucas chuckled, pulling back to look at her and to run a hand down her cheek.

"Yes, and now whenever you remember getting stuck in a Delta jet on the tarmac in Atlanta you'll remember that crazy guy who kissed you in the dark."

"Perhaps I will." She had to smile at his words.

Before he could kiss her again, or before Mallory could decide if she wanted him to, the plane's engines revved and the captain's voice came on telling them they were clear for takeoff. The lights blinked on more brightly then, and everyone began to talk and prepare to move out on the runway.

Looking out the window as they taxied through the rain, Mallory felt a secret smile touch her thoughts. Lucas didn't know any of the things she'd been through recently, and he would probably never know what his impetuous move did to restore her confidence and sense of worth. Wasn't it funny how an impulsive kiss from a handsome man could do more for a woman's self-assurance than a sweep of therapy sessions?

"Kissing is highly underrated as a tension-relieving activity," she said without thinking.

"Kissing a beautiful and smart woman is never underrated to me." He smiled at her, settling back in his seat, looking smug. "And I'm expecting you to get that crossword book out again once we get in the air. It's building my ego to beat out an editor with words."

She put a hand on one hip. "You've hardly beat me out, I'll have you know. I simply let you help me a little."

"Is that so?" he teased, and Mallory felt more of the last month's tensions ease away with their banter. This interlude stranger was good for her.

# CHAPTER 2

**D**espite the late flight and the delay in Atlanta, Lucas slept well after returning home to the resort near Gatlinburg. And now a new day had begun.

After digging out his five-year old's shoes from under a chair, Lucas turned to find his child hanging upside down over the side of the bed.

"Sit up Suzannah, so I can get your shoes on. We need to walk over to Nonnie's so I can get to the golf course. I'm giving a lesson this morning."

Suzannah glanced up at him with bright blue eyes and an impish grin. "I was pulling the string for Babycakes. She's under the bed."

Lucas saw a cat paw swipe out from under the bed skirt to snatch at the yarn string that Suzannah dangled over the bedside.

He grinned. "Well, Baby will have to wait for games until you get home later today. Let's get your shoes on now."

She sat up on the bed, pushing her stockinged feet toward him. Lucas dropped to one knee and began putting her tennis shoes on over her socks.

"I can almost tie my own shoes now, Daddy," Suzannah said, watching him.

"Yeah, I know you can. You only need a little more practice and you'll have it down flat." He leaned over to kiss her knee, making her giggle. "Tell me our rhyme for tying shoes."

"Right over left and left over right," she recited. "Makes the knot neat and tidy and tight." She squinted her eyes, watching him tie the bow on the first shoe. "Maybe I can tie the other one, Daddy."

"You probably could, pumpkin, but we need to hurry, so we'll work on it more later." Lucas finished tying off the second lace quickly. "Maybe you can ask Nonnie to help you after breakfast."

"Are you eating breakfast with Nonnie, too?" she asked.

"I am, and that's another reason we're trying to hurry. Nonnie and Beau invited us to eat with them this morning. I don't want her to have to wait for us or for our breakfast to get cold." He lifted her off the bed in a swoop that made her giggle again.

"Find your doll EdithAnn and whatever else you want to take so we can go." He handed her a child's tote bag he'd already loaded with a few items, watching her stuff her favorite doll into the top so the doll's head stuck out. She sure came up with odd names for her dolls, stuffed animals, and pets.

"Do EdithAnn and I need a jacket?"

"No, with June here now the mornings are warm. I don't think you'll need one." He leaned over to pick up the fluffy brown-striped cat from off the floor as he answered. "I'll drop Baby off on the screened porch as we leave. Since it's sunny, she can go in or out the cat door as she pleases today. She likes to do that."

"I think Babycakes is getting fat like Mrs. Mertz," Suzannah said as she followed him down the stairs.

He chuckled. "Well, don't tell your Sunday School teacher you think she's getting fat, okay? It might hurt her feelings."

"Doesn't she know it?"

"Yeah, she probably does, but people don't like you to tell them things about their appearance that are critical or unflattering."

"Even if it's the truth?"

"Even if."

She considered this as they let themselves out the screen door and started down the quiet walkway leading from their backyard through a patch of open woods to the Wingates' house nearby.

"I don't get mad when you tell me I have peanut butter on my face or dirt on my bottom from playing outside."

"Well, that's different." Lucas frowned, trying to figure out how to explain.

"Maybe Mrs. Mertz doesn't want to be fat but she is and she doesn't want anyone to say anything about it." Suzannah tucked a hand into his. "Do you think that's it, Daddy?"

"You've got the right idea, Suzannah." Her Twinkle Toes tennis shoes sparkled in the sunshine with each step as the colorful lights blinked on the toes of each shoe. "Like your story book, most of the time if you can't say anything nice, it's best not to say anything at all. Then you're safe."

"Okay." She skipped to keep pace with him and changed the subject as she did. "I'm staying with Nonnie until I can go to Aunt Elizabeth's after she gets back from taking Abby to the dentist and maybe getting Abby new shoes. Abby said she wants Twinkle Toes like mine."

Lucas grinned. Abby and Suzannah, like two peas in a pod, liked many of the same things.

Suzannah looked up at him with big blue eyes, her fine, blond hair shining in the sunshine. "Abby has a birthday this week and she will be five like me, and this fall we'll go to kindergarten."

Lucas looked forward to that in some ways, even though he hated to see Suzannah grow up. Shuffling her around every day to stay with his sister Elizabeth, or to stay with Nonnie or another friend or sitter when Elizabeth was too busy or Abby sick, took a lot of planning and thought.

"I guess we need to think about what to get Abby for her birthday," Lucas said, slowing as they passed by Nonnie's famous Butterfly Garden. The garden lay to the back of Wingate House right behind the Butterfly Tea Room where Nonnie held small women's luncheons and events.

"Nonnie's garden is getting pretty," Suzannah said, in tune with his thoughts. "Look, I see some butterflies."

They stopped for a minute to look over the white, picket fence, Lucas making an effort to name the butterflies he knew. Small children always wanted specifics. Because a rural train crossed a road nearby, often stopping their car with a crossbar at the tracks, Lucas had needed to research all the names of the train cars that passed to satisfy Suzannah's avid curiosity.

She turned to shoot him a question, not related to butterflies in any way, typical for a young child whose active mind jumped from one subject to another. "Nonnie's friend said that Nonnie was like my grandmother, but she's not my real grandmother, is she?"

"No, Nonnie is a friend, but she and her husband Beau are like grandparents to you. They've loved you since you were only a little thing from when you first came to Millhouse Resort."

"To live with you because Mommy died."

"Yes." Lucas hoped they wouldn't need to get into this subject more today.

"But I have two *real* grandmothers," she added.

"Yes." Lucas jumped onto that topic, relieved. "You have your Gramma Louise, my mother, who lives nearby in Knoxville."

"She lives with Grampa Clinton," Suzannah interrupted. "And they are Abby's Gramma and Grampa, too."

"That's right, because Abby's mother Elizabeth and I are sister and brother."

"I'd like to have a brother or sister."

"Well, there's not much I can do about that right now, but you have Abby. She's almost like a sister."

"Almost." She considered that, reaching out a hand so a blue butterfly could light on it.

"You also have your Grandmother and Grandfather Bernhard out west in Nevada, your mother's parents."

"I don't hardly ever see them though. They live far."

"Yes, they do live far, but they love you." Her took her hand again to lead her toward the house now. "You have a lot of people who love you."

"Nonnie says I am blessed."

"That's true. You are," he replied, opening a side gate and starting across the patio to let himself into the back door of Wingate House.

The sunny kitchen of Nonnie and Beau Wingate's home felt like a second home to Lucas. Not only had Beau Wingate offered Lucas a job at Millhouse Resort as the golf pro and assistant resort manager, at a time when he felt undecided about his future, but the couple had also taken him under their wing almost like a son from the first. When Cecily died, they'd taken Suzannah into their hearts, too. She'd been barely two then.

"There's my favorite girl!" Nonnie squatted down and held out her arms to Suzannah for a hug. Beau Wingate got up from his seat at the kitchen table to swing the little girl into his arms, too, giving her a big bear hug.

"You forgot to growl." Suzannah pushed her lower lip out at him in a pout. Beau rumbled a good bear growl for her in response, snuggling her and trying to take a chomp out of her shoulder, making her squeal.

"Put that child in her seat," Nonnie said. "I've got breakfast ready to serve."

She brought a platter of scrambled eggs and linked sausages to the table and then returned with a big bowl of cream gravy and another of grits. When Nonnie Wingate decided to cook breakfast, she did it right.

Lucas snagged the platter of homemade biscuits from the counter and put them on the big kitchen table to help her out. "This looks wonderful," he said, putting Suzannah into her booster seat and then sitting down in the chair beside hers.

They settled in to eat breakfast then, Suzannah chattering happily. Lucas loved Nonnie's big breakfasts and ate with relish.

"There are butterflies outside and butterflies inside," Suzannah chirped, pointing all around her in the kitchen.

Lucas hid a smirk by lifting his coffee cup to his mouth. Nonnie Wingate had a passion for butterflies and had indulged herself especially in her kitchen and tearoom décor. The large Wingate kitchen, crisp, white, and sunny, with a multitude of tall windows, was lavishly decorated with butterfly prints on the walls, butterfly and pansy wallpaper, and an array of white dishes embellished with colorful hand-painted moths and more butterflies. As typical, a flurry of bright butterflies circled the borders of Lucas's plate this morning and a large green butterfly decorated his coffee cup. Nonnie had even ordered plastic butterfly child ware for Suzannah with her name imprinted on her cup, plate, and bowl.

"Butterflies make your kitchen happy," Suzannah said, holding up her pink butterfly mug to show it off.

Nonnie smiled. "I've always thought so."

Beau nodded, reaching for another helping of grits. "And I've always called you my Butterfly Lady, Nona Nelle."

Lucas knew that Beau, loving Nonnie as he did, had given her a free hand in decorating, but Beau told Lucas once that he'd put his foot down about having butterflies in more than the kitchen, tearoom, one guest room and a bath.

"Enough's enough," he'd said with a twinkle in his eye. "I told Nonnie if she needed more butterflies, I'd build her a danged insectarium."

Sometimes when Lucas looked across the room at the short, stocky, balding man across from him, white haired and full-faced, it was hard to remember a formidable businessman lay underneath the soft exterior. And although Beau's manner appeared easy-going and friendly, you wouldn't want to cross him or pull anything on him. He possessed a keen discernment and had a brilliant business mind. He'd proved it continuing the growth of the Millhouse Resort he inherited and he'd taken it to even greater heights.

"Lucas, have another biscuit and gravy," Nonnie said, passing him the platter of biscuits across the big table in the kitchen's eat-in area.

"Gosh, no, Nonnie. I'm already stuffed, but thanks." He got up to get himself another cup of coffee.

"Ah, here's my *other* favorite girl," he heard Nonnie say behind him. "I didn't even set a plate for you, sweetie, thinking you'd be worn out after your trip."

"All the wonderful smells from your kitchen woke me," Lucas heard a low throaty voice say.

Feeling an odd prickle, he turned around to see the girl from the airplane standing in the doorway, wearing a long, flirty pink skirt and a white camisole top, her feet bare and her dark honey-colored hair loose around her shoulders. Lucas felt sure his mouth dropped open, and he noticed her eyes pop wide.

Nonnie smiled at him, apparently not noticing his unease. "Lucas James, this is our granddaughter Mallory Wingate. She's come up from Savannah, Georgia, to spend six to eight weeks with us." Turning her eyes to the girl, she said, "Mallory, this is Lucas James, the golf pro and assistant manager of the resort. I'm sure you remember me writing when he came to work here."

Oblivious to the shocked expression still on her granddaughter's face, Nonnie gestured to Suzannah. "This is Lucas's daughter Suzannah, the other love of your granddaddy's and my life. They live on the resort in Ivy Cottage."

"I've seen your picture in Nonnie's scrapbook," Suzannah said, sending Mallory a sunny smile. "Nonnie tells me stories about you and reads me books she used to read to you."

Lucas cleared his throat, glancing toward Mallory. "I think we might have met on the plane last night," he put in, deciding to smooth over this awkward moment. "I must have remembered your name wrong. I thought you said M.T."

"That's the girl's work name, M.T. Wingate, short for Mallory Taylor Wingate," Beau put in. "She uses it for business with her editing work with Whittier Publishing House. She's an associate editor there." He said the last words with obvious pride. "But around here she's just our Mallory." He got up from his chair to give her a warm hug and then directed her toward the seat where Nonnie had finished setting out tableware and silver for her.

"I think everything is still warm, darling," Nonnie said, sitting back down and beginning to pass dishes Mallory's way.

Lucas decided he'd had about all this domestic scene he wanted for the morning. "Look, I've got a lesson with Hap Mullins at ten, so I'm going to head on over to the golf course." He glanced at Beau. "I need to meet with Dale and Andy, too, about those problems we've been having around the resort. I'll talk to Barry afterward, as well."

"You do that," Beau said. "I'll come over later when your lesson with Hap is finished and you can fill me in."

Nonnie sent a smile his way. "Lucas, when Elizabeth gets back, I'll walk Abby down to her house if she doesn't stop by here and pick her up first." She waved a hand. "So don't you worry about her one little bit. You just pick Suzannah up as usual at Elizabeth's when you get off from work."

"Thank you for keeping her for me this morning," he said, walking over to give Nonnie a peck on the cheek. "And thanks for the wonderful breakfast, too."

Seeing Suzannah raise her arms, he walked around the table to wrap her in a big hug and give her a kiss, too, before he left. The thought of strolling over to give M.T. a kiss crossed his mind, as well. As he looked across at her with a quick grin, he knew from the flush on her face she'd read his thoughts all too clearly.

"Nice to see you again, M.T.—or perhaps I should call you Mallory, too."

"Nice to see you again, too." She paused. "Was it Lucas?"

He bit back another grin, seeing that she wanted to present their relationship to her grandparents as passing casual. "Yes, Lucas James."

She smiled then. "I'm pleased to meet you and your daughter."

"I'm sure I'll see you again." He dropped his voice, loving the way her face colored up at his words and tone.

Lucas let himself out of the kitchen and headed down Millhouse Road. Away from the house, he let out a deep breath and then laughed out loud. Of all the coincidences in the world to happen, this had to be one of the most remarkable ones he'd hit yet.

Checking his watch, he lengthened his stride and soon cut across a well-worn path below the tennis courts to reach the curved driveway running from the main road to Millhouse Lodge. The golf pro shop and administrative office lay to the east end of the lodge building, with the golf course beyond it, so Lucas's path took him across the full length of the front of the long rock lodge.

He never wondered why people were attracted to this resort spot. Millhouse Resort lay nestled to the east of Gatlinburg off Highway 321 on a beautiful expanse of land amid rich green hills with the grandeur of the Great Smoky Mountains behind it. The lodge itself, built in the 1800s and added to many times over, was a long, mountain stone structure sprawling across the top of a verdant rise above Mill Creek, with a view of the old millhouse and waterwheel the resort was named for. The historic Millhouse Lodge rose three stories high with picturesque arched entry ways on the ground level, a long expanse of glass windows on the second floor level—offering panoramic views of the mountains all around—and a slate gray gabled roof hiding the third floor.

After cutting through the pro shop, Lucas found Dale Buchanan, the resort's golf course superintendent and turf manager, outside the pro shop talking with Millhouse Resort's previous golf pro Andy Kiley. Andy, Lucas's predecessor, had stepped down from full-time work when Lucas was hired, but he still helped out in a part-time capacity.

"Ah, to be young and good looking again," Dale said as Lucas walked over to join them. Dale sat propped on the back of one of the golf carts beside Andy, and Lucas took a seat on the rock wall across from them.

"I just finished one of Nonnie's famous breakfasts," Lucas said, putting on the golf cap he'd snagged coming through the pro shop. Like his colleagues, he was dressed in the trademark forest green golf shirt all the employees wore, paired with khaki slacks and matching golf hats with Millhouse Resort embroidered across the front of them.

"Man, you should have called and invited us over," Dale groused.

"I was dropping off Suzannah," Lucas said in answer. "What's the recent news on that last car theft?"

"The sheriff came by this morning to tell us they don't have any leads yet. This rash of car thefts around the area has them totally baffled." Dale scratched his chin. "Most of the thefts occurred in public places where a lot of cars are parked for the day—at ball game lots, shopping mall areas, over at Dollywood, and at local event arenas. It's only recently that the finger of thefts reached into our Greenbrier area."

Andy leaned forward. "The sheriff said this was the first theft reported at a public place in Greenbrier and Pittman Center. Most of the other car thefts here happened at remote spots, like where tourists and locals park their cars to hike for the day. He said the parking area near the Maddron Bald Trail is a favorite."

"That's true," Dale put in. "Even one of those recent hiking books *The Afternoon Hiker* warned that cars might not be safe parked at that spot."

Andy shifted on his seat. "Most people think that the stolen cars are being recycled at a local chop shop, but the police departments in both Gatlinburg and Cosby have no clues about who is behind this racket."

"You'd think they might have nailed a lead on all this by now." Dale pushed his sunglasses up, shaking his head.

Lucas glanced restlessly at his watch. It was a challenge to keep these two on track. "Listen," he interrupted at last. "About the car stolen from the resort night before last. What did the sheriff say about that?"

Andy swatted at a mosquito trying to settle on his arm. "He figures it's the same bunch. Same *modus-operandi*. The pattern was the same as in all the other times."

"Nice car they took, too," Dale added. "New black Cadillac Escalade, one of those fancy SUV models. Belonged to that Harkins couple from up in Michigan. They weren't real happy about it, as you can imagine."

Lucas frowned. "We'll need to put on more security at night." He glanced toward one of the parking lots below the golf course. "We could install more lightning as a deterrent, too. We may need more security on the main gate into the resort, as well. The thieves must be technically savvy to trip and open security gates, get into locked cars, hot wire them to steal, and then slip out without anyone seeing anything."

"We questioned everybody," Dale said, picking up on that last thought. "Nobody heard anything or saw anything. Nobody even knew the car was gone until the Harkins went out to the parking lot yesterday around noon."

"Where are the Harkins now?"

"Headed back home to Michigan in a rental car. The sheriff got all their information yesterday afternoon and said they could go on home today. He'll stay in touch with them if anything turns up." Dale shifted off the seat to stand up. "Here comes your ten o'clock student, Lucas. I'll work on some of the security aspects we talked about while you work with Hap."

"I'll do a little more looking and asking around, too," Andy said. "Maybe I can pick up a clue someone else missed."

"What does Beau think about this?" Dale asked as he started toward the pro shop.

"He'll be over later to talk with me about it. To get an update."

Andy stood up and moved into the driver's seat of the golf cart. "Let me know if you want me to come back today to sit in on more talks about this."

"I will, Andy," Lucas said, glancing over at Hap Mullins waiting for him. He didn't look forward to this lesson. The guy had swing flaws and a bad grip which all of Lucas's coaching hadn't affected much at this point and Hap always overanalyzed his game, too. Maybe today he could convince Hap to position his hands properly with his grip. Maintaining the right grip alone would do wonders for the man's swing.

An hour and a half later, Beau walked into Lucas's office above the pro shop. Lucas had just started to sort through a pile of paperwork on his desk.

"Is Hap doing any better with his swing?"

Lucas shrugged. "I think he'll see improvement if he'll remember to use the right grip."

Beau laughed. "Every ham-fisted gorilla thinks he can grab a golf club and whack away at a ball with success. It always surprises them when their personal idea of approaching the game of golf doesn't work out."

Lucas laughed. "Tell me about it. And they usually come to me *after* they've already established bad habits. It's harder to change them at that point."

"Especially if the player has an attitude." Beau knew Hap Mullins well. Hap, now retired and living in the Greenbrier and Pittman Center area, played regularly at the resort.

Lucas saw Beau's eyes move to catch him rubbing his arm.

"Arm bothering you today?" Beau asked.

"Only a little." Lucas shifted his hand away, not wanting to get into that discussion right now.

Noting Beau's ease, it seemed obvious, to Lucas's relief, that his granddaughter hadn't enlightened him about their little interlude on the airplane yesterday. Lucas worried how he might handle that if she did.

"Suzannah behaving herself?" Lucas asked, shifting the subject.

"Ah, you know that child of yours could charm the bees out of the trees." Beau settled into one of the armchairs in front of Lucas's desk. "She's entertaining Mallory now. Making her laugh. That's good for Mallory after all she's been through."

Lucas raised his eyebrows.

"Mallory's a strong girl," Beau said, crossing one ankle across his knee and making himself comfortable. "Smart, hard-working, ambitious, resourceful, and caring. But she went through some tough times this last year with her mother dying and then had a nervous breakdown recently."

Lucas felt himself tense, the words bringing back a swirl of bad memories he didn't want to remember or dwell on. "Sorry to hear that," he made himself say.

"From what I hear, she just cracked—started shaking, crying and couldn't stop. Staff at her publishing house couldn't help her calm down. Finally called an ambulance, and they took her into the hospital for a couple of days. Doctors called it a minor breakdown, mostly caused by an overload of care and stress."

Lucas's mind wandered as Beau talked, thinking about Mallory back at Wingate House, playing with his daughter. He hoped nothing happened in front of Suzannah. Hadn't the child seen enough emotional volatile outbreaks in the past? And hadn't he?

"The doctors thought Mallory ought to take a long break, to get away and get some rest." Beau's voice droned on. "We're tickled she chose to come here. We haven't had Mallory with us for a long holiday since she was in high school." He rubbed his neck. "I thought you ought to know she's been ill in case she has an emotional moment or something."

"Yeah," he said, searching for something to say. "I'm sure time with you and Nonnie will be good for her."

Beau smiled. "Good for us, too. We love that girl. I'd say Nonnie will be encouraging her to stay as long as she can."

*Great*, Lucas thought. He'd flirted with this girl and kissed her on the airplane. *Terrific*. He hoped she wouldn't expect him to start a relationship with her, because he had no plans to go there. Especially knowing what he did now.

Glancing out the window toward the parking lot, Beau changed the subject. "Tell me what the sheriff said about the car theft when he dropped by this morning."

Lucas spent the next twenty minutes filling Beau in on the theft and they discussed what they might do to tighten security throughout the resort.

"Stealing is never something I've understood well," Beau said, running a hand over his short stubble of a beard. "There are so many honest ways a person can make money to buy the things they want. I've never understood why a person would take things from another rather than finding a way to make his or her own money to attain it."

"Well, there's been stealing since the beginning of time, Beau. People steal for greed, for hatred, sometimes for want or to meet basic needs. Some people steal because they have a disorder in their lives or need money for drugs, and some steal just for kicks or to fill a void. With young thieves, sometimes they steal because of jealousy, peer pressure, or to act out." Lucas shrugged. "There are a lot of reasons."

"Yeah, I know that. I watch the movies and read." Beau ran a hand through his hair. "But it's still psychologically hard to wrap my mind around."

"Fortunately, most of the time thieves get caught." Lucas drummed his fingers restlessly on the table. "That's what we're hoping for here."

"Horace, one of the old Latin poets and philosophers, said 'The covetous man is always in want.'" Beau liked quoting bits of philosophical wisdom. "I'd say he's probably right. I've always found a greedy person would rather get than give. Greed is probably the root behind most theft, don't you think?"

"You have a point," Lucas said. "Listen, I need to go down and update Barry and Denise in the pro shop about this car theft business and some of the precautions we're planning to take. I'll also talk to the grounds people—Earl, Wylie, JoJo, and Billie." He paused. "Do you want me to talk to the staff at the lodge, too?"

Beau stood. "No. I'll walk over and update Dick at the lodge and then let him talk to Ruth, Evelyn, Lois and any others."

Lucas nodded, knowing this would get the word out. Dick Kemp was the manager of the Millhouse Lodge, with Ruth, Evelyn, and Lois the other primary staff members.

"We want everyone on board, all being watchful about this issue." Beau continued. "If anyone has seen or heard anything suspicious we need to know about it, too. If a rash of thefts gets started at the resort, word will leak out and it could hurt business. You know how people panic over little things like that."

"Yeah, I do." Lucas agreed as Beau left. Turning back to his desk, he started sorting through the last pieces of his mail.

He soon found himself, however, looking out the window instead of focusing on his work, thinking about Mallory Wingate—M.T. of the airplane interlude. She hadn't acted like an unstable woman. But then neither had Cecily when he first met her and look what came of that? Lucas shook his head.

Admittedly, when he saw Mallory again, realized she'd be staying at the resort, he'd felt pleased. He'd looked forward to further pursuing a relationship with her since they'd been thrown unexpectedly together again. He liked her; he felt attracted to her. In fact, he lay awake for an hour when he got home last night thinking about her, remembering how she looked, hearing her deep voice again, seeing those thoughtful eyes, and remembering the feel of her full lips on his.

She'd touched at something in him when Lucas thought he'd moved his emotions to a safe, distanced place so that wouldn't happen again. Furthermore, he'd enjoyed Mallory's company. He'd liked talking and laughing with her. He hadn't enjoyed a woman's company like that for a long time. Even now he found himself remembering some of her expressions, her scent, how she'd twisted her hair or tapped her chin while thinking. He'd loved the big words she used and how well read she was. Lucas, bright himself, enjoyed a woman he could match minds with.

"It's a shame," he said to himself as he walked over to the hat rack by the door to pick up his golf cap. "But I won't go there again with a woman who is unstable."

# CHAPTER 3

**M**allory ended up spending her first morning back at Millhouse Resort playing with five-year-old Suzannah James, the daughter of the man she'd met on the airplane. The man she *never* expected to see again. She wouldn't have imagined in a million years—even with all the fiction books she read and edited—that she'd discover that man here at Millhouse, her grandfather's right hand aid, no less, the new golf pro and assistant resort manager. After Lucas left, she tactfully got a few facts from her grandmother clarifying that Lucas, now widowed, brought Suzannah, at two, to live with him after his wife died, but little else.

*Oh, well.* Somewhere in a past letter one of her grandparents must have mentioned the man's name but Mallory couldn't recall it. She couldn't even remember when he came to work at Millhouse. Five years ago? Six? It made her realize how busy she'd been with her own life over the last years, to be so out of touch with her grandparents' lives.

She sat now in a white metal chair on the patio off the kitchen, keeping a watch on Suzannah James. The child was walking down one of the garden paths looking for the latest object in a color game Mallory created to entertain her.

"Here's something pink!" the child called, running back in her twinkling tennis shoes, her face excited, to drop a pink cluster of slightly crushed flowers into Mallory's lap.

"You're right. This is pink." Mallory laid the spiky pink shoot on the patio table beside the child's other finds. "It's a shrub called

Fireweed, and the birds and butterflies love it."

"Write the *color* word for it," Suzannah directed.

Mallory reached for the pad of sticky notes she'd brought outside and began to print the word "pink" with a black pen on the top sheet. "It's P-I-N-K." She spelled out the letters to the child as she wrote, sounding out the whole word afterwards. "Let's see if you remember the other colors."

Suzannah frowned in concentration at the collection of items and notes on the metal table. "The berries are red," she said pointing to a cluster of japonica berries. "And the leaf is green, the pine cone is brown, the rock is gray, and the daisy flower is yellow." She recited her list in a singsong voice, pointing to each item as she identified its color.

"Very good." Mallory drew a little star on her hand, making Suzannah giggle.

Mallory pointed to the yellow flower on the table. "This flower's big name is Marguerite Daisy. Birds, bees, and butterflies really love it, and if you remember we walked over to sniff the leaves and they smell really fragrant."

Suzannah flounced into a chair beside Mallory's at the table. "You know all about the flowers in the Butterfly Garden, just like Nonnie does."

"Nonnie taught me," Mallory said, remembering her grandmother playing this same game with her as a child when she spent her long summer vacations here.

"Who taught Nonnie?"

"Her mother, when she was a little girl, and later Beau's mother who helped to create this garden. Beau's mother's name was Alva Wingate. She and her husband Norton used to live in your house, in Ivy Cottage."

"Did she plant all the flowers behind our house, too?"

"She did."

"Did they make the resort?"

"Yes. Norton and Alva developed most of the Millhouse Resort. But the original rock lodge building, the mill and millhouse, and an old store were built on the land by Norton's parents, Gareth Truett Wingate and Annalise Mayes Wingate, in the 1920s. That was a long time ago."

Mallory tried to think what a small child might understand about this history. "When the Smokies became a national park, Norton and Alva began to make the resort bigger and nicer so people could come from all over the United States to stay here and enjoy the mountains. Beau and Nonnie are still doing that, still welcoming people to Millhouse Resort."

"It's pretty here, and I like our garden and Nonnie's garden." Her eyes moved to the collection of items on the table. "Tell me another color to look for." She put a small hand on Mallory's in a sweet gesture.

Mallory smiled. It took so little to entertain a child and they were so carefree. "How about orange," she said.

"I *know* orange." Suzannah pointed to one of the polka dots on the white knit shirt she wore over her shorts.

"Yes, that's orange."

Grinning, Suzannah set off down the pathway, looking around her "for something orange" as she walked.

Mallory closed her eyes for a moment, enjoying the peace of this place where she'd always found so much love and joy. She could hear the birds chirping in the shrubbery, the summer breeze whispering in the trees, and a cricket chirping somewhere near the rock wall not far away. It felt good to be here. Dr. Henry had been right to push for a vacation and a rest.

A voice interrupted her reverie. "Hello. Is Suzannah out here with you?"

Mallory glanced up to see a smiling, round-faced young woman letting herself in the side gate beside the patio. She wore navy capris and a long, pin-tucked overshirt in pale blue, setting off her summer tan, with her brown hair tied back casually in a ponytail. Behind her, a small girl, who looked very much like her, paused and slipped behind her mother's leg in shyness as she saw Mallory.

"You must be Elizabeth McGill and Abby," Mallory said.

"Nonnie is in the kitchen fixing lunch. Suzannah is down the pathway looking for something orange." She pointed.

Abby's eyes lit at those last words and Elizabeth laughed. "Sounds like one of Nonnie's games. Are you her granddaughter?"

"Yes, Mallory Wingate." She held out a hand and started to stand but Elizabeth waved her back into her seat.

"Please stay where you are. I'll sit down for a few minutes if it's okay, and then we'll go in and collect Suzannah's things." She blew out a long breath as she dropped into the chair across from Mallory at the metal table. "We visited the dentist in town today for a cleaning for Abby and it proved an adventure I am *not* interested in pursuing anytime again soon."

Seeing Abby looking down the path, Mallory said, "Why don't you go and look for Suzannah? Maybe you can help her find something orange."

Abby's shyness quickly evaporated at Mallory's words, and at a nod from her mother she took off down the path in a gallop, calling to Suzannah.

Mallory watched a small hugging reunion occur in the pathway, and then the girls began the pursuit for something orange again.

"Did you get in last night?" Elizabeth asked her.

"I did."

"How did you manage to get stuck minding Suzannah so soon?" She grinned, her warm brown eyes sparkling.

Mallory leaned back in her chair. "I offered. Nonnie had a ton of cooking to do for one of her women's luncheons tomorrow."

"She doesn't really think of that as work, you know." Elizabeth smiled. "She loves hosting her ladies' meetings in the tearoom. She makes a nice profit from it, too."

Mallory glanced toward the long, floor to ceiling picture windows of the Butterfly Tea Room, stretching across the back of Wingate House. Through the windows they could see square tables scattered across the long porch room, each covered today with pink cloths under plate glass table tops, already partially set for tomorrow's luncheon. The chairs were a mismatch of light and dark wood, some painted white or leaf green—a charming eclectic look, set off by a backdrop of floral wallpaper covered in twining vines and busy butterflies.

"Even when I was a little girl, I remember Nonnie fixing lunches and hosting her local ladies' groups here. I loved setting the tables with Nonnie's butterfly dishes, putting out the pretty napkins, and helping her serve. All the ladies fussed over me and made me feel special, too."

The memory almost made Mallory's eyes prick with tears. *Honestly.* Her emotions were still so ragged and raw. She straightened, clearing her throat. It wasn't like her to cry over things, even something sentimental.

"That's a good memory." Elizabeth's eyes followed Mallory's to the windows of the tearoom by the patio. "Nonnie has been so excited about your visit. She said you'd been through a rough time lately and needed a vacation."

Mallory glanced away.

Elizabeth crossed a leg, showing Mallory a sandaled foot and a golden tan at the bottom of her capris. Not seeming to notice when Mallory didn't answer quickly, Elizabeth fingered the items on the table. "Abby loves this game."

Mallory knew at that point Elizabeth would easily let the subject go if Mallory didn't want to talk about her past. That ease encouraged her to speak. "Two years ago my mother contacted me and said she wanted to come and stay with me for a time, that she wasn't well and needed my help." She paused. "My dad died when I was only ten, so Mother lived alone."

"I heard your father was shot right here in Greenbrier while out hunting and that no one ever learned who did it or how it happened." Elizabeth said.

"That's true." Mallory picked up the pinecone on the table and turned it in her hand. "It made my mother angry at this place and at the people here. She seldom came back to visit after that, although she let me come to stay with my grandparents every summer and sometimes for holidays when her workload was heavy. She worked as an events coordinator for big hotels."

"So it was only the two of you."

"Yes, so naturally Mother came to me. I learned after she arrived that she had lung cancer and was dying. It proved a really hard and complicated time." Mallory found her voice catching.

"What stage was she in when she came?"

Mallory turned to Elizabeth in some surprise at the direct question.

"I'm a nurse." Elizabeth smiled and leaned back in her chair. "Or I was. Nothing you say will be hard for me to hear. My husband is a doctor. He practices in the clinic on the highway. Sometimes I help there in a pinch."

Mallory looked out across the flowering shrubs and plants in Nonnie's lush garden, heard the girls giggling as they played, saw the bright colors of their clothes flitting in and out among the winding pathways. Pain and the day-to-day responsibility of watching someone suffer and grow worse—the chill and smell of hospitals, the sad, weary faces of the ill and their tired loved ones, the sounds of crying, the feelings of grief—all seemed so far from this bright, sunny place full of the smells of flowers, freshness, and life.

"It was the worst time ever," Mallory said at last. "Mother came to me already heading into stage four. She didn't recognize her symptoms before. A smoker since her teens, she was used to coughs that lingered, feeling short of breath, having frequent attacks of bronchitis in the winter, occasional aches and pains, or hoarseness in her voice. With the stress of her job, she often experienced headaches or felt tired. She didn't realize ...." Mallory's voice drifted off.

"Lung cancer is difficult to diagnose and to treat. It often doesn't produce symptoms until it is too late and has spread beyond the chest to the brain, liver, or bone. Did her oncologists try chemotherapy?"

"Yes, but it didn't help. The tumors weren't impacted by chemotherapy so it was stopped. They tried drugs, too, lots of different ones. Nothing worked. She only got worse." Mallory sighed. "Mother shifted in and out of the hospital. I used care at the apartment when she could be at home. But problems began to occur. She kept forgetting things and it frustrated her. It made her angry, struggling with her memory. Nothing prepared her— or me—for the pain that set in later, the vomiting, rashes, and seizures." Mallory shut her eyes.

"It spread to her brain." Elizabeth put a hand over Mallory's on the table. "That's difficult."

"Yes, it was. By the beginning of the year, with the treatment options exhausted, they moved Mother to palliative treatments to minimize pain and to improve comfort. It was downhill after that, a back and forth seesaw of home hospice care alternated with times in the hospital when complications set in. Eventually her body simply began turning off."

"It's called active dying," Elizabeth said in a matter-of-fact voice. "You've gone through a very stressful and hard time being the only care giver and continuing to work through it all. Nonnie said you were an editor with a lot of responsibility with your job."

"Yes." It seemed so nice to have someone to understand in such a quiet, unemotional way. It also seemed easier sitting and talking about it with a virtual stranger here in the beauty of Nonnie's garden so far away from where all the memories still lay.

The girls ran up again then, each carrying clusters of orange butterfly weed, which Elizabeth identified and made a card for. Mallory listened to their chatter without saying much. As the girls clamored for another color to search for, Elizabeth sent them off to look for purple.

"Are you okay?" she asked Mallory as the girls scampered away. "I didn't mean to pry when we've only just met."

"No, and I didn't mean to dump all this on you." She suddenly felt embarrassed.

Elizabeth smiled at her, a sunny, natural smile. "It often helps to share, and your story made my trials at the dentist with Abby suddenly fall into place as trivial." She laughed. "She actually bit the hygienist's hand and drew blood. Talk about being embarrassed."

Mallory laughed, and the ring of her own and Elizabeth's laughter sounded good on the warm summer air.

"I like you," Elizabeth said matter-of-factly. "A lot of people annoy me so that's a compliment. I hope we can be friends. Nonnie said you might stay for a month or more. I hope you'll come over and visit with me. I live in the white farmhouse you can see on the hill right across the highway from the resort." She pointed with a hand in the general direction. "It has a big sign by the driveway that reads Whitehouse Farm. There's a vegetable stand on the roadside by the turn and you can see some barns in the fields. I raise herbs, plants, and flowers, and I sell them at my road stand and to a few retailers I know around the area. My husband Robert is Pittman Center's only doctor. He works in the Pittman Center Family Clinic on the road in front of our property—a renovated white farmhouse with a long porch across the front and a black roof. I'm sure you've noticed it as you've driven by."

"I've seen it. And the farm is a pretty property."

Elizabeth grinned at her. "You can help me in the garden and at the stand if you want. It's very therapeutic." She laughed. "I can affirm to that since I worked before as an ER nurse—dealing with trauma, suffering, and pain around me all the time. I do know where you're coming from, Mallory."

Mallory liked Elizabeth's calm, fresh-faced ease. She was easy to talk with and she hadn't made Mallory feel like a leper for passing through a rough time the last two years.

Abby and Suzannah came skipping up the garden path again. "Mom, look! We found purple," Abby called, waving a stem of lavender.

"Purple is hard to find," Suzannah added with a small frown, putting her own cluster of flowers on the table. "We finally found it in the very, very back of the garden by the fence."

Nonnie came out the door to hear those last words. "Yes, and those lovely wands of purple flowers you found are called lavender, girls. Did you sniff of them? Their pungent, anise-like smell, making your nose wrinkle, runs the deer off. It's a stinky smell to deer, and they don't like it. I don't want any deer in my garden so I plant lavender along the back fence lines."

Nonnie turned to Elizabeth. "You and Abby come in and eat some lunch with Mallory, Suzannah, and me before you head back to your place. I made macaroni and cheese and both the girls love it. I also stirred up a little slaw on the side and sliced some fresh tomatoes. It's a quick and easy lunch. Beau is eating over at the resort restaurant in the lodge with Dick today talking about business."

"Oh, you don't need to feed us lunch," Elizabeth said. "You have Mallory here. I'm sure you two would love to chat and visit without two noisy little girls filling up the air."

"Pooh, Mallory and I will have plenty of time to talk after lunch and for weeks to come." She leaned over and dropped a kiss on Mallory's forehead. "It's doing both of us good to see each other and be together again. It's been far too long since Mallory last visited here."

Mallory knew the truth of this and she readily agreed with her grandmother, urging Elizabeth to stay. She wanted to get to know this easy, calming woman more. She liked her and she liked little Abby, too.

"No more urging necessary," Elizabeth said, following them into the house. "I can spend more time in my garden this afternoon if I don't have to stop to fix lunch when we get back." She retrieved cushioned booster seats from the kitchen closet, plopped them onto two chairs at the kitchen table and then helped the girls climb into them, obviously familiar with Nonnie's house.

Mallory helped to pour lemonade and tea, and distributed it around, and Elizabeth got butter out of the refrigerator to go with the rolls Nonnie had baked.

Glancing at the stick of butter as she put it on the table and settling into a seat, Elizabeth said, "Nonnie, I found a recipe for herb butter in a magazine in the dentist's office this morning while waiting."

She pulled a slip of paper out of her pocket to read it. "It says to add four tablespoons of dried herbs and a dash of lemon to one-fourth pound of softened butter. Then you beat it until light and fluffy and store it in the refrigerator. Do you think that would be any good?"

"Yes, I do," Nonnie said, sitting down after dishing out hot macaroni and cheese onto their plates. "You write that recipe down for me. It sounds very easy and I could put it on the tables as a spread for homemade breads with my tea luncheons."

Their conversation drifted to a discussion of recipes, herbs, and gardening. Comfortable, normal, and easy topics. Mallory sighed and dug into her plate of macaroni and cheese, dishing out a big scoop of Nonnie's homemade slaw to go with it and adding a juicy slice of red tomato beside it.

She'd forgotten how nice it was to simply sit around a kitchen table, talking about lackadaisical things, with no big cares or worries hanging over her head. Three days ago, she'd still felt like a frayed electric cord, and now—just being here at Nonnie and Beau's—she already felt so much better and so much more relaxed.

Elizabeth had listened earlier and not made a big deal out of learning what Mallory passed through with her mother during the long siege of illness. Now, even knowing she'd broken down and gotten a little emotional afterwards, Elizabeth wasn't acting differently toward her, tiptoeing around her like she might freak out in the next moment. That was nice. She also said she liked Mallory—even knowing about her breakdown.

Mallory smiled, looking across at Nonnie and Elizabeth. *I do feel better,* she thought. Her eyes moved to Suzannah and the child sent her a big grin. *And it looks like I've made a new small friend, too.*

Nonnie passed her a jar of homemade pickles, interrupting her thoughts. "I hope I can get Mallory to help me make Coca-Cola cakes after lunch," she told Elizabeth. "I need two big sheet cakes to feed the Smoky Mountain Red Hat Group tomorrow. I believe that dessert will go nicely with the two extra pans of macaroni and cheese I baked this morning. Plus I made extra slaw and I plan to do pretty fruit plates on the side. Don't you think that will make a nice luncheon?"

"I do," said Mallory.

Elizabeth agreed and Abby added, "I love Coca-Cola cake."

As the talk flowed comfortably around her, Mallory decided she would tell Nonnie, too, about what she'd been through with her mother. Finding it so easy to tell Elizabeth what she'd experienced gave her new confidence that she could talk about it more with her grandmother and perhaps her grandfather, too. She'd held things in so tightly for so long, needing to be strong. Perhaps getting everything out on the table with the people she cared about would help her to move on and not dwell too heavily on all that had occurred.

Mallory sighed on the thought. She probably needed to tell Nonnie and Beau about Ethan, too, at some point. What a deep, bitter betrayal that had been on top of everything else.

# CHAPTER 4

Lucas felt glad to see the longer days of summer beginning. It gave him extra time for outdoor fun, walks, and time with Suzannah after work. After picking Suzannah up today, they'd cleaned out the little tree house at the back of the garden so Suzannah could enjoy it on sunny afternoons and weekends. It was a charming one-room structure with dusty green French doors, more like a garden house than a typical child's tree house. It sat on high stilts under two large maple trees with wooden stairs leading up to it and a neat, railed deck across the front.

"I want Mallory to come to see my tree house," Suzannah said as Lucas finished drying her off from her bath and began to tuck her into pajamas.

He avoided commenting on her remark, as he'd endured a constant stream of babble about Mallory ever since picking Suzannah up after work. Evidently M.T. Wingate played with Suzannah earlier in the day while Nonnie baked for her luncheon. He'd heard *Mallory this* and *Mallory that* all evening.

"Let's go down to the kitchen to get our snack," Lucas said, hoisting Suzannah onto his back to ride her down the stairs.

"I want graham crackers and peanut butter," she told him.

"Sounds good to me." He bumped her up and down, making her laugh, as he made his way down the stairway.

In the kitchen, he parked his daughter on her booster seat and started getting out the fixings for their snack. Elizabeth had taught him that active children often needed a bedtime snack to hold them through the night, especially during growth spurts. Suzannah cherished several favorite options, like grahams with peanut butter or saltine crackers and cheese, which she ate with a small glass of milk—the rule being no sugar or chocolate in the snacks.

The back doorbell rang, and Suzannah jumped down from her booster seat and raced through the laundry area to the back porch to answer it.

"Suzannah, wait to open the door for me," Lucas called, starting after her. A backdoor caller was usually someone they knew, but still…. It was dark out now. And there had been thieves around the property.

"Mallory!" Suzannah cried, hopping up and down with excitement.

*Great,* thought Lucas, putting on a smile as he unlocked the screen door.

"Nonnie asked me to bring Suzannah's doll over." Mallory held it out. "We found it after dinner, and Nonnie thought Suzannah might want it before she went to bed. She said you might get frantic looking for it, before you realized she probably left it at Wingate House."

Suzannah grabbed the doll to hug it. "This is EdithAnn," she told Mallory. "I didn't even know she got lost."

"Thank you," Lucas said, trying to be gracious. "Tell Nonnie she helped me dodge a major crisis bullet by sending the doll over."

Mallory passed him a cookie tin with pink and yellow roses on the lid. "Nonnie sent Suzannah some of her Bedtime Bars, too."

"Oh, goody." Suzannah bounced in place again. "We love those, and we haven't eaten our snack yet, so we can have some right now." She opened the screened door. "Come in and eat some with us, Mallory. We're having milk, too."

Lucas watched a little smile tweak the corners of Mallory's mouth.

"Please come in," he said, bowing to the inevitable. "I'll make coffee if it won't keep you awake this late."

He saw her hesitate, look at Suzannah's excited face, and then said, "Yes, coffee would be nice. Thank you."

Suzannah took Mallory's hand to lead her to the kitchen, directing her across the cozy, old-fashioned room to the eat-in area. Mallory slowed several times to look around the kitchen, and Lucas found himself running his eyes down the back length of her, liking what he saw.

She was tall and moved with a swaying grace when she walked. He noticed she wore the same pink linen skirt and white cotton top she'd worn earlier this morning, but she still managed to look fresh and pretty even at the end of the day. She wore slip-on mules on her feet, and they made flipping sounds as she walked across the old tile floor in the kitchen.

"I've always loved this kitchen," she commented, helping Suzannah back into her seat and looking around fondly. "The green wood cabinetry is so unique with the glass front doors, and I love the rustic beams overhead in the ceiling. It gives the whole room that special cottage feel, don't you think?"

"I forget you've been a part of Millhouse Resort since only a small child," he said, stopping to put the colorful tin of snack bars on the counter in the kitchen. "You probably spent a lot of time in this house when Beau's mother Alva Wingate still lived here."

"I did. It's my favorite place in the resort," she said, leaning against the counter while he started fixing their coffee. "Daddy and I came here to Ivy Cottage every holiday, or whenever he could get a long weekend until he died, and then I came for summers and holidays until I went away to college. We always stayed with Great-Grandmother Wingate until she died, and afterward the two of us continued to stay at Ivy Cottage until Daddy died. Daddy always wanted to come back and live here."

He heard her sigh. "Your mother didn't come with you?"

"No. She never liked the resort, and after Daddy got killed in a hunting accident nearby, she refused to come at all."

Lucas watched a mixture of emotions cross her face with these words. He opened the tin of Nonnie's bars and began to put a selection on a dinner plate.

"It was fun helping to make those Bedtime Bars this evening." Her eyes took on a faraway look. "Nonnie insisted we make them before I brought the doll over. She used to make the same Bedtime Bars for me when I was little."

"Well, they're great. Suzannah and I both love them." He glanced down at the plate. "What's in them, anyway?"

"Oats, puffed cereal, eggs, peanut butter, raisins, dried fruits, some chopped nuts, and Nonnie's secret ingredient."

He raised his eyes.

"I'll tell you later," she whispered, glancing toward Suzannah.

"Oh," he said, deciding the ingredient must be one of those healthy foods kids tried to avoid.

A few minutes later when Suzannah's back was turned she mouthed the word "squash" to him with a grin.

He gave her a thumbs-up at the answer, surprised to learn the bars contained that particular vegetable. Lucas didn't like squash much himself and knew Suzannah didn't, but fortunately you couldn't taste the squash in Nonnie's bars.

"We cleaned up my tree house in the back yard today," Suzannah told Mallory as she sat down at the kitchen table for their snack. "I want you to come see it. I have two chairs and a table in it, dishes, and a little kitchen, too." She glanced out the window and frowned. "But it's too dark now."

"Is it the old treehouse under the maples with the faded green door?" Mallory asked her.

Seeing Suzannah's surprised face, she added, "I used to play in that tree house when I was little, too."

Lucas watched Suzannah process that statement. Children had a hard time imagining adults as kids. "Was that when your grandmother lived here before us?"

"That's right." Mallory smiled at her. She crossed one long leg over the other, her backless shoe dropping away from her foot.

Lucas let his eyes slide over her while she talked to Suzannah. That long, thin, loose skirt she wore with that skimpy sleeveless top and her bare legs made her look sexier than if she'd simply worn jeans or shorts. He turned back to make their coffee, busying himself, trying not to let his eyes skim over her again. She was a sexy, good-looking woman—that was a fact—but totally unaware of her own appeal. He'd seen that on the airplane.

Mallory had the warm olive complexion, like a golden tan, some women possessed naturally—beautiful, too, with her shoulder-length sun-kissed hair and those deep gray-blue eyes. Her hair, mussed now from the walk over and coming out of its clasp in back, made his fingers itch to touch it. As if sensing his eyes on her, she ran a hand through her hair now, twisting a strand of it absently, as he'd seen her do often on the airplane.

He looked away, working on the coffee, and then back again. As she talked to Suzannah, the light filtered through the thin material of her skirt, outlining her legs. *Dang,* he wished this woman hadn't come over here tonight to parade around his kitchen and beguile him so.

"Can I help you in the kitchen?" she asked, glancing his way.

He shook his head, trying to steel his emotions. Despite how normal and nice Mallory acted, he knew she wasn't well. How many times had he watched Cecily seem normal and then skip out emotionally and make his life a misery?

He glanced out the window, lost in his thoughts, only half listening to Mallory and his daughter talking now.

"Mallory says she'll come up and read me some bedtime books, Daddy," he heard Suzannah say.

He scowled. "You don't need to do that, Mallory."

She shrugged. "I don't mind, and I'd like to see what books she cherishes and enjoys. Part of my job at Whittier is to help with acquisitions for our children's line, the Colorstone Press."

Seeing Suzannah's excited face, Lucas could hardly find it in himself to say no. "Okay. She'll show you the way upstairs to her room. You can come get me to tuck her in after two or three books." He sent a stern glance at Suzannah. "That's our limit, so don't let her talk you into more, Mallory. I'll sit out on the screened porch, drink my coffee, and glance through the newspaper I never got to read this morning until you're done."

"Thank you, Daddy." Suzannah leaped down from her chair and ran around the table to fling herself into his arms. He hugged and kissed her and then swatted her playfully on the bottom, watching Mallory's thoughtful eyes on him the entire time.

A little later, after finishing off his coffee and reading the news, Lucas leaned back in one of the rattan chairs on the porch and closed his eyes, enjoying the quiet and the small sounds of the night. His life had grown much simpler and smaller than the pro life he'd once lived, but in many ways it was far better.

He heard the door to the porch open, and looked up to see Mallory coming out onto the screened porch, carrying a cup of coffee she'd gotten for herself in the kitchen.

"No need to get up," she said. "Suzannah fell asleep on the last book saying goodnight to everything in the room while we read the story."

Lucas smiled. "You read *Goodnight Moon*."

"Yes, and obviously you've read it to her often yourself."

He couldn't help grinning. "We've made rather a game of saying goodnight to everything in Suzannah's room as an ending to that one."

"So I learned." She settled herself onto the rattan sofa, adjusting a striped pillow behind her back. Then she slipped off her shoes to put her bare feet on the coffee table.

The intimacy of the gesture bothered Lucas.

"I tucked Suzannah into bed with her doll, EdithAnn, who she insisted had to be changed into appropriate pajamas, and then we settled the cat dolls all around her, each of them with distinctive names and stories she filled me in on."

"Yeah. Her handcrafted *Ruffing's* cat dolls, Lillie, Tommy, and Meredith. Each of them has a unique name and story created by the artist that designs them. One of Suzannah's grandmothers sends them to her at her birthdays. It's started a tradition."

"I see." Mallory sipped her coffee. "The child has a very vivid imagination, and she is very smart."

"Yes, to both," he agreed.

"And she's obviously foolish about you."

He glanced over at her then. "Did you expect her not to be?"

She gave him a puzzled look. "I didn't have any expectations, Lucas. I didn't even know you had a child until this morning."

He chuckled. "That was a danged coincidence meeting again in the kitchen today, wasn't it?"

"Yes, it was." She tucked a leg up under her now, changing her position to curl into the corner of the wicker sofa. "It's the main reason I offered to bring over Suzannah's doll rather than letting Nonnie or Beau do it. I wanted to thank you for not telling my grandparents more about our meeting."

He let his eyes rove over her. "I guess I could say the same to you. Your grandfather is my boss, after all, and he might think less of me for flirting with his granddaughter on so little acquaintance."

A little blush stole over her cheeks.

"Actually for doing a little *more* than flirting," he added.

The blush deepened. "Well, as you said it was only an interlude."

"Or so we thought." Lucas decided it time to make a few things clear. "Listen," he said, trying to think how to begin. "Your grandfather told me you'd been through a rough time lately. I didn't know that. It wasn't something you told me. So I don't think we need to complicate things while you're recovering here with some sort of relationship."

"Relationship," she repeated the word without any expression.

He rubbed at his neck, uncomfortable. "Yeah, you know, trying to continue a relationship like we started on the plane."

Her facial expression grew chilly now. "And what sort of relationship did we start on the plane that you're worried we might continue?"

Annoyed, Lucas leaned toward her. "Mallory, I don't want to get into a relationship with any woman who isn't emotionally stable. I don't think that would be good for Suzannah."

She sat up, tensing, tight-lipped, her voice sounding oddly brittle in reply. "What exactly did my grandfather say to you?"

*Did she think he didn't know?* Lucas crossed his arms. "He said you had a complete emotional breakdown." He searched his memory for Beau's words. "He told me you cracked, started crying and couldn't stop at your workplace; he said nobody could calm you down, so they had to call an ambulance to carry you off."

"Grandad certainly told that story with dramatic detail, especially when he wasn't even there." Her eyes flashed with anger now and it looked like she was making an effort not to cry.

"Wasn't it true?" he asked, deciding to give her the opportunity to offer her own version.

"It was more or less true." She looked away, embarrassed. "Did he happen to mention what caused this breakdown?"

The way she pronounced that last word *breakdown* let him know she hated the sound of the word. Lucas tried to remember. "An overload of stress and care, I think he said."

Her eyes moved to his. "And I don't suppose you ever went through a time in your life where you experienced an overload of stress and care?"

The question annoyed him. "Yes, but I handled it differently. We all have different emotional constitutions."

"Is that right?"

Her tone piqued him further. "Listen, we're not talking about me. We're talking about you. And you may not know it, but Suzannah has been through enough in her past already with emotionally unstable people. She doesn't need to be around anyone who creates emotional scenes. She doesn't need that in her life. I felt it was really important for me to tell you that."

She sat very quietly for a few minutes. "Are you telling me you don't want me to spend time around your daughter because I've had a breakdown?"

It sounded harsh even to Lucas, but it was how he felt. "I think you should limit your time around Suzannah until you know you're better and in control. Until you're well." He paused. "If you can get well."

When she didn't reply, Lucas looked over to see her crying.

"Look, I didn't mean to hurt your feelings."

"Didn't you?" Her eyes flashed.

"Like I said earlier, you don't know what Suzannah dealt with earlier in her life. Her mother had mental problems and she killed herself." Lucas snapped the words out at last, tired of Mallory's tone and of this conversation.

The words hung between them for a moment.

"I'm very sorry to hear that," Mallory said, her eyes staying steady on his.

He jerked out of his seat and paced over to look out into the dark. "Cecily was bipolar. Sometimes she acted totally normal. A beautiful woman at those times—lively, creative, vivid, and happy." He sighed. "Too happy sometimes, too buoyant, like someone on a high. Then without warning she'd drop unexpectedly, like a thermostat on a cold day, and go in the opposite direction. Become broody, overly emotional, depressed, take crying spells that wouldn't stop. She often felt victimized for no reason, thought no one understood her."

Lucas ran a hand through his hair. "I had to hire a full-time housekeeper after Suzannah was born. Sometimes Cecily locked herself in her room, forgot to take care of Suzannah or herself. Other times she took off. We didn't always know where." He paused. "During one of those times the police found her dead in a motel room. She'd taken too many drugs mixed with alcohol."

"Again, I'm very sorry," she said.

A small space of quiet descended over the porch.

He turned back to her. "So you can see why I need to keep Suzannah safe, to keep her from more emotional problems. To keep her from being around unstable people."

She stood up and walked over closer to him to look into his eyes with those deep gray-blue eyes of hers. "Why don't you admit the truth instead of trying to foist your excuses and fears off on a small child? You don't want to pursue any kind of relationship with me because you know I experienced a minor breakdown and because you're afraid I might be like your wife."

"That's not it." He shot her a dark glance.

"Isn't it?"

He looked away from her, out the window into the gathering darkness and then back to her eyes again.

She crossed her arms. "You know, I liked you when I first met you. You were kind and funny and smart. I regretted afterwards I wouldn't see you again, that you were only an interlude." She stepped back, and started toward the door. "But I don't feel that way anymore."

He moved to follow after her. "Look, I hope you don't go home and tell your grandparents I was unkind to you."

"Weren't you unkind?" She paused at the door to look at him.

"I was simply trying to be honest," he said.

"You may be *very* sure Lucas James that I will keep this little conversation to myself." She lifted her chin.

He saw the tears in her eyes again.

She hesitated. "As for Suzannah, perhaps we both need to think on that one. I'll try to keep a little distance between Suzannah and myself if you insist, but I will not deliberately hurt that child for no valid reason."

"I didn't ask you to."

Her temper flared. "Yes, you did. You asked me to ignore her and try to stay away from her when you know she's fond of me. If I act distant and uninterested around that little girl or try to ignore her, it will hurt her feelings and it will hurt my grandparents who adore Suzannah. I will not discredit myself in their eyes by ignoring or avoiding that child without explaining all of this conversation to them. Do you want me to do that?"

Her words set off small alarms in his head. "No. I have a good relationship with Beau and Nonnie Wingate. I don't want anything to jeopardize it."

"I feel exactly the same way." She put a hand on the doorframe. "So I think we'd better pretend we entertain a cordial and respectful relationship, don't you, Mr. James?"

"I can do that."

"I won't be here at Millhouse very long and then you can stop worrying about my influence on your daughter. Or worrying I might break down in front of you some time and remind you of your past problems with your wife."

"That was a little nasty," he said, scowling.

"Well, then perhaps we're even for all of your earlier nasty remarks to me." With that statement she turned, letting herself out the door and disappearing quickly down the dark path.

Lucas slumped back into his chair and tried to think. Somehow all he'd intended to say hadn't turned out well. And Mallory's mobile face, with its alternating expressions of joy, surprise, hurt, and anger, floated before his eyes again and again.

The Maine Coon cat, Babycakes, let herself in the cat door and came to jump on Lucas's lap, purring.

"I think I muffed it, Baby," he told the cat. But how could he go back?

# CHAPTER 5

**M**allory cried herself to sleep after leaving Lucas's house. She hated that he'd rattled her emotions and gotten her upset enough to cry again. How had she become a woman who cried so easily? Before her breakdown she could hardly recall crying over anything. The last time she remembered crying at all was years ago over some teenage angst.

Despite a fitful spell of tossing and turning, Mallory finally fell asleep and woke the next morning feeling a little better. Smells of Nonnie's homemade sweet rolls and hot coffee drifted on the air, encouraging her to head downstairs, purposed to enjoy a good day. After breakfast she stayed busy through the morning helping Nonnie prepare for her ladies luncheon for the Red Hat group. Then later in the afternoon, Mallory spent a few quiet hours resting and reading, gaining back the peace Lucas stole from her the evening before.

Now she listened to Nonnie chatting in the kitchen as her grandmother put dinner on the table for the three of them.

"What were you reading this afternoon?" Nonnie asked.

"Some absolutely horrible books," Mallory answered honestly, shaking her head. "I tried reading two or three of the books in your bookcase, the ones with intriguing titles, but all of them were riddled with errors. It made me itch to start editing them. I don't mean to sound critical, but I couldn't help seeing the mistakes and problems." She smiled. "You know I love working with authors, helping to make their writing better."

"Which books did you read?"

Mallory listed off the titles.

"Oh, those books are by some of our friends around the area here. A number of the ladies in my women's groups and their husbands have published novels locally, so of course I needed to buy copies of their books when they came out."

Mallory got up to begin setting the table to help her grandmother. "Nonnie, you know I'm pleased to see so many options for publishing available today—traditional along with all the innovative, new self-publishing opportunities—but some of the new venues have opened the door to a sweep of poor quality work flooding the market. It isn't helping the reputation of authors as a whole, or of publishers, and it makes people more leery of buying books, not certain what they might be getting."

"Well, I admit I noticed an awful lot of problems in those books and I'm certainly not an editor like you." Nonnie wiped her hands on the checked apron she wore around her waist. "Why do you suppose these problems are happening?"

"One reason is that many authors publish their own books without paying a good, qualified editor to help them strengthen their work. Some small presses do the same thing." Mallory paused with a fistful of silverware in her hand. "New authors, kind of like new parents with a new baby, don't see the flaws in their precious, novice creations. New to the publishing world, too, they don't realize what an editor can do to help improve the style and flow of their books and to correct errors—in point-of-view, chronological order, grammar, spelling, and more. That's where I come in." She grinned. "I love to help authors make their work the best it can be, to provide a fresh set of eyes for their writing."

She began to put silverware around the plates as she talked, in her element now. "At Whittier, a book passes through several editorial stages before publication. Many expert sets of eyes go through every book, even books by well-known and very well established authors, before they are allowed on the market."

"That sounds sensible," Nonnie said.

Mallory paused, leaning against the table. "Some of our authors have gone hybrid now, starting their own publishing companies, and are doing well. They have taken what they learned and continue to apply it. One of our editors Doreen Paul, who retired, does freelance editing for many independent authors." Mallory glanced around the table to see what else she needed to do. "It can be done the right way but so many rush the process without going through the stages to ensure they have an excellent product first. Then they wonder why things don't go well."

Nonnie opened the oven door to check on her rolls. "Don't all publishing companies look at the books carefully to see if they meet some standard before they put them out?"

"No, although I really wish the answer was yes to that question." Mallory paused. "If an individual is willing to pay the on-demand publisher or distributor to print a book, most will print virtually anything they receive from a writer, even a book formatted incorrectly with a poor quality cover and filled with editorial problems and uncorrected errors."

Nonnie looked shocked. "You mean I could simply sit down and write a book and then pay some company to publish it—and that no one would check it to see if it was even of a good quality?"

"That's about it."

"Well, my lands. That explains some of the mess in the books I've been picking up around here lately." She took the rolls and a green bean casserole out of the oven and checked the roast simmering in the big crockpot on the kitchen counter before turning back to Mallory. "That is just not right. There ought to be some kind of law that governs that sort of thing. You know, like the USDA and the FDA that make sure our food is okay."

Mallory laughed. "Well, actually that's a great idea, Nonnie. But there are no regulatory boards about book quality."

"What are you girls talking about?" Beau asked, letting himself in the back door.

"The need for regulatory boards to see that only books of good quality get published," Nonnie answered. "Mallory has been telling me that anybody with the money to publish a book today can get one published, even if it's of poor quality and not corrected or edited well."

"Hmmm … I guess not all progress is good progress sometimes." Beau walked over to give Nonnie a kiss on the cheek and then crossed the room to give Mallory a hug and kiss, too. "Maybe in time it will straighten itself out."

Nonnie took out the roast, potatoes, and onions from the crockpot and put everything on a big platter to bring to the table.

Mallory helped carry over the green bean casserole and the basket of rolls. A bowl of fresh strawberries mixed with sliced bananas already sat on the table.

After sitting down, the three Wingates held hands and Beau asked the blessing.

"Any news about the police catching those car thieves?" Nonnie asked, changing the subject after their prayer.

"No." Beau shook his head as he loaded his plate with food. "Now we've had some petty theft around the lodge, too. Mostly in the golf pro shop."

Nonnie looked surprised. "Well, my goodness. What did they take there?"

"Primarily money, from what we can discern." He began to cut his roast, talking around bites. "After the car theft, we began to systematically check other areas of the resort for possible theft and discovered the books were off in the pro shop."

Mallory paused after a mouthful of Nonnie's green bean casserole, so good with fresh mushrooms and little almonds tucked in. "How could car thieves have gotten into the cash register of the pro shop?"

Beau frowned. "We're not sure the thefts are linked."

Nonnie made a tsk-tsking sound. "Trouble comes in threes. The women at the Monday Group luncheon were talking about some petty thievery we've noticed here at the house and tearoom, too."

"What thievery?" Beau looked up in alarm. "You haven't told me about this."

She waved a hand dismissively. "Oh, it's only small things—little jewelry items, curios—but it's starting to add up and look suspicious. I think everyone talking about the car theft brought this to the surface. Several of the women have noticed things missing."

Mallory spread butter on one of Nonnie's homemade yeast rolls. "I didn't hear any of the women at the Red Hat luncheon today talking about items being stolen from them," she said.

"No, it was only at the Monday Group and you didn't arrive until late Monday evening so you didn't hear about it."

Mallory looked at her grandfather. "Do you think all these thefts are related?"

"It seems unlikely, but it's an odd coincidence they've all come to pass at one time." He rubbed his neck. "I don't like all these goings-on at the resort, that's for sure."

Their conversation moved into other areas as they finished their dinner. Then Nonnie got up to get the dessert she'd made, a pretty Orange Crush pound cake with a confectioner's sugar glaze dripping down its sides.

"Is that the new cake recipe you've been wanting to try with orange soda in it?" Beau asked.

"Yes, and if you both like it, I'm planning to make it for one of my luncheons next week." Nonnie began cutting pieces of the cake for them.

"Please. Just a small piece for me," Mallory said. "If I keep eating as heavily as I have since I got here, I'm going to gain weight."

Beau's eyes drifted over her. "A little weight wouldn't hurt you, girl. You've lost some weight through this bad time."

"I have, but not much." Mallory used this change in the dinner conversation to her advantage. "And if it's okay, I want to tell both of you a little more about these past months."

"I hoped you might share more with us when you felt a little stronger," Beau said, reaching across the table to pat her hand.

Mallory gradually repeated the story to them she'd told Elizabeth earlier. "Too much happened to me in a short time," she finished.

"Mother was in the last stages of her life and then died. I had the funeral to deal with and then so much afterwards. I got behind at work, tried to catch up at night. I wasn't sleeping well or eating well with all the stress and the overload of work and care. I got terribly run down, then I picked up the flu, and I couldn't seem to get my strength back afterward. I guess my body simply finally had enough and broke down on me."

She paused, trying to decide what else to say. "It was hard for me to watch Mother grow worse, so slowly and painfully, month after month. I should have reached out more to you. I realize that now, but I was so focused on managing everything myself. Neither of you were close to Mother either, with the problems of the past. I kept thinking I could handle it all and spare you."

"Well bless your heart," Nonnie said, tears in her eyes.

Beau sighed. "Nonnie and I thought you looked worn out and tired when we drove to Savannah for the funeral. Perhaps we should have stayed longer to be more of a help to you then."

"No, you both needed to get back, but I was grateful you came that weekend." She smiled at her grandparents. "Don't feel guilty you didn't stay longer."

"But we do, darling," Nonnie added. "Beau and I talked about it several times. We knew you were going through a trial with Delores. Perhaps we should have come earlier and been more of a support to you."

Beau gave a disgusted snort. "Delores wouldn't have welcomed us around her sick bed any more than she welcomed us in her life when all was well."

"You shouldn't talk disrespectfully about the dead," Nonnie admonished.

Beau shot her an irritated look. "Mallory is a grown woman now. She knows Delores held no fondness for us."

Nonnie sighed. "Yes and I always regretted that. We tried so hard to be loving and welcoming to Delores when she married Jarrett."

"Don't feel bad that she wasn't more fond of you," Mallory put in. "In many ways she wasn't very fond of me, either. Oh, she loved me, of course, like she did Daddy, but she didn't possess a very warm heart. It took me a long time to see this and to not feel I'd done something wrong to not receive more of her affection."

"You know Beau and I always loved you with all our hearts, don't you?" Nonnie reached a hand across the table to put over Mallory's.

"Yes, and I'm so grateful for that. Here at your home I always felt loved and accepted just as I was. Your unconditional love was a great solace to me." She twisted at a strand of her hair, thinking back. "With Delores—and that's what she liked me to call her more often than Mother—I always felt like I fell short in some way. Delores was demanding and often critical. She policed my life, my friends and activities more than I liked. She seldom understood any of my interests. She did encourage me to excel in school, though. And she praised me for the things I did well at home— cooking, housekeeping, taking care of the bookkeeping as I grew older, running errands."

Beau laughed. "That's because Delores never cared for any of those home related chores. She was eager to see you take them over so she wouldn't need to do them."

Mallory grinned. "Even I figured that out, Grandad."

"I could never understand why Delores was so against coming to live at the resort." Beau scratched his head. "I know Jarrett wanted to come back home."

"Yes." Nonnie put in. "And Jarrett came back from Nashville whenever he could, even when Delores wouldn't come with him or was working. He always brought you with him too, Mallory. We so loved having you both."

"Did Delores ever tell you what she had against the resort or us?" Beau asked as he got up from the table to cut himself another small slice of Nonnie's cake. "Why she manipulated and schemed so hard to keep Jarrett from coming back home?"

Mallory considered his questions. "Here's what I learned over time about that. Mother came from McMinnville, a small town in Tennessee. Her father owned the only funeral home in town, Taylor's Funeral Home. Perhaps you remember Delores had three older brothers. She was a late child and her parents spoiled her when young, but then clamped down on her when she began to show too much spunk and rebellion in her early teens."

She smiled a little, remembering her mother telling this story. "Delores's mother Idelle told her it was time she grew up, remembered who she was, and began to act accordingly. Idelle, who Delores already had a poor relationship with, began to push her to help with the cooking, cleaning, gardening, and household tasks—none of which Delores held any interest in. Although earlier Delores had been her father's 'little darling,' now Delores father shifted all responsibility for rearing Delores over onto his wife. Delores began to rebel, especially when watching her older brothers enjoy so much more freedom and such different life expectations."

"You know, I remember Jarrett said Delores had a very poor relationship with her mother and family in McMinnville," Nonnie put in. "Jarrett told me she seldom wanted to go to see them for a visit."

"That's true. I hardly know that side of my family at all." Mallory spread her hands with the words.

"So how did this problem with Delores's family impact how she saw us?" Beau asked, confused. "We never had unrealistic expectations of Delores or pushed her to be anything other than what she was."

"I think Delores transferred her feelings about her family and the restrictions they imposed on her over onto you and Nonnie—and even onto Daddy and me." Mallory tried to think how to explain what she learned about her mother over the years.

"A defining moment in Mother's life occurred when she got caught smoking behind the funeral home by Mrs. Beard, the widowed bookkeeper at Taylor Funeral Home," Mallory said. "Mother told me the words Mrs. Beard said to her that day changed the course of her whole life. I believe it's true, too, because Mother told me those exact words herself so many times that I practically memorized them."

She paused, pulling up the words from her memory. "Mrs. Beard said, 'The way out of this little town, Delores Taylor, is not accomplished by rebelling. With that you'll guarantee your life will remain small, limited, and that you will end up right here for the rest of your days—just like me. The way out is to go along sweetly for a few years, study hard to make excellent grades so you can get a scholarship, and then go off to a posh college like Vanderbilt. You start reading what they want in those scholarship guides and you become that, Delores. That's the way out. This route of smoking and rebelling is a dead end road and it will cause you to end up spending your life exactly like me or your mother right here in McMinnville—and probably married to someone like Lester Barnes.'"

Mallory laughed as she finished her recitation. "Lester Barnes was a creepy boy with a big crush on Delores at the time, ugly and a real loser from all I heard. Mother said the concept of ending up married to someone like Lester, who she knew had a crush on her, or of becoming a clone of Mrs. Beard or her mother shook her down to her roots." She giggled. "Mother said she began to read what those scholarships wanted and she worked to excel in her academics and in clubs and extracurricular activities. She focused on a new goal after that. She wanted out. She made it, too, graduating near the top of her class with a whole paragraph in her high school annual listing clubs and offices, as well as beauty contest awards. Mother won a full scholarship to Vanderbilt, too."

"Delores always was a smart woman— at least in some ways," Beau put in.

"Yes," Mallory agreed. "She majored in business management and marketing in college, with a focus on public relations. She'd learned already—as she often told me—that she was good at managing people and things."

"There's a fine line between managing and manipulating," Beau interrupted.

"You're right, Grandad, and Mother crossed that line all too many times. She always told me: *A person can always be what they need to be in order to get what they want.* It was one of her favorite personal sayings. After all, it had worked for her. The fact that she might be less than genuine in the process, or that she might use, hurt, or exploit others, seldom mattered much to her. Mrs. Beard set her on a whole, new course she would follow for the rest of her life."

"That's a little sad to hear." Nonnie shook her head. "We saw some of what Delores was like when Jarrett first brought her to visit us, but I don't think Jarrett ever saw the problems we did."

"He saw them later," Mallory said. "Daddy didn't mind getting a job in Nashville right after he and Mother graduated from Vanderbilt at first. He told me he agreed with Mother it might be good for him to experience some years in the business world on his own before coming back to help run the resort. He enjoyed his job with the new Opryland Theme Park in suburban Nashville. Daddy was gregarious and entertaining by nature, and a hard worker, and he quickly moved up in management responsibilities, which thrilled Delores."

"That woman was always ambitious." Beau refilled his glass with iced tea from the pitcher on the table and then passed the pitcher Mallory's way.

Mallory poured herself another glass of tea, too. "Yes, Delores was ambitious, and she soon got into a good job situation herself working at a big downtown hotel but then got pregnant with me. She told me many times that getting pregnant at that point in her life was *not* in her plans."

Nonnie snorted. "Delores didn't waste much time getting back to work, either, after you were born. That was at a time, too, when most young women stayed home with their babies for a few years if they could." Nonnie carried some dishes over to the sink while she talked.

"Well, Delores didn't enjoy motherhood any more than she did handling other domestic duties. She soon found a good housekeeper/sitter shortly after I was born and went back to work.

Although Daddy wanted more children, Mother never did. When Daddy began to yearn to come back home to the resort to work and live, Mother found excuses to postpone a move, too."

"I remember when Jarrett began to grow discontent in Nashville," Nonnie said.

Mallory paused, remembering. "Yes, and those cross desires began to cause a big rift between the two of them. You two may not know that, but I recall a lot of fights and angry scenes between them as a girl."

"I'm sorry for that," Nonnie said. "Beau and I knew Jarrett was unhappy. He came home more and more often in those last years before he got killed."

Beau frowned. "Yes, and Jarrett's death put the icing on the cake for your mother in cutting off all ties with us. She used Jarrett's death as an excuse to never want to come back here again."

"Yes, but blessedly she allowed you to come." Nonnie reached a hand across to put it over Mallory's again. "We're so grateful for that. It helped our sorrow after losing Jarrett. To have lost you, too, would have been simply horrible."

"You know we tried to get Delores to allow you to come live with us permanently," Beau told her.

Mallory smiled at him. "Mother told me that once. But I'd already become useful to Delores, even at ten years old. I'd started doing some of the housework and cooking. I think Mother feared being totally alone, too. Deep down, she wasn't happy. I think that's why she moved from one relationship to another over the years and from one job to another."

"You did move often," Beau agreed.

Mallory sighed. "Yes, and usually very unexpectedly because one of Delores's relationships went sour and she wanted a new start in a new place. I never got to put down roots anywhere. Except here." She smiled at her grandparents. "This place, your house, was always more home to me than any other. I think that's why I already feel so much better, so much more easy and peaceful, since I came here to stay with you."

"Oh, honey, I'm so glad." Nonnie put a hand to her heart. "Going through that hard, hard time with Delores couldn't have been easy for you."

"No, Mother grew terribly demanding—and angry. She had no peace in dealing with the illness that attacked her or in facing death."

"She had no relationship with the Lord, either." Nonnie shook her head as she spoke the words.

Beau chuckled. "I think if Delores could have told God how to run things down here on the earth she might have decided to develop a relationship with the Almighty."

"Now, Beau, that isn't a very nice thing to say," Nonnie chided.

Mallory laughed. "Actually, it's a very honest thing to say. I'm grateful to both of you for helping me to come to know the Lord in a real way at a young age. I needed a strong faith as a girl to live with Delores and to bounce around all those years with her. I especially needed a strong faith to draw on these last two years when Delores grew so sick."

"Child, I know you enjoy your life and your work in Savannah, but I hope you will always think of this as your home." Nonnie got up to walk around the table to give Mallory a hug. "We love you so much."

"Thank you," Mallory answered with healthy tears in her eyes.

Beau cleared his throat. "Girl, are there any business or personal details back in Savannah you need me to take care of for you? I'll be glad to fly down there and handle anything that still needs to be done."

"You are sweet to say that, Grandad. If I think of anything, I might let you handle it for me, but I don't believe you'll need to fly down—just possibly make a few calls for me." She paused, considering her next words. "There is one more thing I need to tell you, though."

"Let's go sit out on the porch then, darlin'," Nonnie said. "It's a lovely evening and the lilac and honeysuckle blooms smell so sweet on the air this time of year."

They carried their iced tea outside and settled into the comfortable cushioned chairs on the outside patio. The peaceful sounds of crickets and night frogs from the pond drifted on the air.

"Are you unhappy with your work?" Beau asked.

"No, I love my job," Mallory said, propping her feet on a nearby chair. "I feel so blessed I got that little summer job at Whittier while in college and then was offered a job with them even before I graduated. I love my work and I actually like Savannah very much. I've stayed there longer than any other place in my life. Savannah is a beautiful city, and I live in a nice townhouse not far from the office. You've visited there a few times."

"Yes, right after you moved in, for two short vacation trips to the coast, and then for the funeral." Nonnie ticked off the times on her fingers.

"So what's the problem?" Beau asked, direct as always.

"The year before Mother came to stay with me, I met someone special, a young man named Ethan Broussard." Mallory paused, trying to decide what she wanted to say. "Ethan's family owns a lovely shop in downtown Savannah called Broussard's that sells European antiques, gifts, collectibles, and accessories. Ethan and I met in a downtown café where we both often stopped for lunch. We began talking over our lunches and soon started to date."

Mallory leaned her head back, closing her eyes and remembering. "We had so many things in common. We enjoyed films, plays, and the symphony. We liked to visit art exhibits and other cultural activities around the city. After a few months, we began to talk about a future together. We didn't get formally engaged, but we talked about marriage often and started to make plans."

"I think you mentioned you were seeing someone." Nonnie tapped her chin. "But I don't remember you telling us much about this young man. Are you still dating him?"

"No." It still pained her to say the word. "When Mother came to me and as her health failed, I had less time. Delores proved difficult to be around, and Ethan soon found excuses not to drop by. We shared what times we could find around our schedules at

Ethan's place or going out to events we enjoyed." She paused. "But as time moved on, these opportunities diminished."

She sighed deeply. "I was simply too drained most evenings to do anything beyond seeing to Mother, getting caught up on household chores, and completing the work I had to bring home from Whittier."

"A man who loves you should stand by you in a difficult time and be a help and support to you," Beau put in.

"Yes, but Ethan *wasn't* a support in that way or in any way." Mallory almost snapped the words. "He was a very fastidious person by nature. He didn't like disorder or unpleasantness. He didn't tolerate sickness well."

"Since you've already popped off at me, I'll risk adding that Ethan doesn't sound like a very good catch if he couldn't offer you support in a time of trouble. If he only thought about himself and how inconvenient Delores's problems made his life then I don't think much of him already." Beau spoke the words matter-of-factly.

Mallory sighed. "I wish I'd seen things that clearly about Ethan at the time," she admitted. "It might have saved me some sorrow."

"We tend to make excuses for those we love," Nonnie offered.

"Yes, and that's exactly what I did." Mallory agreed. "I knew after a time, of course, that Mother wouldn't make it. I thought when everything was over Ethan and I could pick up where we left off before." She looked out into the night remembering.

"And?" Beau asked.

"And I'd ironed a couple of shirts for Ethan one weekend when he missed getting them dropped off at the cleaners." She crossed her arms. "He said he'd run by to get them early on Monday morning, but I decided to surprise him and take them over Sunday evening. Mother seemed quieter than usual that day, and I felt I could leave her to spend a little time with Ethan. I hoped we might take a walk in the park or go to a movie."

Mallory closed her eyes remembering. "I walked up the sidewalk that led to his front door. It passes by his bedroom window. I glanced over. The blind was up part way, and I could see him in bed with another woman." She felt her heart wrench at the memory. "I must have shrieked or something. The window was partly open. They both turned to look right at me."

"Oh, honey, how awful." Nonnie put a hand to her mouth.

"After standing there in total shock for a few moments, I threw the shirts down on the ground, stomped on them, and then ran to my car."

"Atta girl." Beau chuckled.

"Beau, this isn't funny," Nonnie scolded, shaking a finger at him.

"Well, it is a little funny, if it hadn't happened to me," Mallory admitted. "If I'd read it in one of the books I edit, I'd have thought it a great dramatic scene. But it was awful to experience. I was already so tired and worn out from simply everything and it really hurt my heart. I went home and wept, and then Mother passed away the very next day, as if things couldn't get any worse. I had the funeral arrangements to get through and then caught the flu. Through all this, Ethan kept calling me all the time, trying to apologize and explain things."

"What was there to explain?" Beau asked.

Mallory shook her head. "He kept telling me it didn't mean anything he slept with that woman, that it wasn't important. He tried to explain he simply needed some relief from all the strain we'd experienced in our relationship with my mother so sick."

"What a creep." Beau snorted. "You're well rid of him."

"I keep telling myself that." Mallory pushed a swatch of her hair back behind her ear. "I really do."

"Your mind has received the message but your heart hasn't caught up." Nonnie smiled at her.

Mallory sent a forced smile back at her grandmother. "That's it, exactly, Nonnie. I know Ethan wasn't faithful, and I know, too, I don't want to spend my life with someone I can't trust or who wouldn't stand by me in trouble, but it's still hard and hurtful. I carried strong feelings for Ethan."

"I'm so sorry you got hurt, honey." Nonnie got up to give her a kiss on the forehead. "I hope time will heal your heart."

"Hmmph." Beau leaned over to pat her arm. "It's no wonder the bottom of your emotions dropped out after that romantic fiasco—coupled with Delores dying and you getting sick with the flu. That's a lot of strain all at one time even for a strong and healthy person."

"I didn't even realize I'd hit the end of my leash until I suddenly started shaking and crying and then completely fell apart." She covered her face with her hands. "I was so embarrassed. It happened at work, and my colleagues at Whittier simply didn't know what to do with me."

Beau scowled. "You probably pushed yourself, while sick and run down, to go back to work too soon. A person can only stand so much strain without breaking down in some way, Mallory."

"Yes, I think I've learned that, Grandad."

"Well, I feel much better after hearing this story," Beau said. "You didn't give us much information on the phone when you called and asked if you could come and stay here for a time to recover." He paused, his eyes studying her face. "You do seem to be feeling better already, too."

Nonnie reached a hand across to pat Mallory's knee. "I know you're better, darling, but I did hear you sniffling in your room last night. The nights are the hardest sometimes when you've been hurt."

Mallory had no intention of telling her grandmother that the hurtful remarks made by Lucas James last night brought on that stint of tears she'd heard.

"I am truly better," she said instead, giving them both a genuine smile. "Just being here with the two of you is like a healing tonic."

Nonnie sent a warm smile back at her. "Well, your grandfather and I want you to take it easy and rest while you're here. Feel free to stay for as long as you want, too, and to come stay with us anytime you can, do you hear?"

"I hear, Nonnie, and thank you." Mallory got up to hug them

both. "Now I'm going to go inside and clean up the kitchen while you two sit out here and enjoy the night air."

"Nonsense, I'll go in and help you," her grandmother insisted, getting up to head toward the kitchen door with her. "Beau can go fill the bird feeders in the garden, and then we'll all watch that nice TV movie I marked in the newspaper this morning. It's a comedy and it will do us good to laugh a little."

Mallory followed her grandmother back into the kitchen with her heart a little lighter. It seemed to help to talk everything out. To see that most people understood the problems she'd passed through, saw her breakdown as temporary—brought on by too much strain—and saw no reason not to expect her to be back to her old self soon.

*Most people, that is,* she added in her thoughts. Mallory's heart still hurt from the harsh words Lucas sent her way last night.

She could hear Delores words slide through her mind, too: *All men are unreliable, Mallory. Trust in yourself and your own abilities. Men will only hurt you. Guard your heart. Keep your independence.*

Mallory heard these words often in her thoughts whenever she felt attracted to a man, making her hesitate to trust. Ethan wasn't the first man to hurt her heart, either. *Was her mother right?* She wondered. *Perhaps so.* It seemed that most of the men Mallory found attractive proved to be hurtful and unreliable just like her mother cautioned. How sad.

# CHAPTER 6

Two weeks passed without Lucas encountering Mallory Wingate again. He knew he should feel glad about that, but he didn't. A niggling sense of guilt lingered in his mind that he might have been unkind to Mallory at a hard time in her life. She might have been right, too, about his real desire to avoid her. Learning about Mallory's breakdown brought back a sweep of old memories of his years living with Cecily.

"Dang it," he said to himself as he took a club out of his bag and lined up for a long drive down the fairway on Millhouse's eighteenth hole. He didn't like this jumbled mix of feelings and impressions continuing to haunt and follow him.

Finishing his afternoon practice round, Lucas made his way through the pro shop on the way to his office. He found Barry Short, the pro shop manager, and Denise Ogle, the shop's assistant manager, both working today.

"I thought you were off today, Denise," Lucas said.

She flashed him one of her homespun smiles that always made customers and clients want to linger for a chat. "I came in to update the website." She leaned forward to study the computer screen in front of her. "It's hard to find time to work on it when I'm running the shop."

Lucas turned to Barry. "Beau's accountant is coming to review the shop books more carefully. Probably next week."

Barry frowned. "I've looked through them, Lucas. I'm sure I can pinpoint where the trouble is. It's probably only a math error."

"Maybe so, but with all the thefts around the resort right now, Beau wants his accountant to check everything." He watched Barry continue to scowl. "It's no reflection on you, Barry. He's looking at the books and records in every department around the resort."

Denise glanced up. "Have you uncovered more thefts around the resort besides the car?"

"Nothing major, but Beau told me Nonnie reported a rash of petty thefts at the tearoom, too." He paused, glancing around the rustic shop with its rich oak shelves and furniture, rock fireplace, and green plaid carpeting. "We should probably do a full inventory check at the pro shop, too."

"I can't see how there's any link between a car theft, our books at the shop being off, and lost items at the tearoom." Denise wrinkled her nose.

"Beau and I don't see a link between any of the problems either. They seem so unrelated. But all of these concerns affect the resort and all of them need to be resolved," Lucas said.

"Okay. I'll start an inventory check today," Barry said, but Lucas could tell he wasn't happy about doing it.

Lucas headed upstairs to his office above the pro shop. The thefts and problems around the resort were certainly making everyone feel edgy. If the thefts weren't coming from outside, then the fact had to be faced they could be coming from within. That wasn't a pretty thought. The staff at Millhouse had always been like a warm, cooperative, and trusting family.

After finishing needed work in the office, Lucas headed to his sister Elizabeth's to pick up Suzannah. He found Elizabeth sitting on the broad front porch of her big white farmhouse making herbal sachet bags, and he could see the girls playing on a quilt under the shade of a big maple tree in the yard.

"Have a seat, Lucas," Elizabeth said, gesturing to a chair across the table from hers. "There's a pitcher of lemonade and some glasses on the side table." She pointed. "You'll find a cooler with some ice underneath the table."

"You're well prepared," he commented, going to get ice from

the cooler, plopping it into a tall glass, and then pouring lemonade over it.

"Little girls get thirsty and if I keep the lemonade here on the porch, I don't constantly need to run into the house to get drinks or ice while I'm working."

Lucas glanced toward the yard, wondering what the girls were so involved with.

"The girls are playing paper dolls," Elizabeth said, following his glance.

He lifted an eyebrow.

"Don't worry. These are the no-scissors type—with magnetic paper dolls the clothing pieces stick to. According to the box they came in, the paper dolls are perfect for ages four and up."

"Wow. Where did you find those?"

"They were a birthday gift from Nonnie, one of the many gifts Abby opened at her little party on Friday."

"I'm sorry I couldn't make it over for that."

"Don't be." She laughed. "It was a crazy time with ten little girls under school age running all over the place shrieking and giggling. I aged three years that day."

Lucas grinned. "Suzannah said it was fun."

"Yeah, the girls had a good time. And thanks for the Twinkle Toes tennis shoes. I never got a chance to buy some the day Abby and I went to the dentist. Abby has pouted ever since over not getting by the store."

"Well, I'm glad you mentioned the shoes last week. I never know what to get for these birthday occasions." He leaned over to sniff at one of the bowls of dried herbs on the table.

"This one smells like Christmas trees." Lucas took a pinch of herbs from the bowl to hold it closer to his nose.

"Actually it's rosemary," Elizabeth said. "It has a pungent, evergreen smell much like Christmas trees."

"What are the others?" He gestured to the other four bowls.

"I'm making five different kinds of sachet bags today—rosemary, lavender, mint, a rose petal medley, and lemon balm." She picked up a small organza bag while she talked and spooned it full of dried herbs.

"Pretty bags," he commented.

"I order these bags online since I can get them cheaper in bulk than I can make them. They even come with little ribbon drawstrings." She demonstrated tying up the little organza bag and then picked up another red-gingham bag to show him. "I order these, too. Aren't they cute?"

Lucas studied the assortment of finished sachet bags Elizabeth had piled into two big baskets on the porch floor. "You've been busy today."

"Here." She pushed a pile of bags she'd finished filling in his direction and handed him a stack of small cardstock labels. "Make yourself useful and tie business labels on each of these bags. Just tuck a twist tie through the hole in the card and tie it around the top of the bag."

He scowled as he eyed the decorative labels she'd given him. Each had the words "Lavender Sachet" in calligraphy script with her business name Whitehouse Farm underneath. "I'm not very good at these crafty things."

She crossed her arms. "If you can put a twist tie on a bread bag you can do this, Lucas. I'm handling the crafty part."

"Okay, but if you're not happy with the results, don't say I didn't warn you." He studied the example she'd given him and worked to duplicate it, hooking the label onto the bag with one of the ties.

"Pretty good, Brother. I'm glad to see those talented golf hands of yours have other uses." She sent him one of her saucy smiles. "Besides if I didn't give you something to occupy those hands, you'd soon be fidgeting or drumming your fingers on the table and driving me crazy. You have so much restless energy."

"Who came to Abby's party?" He changed the subject.

Elizabeth named off a list of little girls who lived nearby in the Pittman Center area or who attended Beech Grove Baptist Church with them. "Ten is a big group, but thank goodness Mallory Wingate came to help me with the party."

Lucas worked on another bag, not making a comment to that.

"You have met Mallory Wingate, haven't you?"

"Yes, I did—over at Nonnie and Beau's." He rubbed his neck, hoping this conversation wouldn't lead to more talk about Mallory.

Elizabeth grew quiet and Lucas glanced up to see her watching him thoughtfully.

"What?" he asked.

"It's not like you to practically dismiss meeting a beautiful woman like Mallory Wingate." She tied off another sachet bag. "Besides, I happen to know from Nonnie the two of you met on the airplane coming back from Savannah and that Mallory spent an evening at your house, as well. Suzannah is crazy about Mallory and talks about her all the time, including telling me lots of details of her evening visit at your place."

Lucas scowled. "Mallory brought over Suzannah's doll she left behind at Nonnie's and Breakfast Bars Nonnie baked. It wasn't exactly a social event."

"You're acting very odd and prickly about this. Why is that?"

"I'm *not* acting odd and prickly." He felt his voice rise. "You're just trying to make more of my casual meeting with M.T. Wingate than there was."

"M.T.?"

"That's her work name at Whittier Publishing. I assumed you'd know that since you seem to be so well informed." Even he could hear the sarcasm in his voice and he immediately regretted it.

Elizabeth caught his eyes with hers. "Did you and Mallory have a fight?"

"What makes you ask that?" He glanced at his watch, trying to think of an excuse to leave.

"Because you're acting snippy about my questions and because Mallory acted odd, too, when your name came up." She pushed a few more sachet bags his way. "And don't you dare offer me some lame excuse as to why you suddenly need to leave. I want to know what happened between you and Mallory Wingate."

Lucas straightened. "It's really not any of your business, Elizabeth."

Her mouth dropped open in surprise and she stomped her foot under the table. "I can't believe you said that to me. I'm your only sister. I help take care of your child every day. I feed you many nights of the week. I share my life and thoughts with you. And suddenly you have the nerve to tell me I have no right to ask why you and the Wingate's granddaughter aren't getting along?"

"No one said we weren't getting along."

"No one said you were either."

Yielding to the inevitable, Lucas pushed back his chair with annoyance. "Okay. I met M.T. on the airplane. All we exchanged were first names. She's an attractive woman and smart. We got to talking." He shrugged. "We shared dinner in the airport in Atlanta. Flirted a little." That was all he intended to say about that.

Lucas rubbed his neck nervously. "I had no idea she was Beau and Nonnie's granddaughter until she walked into the kitchen the next morning dressed in this flimsy little skirt and a skimpy top."

Elizabeth laughed. "You like her."

"Yes," he answered without thinking. "I mean no," he amended.

Elizabeth always had a way of getting things out of him he didn't want to confide. She'd been clever like that since they were kids.

"So which is it, yes or no?" She gave him a catbird smile of triumph.

"It's no because Mallory has problems Suzannah and I don't need right now."

Elizabeth looked baffled. "What are you talking about?"

Lucas twisted a tie onto a sachet bag a little too savagely, almost tearing the thin material. "Didn't anyone tell you Mallory had a nervous breakdown?"

"And this affects you and Suzannah in what way?"

Lucas frowned at her. "Don't be dense, Elizabeth. You know what Suzannah and I went through with Cecily."

Her mouth dropped open. "And you're relating the two health conditions?"

"They're both mental health issues."

She drew in a sharp, indignant breath. "Actually the two conditions are about as remotely linked as a head cold to pneumonia."

"Both are emotional sicknesses," he argued.

Elizabeth studied him thoughtfully. "Let me guess," she said at last. "You said words something like this to Mallory Wingate."

He fidgeted in his seat. "I simply suggested to her it might not be a good thing for Suzannah to spend too much time with her since she hadn't been well."

"You told her about Cecily?"

"A little."

"How did Mallory take this?"

Lucas glanced out toward the girls playing under the tree, not answering. Her questions were getting too personal now.

"You hurt Mallory's feelings," Elizabeth said quietly. "That poor girl. Do you have any idea what she's been through lately? What strain she's been under? Then you made her feel like a pariah because she broke emotionally under all the stress she carried."

"Maybe I didn't think it through carefully or have all the facts," he admitted, feeling chastised now.

Elizabeth sat making more bags for a little while, not talking.

"So, what? You think I'm a creep for worrying about Suzannah?" Lucas said at last.

She lifted her eyes to his. "I don't believe you were really thinking about Suzannah."

He ran a hand through his hair, irritated. "Gee, you sound like Mallory. Did she tell you what she said to me?"

She watched him. "Actually she said nothing to me. But I could tell from how she skirted the very subject of your name that something must have happened. It contrasted too radically from Suzannah's ongoing, rapturous babblings. Suzannah really likes Mallory."

"I've seen that." Lucas busied himself tying labels on the little sachet bags.

"Let me clarify something to you as a nurse, Lucas," Elizabeth said. "Bipolar disorder, which Cecily had, is a manic depressive illness that can cause drastic changes and intense emotional states or episodes, very different from the normally expected moods and behaviors of most people."

"Oh, really?"

She ignored him. "The cause of bipolar is not known. Some medical studies suggest it may be genetic. Others think it is linked to differences in brain development, especially as related to the development of the prefrontal cortex. That's why it often appears first in the teen years." She continued stuffing sachet bags while she talked. "In individuals with bipolar their moods and behavior often alternate between two extremes—a manic, overly exuberant stage and a depressive, overly sad, and often reclusive stage."

"Elizabeth, you're not telling me anything I don't know."

"I'm just reminding you that this mental disorder is defined in the DSM-IV, the *Diagnostic and Statistical Manual of Mental Disorders*, which includes all recognized health disorders in the mental health field. And this disorder, once diagnosed, requires psychotherapy and medications. It doesn't resolve itself naturally over time. However, many people with bipolar are able to lead stable, productive lives, but not all can or do, as you learned with Cecily."

Lucas felt himself getting annoyed as he always did with any discussion about Cecily. "Your point is?"

"My point is that a minor emotional breakdown, like Mallory experienced, is on the opposite end of the mental health continuum from conditions like bipolar. People experience nervous breakdowns, or disambiguations, from stress-induced situations. A mental breakdown like Mallory had is defined as temporary in nature, usually occurring to an individual with otherwise sound mental faculties. It is not listed in the DSM-IV for that reason. It resolves itself with recognition, time, life changes, rest, healthful activities, and understanding." She stressed the last word in particular as she finished.

"You think I wasn't understanding."

"It sounds that way." Elizabeth started filling yellow organza sachet bags from a new bowl, the scent of the lemon balm herbs crisp and tangy on the air. She passed Lucas new labels to use.

They worked in silence for a few moments. "I've always felt so sad for you over what happened with Cecily," Elizabeth said after a time. "She was so beautiful but so emotionally fragile in many ways. I always felt her parents should have told you clearly about her condition before you married."

"They thought marriage might stabilize her, be good for her."

"They were in denial about her condition." Elizabeth frowned. "From what you shared with me later, they protected her, covered for her after her symptoms and condition began to manifest. They never saw to it that she got the help she needed. They kept hoping she would outgrow it, like a teenage aberration."

Lucas scowled. "I always felt they were disappointed in me because Cecily didn't get better after we married."

"That was wrong of them to think that." Elizabeth paused in her work. "And you've always felt guilty you couldn't fix things for Cecily. You need to look back realistically and remember Cecily was often her own worst enemy. She refused to take her medications regularly, and she often enjoyed being a victim to her condition."

"That's a rather mean thing to say."

"Yes, but it needs to be said. That attitude kept Cecily from handling her mental illness successfully. She often liked being 'poor little Cecily.' She liked having an excuse for any selfish, immature, or irresponsible behavior she wanted to engage in."

"Why are we having this conversation?" Lucas felt his temper rising.

"Because you still haven't come to terms with the ways in which Cecily hindered herself from living a life with positive quality. It wasn't only the bipolar condition that got in Cecily's way. She was also a spoiled and selfish girl."

"Haven't you ever heard it's not nice to talk ill of the dead?"

"Yes, but you continuing to hold false conceptions about Cecily is worse. As I said before, many people with bipolar and other mental illnesses handle their medical conditions very effectively and live productive lives. It isn't your fault that Cecily didn't."

He threw down the bag he was working on in annoyance. "But I was gone when she died. I was here at the resort. I'd left her." The words flew out of his mouth before Lucas could stop them.

She reached a hand across the table to put it on his arm. "If you had been there, it wouldn't have changed things. You know that. Think how many other times Cecily slipped out of the house and took off to engage in unhealthy behaviors when you were at home before you came here. You know it's true."

"But maybe if I'd been there, we might have found her in time."

"And maybe not." She patted his arm. "You need to let go of the guilt that you could have changed what happened. You also need to let go of the fear of becoming involved with anyone else."

He bristled. "I've gotten involved with other women."

"Only casually," she answered. "And to fear Mallory because she experienced a minor emotional breakdown shows clearly you still harbor unresolved feelings about Cecily's death."

Lucas scowled at her. "You don't simply *forget* that someone you loved has died—and tragically. She was my wife, Elizabeth."

"Yes, and it's been over four years since Cecily died. And she was very unstable for several years before that."

Lucas heard Suzannah and Abby's childish giggles floating across the summer air.

"Mallory recently lost someone she loved, too, Lucas. She nursed her mother through two years of debilitating lung cancer. She couldn't stop the cancer from taking her mother's life or stop it from causing her mother's suffering and anguish. She understands the grief of death, too. And her grief is much fresher."

"You think I rubbed salt in the wound."

"Well, I didn't hear your conversations, but it sounds like you didn't apply healing salve and kindness."

"Mallory said I was unkind."

"Then perhaps you owe her an apology."

Lucas hated to consider that thought. *What could he say?*

He sighed. "Listen, I need to head for the house." He got

up, stretching as he did. "I took off early today so I could take Suzannah on a walk I promised her."

"Yes. She told me you promised to take her to Rock Creek Falls and the old cemetery one day." She hesitated. "You're not mad at me for our talk today, are you, Lucas?"

"No, only mad at life sometimes." He walked over to give her a kiss on the forehead. "You've always talked straight to me and I appreciate that. It's helped me in some rough times when I couldn't find my way."

"I love you, Lucas. I hope you know that."

"I know you do." He patted her cheek. "I'm truly grateful for all the love and help you've given me with Suzannah, too."

"She's a joy and she's my family." Her eyes moved to the girls playing under the tree. "It's been a blessing to me in many ways to keep Suzannah these last years. It's given Abby someone to love and someone to play with every day. Abby's days might have been a little lonely out here in the country without Suzannah. And the girls get along so well together."

"They both love those Twinkle Toes shoes, too," he added, watching the girls running across the yard toward them now, their bright shoes blinking multi-colors in the sunshine.

# CHAPTER 7

**M**allory had been at her grandparents for two weeks now. A quiet peace had settled over her. Her emotions had calmed down and the nightmares, which previously robbed her sleep, had stopped. Dr. Henry had been right that she needed this rest and change.

Today she was helping Nonnie with the luncheon for the Monday Group, giving her grandmother extra time to enjoy the lunch and a visit with her group of old friends. After cutting slices of Orange Crush cake in the kitchen, Mallory put a sprig of mint and a scoop of orange sherbet on each cake plate, loaded the dessert dishes onto the dessert cart, and then pushed the cart out to the group in the tearoom.

The women in this group had known Mallory since her childhood, and she looked around with fondness at the twelve familiar women, seated around three tables. Each table was decorated with gay floral tablecloths and green hobnail Depression glass vases filled with pink, white, and magenta roses from the garden. Nonnie sat with three of her friends— Leona Davis, a regional photographer and wildflower expert, Dottie French, retired teacher and principal, who also headed the monthly Book Club at the tearoom, and the quieter Esther Dagley who worked with her husband in his veterinarian's office. Nearby at the second table sat the socialites and community activists, Betty Lou Reagan, Annabel Trotter, Ina Ruth Stafford, and Jackie Cardwell, all dressed to the nines and full of gossip and chat. At the last table were the women whose roots reached deepest into Pittman Center's past, Gladys Whaley and Ellen Jean Kiley, whose families farmed in the area, Polly Trentham, a local pastor's wife, and Tilly Buchanan Walker, who Mallory always thought of affectionately as the ditz, a slightly neurotic and self-absorbed worrier.

"I sure remember your father Jarrett Wingate with fondness," Leona Davis said, sending Mallory a smile as she put a plate of dessert in front of her. "I watched your daddy grow up, you know, and he and my son Waylon were fine friends."

"Nonnie told me many stories about Jarrett and Waylon's boyhood adventures—and stories about the two of you as girls, too," Mallory said, smiling at Leona, who'd been her grandmother's best friend since girlhood.

Gladys Whaley, always the more outspoken in the group, glanced up at Mallory as she passed by. "It's a shame they never found out who killed your father, Mallory."

"Gladys, honestly." Nonnie gasped. "Jarrett's death was *not* a murder."

Dottie French shook a finger at Gladys. "They ruled it a hunting accident from the evidence they found. If you remember, my husband Don served as the primary police officer in the investigation."

"Oh I remember all that." Gladys waved a hand with annoyance. "But I always felt if Jarrett's death had *only* been an accident someone would have come forward to confess to it."

"Oh, Gladys, don't create drama where there is none," Annabel Trotter said, sending a frown her way. "The person probably feared coming forward. My husband Jim always said whoever shot Jarrett by accident worried that any admittance, even if honorable and contrite, might turn into a criminal investigation and charge." Annabel's husband Jim was an attorney and Mallory knew Annabel's words were true. She'd heard them often enough when people talked about her father's death over the years.

"Annabel's right," Dottie agreed. "It would have hit the news and been a big scandal if anyone confessed to an accidental shooting."

Gladys crossed her arms. "All that's true enough, I suppose, but I often wonder how that shooter has lived with himself all these years, knowing he killed someone but that no one knows about it. I still don't like the lack of resolution of it for Nonnie and Beau's sake either."

Tilly piped in, her eyes wide. "It worries me to think that person is still living in the area. What if he isn't stable and should shoot at one of us?"

"Leave it to you to worry over that," Betty Lou said, rolling her eyes. "The accident happened over twenty years ago. The shooter is probably dead by now."

Tilly lifted her chin. "Well, you never know. And I don't feel nearly as safe living alone since Bobby Joe left." Mallory knew Tilly's husband left her and filed for divorce in the last year, and Nonnie said she wasn't handling it well.

The women chattered on, remembering other facts about Jarrett's hunting accident before their conversation moved on to a new topic.

After the women left, Nonnie gave Mallory a hug. "I'm sorry the girls brought up Jarrett's death today, honey. You didn't need to dwell on that right now. The girls didn't mean to be unkind to you by talking about it."

"I know." Mallory carried a stack of dishes from the tearoom into the kitchen to stack them on the counter.

Nonnie followed her with the last load of the dessert plates.

Mallory smiled at her grandmother. "Your friends haven't changed much in all these years."

Nonnie's eyes twinkled. "Oh, we've all grown a little older, but the girls were pleased to see you today."

"I was glad to see them, too. Those women have been your friends for as long as I can remember."

Nonnie rinsed off a few more salad plates and loaded them into the dishwasher. "We started our Monday Group when we were all young mothers. It was our day to get out of the house and take a break from our busy lives."

"Like a Mothers-Day-Out." Mallory rinsed a handful of silverware and added it to the dishwasher.

"Yes, and our little group of twelve have continued as friends for many years now. Most of us have grandchildren. Some are widowed, like Dottie. Some divorced, like Tilly."

"Tilly seems to have taken that hard."

Nonnie leaned against the counter. "Well, Tilly's a worrier by nature and she takes everything hard. She's been real unhappy this last year since Bobby Joe left and more anxious than normal."

"I heard the women talking about another theft again, too." Mallory changed the subject.

"Yes and that upsets me." Nonnie turned back to the sink to rinse more plates to put in the dishwasher. "Betty Lou took off her rings in the bathroom when she washed her hands last week, and she accidently left behind her brand new, blue sapphire eternity band when she put her rings back on. She wears a lot of rings. Later when she realized she left it by the sink, she dropped by to get it but it was gone. She felt sick about losing it because Wayne only recently gave it to her for their fortieth wedding anniversary."

"Is she certain she left it here?"

"Yes, and she knew right where to look. No one uses that half bath near the tearoom except the women who come for my lunches and events." She paused. "I didn't even go in there to clean after the luncheon. I can't imagine who could have slipped into the house to steal that ring. It makes me a little nervous to think about it. I suppose someone could sneak in one of the side doors into the house. I'm careless about locking up."

"What else has gone missing from the house?"

"Only little things." She stopped to think. "An old filigreed butterfly pin with a lovely turquoise in the middle that Beau bought me at an estate sale. I left it in a glass dish in my bedroom after wearing it to church one Sunday. Then Ina Ruth lost one of those pretty charm bracelets with the colorful beads on it. She showed it to us at the Monday group because she'd just added a new bead to it, one Vick bought her for her birthday, a pretty white porcelain bead with a pink rose painted on it. She took the bracelet off after showing it to all the girls at the Monday Group and then put it in her purse in my bedroom when we started lunch. The girls always put their purses and coats on the bed in my downstairs bedroom."

Mallory bit on a nail. "Nonnie, that's three different thefts."

"Well, actually there might have been a few others, but those are more iffy because the girls couldn't remember exactly whether the items got lost at our group or at some other time." She took her apron off to hang it up. "It's odd, isn't it?"

"Yes, more than odd." Mallory closed the full dishwasher and started it. "You and I both need to start locking the doors more conscientiously. Here in the country we often forget to do that."

Nonnie covered the remains of the cake. "I simply hate thinking someone would come into our house and take things. Whoever do you think would do that? It seems unlikely these little jewelry thefts are a part of the same group stealing cars or taking money from the pro shop."

Mallory considered this. "Well, sometimes people who become involved in drugs get desperate for ways to fund their habits and they begin to steal in all sorts of ways."

"You're right. I've seen shows on TV about people like that."

Mallory tucked the glassware and dishes they hadn't used into Nonnie's china cabinet. "The thefts could be unrelated, too. It might only be a coincidence they're occurring at the same time."

"That seems unlikely doesn't it?"

Mallory agreed it probably did.

Nonnie looked around in satisfaction at the clean kitchen. "Well, we're all finished here. What do you plan to do this afternoon while I visit our Sunday school teacher at the hospital in Sevierville?"

"I think I'll walk up to the old cemetery to Daddy's grave. The girls talking about Daddy got me to thinking I haven't been there for a long time."

Nonnie glanced out the window. "Well, it's a beautiful, sunny day for a walk. It will do you good to get outside. Take some flowers from the garden, if you'd like. The zinnias are pretty right now.

There's a bronze flower vase beside Jarrett's stone in the cemetery. I take flowers some days, too."

An hour or so later, Mallory followed the well-worn trail that wound through the woods behind Wingate House to the old cemetery. The property behind the Millhouse Resort rose gradually uphill over the low ridges leading to the boundary line of the Great Smoky Mountains National Park and the deeper forest beyond.

The Wingate family cemetery lay on an open knoll off the side of the trail. Mallory always liked coming here to see the old family graves and to read the personal inscriptions on many of the stones. She carried a big handful of Nonnie's colorful zinnias to decorate her father's grave and, after tucking a few into the bronze vase, she walked around the cemetery to put a few flowers on her great grandparents' graves, also.

A sound on the path made her turn, and she saw Suzannah James skipping into the cemetery, waving to her, with Lucas not far behind. He was certainly one of the last people she'd hoped to run into today.

"Hi, Mallory." Suzannah greeted her in obvious pleasure. "What are you doing here at the cem-tree?" She mispronounced the word cemetery, making Mallory smile.

"Putting flowers on some of the family graves," she answered.

Lucas nodded to her as he walked closer, acting uncomfortable to see her again.

Suzannah looked around at the stones and gravesites. "Do dead peoples like flowers?"

"I think they do," Malloy bit back on a grin.

Suzannah cocked her head, thinking about this. "How do you know if they do or not since they're dead and can't tell you?"

"Suzannah, watch your manners." Lucas frowned at her.

"I think everyone likes flowers," Mallory answered. "Plus I like bringing them as a way to say I'm thinking about the people I bring them to."

Suzannah nodded. "I like flowers, too," she said, seeming satisfied with Mallory's answer. "Can I put your extra flowers on the other graves that don't have any?"

"I think that would be nice," Mallory said, handing her the bunch of remaining zinnias.

"I'll say *Bless you and be happy in heaven* to everyone," she said, making Mallory smile again.

Lucas rolled his eyes as she skipped off.

Mallory couldn't help giggling. "She must keep you laughing and smiling all the time."

"She does tend to brighten the day." He traced his fingers across her father's gravestone. "I've heard only the finest things about your father from those who knew him. Dale Buchanan, our turf manager, and Andy Kiley, the golf pro before me, talk about your dad with only good memories."

"Thank you." She looked across at him. "Why did Andy Kiley leave as the resort's golf pro?"

"He has Parkinson's. Didn't you know?"

She winced. "No, I didn't. If Beau or Nonnie told me I don't remember it. I'm sorry to hear that."

"It's not too bad most of the time. He's taking some meds that help, but the symptoms keep him from carrying the job full-time anymore. He still works part-time for Millhouse. I value his wisdom and experience."

"And here I thought you might have pushed him out of his job." She grinned at him. "I'm sorry for thinking that."

"I'm sorry for how unkind I was to you Friday night at my house." He closed his eyes on the words. "I was out of line and I regret it."

She studied him. "What changed your mind?"

"Thinking over some of my own words afterwards and remembering yours." He hesitated. "And getting chewed out by my sister today."

Mallory knew her eyes flew open at that. "You told Elizabeth about our conversation?"

"No, Elizabeth guessed from her candid observations and questions that some misunderstanding occurred between us."

"A misunderstanding." Mallory pronounced the last word slowly.

Lucas frowned, knowing Mallory was considering the appropriateness of the term. "Let's don't get into semantics on this." He ran a hand through his hair. "She figured out there had been a problem and wormed some of the facts out of me and guessed the rest. It's hard to keep a secret from that woman. She's always been able to read me like a book. It ticks me off sometimes."

"I imagine." Mallory tried not to smirk.

Suzannah came skipping back to them. "I saved one flower for you, Mallory, since you said you liked them." She handed her a slightly wilted zinnia.

Touched, Mallory tucked it into her hair, that she'd pulled up and clasped in a big clip behind her head today. "Thanks, Suzannah."

Lucas lips twitched. "It matches your shirt."

"So it does." She glanced down to notice the coral cotton shirt, the same color as the zinnia. She'd worn boots today, too, to hike up the trail into the woods. When walking in the mountains, even on maintained trails, it was easy to twist your ankle without good shoes.

Copying Mallory, Suzannah picked up a dropped flower from the ground and tucked it into one of her stumpy pigtails. "We're going walking to Rock Creek Falls. Do you want to go with us, Mallory?"

She hesitated. "I probably need to start back to the house."

Suzannah made a sad face at her words.

"Please come," Lucas put in. "I could use some adult company."

"Okay," she said after a few moments of thought. "I haven't been to the falls at Rock Creek in years."

He smiled at her, turning to lead the way out of the cemetery.

Mallory considered saying no to Lucas's offer, but then changed her mind. The man did work for her grandparents and was their neighbor. She needed to manage a cordial relationship with him. Meeting him halfway might help.

After walking a short distance up the dirt roadbed away from the resort, Lucas turned onto a side trail. It began to descend gradually toward the falls through a shady and picturesque woodland of predominantly hardwoods and poplars.

"This trail section is a virtual glory of yellow in the fall when the tulip poplar trees change color," Lucas said, slowing his pace so Suzannah could stop to study a fuzzy caterpillar on a log by the trail. He turned to grin at her. "I'm afraid our pace will prove slow following a five-year-old with short legs, who stops to look at every natural wonder along the pathway."

"I don't mind, and it brings back good memories of hikes in these mountains when I was a young girl," she replied, as they moved on. "I used to walk all the trails around the resort with Daddy or one of my grandparents. Daddy often took me to the Old Settlers Trail higher up the mountain inside the park boundary. I still remember the old rock walls and the crumbling chimneys of pioneer homes we found along the trail side on those walks."

"I've hiked parts of that long trail many times myself—to Campsite #33 and Overlook Point on the west and to Maddron Bald and the Albright Grove on the east."

Mallory reached down to pick up an interesting pinecone to study it. "I love the hike to Albright Grove. The upper loop on that trail has so many virgin trees with vast diameters and the forest there is so rich and green."

Their conversation continued like this, in a casual, easy vein, on their short walk to the falls. There they took pleasure in Suzannah's excitement at seeing the waterfall and wading in the cold pool below it.

The cascading plume of water dropped in an impressive fall of twenty feet over a sandstone bluff to splash into the green pool below. Large boulders lay scattered around the streamside, and Lucas and Mallory climbed onto one of the boulders where they could enjoy watching the waterfall and keep an eye on Suzannah at the same time.

Lucas wore khaki shorts today in the June heat with a forest green Millhouse Resort shirt over it, a golf cap tucked on his head. He also wore boots for their walk and he'd stopped once along the way to tie the laces on the charming pair of pink hiking boots Suzannah wore. Mallory grinned when she noticed the child's boots, sure that Suzannah, in some way, had been a party to this fanciful choice.

"Wherever did you find cotton candy colored hiking boots for Suzannah?" She watched the child climb boulders by the stream in her cute shoes.

"Don't ask." He rolled his eyes. "As soon as she saw them, there was no point in even looking at any of the other selections."

"She likes pink?"

"Pink is her favorite color. You saw her room." He flicked small rocks into the stream in his usual restless manner while he talked. "A girl I dated once said we culturally program boys and girls about interests and colors, but I don't believe it after Suzannah. I bought her cars, trains, and toy guns, but they were soon relegated to the bottom of her toy chest. She likes dolls, kittens, flowers, ruffled panties, lace-trimmed socks, sparkly bracelets, fanciful baubles, and anything pink instead. Go figure it."

"Perhaps a lot of gender preferences are genetic or culturally ingrained." Mallory watched a dragon fly settle on a quiet spot in the water. "I think about that a lot when I consider books for acquisitions for our children's line. When I can, I try to select books that show alternative interests for girls."

He stretched out his legs on the flat rock. "Tell me about how you became an editor."

"I majored in English in college at Armstrong State University in Savannah. It was close to home, and I could commute." She tried not to let her eyes drift over his long tan legs. "I thought I might work as a teacher or continue to get a master's degree to work as a librarian. But the summer before my junior year, my advisor recommended me for a summer job opening at Whittier Publishing."

Lucas interrupted to call out a word of caution to Suzannah and then turned back to her. "I thought all the big publishers were in New York."

"Most are. Whittier's main publishing office, started by David Whittier's father, still has a small office in New York. But David loved the south and moved the primary offices of Whittier to Savannah after his dad died. With the world so connected by technology today, it's easier for a major publishing company to function in another city."

"I gather that's worked out successfully. I googled Whittier and they are one of the larger independent publishing houses in the United States."

Mallory felt unexpectedly pleased he'd researched her employer. "Whittier publishes about 400 titles a year. It has several imprints. I went to work that summer filling in at the front desk for the receptionist on maternity leave. David Whittier soon realized I possessed good proofing and copy editing skills and he, and his associate editor, Nancy Franklin, began to train me to review publications and galleys." She smiled at him. "I loved working at Whittier from the first day, handling books, getting paid to read books, listening to people talk about books, and meeting authors."

"You found your niche."

"Yes, although I didn't fully realize it at the time. I kept working with Whittier part-time through my junior year and into the next summer." She stopped then. "Mother decided at that point to change jobs again. We always moved a lot. I felt heartsick to think of moving again with my senior year coming up at Armstrong and I hated to consider leaving Whittier."

"Did your mother need to change her job at that time?"

"No, but she wanted a change. Whenever Mother wanted a job change, we always moved. That's the way it was." Mallory traced a hand through the cold mountain water, remembering that time. "When I told David Whittier about the move, he offered me a full-time job. He said he intended to offer me one at graduation, but that he'd hire me sooner to keep me. He suggested I could finish my senior courses at night or on breaks around my work schedule.

He hired me as a full-time copy editor."

"And your mother moved on alone?"

"Yes, and furious at me for staying, for not moving with her. It had always been the two of us since Daddy died after I turned ten." She sighed. "It caused a big rift between us for a long time that I chose to stay behind."

"Parents don't always celebrate or understand their children's goals," he said. "I was lucky my folks saw I loved golf at an early age and let me go at it with my whole heart." He chuckled. "It didn't hurt that my family lived two blocks from the country club golf course."

Suzannah came over to show them some special rocks found by the stream bank.

"So you stayed at Whittier in Savannah when your mother moved," he said after Suzannah went back to hunt for more rocks.

"Yes. I settled into a small, shabby furnished apartment for the first few years until I could graduate and get on my feet, but then afterward I moved up in position at Whittier and bought my townhouse." She smiled. "It's in one of those marvelous old historic buildings and within walking distance of the Whittier office, parks, shops, and restaurants. I really love living in downtown Savannah."

"And now you're an associate editor instead of a copy editor."

"Yes. I also do acquisitions for our children's imprint, the Colorstone Press, and for our romance imprint Full Moon Books. Whittier also has a mystery and adventure imprint, Quicksilver Books, and a nonfiction, imprint for predominantly coastal books called Seaside Press along with the general Whittier label." She turned to look at him where he sat on a large boulder by the stream across from her. "What about you?"

He shrugged. "My story is a lot like yours; it simply started a little earlier. My talent swung into place as a kid, led to youth tournaments and later to a golf scholarship at The University of Tennessee. At graduation, I qualified for the Web.com Tour. I stayed on that about a year, won some tournaments and got promoted to the

PGA Tour." He paused. "I was lucky. I played well, the right doors opened, and I thrived on competition and tournament play."

"I looked you up on the internet. You became a very well-known and successful professional golfer." She shrugged. "Being more bookish minded than sports minded, I didn't even recognize your name when I heard it before. I'm sorry for that."

He flashed a smile at her. "It's nice to be liked simply for yourself sometimes rather than because you play golf well."

"Or because you're famous," she put in.

"I guess I was a little famous."

"More than a little," she said. "So what brought you to Millhouse?"

"A combination of three things." He looked out across the mountain stream, watching Suzannah play for a moment. "I had an accident and hurt my arm. It would get better and then kick back up again. It began to affect my game. Even when it didn't and I played heavily, I often paid with pain afterward."

"I'm sorry."

He shrugged. "Two years before that, I'd met Cecily Bernhard out in Las Vegas, where she worked the desk at a spa her parents own and run. She was beautiful, we hit it off, and I felt flattered at how much she seemed to lean to me and need me." He took off his hat and fiddled with it. "We got married somewhat impulsively. Traveling the road is lonely; I think I was hungry to settle down. But in the first year, I realized Cecily had problems. As I told you, she was bipolar."

"She didn't tell you about it before you married?"

"No." Mallory saw a frown cross his forehead. "Her parents didn't tell me either."

"I see."

"Some people handle bipolar well. Cecily wasn't one of those. She didn't handle her life well, either." He blew out a breath. "I wasn't happy when I learned she was pregnant. But I thought becoming a mother might help her grow up, mature, become more responsible. It didn't."

He got up to help Suzannah over a rock and then came to sit back down, picking up his story. "Cecily wasn't reliable with the baby. I told you I had to hire a housekeeper to help out. I was having problems at home and trouble with my arm on the tour. I became discontent with my life." He toyed with his hat again. "I didn't much like who I'd become, either. I'd slid away from my faith and my solid upbringing. When I attended one of those big religious meetings with a friend, it turned me around."

Lucas put his hat back on and began to toss rocks into the stream. "My pro tour season for the year was ending, and I came home for a visit with my family and brought Suzannah with me. Cecily didn't want to come. My parents live in Knoxville and they work long hours at their travel business downtown, so I stayed with Elizabeth and Robert at their farm. Because Elizabeth had Abby, I knew she could help me with Suzannah, too. I was still a little awkward with small babies."

"How long did you stay?"

"About a month. I got to know Beau and Andy Kiley while keeping my game up over at the resort. I let my hair down to Beau and he realized I wasn't totally happy on the tour. He offered me a job at the club."

Mallory waited. Listening had always been one of her strong points.

He laughed, looking out across the stream. "Cecily refused to move here with me. She wanted to stay at our place out west in Scottsdale, Arizona. So we separated. I didn't fight her over the baby. At the time, I still felt it better for Suzannah to stay with Cecily. I flew to see Suzannah often, though. Most of the time Cecily was a good mother, and when she hit her bad times, the housekeeper Agnes Moore helped. Agnes was wonderful to Suzannah and patient with Cecily. We were lucky to have her. I still stay in touch with her."

"And then Cecily was found dead." Mallory added.

"Yes, and I brought Suzannah here. You know the rest." He looked over to her. "As Elizabeth reminded me, you and I have both lost someone we loved and both known problems."

"Yes, life can be difficult sometimes."

A small silence fell and then he flashed her a sudden wide grin and flipped a handful of cold water her way. "Do these confessions mean we're friends again, M.T.?"

Taken aback at this abrupt change from serious to playful, Mallory could only laugh and shake her head. "You sometimes act like a big kid, you know."

"I don't count that a criticism." He wrinkled his nose. "Too much seriousness takes all the fun out of life. It'll make you old before your time."

"Is that so?" She tried to keep from giggling.

"Yeah, that's so." He flipped more water at her, and they soon began a small water fight with Suzannah joining in with a whoop.

On the way back down the path heading home later, Lucas asked, "Why don't you come over to eat with us tonight? I'm grilling burgers. You can apply your culinary skills to heat a can of baked beans and put some chips in a bowl, if you like, or you could make potato salad. Think you can handle that, city girl?"

"You're forgetting all the summers I spent with Nonnie. Also since my mother lacked any skills in the kitchen, I learned to cook at an early age. You might be surprised at what this city girl can do in a kitchen."

Hearing their conversation, Suzannah began adding her persuasions. "Please come, Mallory. Please?" She came to take Mallory's hand. "I want you to see my tree house and maybe you can read me my stories again."

As she danced out of hearing a few minutes later, Mallory sighed. "I hardly have any choice now with you asking me in front of Suzannah. She'll be really disappointed if I refuse."

He feigned an innocent look, letting Mallory know he knew exactly what he'd done inviting her in front of the child.

"Listen, I want us to be friends, Mallory," he said in seriousness.

Resigned, she gave in. "All right. I'll go over to the house to see if it will be okay with Nonnie and Beau. If it is I'll bring some of

Nonnie's Orange Crush cake from the luncheon today for dessert. There was plenty left. She'll probably send me over with other leftovers in addition." She paused. "Do you have the ingredients for potato salad if I decide to make some?"

"I think so." He named off a list of ingredients. "I've tried to make it a few times myself but I usually get too much mustard or too much of something else in it. Or I cook the potatoes too mushy."

She grinned at him. "I gather you like potato salad if you've tried so often to make it."

"I do," he admitted, pulling Suzannah up to ride on his back since she was growing tired.

"Well, I'll see what I can do."

Soon, at Suzannah's urging, Lucas began to sing "Oh, Suzannah" to the child, and Mallory marveled again at the natural spontaneity of the man.

As if reading her mind, Lucas said, "I know all the verses to the song, too. It's one of Suzannah's favorites for obvious reasons." He then launched into several verses Mallory didn't remember, Suzannah singing along on the choruses.

Mallory laughed listening to them. It was hard not to. She decided then, also, to make the best of this day and the evening to come. In all honesty, she hated that she and Lucas had quarreled and said such harsh words to each other earlier. By nature Mallory was a peaceable person and disharmony always upset her. Maybe they could move past their disagreement.

# CHAPTER 8

Lucas felt relieved he'd run into Mallory at the cemetery earlier. The encounter offered him an easy opportunity to apologize and to straighten out their relationship. He decided, after their walk to the falls, to invite her to dinner, too. Nonnie and Beau would appreciate the friendly gesture and Elizabeth would hear about it and get off his back. Admittedly, he'd enjoyed spending time with Mallory today. She had a calm, easy way about her for someone who'd recently experienced a breakdown. And she kicked up his male hormones.

"That was great potato salad you made," he told her after dinner. "Even better than Nonnie Wingate's."

"Well, don't tell Nonnie that." Mallory smiled across at him. "She prides herself on her cooking and feels a little rivalrous about her reputation."

Like the last time when Mallory visited, the two sat out on the screened porch now, after getting Suzannah to bed.

"Suzannah loved that you played in the tree house with her and read to her again."

"She's an easy child to enjoy and she makes me laugh and smile."

"I guess that's a help for you right now."

She speared him with a sharp look across the room. "You could have left that comment out, Lucas."

He looked away, not sure what to say. "Do we always need to tiptoe around your illness?" he asked. "Cecily never wanted to talk about hers either."

"I don't *have* an illness, Lucas. I had a temporary health problem—Dr. McGill's words, not mine." She continued to pin him with that steady gaze of hers. "I believe you know Dr. Robert McGill. He's your sister's husband. He pronounced me in excellent health at my last checkup. My only symptoms now are bad dreams once in a while, an occasional sweep of grief, and some minor stomach trouble. It seems I kept my problems all to myself for too long, and they internalized into a condition almost like an ulcer. Dr. McGill gave me some meds and a little diet sheet for that."

"I didn't mean to tick you off." He drummed his fingers on the chair arm.

"Lucas, it's not so much *what* you say—which is often impulsive—but what you imply. Your underlying feelings aren't very subtle. You still classify me as a mental patient."

He tried to think what to say. "I do admit you seem better."

She laughed. "I feel like you've bestowed an honor on me with those words. Maybe I should kneel down and let you knight me with your sword."

He scowled. "You read too many romance books."

"Not lately." She pulled her long legs up to tuck them under her on the sofa. "And I miss my work. I'm going to call David Whittier tomorrow to see if he'll send me some editing to do."

Lucas felt a prickle of unease. "Do you think you should do that?"

"Do you think I *shouldn't?* Are you afraid I'll run screaming from the room over editing a romance novel?"

He glared at her. "Now you're being sarcastic."

She rolled her shoulders. "I am, but I get tired of you picking at me over this little problem I experienced. I admit it scared me at the time. I'm never sick and I'm ordinarily very calm and easygoing. But I feel worlds better now."

"Worlds better."

She grinned at him. "You like that expression? So do I. It brings up pictures. The mind sees a transition from one very different setting to another, like from a dark and grim place to a bright and fair one."

"That's how changed you feel?"

She leaned back against the sofa. "It's a nice comparison. Not only was my mother sick the last two years, but Delores Wingate was a very difficult woman. I felt trapped in a dark and unhappy world with her. And a sad one."

"I know that feeling."

"Living with Cecily was difficult, too, wasn't it?"

"Yes." He thought how to explain it. "Living with Cecily was like flicking from one movie to another all the time. I never knew when the switch would flip, when the channel would change, and when she would become an entirely different person." He paused. "Once she went on a manic spending spree. She ran up over five thousand dollars before one of the credit companies contacted me to be sure someone hadn't stolen my card."

"What did she say?"

Lucas shook his head. "She was still so high on that spending phase she threw a fit when I put stops on all the credit cards. She said I always spoiled all her fun."

The Maine Coon cat pushed her way through the cat door at that moment and walked over to leap on Lucas's lap with a roaring purr.

"That cat obviously likes you." Mallory laughed, and Lucas felt glad for the change of subject and the interruption to their overly serious conversation.

The cat circled around on his lap before settling with her paws across his knees. Lucas glanced down at her with a frown. "This dang cat is getting fatter every day, too. I wonder if I ought to put Baby on a diet."

A yellow tabby head pushed into the cat door then as he finished his words, looking around. Spotting Baby, he began to edge cautiously into the porch.

"Who is this?" Mallory asked.

"That's Mr. Tom. He showed up here a few months ago. He looked pretty ratty then, acted shy of us. Suzannah and I started feeding him, talking to him, and he's come around. I don't think he's feral, maybe just got lost or dropped off." He reached a hand down and the big tabby moved under it, pushing up against Lucas's hand with his head to get petted.

"He looks like Morris in the cat commercials."

"Yeah, he's become a handsome boy since we cleaned him up and fed him. We checked around the valley, put up signs, but no one claimed him. I'm thinking we've found ourselves another cat."

"Where did the name Mr. Tom come from?"

"Suzannah was considering Thomasina, like in the old Disney movie, but I suggested a male cat name would be a better choice." Lucas chuckled. "I had to explain why Thomasina was a Mr. Tom versus a Miss Thomasina, too." He shrugged. "The rest is history."

"Suzannah is very creative."

"That's one gift Cecily really had in spades. She sang, played piano, painted. It was a shame she couldn't settle in consistently to really develop or use any of her gifts. Suzannah looks very much like Cecily ...." He let the words drift off, not saying more.

Mallory's eyes met his. "Just because Suzannah looks like Cecily does *not* mean she'll be bipolar when she's older."

"I didn't say she would." He snapped out the words.

"No, but you were thinking it," she pronounced in that calm, direct way of hers. "I edited a book about bipolar once and learned that only about two percent of people around the world are bipolar and there's only scant research to suggest genetics has anything to do with its occurrence."

He regarded her with interest. "Sometimes hanging around with a smart woman is very comforting."

Mr. Tom pushed his way onto Lucas's lap and Baby leaped down, ears laid back for a moment, and then waltzed over to leap on Mallory's lap.

"I guess you've made a new friend," he said, watching Baby roll over so Mallory could stroke her stomach.

"Ahhh," Mallory said with a small smile. "I think I know why

Baby is gaining a little weight. I think she's going to have kittens."

"What?" He almost knocked Mr. Tom off his lap in surprise. "Why do you say that?"

She studied the cat's stomach. "Her nipples are distended. See?" She pointed. "And all her weight is right here in her middle."

"Dang, just what I need. More cats!"

"Suzannah will be thrilled, but why haven't you gotten Baby spayed?"

"We've only had her a few months. She belonged to a lady across the highway who moved away. She sometimes kept Suzannah for me and knew Suzannah was crazy about the cat. So she talked us into taking her. She'd taken Baby for her shots and everything, and she did mention we'd probably need to get her fixed. I've been meaning to get around to it."

She snickered. "That plan will have to wait until a little later now."

"When do you think she'll have kittens?" He frowned.

"It's usually nine weeks or so until a cat delivers versus our human nine months—probably a month or more from now. Baby will need to nurse the kittens then until they can begin to drink milk and eat food on their own. Once you find homes for them, you can get Baby spayed." Her eyes moved to the tomcat on his lap. "With Mr. Tom as a new resident, however, it might be a good idea to keep a close watch on mama after the birthing or to consider taking Mr. Tom to the vet for a neutering visit."

He eyed the female cat with apprehension. "What do I need to do when it's time for Baby to deliver?"

"She'll take care of things. But it would be a good idea for you to prepare a soft bed in a box for her and to put it in a quiet corner or in a closet she can get to easily. Take her and show the bed every now and then so she'll know where it is. She might use it, or she might have other ideas. Usually cats that live indoors with people want to birth their babies inside."

Lucas stroked a hand down Mr. Tom's back. "I remember when I was a kid our neighbors' cat had kittens in our garage. We took them over to the Thurstons' and put them in their garage, but she kept bringing them back."

Mallory laughed at his story. "Animals often have their own ideas about things."

He frowned. "Mallory, do you think you could tell Suzannah about Baby? It seems like a girl thing to talk about."

"I can but as Suzannah's only parent, you need to get comfortable talking to her about sensitive and private issues. It comes with the territory of parenting."

"Believe me, I get my share of uncomfortable, sensitive conversations with Suzannah. That child has questions about everything."

"I'll bet she does. You're blessed to have her, you know."

"I know." He shifted subjects. "That call I got earlier was to tell me there's been another car theft on the back property behind Retreat House."

She sat up abruptly, unsettling the cat on her lap. "That's not far from our homes and especially close to your place."

"That's why I didn't mention it earlier. I didn't want to upset you or Suzannah. A Christian retreat group is staying in the Retreat House this week, so all the guests parked their cars in the small parking lot beside the house. Someone must be keeping a diligent watch on the Millhouse Resort as a whole to know a group was staying there. We put a guard on the big parking areas near the lodge and golf course after the first theft, but Beau and I didn't consider thieves would risk coming this deep back into the resort property."

"Did you tell Beau and Nonnie about this?" She seemed agitated.

"Yes." He watched her fidget. "But maybe I shouldn't have told you about it."

Her eyes moved to his. "Your child sleeps only a short distance from that parking lot and Retreat House. Only a wooded area lies between the two properties. Suzannah plays in the yard, the garden, and in that woods every day."

He smiled then. "You're worried about Suzannah."

"Aren't you?" She crossed her arms in annoyance.

"As you've learned, I worry about Suzannah more than I should sometimes, but it's nice you've grown fond enough of her to care like this."

"Anyone would." She lifted Baby off her lap to put the cat on the sofa and stood up. "I really need to head back home now. With this new theft happening so nearby, Nonnie and Beau will worry about me until I'm home safe."

"I'll walk you through the garden and then stand by the gate until I see you're safely back to Wingate House." He shifted Mr. Tom onto the chair as he stood. "I would walk you all the way home, but I don't want to leave Suzannah here by herself."

"You don't even need to even walk me to the gate."

"I know, but I'd like to." He pushed the screen door open to let her out in front of him.

They walked down the winding flagstone pathway between flowering shrubs and plants on all sides. Mallory pointed out different plants to him even in the darkness. A full moon overhead made many of the white flowers glow in the night.

"Suzannah says you know all the names of the flowers and plants like Nonnie." He inhaled the scent of a rose bush as they passed by it.

"The things you learn and memorize when you are very young tend to stay with you. Have you noticed that? You remember those facts more vividly than many things you learn later on."

He laughed. "Like remembering the first phone number your family had better than the algebraic formula you had to memorize in high school."

"That's it exactly." She paused at the gate, turning to smile at him. "Thanks for being nice and inviting me over. Like you said, I want us to be friends. I felt bad that we argued and said unkind things before."

"Yeah, me, too." He found himself fingering a drooping branch covered with crimson flowers on a shrub by the gate. "What's this flower?" he asked, grinning at her and diverting the subject. "If you're the resident flower expert, you probably know its name."

She studied it and then a deep flush rose up her neck. "It's an old-fashioned plant, probably one that my great grandmother Alva Wingate started. The crimson pink flowers hang down in chains and it can self-seed itself in the garden."

"You don't know what it's called?" He teased her now, enjoying finding she didn't know the name of the shrub and felt uncomfortable about it.

"I do, it's only that I didn't want to say the name." She stuck her chin up and gave him one of those looks of hers. "It's called Kiss Me Over the Garden Gate."

He laughed out loud. "You made that up."

The flush ran up her face now. "I did *not* make it up. It's simply one of those crazy coincidences, especially when we're standing right here at the gate."

Her voice was breathy with nervousness. Lucas loved it. "It's too much coincidence for me to handle," he said and leaned over to kiss her, pulling her against him in a quick, smooth motion.

Like on the plane, she resisted at first. Shocked again probably. But then she leaned into him, her body molding up against his. He loved how they fit together, with Mallory nearly as tall as he was. He barely had to lean down to kiss her and it made it so much easier to nuzzle and to meld closer in all the right places when he pulled her tighter.

"I thought we'd decided to only be friends," she whispered in a breathy tone when his lips drifted away from her mouth to move down her neck.

"We are friends. This is only another interlude, determined by coincidence."

She gave a soft whimper as he ran his hands up under her hair. Such glorious hair—thick and honey-colored—and he could smell the musky scent she wore even now at the end of the day.

"Just another interlude," she repeated his words softly. "Determined by coincidence."

The woman loved words and that was a fact.

Mallory pulled back, moving to put the gate between them, but her eyes traveled over him and she wet her lips as she studied him.

"You do that one more time," he said, reaching a hand out to touch her lips, "and I'm going to climb over that gate."

She dropped her eyes and hugged herself. "I had a nice time tonight."

"So did I." He glanced back toward the house. "Sure you don't want to come back for a little while?"

"No, and you'd better go back to check on Suzannah." She leaned over to give him a quick kiss of her own, which he quickly turned into a longer one by fisting his hand into her hair. But then afterward she turned to walk away down the path, sending him a little fingertip wave over her shoulder.

He watched until she let herself in the back gate of Wingate House, watched her swaying walk in the deepening darkness and saw the flecks of moonlight touch her golden hair. He could still smell her scent on the air and the taste of her still lingered on his mouth, making him run his tongue across his own lips, remembering. The woman turned him on and that was a fact. And, he reminded himself again, she was his boss's cherished granddaughter.

Lucas spoke to himself in caution then. "You keep in mind who she is, Lucas James, and you remember, too, that since she's feeling better, she'll soon be going back to Savannah to her own life."

He sighed as he opened the screened door to the back porch. "I guess I'll need to try harder to keep a little safe distance between the two of us and hope no more coincidences and interludes come up." But he smiled on the words, even as he said them, and wandered into the house whistling.

# CHAPTER 9

Mallory sat at the kitchen table with Beau and Nonnie the next morning, enjoying their pleasant, easy chatter over breakfast. She loved both of them so much and it was a pleasure to spend time with them again.

"How did you enjoy your dinner at Lucas's last night?" Nonnie asked. "Did he and Suzannah like that Orange Crush cake you carried over?"

Mallory finished her last bite of toast, smothered in Nonnie's homemade apple jam, before answering. "It was a nice evening and they both loved the cake. It was Suzannah's first time to try sherbet as well. Having sampled the orange you sent over with the cake, Suzannah is now pushing Lucas to buy her lime and pineapple sherbet to try out."

"Sherbet comes in raspberry, too," Nonnie said, as she got up to pour Beau another cup of coffee. "I love to pair it with my Raspberry-Buttermilk Cake."

Beau glanced across at Mallory with a surprised expression. "I didn't know you went to Lucas's last night."

Nonnie waved a hand. "Oh, you were gone all day to those civic meetings in Sevierville. Mallory went to the cemetery to put flowers on Jarrett's grave. She ran into Lucas and Suzannah there. They took her on a nice hike to Rock Creek Falls and then invited her to dinner. Suzannah wanted Mallory to see how Lucas and she had fixed up the tree house. You remember that sweet little tree house under the maples? Mallory used to love playing there when your mother lived at Ivy Cottage. Remember? Mallory liked seeing it again and telling Suzannah stories about her own play there as a little girl."

She passed him the plate of eggs for a second helping without a pause in her conversation. "Lucas cooked hamburgers on the grill for them and Mallory made potato salad at Lucas's house using my recipe. She said it turned out real nice. Suzannah loves Mallory and begged her to stay and read bedtime stories to her again. Suzannah told me Mallory reads bedtime stories better than anyone, and that she uses voices for the characters that make them seem alive."

Beau listened to all this with interest, and then glanced at Mallory with a question in his eyes. "Hmmm… it's interesting to learn you're seeing Lucas."

Mallory could feel a flush steal up her neck. "I simply had dinner there after running into him and Suzannah on my walk. We're not dating or anything Grandad, so don't get the wrong idea."

"I see." She could feel him studying her face. "Well, Lucas is a fine man, and Nonnie and I don't mind for you to spend time with him." He spread jam on the last bite of his biscuit. "I count myself real lucky that Lucas decided to accept my offer to be the golf pro here at Millhouse Resort. Andy felt excited about it, too. Getting a well-known pro like Lucas has really put Millhouse Resort on the map for golfers. Many come simply to meet Lucas or because he's associated with our resort. We've drawn in more conference groups, too, because of him being here. One group of business executives that came to the resort asked Lucas to be the keynote speaker at their main dinner. He could have gone to work for a lot bigger and more prestigious resorts than Millhouse."

"Yes, he mentioned he was at a crossroads in his life at the time he made the decision and he also mentioned he was having problems with his arm," she said. "Do you know what the injury is? He didn't seem to want to talk about it much."

Beau made a face. "The boy never likes to talk about his arm much, but it still bothers him sometimes, especially with overuse."

Nonnie propped an elbow on the table. "Elizabeth told me the name of the condition, but I can't remember it...."

"The medical term is *medial epicondylitis* or golfer's elbow in more layman's terms," Beau put in. "Basically it's an inflammation of the tendons that attach the forearm muscles to the inside of the bone at your elbow. Lucas's problem was initiated by a ski accident and then made worse by him heading right back onto the tour without enough rest for full healing. The injury kicked up again and inflammation set in. Healing proved difficult with repetitive golf swings and continuing overuse and stress to the arm. More tears in the tendon occurred, scar tissue developed; it's like a cycle."

"And this affected his game?" she asked.

"Yes. Repetitive activities make golfer's elbow worse. The condition causes tenderness, soreness, pain at the elbow and down the forearm." Beau frowned. "For a golfer on tour this is bad news. Gripping hurts; there is less arm strength. When problems and inflammation kick up, the condition affects range of motion and function, and it impacts strength and movement patterns."

"That all sounds very technical and complicated." Nonnie sighed. "How did you learn all that?"

"Well, Andy and I read up on it when we began to consider asking Lucas to come to work at the resort."

"But Lucas still plays golf most every day." Nonnie interrupted. "Doesn't that hurt his arm?"

"It's not *use* that causes the problem, Nonnie, but overuse. Here at Millhouse, Lucas can pace himself. He can rest the arm when there is a problem. The man doesn't need to give up golfing altogether, and he probably could have continued on tour even with the problem. But he knew it negatively affected his game. He also wasn't as happy with life on tour as at the beginning."

"How long did Lucas play on tour?" Mallory asked.

"Hmmm." Beau scratched his head, searching his memory. "He played in high school and college tournaments, then on the Web. com tour, qualified for the PGA Tour and then played on the PGA until he came here. He's thirty-nine now, came here at thirty-three. I guess Lucas played on the PGA Tour about ten years; he's been here six years now."

"He was very successful on tour, too." Nonnie added. "Suzannah showed me his scrapbooks and all the trophies and pictures in his study at Ivy Cottage. I saw more at his office in the pro shop."

"That's true. Lucas was very successful. A lot of money is made on the PGA Tour for those who rise to the top like he did." Beau sipped at his coffee. "Financially, Lucas didn't need to work again when he left the tour, but he's not the sort of man who'd want to live idle. Some would."

He reached for another of Nonnie's biscuits. "Like I said, we're lucky to have him. Not only is Lucas still a crackerjack golfer and a charismatic, friendly person with all who visit the resort and golf course, but he has a keen business head, too. His father and mother run their own travel business in Knoxville and Lucas majored in business at college. I guess he inherited good business genes."

He looked at Mallory then, studying her.

"What?" she asked, seeing him watching her with that old familiar look of his that meant he had some idea or other on his mind.

"It could work out real nice if you and Lucas James got together." Beau smoothed the small, white mustache over his upper lip in thought. "Solve two problems at once. I know Lucas wants to buy into the resort and I need to think about who will take over, and run the place for me, as I get older. With Jarrett gone, you're my only direct heir and you haven't shown much interest in coming back to work with Millhouse in any way."

Nonnie shook a finger at him. "Beau Wingate, don't you put pressure on this girl while she's here to heal and rest. She doesn't need to be dealing with these problems right now."

Mallory knew her eyes widened. "I guess I never thought about what you would do with the resort one day. I assumed you'd probably sell it at some point."

"Honey, it's not simply our business, it's our home and our life," Nonnie said in a soft voice. "All our roots and memories are here. Our people are buried in the cemetery on the hill. We built this house as a young couple. I grew the gardens and developed my tearoom. Beau enlarged and expanded the resort. It's not easy to walk away from all that. I suppose I hoped we'd continue to work, at least in a part-time capacity—like Andy Kiley does—even when we grew older. And that maybe we could stay here."

Mallory felt a little stunned at these revelations. "Are you saying you'd like me to come and learn how to run the resort?"

"No." Beau bit out the word gruffly. "We're not asking you to give up your life. Delores used you enough in that capacity, always putting herself first, dragging you all over the country, never thinking about what was best for you. Nonnie and I know you've found your place in the publishing world, but you might want to add marriage and a family to that mix someday, and I couldn't help but think how nice it would be if you and Lucas linked up. Then he'd be family."

Mallory felt her head reel at this idea. "You haven't talked about this with Lucas, have you?" She certainly hoped not.

"Of course not." Beau scowled at her. "The idea only just occurred to me when I heard you and Lucas were seeing each other."

Mallory leaned forward. "Again, we are *not* seeing each other. We simply shared a little time together yesterday. I thought you and Nonnie would be pleased if I developed a friendship with Lucas and Suzannah, since you're so fond of them and since Lucas works for you."

"We are pleased, darling." Nonnie rose to start cleaning off the table. "Aren't we, Beau?"

"Absolutely." Beau pushed back his chair as well. "And I need to get over to the lodge for a meeting now." He walked around to give Mallory a kiss on the cheek. "You have a nice day, girl. We're so glad to have you visiting with us for a little while. I can already see the roses back in your cheeks and those dark circles are gone under your eyes. I'm real glad to see you feeling better."

"Thank you," she said, her mind still reeling with the thoughts Beau planted there. She couldn't help but wonder now if Lucas carried some idea of linking up with her because she was Beau and Nonnie's only granddaughter. Was he the type of person to show interest in her for a reason other than genuine affection? She didn't know. It made her uncomfortable to think about it, just as it made her uncomfortable to hear Beau and Nonnie discuss their regrets of not having an heir to take over the resort. For some reason, she'd never considered before what would happen to the Millhouse Resort when they grew older. As Nonnie said, Wingates had lived here for over three generations. It would feel sad to see the land pass out of the family.

She helped Nonnie clean up, listening to her chatter as she worked, but not really attending. Her mind was too crowded with mixed emotions to catch more than the basics of Nonnie's words. But she nodded, smiled, and made appropriate comments, sort of like she did when people dropped into her office at Whittier when she was lost in a book and editing.

With her mind moving to thoughts of work now, she went to get her laptop as soon as Nonnie left the house to run errands. With the day warm and sunny, she carried it out onto the covered side porch that arched across the east end of Wingate House. Her grandparents' charming, older home, built of gray stone quarried in Tennessee, had several lovely porches tucked around the two-storied structure. Mallory had always loved sitting out on this side porch with its views stretching down the green hillsides toward the woods. Summer flowers bloomed in gay clumps around forsythia and japonica bushes, which in spring created a colorful show under the pink and white dogwood trees scattered around the yard.

She sat her laptop on the white wooden table on the porch and settled into the ladder back chair behind it. Mallory checked her email then, responding to notes from friends and business associates as needed. She deleted all the messages from Ethan, not even opening them. Hadn't she made it clear to him their relationship was over? It amazed her that he kept sending her notes at all.

Mallory read her emails from Nancy Franklin and Sherman Rhodes, the other editors at Whittier helping to handle her work while she was away. She answered a note from Rae Litz, Whittier's sales and marketing director, about an event planned for one of Mallory's authors, and she sent back replies to Virginia Conklin, Whittier's production editor, and Sue Brenner, the new copy editor they'd snagged from a big New York company. Her last email came from Amil Devrat, the design and production director. He'd attached the final cover design for Avery Briley's new book. Mallory jetted him back a note to tell him she loved it. She knew Avery would be thrilled with it, too.

As good as it had been to take this break, Mallory missed being at Whittier every day. She missed being a part of the weekly staff meetings, the buzz of the office, and the interaction between colleagues about the work they were all involved in. With this thought in mind, she picked up her cell phone and called David Whittier.

"Hey, M.T.," he answered. "Is everything all right?"

"Everything is great." She smiled to hear his voice. "I'm feeling more like myself again and the doctor here gave me an excellent five star report."

"Wonderful. We were all worried about you."

Mallory felt embarrassed to remember the meltdown she'd had in the Whittier office only a month ago. "I really am okay now, David."

"I believe you. I've worked with you since that first internship when you were a student at Armstrong. The only times I remember ever seeing you cry was when you came to tell me your mother planned to move—or a few times over a good book you were reading." He chuckled.

She smiled. "Listen, I'm getting restless and bored and thought you could send me some work to do."

He hesitated. "I haven't gotten a go-ahead from Dr. Henry that you're ready to work again."

"I'm not seeing Dr. Henry here, but I'll be glad to have Dr. McGill phone you with a positive report." She wrinkled her nose in annoyance. "A little editing won't hurt me."

"A little rest and relaxation won't hurt you, either. We're good here. There's nothing pressing. Nancy is doing Cleo's edit for the third book in her series. Sherman is checking back over Dorothy Paton's edit changes you asked her to make before you left. No problems there. Nancy and I are looking at any submissions coming in." His voice sounded firm and determined.

Mallory sighed. She knew that voice.

"M.T., I want to see you take some time off before I send you any work. Your voice sounds better, and I'm glad to hear you're coming back so quickly. Maybe next week I'll send you a novel to read from a new author we're interested in, possibly a few editing jobs after, and in August you can head back home if this good recovery continues."

"David, I don't think I'll need to stay here two months."

"Think of it as a short sabbatical," he interrupted. "Besides, if anyone deserves a nice, long vacation, you do."

"Very well." Mallory knew better than to argue once David made up his mind about something.

"Listen, before we hang up, I think I should let you know Ethan Broussard came by the office."

Mallory groaned.

"Most of us were out that day and Tina talked to him." Tina Brassi, the administrative assistant at the front desk, was a young, part-time student like Mallory had been when she first started to work at Whittier.

"And?"

"Tina didn't know about your relationship with Ethan, and Ethan didn't fill her in. I think Tina said a little more than she needed to."

"Like what?"

"When Ethan indicated you and he had a serious relationship, Tina sort of assumed he knew about your breakdown and that you were at your grandparents for a vacation and rest."

"Oh, great," Mallory said. She knew Tina could definitely be chatty. "I noticed a lot of emails from Ethan in my in-box."

"What did Ethan say?" David asked.

Mallory's voice hardened. "I deleted his emails without opening them, like I've done with all the other emails he sent me before."

"Hmmm. Well, I'm not going to make any comments about your love life but I thought you might want to know Tina talked to Ethan." He paused. "Tina made me promise to tell you she was *so sorry*." He mimicked Tina's familiar tone with the last two words.

Mallory couldn't help but laugh. She could visualize Tina's words and expressions so easily. "Well, Ethan can be rather charming and persuasive when he wants to. Tell Tina not to worry about it."

However when Mallory hung up, she worried about it herself. She hadn't wanted Ethan to know about her breakdown and she hadn't wanted him to know where she was. It seemed unlikely he'd drive all the way to Tennessee, but she still didn't like him knowing where to find her. The location of Millhouse Resort could easily be located with any quick Internet search.

Her cell phone rang and Mallory looked at the number with caution before answering.

"Hi," said Elizabeth. "What are you doing for dinner? One of Robert's patients gave him a honey glazed ham as a thank-you gift so I decided to cook some sides to go with it. Now I have too much food for only Robert, Abby, and me. Do you want to come eat with us tonight?"

Mallory grinned. "What else did you fix?"

"I made a linguini salad with pasta, fresh vegetables and my homemade herbed Italian dressing, and I baked a Mississippi Mud Cake. Abby loves that cake because it's full of chocolate, marshmallows, and nuts and has this drizzly chocolate icing over the top."

"Who wouldn't love that?"

"I'm popping scalloped potatoes into the oven closer to dinner, the kind with two cheeses," she continued. "Robert loves those, and I'm making this luscious green bean dish with fresh green beans, herbs, mayonnaise, eggs, onion, bacon, and a little bit of horseradish. It's called Green Beans Horseradish Casserole since the touch of horseradish gives it a secret zip." She paused for breath. "And I'm making sunshine carrots. You put a little brown sugar, cornstarch, ginger, orange juice, and butter in with fresh carrots, and it is so good, Mallory."

"How could I say no? It sounds like a feast." Mallory laughed. "What can I bring?"

"Bread and wine. Nonnie should have both on hand without you needing to drive in to Gatlinburg to pick up some. I think we'll celebrate."

"For what?"

She hesitated before answering. "I'm going to have another baby."

"Oh, Elizabeth, how wonderful. Then I'll certainly come."

"Listen. I haven't told Abby yet, so don't say anything around her." She dropped her voice. "Robert and I thought it would be better to tell her later when I started to show; I'm only two months along now. It's hard for children to wait when they're excited about something. At five years old, seven more months can seem like a long time."

Elizabeth's call took the edge off Mallory's disappointment in not persuading David to send her any editing work and in learning Ethan knew about her health issues. She wasn't surprised in some ways David wanted her to take a long rest. He'd heard Dr. Henry's suggestion for that. But here at Millhouse, her peace and calm had returned more quickly than expected.

Mallory finished scanning her personal emails and notes, paid a few bills online, and responded to a letter from the funeral home that had handled her mother's service. Then she stretched her neck and looked out over the green lawn. She could hear an assortment of birds twittering in the trees and watched idly as a robin made its way across the lawn, listening and occasionally pecking in the grass. A pair of hummingbirds darted in and out of the feeder Nonnie had hung from a hook at the end of the deck. Mallory smiled. She could hear their tiny wings in the quiet of the June afternoon and could hear the hum of the bees working the hollyhocks and rose bushes clustered around the porch foundations.

Feeling the warmth of the afternoon sun spreading its fingers onto the shady porch now, Mallory decided to put on her swimsuit and walk over to swim at the resort pool. It would be nice to lie in the sun and read. How long had it been since she'd done that?

# CHAPTER 10

It was after five o'clock when Lucas pulled up at his sister Elizabeth's house to pick up his daughter Suzannah. Seeing his sister maneuvering out the front door with an armload of boxes, he sprinted up the porch steps to catch the door for her. "Sorry I'm a little late," he said.

"No problem." She pushed the boxes into his arms. "You're just in time to carry these boxes down to those tables in the yard." She pointed to a cluster of tables set up under the shade of two big oak trees.

"What's the occasion?" he asked, taking the boxes and following her to the table she indicated to deposit them on top of it.

"One of Robert's patients gave him a big honey glazed ham today so I decided to make some sides and have a garden party out under the trees. It's so beautiful outdoors this time of year." She pulled a couple of tablecloths from the boxes, spreading one over the largest table she'd set up while she talked. "I hope you and Suzannah will stay for supper. I made a lot of food."

"You feed us far too often," he said, watching her place a vase of pink and blue hydrangeas on the table and then begin to take floral dinnerware from her box.

"I'm cooking anyway," she told him, looking up with a smile. "You can earn your dinner by helping me set up. I need chairs brought from the storage room in the barn, and it would be great if you'd run down to the market and pick up a bag of ice for me. There's a cooler in the storage shed we'll need, too, and if you wouldn't mind hauling out my other long table against the back wall in the shed, I'll use it for a buffet table for the food."

She studied the table she'd been decorating. "This table is for us and the child's table under the trees is for the girls. We'll need four of those smaller children's chairs for their table, too."

"Why four chairs for two girls?"

Elizabeth rolled her eyes at his question. "Abby and Suzannah decided their dolls, EdithAnn and Charlotte, had to attend the garden party tonight, so both dolls will need a chair. You know those girls get seriously into their imaginative play some days."

Lucas grinned. "Yes, I do, and I've been forced to ask restaurants for a booster seat for Suzannah's doll EdithAnn more times than I care to recall." He laughed. "Where are the girls now?"

"They're in the house trying on the sundresses I made for them earlier this week and dressing their dolls." She turned to him and wiggled her eyebrows. "I made two of the cutest sundresses for them with calico fabric layers and little tie strings at the top. I made matching dresses for the dolls, too. The dresses are all so pretty, and I can use the scraps for my sachet bags."

Lucas went over to wrap his sister in a hug. "In case I don't say it often enough, I am very grateful to have you in my life. You do so much for Suzannah and for me."

She kissed him on the cheek. "You're a sweet thing to say that, but you also pay me very well to keep your daughter. It's nice to have a rich brother."

He swatted her on the bottom. "Smarty-pants. You know I'm complimenting you on all the extras you do. They are really special, Elizabeth. I wish I could think of more things to do for you."

She sent him a sunny grin. "Well, I hope you apologized to Mallory Wingate because I invited her tonight, too."

"Actually I took care of that right after we talked yesterday," he told her. "Suzannah and I ran into Mallory when we walked up to the cemetery. She hiked on to the falls with us and ate dinner at our house last night. So all is good."

She studied him as if looking for more beyond his words. "Well,

I'm glad to hear that." Elizabeth glanced at her watch. "Mallory and Robert will be here around six so you'd better bring those chairs out for me now and then head down the road to the W.T. Market to get the ice. I'll finish setting up while you're gone. When you get back, you can help me bring food and drinks out and keep a watch on the girls while I finish up in the kitchen.

"Do I need to pick up Mallory?"

"No, she's walking over, but you can drive her home later. It might be dark when we finish." She began putting plates and dinnerware around the table as she talked. "And since you have that early golf tournament at the resort tomorrow, I thought Suzannah could simply spend the night here. That way after dinner, we can put both girls down early and enjoy a little adult time."

Lucas smiled as he turned to head for the barn. That plan would give him a little one-on-one time with Mallory, too. He whistled as he let himself into the shed to get out the chairs and extra table for his sister.

About thirty minutes later, after setting out the chairs, table, and cooler, and then driving down the road to Harrison Ramsey's small market to get a bag of ice, Lucas drove his black Lexus back up the driveway to Elizabeth and Robert's home. He'd won this car hitting a hole-in-one in a tournament he played his last year on tour, and the car still drove like a dream.

The pretty McGill farmhouse sat on a rise in the middle of the green farmland in a cluster of deep shade trees. It was an old two-storied white home with crisp black shutters and long deep windows marching across the front of the house. A brick foundation gave the house a pretty touch as did a wide covered porch across the front—cluttered as always with an assortment of rockers, chairs, and the outdoor tables Elizabeth worked on. A vintage milk can stood by the front door filled with walking sticks, handmade stick horses, and a spray of colorful peacock feathers. Two giant hanging ferns and an array of lush plants, in a variety of pots and planters, gave evidence to Elizabeth's green thumb.

Lucas spotted Mallory as soon as he got out of the car. He paused to look across the lawn at her where she and Elizabeth chatted. She wore another of her long summer skirts tonight, this one a deep sky blue with darker polka dots all over it. Her simple scoop-neck tee matched the dots, and she wore slip-on canvas shoes tonight. She'd pinned her hair up in a loose knot for the evening and Lucas could see the sunlight dancing over it. Mallory was a pretty woman, but in a low-key, polished, distinguished way, so different in looks from Cecily, who'd always displayed a fragile delicate beauty.

As he walked over with the bag of ice, he saw Mallory reach to pick up a plastic plate from the table. "Where did you get these charming dishes?" she asked. "They look like Victorian vintage wear. I can't believe they're plastic."

"Aren't they cute?" Elizabeth positioned wine glasses around the outdoor table as she talked. "I got them at a local flea market. They were super cheap, too. You learn to use more plasticware once you have kids."

"I imagine that's sensible." Putting the plate back on the table, Mallory pulled two bottles of wine and a long loaf of French bread from the bag she'd dropped on a nearby chair. "Here are my contributions for dinner. Hope they will do. Nonnie insisted I bring both a white and a red wine and she thought this loaf of French bread would be quick and easy to heat." She held it out to Elizabeth. "She suggested you cut slits in it and spread some of that herb butter mixture over it."

"Wonderful idea. I'll go stick it in the oven right now and put the wine in the refrigerator until we're ready to eat." She glanced Lucas's way. "And here's my favorite brother. He can keep you company until Robert arrives. Robert called a few minutes ago to say he was seeing his last patient out the door."

Lucas watched Mallory's eyes meet his with an odd accessing look, as if trying to learn something about him in the glance. What question traveled in her fine mind now, he wondered?

He turned to his sister. "I'll dump the ice into the cooler unless you want me to put it in the kitchen frig."

"No, just stick it in the cooler." She waved a hand toward a battered metal cooler as she headed toward the house.

Lucas grinned at Mallory as he dumped the ice into the cooler as directed. "Elizabeth's been working me like a racehorse ever since I got here."

"Well, everything looks really pretty." Mallory glanced around at the decorated tables and the paper lanterns Elizabeth had hung from the tree limbs. She sat down in one of the chairs by the table. "Elizabeth is so creative."

"That she is. And I don't think I inherited any of those creative genes." Lucas dropped into the chair beside hers and crossed an ankle over his knee.

"You have your own talents and you've developed them well." She glanced toward the driveway. "Nice car. A Lexus?"

"Yes, I won it in a tournament the last year I played on tour." He drummed his fingers on his knee restlessly. "One of the perks of playing pro golf."

"Did you win that tournament?"

"Nope, not that one. I placed third. It was a tight game."

She fingered one of the colorful napkins Elizabeth had rolled in napkin rings beside each plate. "Does a golfer win very much in third place or do only the top winners collect all the prize money? I don't know much about golf."

He laughed. "Most everyone in a big tournament takes home some money. The first place winner, who blew away the field that day and finished with a 9-under, won over 1.5 million. Second place came in around $800,000 and third won $650,000."

Her eyes widened. "Oh, my. I didn't realize pro golfers made so much money. I feel silly now asking what I did."

"It's okay. Most people aren't aware of how much money professional golfers make, even if they don't win every tournament."

She crossed her leg over one knee, drawing his eyes to her long legs, tan now from her days in the sunshine.

"How many tournaments a year does a golfer play?"

"A professional golfer might play twenty or more tournaments in a season. Where each is held depends on the weather. For example, one of the early tournaments in the year, in January, is usually held in Hawaii and then maybe the next in California or Arizona where the weather will be nice."

"How interesting."

He could almost visualize that clever mind of hers sorting and classifying this new information.

She sighed. "It must be lovely to go to Hawaii in January when it's so cold most everywhere else."

He nodded, leaning back in his chair. "The Sony Open, which used to be the Hawaiian Open, is usually held at the Waialae Country Club in Honolulu. It is a pretty place with lush foliage, gorgeous flowers, and tall palm trees. It's on the ocean and not far from Diamond Head, the volcanic landmark. That area of Hawaii is highly populated though. I think some of the other islands are much prettier."

"What is one place you really liked there?"

Lucas considered her question. "I like the golf course at Princeville at Hanalei on the north shore of Kauai. There is more wilderness there, a dramatic coastline, some unbelievable beauty."

She sighed. "I'd like to go to Hawaii. I've read so many wonderful books set there, like Michener's." She smiled at him. "One of our authors, Alana Kane, grew up in Hawaii, and she sets many of her romance novels there that Whittier publishes. Every time I edit one of them, I want to pack a bag and take off." She laughed, that low deep laugh of hers. He loved to hear that laugh.

Lucas thought about suggesting she pack up and go with him. That he'd show her all the beautiful places in Hawaii. But it wasn't the right thing to think or to ask. She wasn't the kind of girl who'd pack up and go off on a trip with a man or even to a motel overnight. He knew that. She was Beau and Nonnie Wingate's granddaughter, too. He needed to keep his thoughts in check.

"Maybe you can take a vacation there one day," he said instead, consciously moving his mind in a new direction.

She twisted a strand of her hair, considering it. "I'd really like that. I can almost picture it."

So could he—and with himself in the picture.

Robert pulled into the driveway in his SUV then, breaking Lucas's thoughts. He waved to them as he got out of the car. The evening moved in a new direction after that, the girls running outside to get hugs from Robert and then skipping towards he and Mallory, eager to chat and tell them about the small events of their day.

"There's a new baby goat in the barn," Suzannah told him, her eyes brightening. "We can go see it. Mallory would like it, too."

"She would," Robert agreed. "It was born only yesterday. Lucas, walk with Mallory and the girls down to the barn to see the goats. I'll go change and then help Elizabeth bring out the food. When I talked to her on my cell coming up the driveway, she said everything was nearly ready."

A short time later, when they returned from the barn, Robert offered a short grace and then everyone loaded plates from the buffet table.

"That baby goat was *so* cute," Mallory said as they all settled into their seats. "All snowy white and as fluffy as a lamb, simply a darling little baby."

"My Mama is going to have a baby, too," Abby announced from the children's table and then covered her mouth. "Whoops. I'm not supposed to know. But Suzannah and I heard Mommy on the phone today." She turned to her mother. "It was an *accident*." She drew out the last word dramatically.

"Oh, well, so much for keeping that secret quiet." Elizabeth made a face and they all laughed.

Lucas laid his fork down and crossed his arms. "And when were you planning to tell your only brother this good news?"

"Oh, don't fuss." She wrinkled her nose at him. "I only found out for sure today, and I planned to announce the news over a toast after the girls went to bed."

"Well, since the girls already know, let me offer that toast now." Robert poured out wine for each of them and passed the glasses around the table.

The dinner conversation then turned to talk about the upcoming baby, later moving to happenings of the day. Lucas noticed that Mallory, in this group setting, grew quiet, enjoying listening to everyone else's dialogue.

He leaned over toward her. "See, I told you that you're an introvert. You go quiet in a group."

"I'm simply enjoying my meal," she said, not rising to the bait of his teasing.

He raised his wine glass to her with a grin.

Mallory deftly moved the conversation back to food. "Elizabeth, everything is simply wonderful," she said.

"Yes, everything is wonderful," he agreed, watching Mallory interact with his family with grace and ease. Family was important to Lucas, and Cecily had never been comfortable with his family or with many of his friends.

# CHAPTER 11

To spare Elizabeth, Mallory tucked the girls into their pajamas and then into the two twin beds in Abby's room. Afterwards she read them several bedtime stories while Robert and Lucas helped Elizabeth clean up the food and dishes.

Now, as she let herself back out the front door, she could see Lucas, Elizabeth, and Robert settled companionably in a group of chairs under the trees, the twinkling lights Elizabeth draped earlier over the branches casting a fanciful glow over them. She stopped to look at them and sigh, hearing their easy voices and warm laughter drifting over the evening air. Life was good here in this simple community in the Smoky Mountains.

"Come and sit down," Robert said as she walked closer. Tall, like Lucas, with short, wavy brown hair, he sat with his feet propped on a battered metal ice chest, relaxed and comfortable. "Pour yourself another glass of wine before you sit down, too." He gestured toward the bottles of wine on the table.

Mallory poured out a half glass of red wine and then settled into the vacant chair in their small circle. With dusk past, she could hear the night sounds beginning to rise on the air—the croak of a frog in the pond behind the barn, the chirrup of crickets, the hum of cicadas in the tree limbs, the soft sounds of the goats settling down in the barn for the night.

She smiled, listening to it all and to the sounds of her friends.

"You're feeling much better," Robert said, catching her eye.

"Very much so."

"I sent the note you requested to David Whittier at your publishing company. I don't see any reason why you can't do a little editing work while you rest and recuperate, as long as you remember to eat well and to get out and enjoy some fresh air and exercise to build up your strength."

Mallory smiled. "With Nonnie and Elizabeth feeding me, I don't think you'll need to worry about me eating well."

Elizabeth reached over to pat her knee. "Your color is so much better than the first day when I met you, and those dark circles under your eyes are gone. You must be sleeping better."

"I am."

"Well, don't get well too quickly." Elizabeth laughed. "I want to keep you around a little longer. I have a shortage of women friends nearby."

"What brought the two of you here to Pittman Center?" Mallory asked, turning her eyes to Robert. "I know from what Elizabeth told me that you both worked in one of the major medical centers in Nashville, both in the ER."

"Yes, I specialized in both emergency medicine and family practice, and I went to work at the same hospital where I completed my internship," Robert answered. "Elizabeth was a nurse in the ER. That's where we met." He glanced across at her fondly. "Both of us were doing some reevaluating of our lives when we connected."

"Amen. Those twelve hour shifts amid all that ongoing trauma in the ER were stressful," Elizabeth added.

Robert paused, as if trying to decide what to say next. "My grandmother had sent me a copy of a small book called *So Sure Of Life* as a Christmas gift, thinking I'd enjoy reading the story of Dr. Robert Thomas, one of our relatives who mother named me after."

"I've heard Beau and Nonnie talk about him," Mallory said.

"He's a very well-known and beloved figure around here," Elizabeth put in. "Dr. Thomas was one of the early doctors to come to this part of the mountains in the 1920s to work in a rural mission established only a few years earlier. This area was unbelievably backward and primitive then. Little existed but the clinic, a small school, church, and a little store. The closest hospital, in Knoxville, lay forty-two miles away and the roads into the mountains at that time were simply terrible. It took six or seven hours for Dr. Thomas to cover the twenty-five miles between Newport and Pittman Center when he, his wife Eva, and their little boy Bobbie first came. The road wound through the mountains like an old wagon trail, rutted and muddy with hairpin curves. After he arrived, he made many of his calls on horseback."

Robert leaned back in his chair, adjusting his feet on the old ice chest. "Dr. Thomas made such a difference as a doctor, was so beloved by all he ministered to. My work in Nashville, although important, seemed more impartial, and I hungered for what he'd known."

Elizabeth patted his knee. "Even at that time I grew plants and herbs on the windowsills and patio of my small apartment. I felt restless for something more, too, and when Robert and I decided to marry I began to wish for a less hectic world for us to raise our children in."

"We came home for a holiday visit one Easter," Robert said, picking up the story. "Elizabeth's family, as you know, live in east Knoxville, less than a half hour down the freeway. My family lives even closer in Sevierville. Dad owns a car dealership and my older sister and her husband both work there. My younger sister, who is an English teacher, and her husband live in Cosby, so our route between family visits often took us along this highway in front of the farm."

Elizabeth sighed. "We noticed a For Sale sign stuck in the ground by the driveway of the farm when we passed. I begged Robert to drive up the farm road so we could look at the house and we both fell in love with the place."

"I began to look around for jobs in the area and learned no medical office or clinic existed anymore in the Pittman Center area where Dr. Thomas once worked. This seemed sad to me," Robert told them, sitting up and leaning forward now. "I began to approach civic leaders in the area, your grandfather one of them, to see if the community had any interest in helping to start a new clinic here."

Mallory interrupted. "Was the smaller farmhouse on the highway, that became your clinic, a part of the farm property?"

"Yes," Elizabeth answered. "The community helped to raise funds to renovate it into a clinic so Robert could start his practice there."

"I guess the rest is history." Robert smiled, ending their story.

Mallory straightened the clasp in her hair, considering this. "I expect it was a big change from practicing in the city. In addition, building a business, of any kind, takes time."

Elizabeth nodded. "We had some lean years starting out, that's for sure, and it took time for the people in the area to trust us, to come to Robert as their doctor."

"We saw a huge drop in income by coming here. Many people still wonder at our choices." Robert winked at Elizabeth.

"But money isn't everything," Lucas put in.

Elizabeth reached across to punch him. "Spoken like a man who has no worries with it."

Lucas scowled. "I gave up a lot to come and settle here, too. Like you and Robert I wanted a simpler life with more meaning and a simpler pace."

He drummed his fingers on his knee. "It's harder than you might think being on the professional golf tour. Golfers on the PGA Tour travel constantly. It's a lonely life much of the time, staying in hotels, sitting in airports, practicing every day and then playing so many tournaments, always doing interviews and constantly being followed by the media. The pressure on a pro golfer is relentless and constant, to continue winning enough to pay your expenses, to pay your caddie, and to keep your reputation strong. The lifestyle you get involved in isn't always wholesome."

"Then you hurt your arm," Robert added. "That made it harder for you. There's no time for sickness and recovery of any long duration on tour."

"Yes." Elizabeth sent Lucas a sweet smile. "I'm so glad you came to us that winter for a break with little Suzannah." She giggled. "You were pretty awkward taking care of that baby on your own without the housekeeper or Cecily to help."

"True, but thankfully you helped me with Suzannah." He grinned at her.

"Well, I had Abby then. I was already used to babies."

Lucas expression grew thoughtful. "Looking back, I believe the timing was perfect for me to come here, to meet Andy and Beau, to get offered the job at Millhouse." He glanced at his sister. "Like the timing for you and Robert to find Whitehouse Farm and for Robert to open the clinic. Maybe God knows what you need and helps you find the way before you even know what you want."

"That's a nice thought." Elizabeth reached across to take her brother's hand. "I'm glad you ended up here with us."

Robert looked at Mallory with a smile. "I think Mallory is finding our little corner of the world a restful, healing place, too."

"It is that," she agreed.

They chatted on until dark began to fall. Mallory glanced at her watch. "I should probably start back or Nonnie and Beau will worry. With all the thefts going on, I know they're a little nervous when I'm out at night alone."

Lucas stretched. "I'll drive you home. I need to get back, too, and it's on the way for me." He stood. "Let me check on Suzannah before I leave." He turned to Elizabeth. "Are you sure it's okay for Suzannah to sleep over? I can tuck her into the backseat and take her on home."

Elizabeth shook her head. "No. If she's sleeping well when you check, just leave her. I promised both of them she could stay over. You know how they are when you make a promise."

Lucas laughed. "Yes, I do."

A short time later, thanks-yous made and hugs distributed, Mallory settled into Lucas's car to start back to the resort.

"I had a good time tonight, "she said.

"Me, too." Lucas started the car and offered her a slow grin.

"Wanna go take a drive somewhere and look at the stars? It's a nice night."

Mallory jerked her head around in surprise to look at him. "You mean like look at the stars and ..." She let her words drift off.

"Yeah." He winked at her. "Actually there's a great place I know about at the top of one of the mountain roads nearby where you can see a zillion stars. It's a clear night with a full moon. It should be pretty."

"I've heard that line about a pretty view before—and a few others."

"I'll bet you have." He chuckled in the darkness as he turned the car around to start down the driveway.

"It *is* a nice night though," she agreed after a few minutes. "I only said I needed to go home because I felt concerned about Elizabeth. She worked hard today for someone pregnant with a new baby. I thought she needed to rest."

"So?" He slowed at the bottom of the driveway before turning onto the highway. "Do you want to go check out the view?"

"Well, as you mentioned before, it is a nice night." A smile twitched at her lips. "You could probably point out some of the constellations to me."

"That I could." She heard another low chuckle from him before he turned to head up the highway.

A short time later, after winding up a steep, twining side road and bumping down a rustic, unpaved gravel drive, they came out into an open field.

"Where in the world are we?" she asked, looking around.

"On the mountain near Rock Creek, not too far from where we walked the other day when we went to the falls. An old settlers' homestead used to sit here." He pointed to a battered mountain cabin to their left at the edge of the woods, surrounded in part by a rock wall, with a small weathered barn to one side. "I found this place one day while taking a hike up the creek. I wondered at the time what sort of person would build high on a mountain so isolated from others like this. But then, when you look out over this ridge at the views over the valley and across to the mountains beyond, you can certainly see one reason for it."

Lucas pulled the car close to the edge of the ridge top, before killing the motor, giving them a stupendous view out over the Pittman Center valley. Behind them, they could see the hazy edges of the Smoky Mountains rising into the darkness.

"It is a beautiful place." She gazed out over the view before her. "Do you come here often?"

"Occasionally. It's a good place to think—and to pray. A good place to find answers when you need them. I often get out of my car and sit on the porch of that old house until I get the peace I need."

"Are we trespassing?"

"Not exactly. This is actually part of the Millhouse Resort property, even on this rough side of the mountain across the creek. Beau knew the old man who once lived here. He let him stay on the place, even after he and his father purchased the acreage when it went up for auction. Beau's father thought the resort might want to expand to build rental homes or villas here one day."

"Well, you certainly couldn't use a mountainous piece of property like this for much else." She paused, a thought coming to her. "Was this Chessy Bohanan's place?"

"I think so. Why? Did you know him?" Lucas gave her a curious look.

Mallory shivered. "Not really. He's the man who found my father in the woods after the hunting accident. Daddy drove over from Nashville that fall weekend to go turkey hunting with a group of old friends." She smiled to herself in memory. "I remember he said he wanted to get a turkey for Nonnie to put away for Thanksgiving."

"Do you mind if I ask what happened?"

"No one knows for sure." She leaned back in the seat remembering. "Daddy and two friends went hunting and then split up. Later at the point where they planned to meet again, Daddy didn't show. The two men waited for some time and then came on back to the resort, thinking Daddy came home earlier for some reason. Realizing later he was missing, Beau, Daddy's friends and others searched to no avail and then the sheriff sent out a search team, too. It was Chessy Bohanan who found Daddy. He'd been shot almost straight through the heart. They said he must have died quickly. It appeared to be a hunting accident—with so many people out hunting that weekend. No one ever came forward, so the police determined it must have been a random shot and that the shooter probably didn't even know he hit and killed Daddy. It's a sad story, isn't it?"

"It is, and I'm really sorry I brought you up here to make you remember it."

"It's okay. But I'm glad I wasn't here that particular weekend with Daddy." She closed her eyes. "I stayed in Nashville for one of my girlfriend's sleep-over birthday parties."

"It must have been hard for you—losing your father so young."

"It was."

He moved over to wrap her in his arms. "I'm sorry to stir up a sad memory for you."

She pulled back to look at him in the darkened car. "One of the women in Nonnie's Monday Group said she wondered if Daddy's death really was an accident."

"I wouldn't pay any attention to that." Lucas pushed a strand of her hair back. "I've always heard the men at the pro shop say the death was ruled an accident. There didn't appear to be any struggle or sign it might have been anything else. Plus no one knew of anyone who might have wanted to kill your father. From all I've been told, everyone loved him."

"Yes. Everyone did love him." She laid her head against his chest. "So did I."

Mallory pulled back, hugging herself again, blinking so she wouldn't shed the tears that threatened. "I'd better not cry or you'll think I'm getting overly emotional. I know that bothers you."

He pulled her back close to him. "Don't worry. Sometimes getting overly emotional is a good thing. Like now." He moved his lips to settle over hers, quickly shifting her thoughts from the past to the present.

Mallory sighed under his mouth. It always felt both exciting and peaceful when Lucas kissed her, such a lovely contrast of emotions. She twined her arms around his neck, kissing him back. "I haven't sat in the dark making out in a long time," she whispered against his lips. "I'm glad you thought of this."

A short time later, Lucas drew back from her. "We're steaming up the windows." He laughed. "And I just had a vision of a frowning policeman shining a flashlight into the window at us."

She giggled. "Has that ever happened to you?"

"Once a long time ago, although not here." He grinned at her. "Probably why the remembrance of it hit me again."

Mallory ran a hand down his face, enjoying the feel of him, turning her fingers to trace them over his mouth.

He kissed her fingers and then leaned over to kiss her again.

"Who was the last man you kissed before me?" he asked playfully.

Mallory felt herself tighten and pull into herself. She looked away from him, not wanting to answer.

"Hmmm… guess I hit a nerve," he said. "Which means it's your turn to confess about your problem man. After all, I told you about my past with Cecily."

Mallory looked out the window at the stars scattered across the dark sky. "That's hardly the same. I'm sure Cecily wasn't the last girl you kissed."

"No, the last girl I kissed was Lorilee Neely in the swimming pool behind the resort one dark night when the two of us took a late swim together. In early May this year, I think."

"That wasn't long ago." She frowned at him.

He smiled at her. "I hadn't met you yet."

"Oh, as if that would matter." She flipped at her hair in annoyance.

"Do you want me to describe that little kiss scene in more detail or do you want to tell me about the last man in your life?"

"Why do you want to know about him?" She crossed her arms.

"What he did to hurt you." He pushed a strand of her hair behind her ear. "Whatever he did, I want to avoid doing the same thing if I can."

"Sweet words." She felt her emotions kicking around, a little anger building at her memories. "Ethan could use sweet words, too, but he failed me when I really needed him to be there for me."

"When your mother was sick and dying?" His eyes held hers.

She nodded. "Yes. He decided he needed more entertainment during that time. I sort of walked in on it." Mallory didn't want to tell him the details.

He lifted her chin to look at her. "He sounds like a stupid man. I think a woman who would care for and love her mother through a long siege of illness and death would be the kind of woman you'd want to keep around."

She turned her face away from his gaze. "Well, Ethan apparently didn't hold the same insight."

"Ethan what?"

"Ethan Broussard." She knew she said the name with bitterness.

He sent her one of his mischievous grins. "That's too pretty a name for a man. Makes me suspicious right away—in the same way meeting a girl named Butchie Beamer or Gloria Galore would make me leery."

Mallory giggled in spite of herself. "Can't you be serious about anything?"

"Sure, but I don't like Ethan Broussard messing up my evening with you." He reached over to give her a quick kiss. "You already know he was a jerk if he acted like that, don't you?"

"Yes, but it still hurt." She dropped her eyes.

"It probably hurt more because you were worn out caring for your mom, not taking care of yourself or getting enough sleep, and still trying to keep up with your workload. I had times like that with Cecily. Her scenes were always worse when I was exhausted from travel, fighting off sickness, or beaten down over the last episode of trauma and emotional overload she'd walked me through."

"You went through a lot with Cecily—much more than I did with Ethan. At least, thankfully, I didn't marry him." She put a hand to his face, watching his eyes darken.

He kissed her again. "Maybe I'll marry you so you won't go back to Savannah." His voice softened. "I'm getting rather used to having you around."

Mallory tensed, pulling back without thinking.

"What?" He spread his hands. "You think I'm such a bad catch?"

She bit her lip. "Beau didn't talk to you about maybe marrying me or anything, did he?" The question tumbled out before Mallory thought.

"Beau?" He looked baffled. "As far as I know, Beau doesn't even know we're more than friends."

Now that she'd gone this far, she watched his face closely as she asked, "I just wondered if he suggested it might be nice if you and I got together."

He regarded her with interest. "Why do you think Beau might suggest that?"

Mallory tried to keep her voice casual. "Because of the resort. Because you're wanting to buy into it ..."

"And?"

"And it would make it easier if...." She couldn't finish out the words.

His jaw clenched. "Are you suggesting I might be showing interest in you because it could pave my way into an interest in the resort?" He grabbed her arm with the words, startling her. "The answer is no, and I'm disappointed you would entertain an idea like that about me."

"Beau sort of mentioned it might be nice and it made me start to think."

"What you're saying is that his words opened a nasty little door in your mind about my interest in you." He turned around in his seat and started the car. "I'm taking you home now, Mallory. I think our little interlude of the evening is finished."

"I hurt your feelings," she said, as he backed the car out of its parking place and started down the dark roadway away from the cabin.

"Believe it or not men do have feelings, too." His voice was laced with sarcasm. "Women don't have a monopoly on that."

They drove in silence the rest of the way down the mountain and up the highway back to Millhouse Resort. Mallory tried to think what to say.

"I'm sorry," she said at last.

"Sorry for what? … that I got mad at you? Or are you sorry you said what you did and thought what you did of me?"

She tried to sort out his words. "I'm sorry for all those things, I guess."

"You guess?" His voice rose. "What kind of sorry is that?"

She made a slight sound of exasperation. "I'm trying to apologize, Lucas."

"Well, maybe I'm not ready to hear it." He pulled the Lexus to a stop by the gate leading to the back door of Wingate House.

She bit her tongue as she considered saying more, not wanting to make him angrier.

"Let me straighten something out for you, M.T. Wingate." He took his hands off the steering wheel where he'd clenched them before and looked at her with hardened eyes. "First, if you'll recall, I initially felt attracted to you on an airplane when I had no idea you were even related to Beau and Nonnie Wingate. Second, I tried to fight that attraction, because you *were* Beau and Nonnie's granddaughter."

Mallory decided it wasn't a good time to remind him he'd tried to fight any attraction to her because he thought she might be mentally unstable like Cecily.

"Third," he continued, practically shaking a finger at her now, his voice rising. "I don't *need* to marry into any well-to-do family in order to buy part or all of a resort. I made a very large amount of money on the pro golf tour. I could buy a posh resort almost anywhere—one much bigger than Millhouse—without even losing sleep over the financial cost of it."

Mallory found herself shrinking back into her seat, wishing she might disappear into it.

He reached across her, opening her door. "I'll let you see yourself to the door. You can be assured I *won't* be kissing you over the garden gate tonight, Mallory Wingate. And just so you're absolutely clear about it, I was *teasing* you earlier when I said I might marry you to keep you here. Note the word is t-e-a-s-i-n-g." He spelled it out. "You like words, so maybe you'll remember that one. I have *no* interest in marrying again—either to you or to anyone after what I went through with Cecily."

She mouthed the words *I'm sorry* again as she walked around the car past the driver's side near him, but she doubted he noticed, since he jerked the car into gear and pealed up the drive.

Watching his car disappear, Mallory let out a slow sigh. This felt like reading one of those romance novels she edited by the dozens, where things weren't going well for the heroine. Assuming she even *was* the heroine anymore.

# CHAPTER 12

Lucas did everything in his power over the next few days to avoid thinking about, or running into, Mallory Wingate. He'd allowed himself to get vulnerable toward her at his sister's home and look where going soft had led him? To joking around that she ought to marry him, a thought he never should have put into words even in jest, and then to be insulted by her about his intentions. How dare she suggest he might want to form a liaison with her to sweeten a buy into Millhouse Resort? Yes, he'd talked to Beau about the possibility. But now he even felt angry toward Beau for bringing his and Mallory's relationship into that mix.

Fortunately, neither Beau, nor his nosy sister Elizabeth, initiated any one-on-one chats with him over the next days, giving him time to cool down. Whatever was he thinking, getting hung up on Mallory? She had her own life in Savannah she'd soon return to. He knew that; she knew that. Hadn't she told him often enough how much her work meant to her, always chatting away about her authors, their books, and her colleagues at Whittier? She wouldn't want to walk away from that life. He was kidding himself to imagine she would. And for what? A golf pro at a rural mountain resort—and one with a ready-made kid in tow? Right.

Lucas pulled his thoughts back to business. He *needed* to focus on business. Another car theft had occurred last week. This made three at Millhouse now, and they'd ramped up security at the resort and hired a guard to patrol the grounds.

Beau held a meeting with all the staff after the last theft to discuss measures they needed to take to see that no more thefts occurred. Today the resort's accountant was coming to go through the books in all departments of the resort, starting with the pro shop. Lucas hated that it was in his arena where problems had first been spotted. He couldn't imagine where the problem could be. Barry Short, the shop manager, and his assistant, Denise Ogle, had worked at Millhouse for years. Andy Kiley filled in part-time in the shop when needed and his legacy at Millhouse could hardly be questioned. Who else could have access to the finances at the pro shop?

Finishing an early practice round this morning, he put his clubs away and made his way into the pro shop. He found Denise looking upset behind the register.

"I'm glad you're here, Lucas," she said in a rush. "Do you know why Barry didn't show up at work today? It's my day off, but Dick Kemp at the lodge called and asked me to come in. Barry didn't show up this morning and Dick couldn't reach him on his cell."

"Barry's not here?" Lucas glanced around the shop in surprise. He'd headed out on the course to practice long before the pro shop opened.

"No, he's not." Denise pulled at the collar of her shirt, obviously upset. "One of the guests at the lodge walked over earlier and then returned grumbling to Evelyn at the front desk because they found the shop closed. Evelyn called Dick, and Dick called Barry and then me when he couldn't reach Barry." She sighed. "I already worked extra days for Barry this weekend, since he wanted to be here when the accountant came today. I had to cancel a doctor's appointment to come in to cover for him."

"Well, I can cover if you need to go, Denise."

"No, no." She waved a hand. "I already rescheduled it. I'm just upset Barry didn't show or call anyone. It's not like him."

"No, it's not. I'll try his cell once more and then call his wife Wilma at the bank. Maybe they had a family emergency or something."

A few hours later, Lucas walked over to Beau's for a talk. It wasn't a conversation he looked forward to.

"Well, hi Lucas," Nonnie said as he pushed open the kitchen door after knocking. "Come on in. Beau and Mallory and I just finished lunch. We're running late because Beau had that civic meeting in Sevierville this morning."

Beau glanced up, his eyes catching Lucas's. "What's wrong?" he asked, picking up immediately on Lucas's mood.

"I have bad news." He regretted Mallory had to sit in on this discussion, but he could hardly ask her to leave. "Barry Short didn't show up for work today. One of the guests came over to the shop while I was out on the course, expecting it to be open, and returned to the lodge grumbling to find it closed. Evelyn called Dick about it, and Dick called Barry who was scheduled to open today. Not able to reach him, he next called Denise. When Denise couldn't get in touch with Barry either, she came in to open, even though it was her day off."

Beau frowned. "That's not like Barry."

"No." Lucas sighed, slumping into a kitchen chair. "I tried Barry again and then called Wilma at the bank where she works as a teller. We thought maybe they had an emergency at home or something...." His voice trailed off.

"And?" When Lucas hesitated, Beau added, "Spit it out, boy."

"Wilma thought Barry was on a buying trip for the shop. She babbled away to me about him leaving Friday morning, said he wouldn't be back for a few more days yet. She seemed to think Denise forgot to tell me."

Lucas watched Beau digest this.

"I had to tell Wilma that Barry wasn't on a buying trip and then ask her some hard questions." He ran a hand through his hair. "Wilma works in the bank. She ran some checks after we talked. She and Barry hold two accounts. Barry cleaned his out. She came over to the shop crying to tell me this. She said Barry had gotten involved with some online gambling. He came to her a couple of times for loans last year to bail him out, but he swore to her after that he'd quit. She hoped he had."

"Sounds like maybe he borrowed from us, too," Beau said.

Lucas nodded, still stunned over the events of the morning.

"Poor Wilma." Nonnie shook her head. "This must be a terrible shock to her. Where in the world do you suppose Barry went?"

"Right now no one knows," Lucas answered. "But the police are starting to investigate. Either Barry panicked and ran, knowing the audit would bring to light the unauthorized withdrawals made at the shop, or he'd carefully planned to leave for some time, possibly arranging for a job in another country and another identity."

Beau shook his head. "I can't quite imagine Barry Short being clever or resourceful enough for the latter. He was a nice steady guy, but not a rocket scientist."

"The officer who came to the pro shop said people can become very resourceful once they get involved in criminal activity." Lucas leaned his head back and closed his eyes. "I can't believe this has happened."

Beau blew out a deep breath before speaking again. "The unexpected is the norm more often than we like to think, but it still catches us off guard."

"No kidding."

"The police will probably track Barry down eventually. It won't help him that he ran." Beau paused. "Did Barry take more from the shop before he ran?"

"Yes, but not much. The overall theft, from all I can determine, probably totaled thirty or forty thousand. We could have worked something out with him and Wilma if he had only come to us."

"I guess he felt too ashamed," Nonnie said.

Mallory fixed Lucas a lunch plate while they talked and put it in front of him. "Here, I'm sure you had no time for lunch with all that's happened."

He picked at the food, having little appetite. "Our accountant, Gary Rodale, wants to know if he should still come to go through the shop records today. I wasn't sure what to tell him."

"I'll call and talk to him," Beau replied. "He might as well come on. The police will want to know an accurate figure of money taken. Our regrets over this situation don't change how we need to deal with it." He put his napkin on the table and stood up. "Let Mallory pack that sandwich to bring with you. We'd better get over to the lodge and meet with all the Millhouse employees before gossip begins to circulate."

He turned to Nonnie. "Why don't you take some of the food left from your Monday Group luncheon over to Wilma's today? Maybe see if the minister wouldn't go with you and possibly one of Wilma's good friends. I think she could use support and company at a time like this."

"That's a nice idea." Nonnie went over to kiss his cheek and then give Lucas a hug, too. "I know this has been hard for you, Lucas, but try not to let it make you feel guilty. None of us could imagine Barry behaving this way."

Beau turned to Mallory. "Girl, help your grandmother with the lunch today, if you would. She'll have her mind divided over all this, and I'm still worried about the little thefts going on here, too."

"Do you think there's any link between the thefts at the shop and here?" Mallory asked.

"I can't imagine how pilfering a few gewgaws would help Barry much with gambling debts." Beau frowned. "But we'll mention it to the officer."

Mallory handed Lucas a paper sack with his sandwich in it. "I put a few of Nonnie's brownies in also."

"Thanks." He met her eyes then, seeing that steady gaze he remembered from the first time they met.

"I'm sorry this happened," she said.

"Me, too." He left with Beau then to start a hectic day filled with meetings, calls, and discussions. At four in the afternoon Elizabeth phoned him. "I sent Suzannah home with Mallory after lunch today. Abby has pink eye. Nonnie told me all that was going on when I called her, hoping she might keep Suzannah. I'm sorry about Barry, but Robert said I should separate the girls because pink eye is highly contagious. I hope Suzannah doesn't get it, but Robert said to call him if you see any symptoms."

Lucas groaned. Just what he needed—a sitter problem with

Suzannah right now and possibly pinkeye to deal with. "You should have called me earlier."

"Why?" she answered. "Mallory offered to help out. I didn't see any problem with letting her."

Lucas could hardly go into the reasons why he wasn't eager to be in Mallory's debt for anything at this time.

"Well, I hope Abby gets better soon," he told her instead.

"Me, too. You know, I think Abby might have picked that pink eye up when we delivered herbs and sachets Saturday. I noticed one of the children looked like she'd been crying. Thinking back, it was probably pink eye. Abby played with her while I unloaded my delivery." Lucas heard her sigh. "You know, Abby could be contagious for several days to a week."

"It's okay, Sis. I'll work something out. You take care of Abby and yourself."

Lucas headed home at nearly six, running late and worn out from the day.

As he let himself in the back door and started into the kitchen, cooking smells met his nose.

He stopped in the doorway to find Mallory at the stove with a dish towel tied around her waist.

"Hey," she said, turning around to smile at him. "I thought you would be tired, so I made dinner."

Suzannah grinned at him from her perch on a stool by the counter. "Mallory and I went to the store and shopped special for dinner," she said. "Mallory bought me a new coloring book and crayons, too." She held up her page to him. "Look at the fairy I colored. It's a fairies and elves coloring book."

He leaned against the doorframe. "You didn't have to do all this, Mallory."

"I know, but I *can* be nice sometimes." She gave him a grin, making him smile despite himself.

"Yeah, I can see that."

Suzannah popped into the conversation once more. "Mallory cooked meat loaf for us. I told her we both liked it."

"That we do." He agreed. "What can I do to help?"

"Go wash up and then come back for dinner. Everything is almost ready."

True to her word, Lucas was soon sitting at the table eating meat loaf, scalloped potatoes, fresh green beans, and sliced homegrown tomatoes, a welcome feast for a tired man.

"Elizabeth gave us the green beans and tomatoes from her garden to take to Nonnie, but there were *lots* of tomatoes and beans so we brought some home to eat here." She speared a green bean with her fork as she talked.

"Everything tastes great," Lucas said, and he meant it. She'd made exactly the kind of meat loaf he loved, firm with a drizzle of warm red sauce over the top and the green beans had bits of onion and bacon in them.

"I helped Mallory make the potatoes," Suzannah said with a smug smile. "You cut up the potatoes and then do layers with potatoes and butter and flour and cheese and other stuff. Do you like them, Daddy?"

"They are excellent." He reached for another helping to please her and also because they tasted terrific. He never had time for fancy dishes like this for Suzannah and himself when he cooked. He'd gotten pretty good in the kitchen over the years with one dish items, a few casseroles, spaghetti, or anything he could grill, but his culinary skills were limited. Many evenings, he loaded Suzannah up and took her to the Millhouse Lodge to eat or down the highway to Palmer's Grill for burgers or pizza.

As Lucas ate his dinner, he listened to Suzannah and Mallory's mixed chatter about fairies and then kittens, enjoying his food and finally beginning to relax after a hard day.

Mallory possessed such an easy manner with Suzannah, listening to her endless talk and chatter, patiently answering her questions, helping her learn something new when needed.

"We made a bed for Babycakes this afternoon in the closet where you come in from the screened porch." Suzannah turned bright eyes to his. "Mallory said it would be an easy place for Babycakes to find when she needed to have her babies. She told me lots about baby kittens."

Lucas felt relieved. He'd put off that conversation.

"We took Babycakes to her bed several times so she could see it and know where it is. She went back and looked at it all by herself later and climbed into her box and everything. That's good."

Lucas smiled at his daughter. "It was nice of you and Mallory to make Baby a special place. But it will be a while before she needs it yet."

"Yes, but it's all ready now. And if we keep showing it to her, she might use it and not have her kittens outside where they wouldn't be safe—or maybe in your bed."

His eyes popped open at that, and he heard Mallory's low laugh. "Cats can be unpredictable," she said, giving him a gamine smile.

"Well, closer to the time, I'll be sure to keep my bedroom door closed."

"Guess what we made for dessert?" Suzannah said, jumping to a new topic. "Strawberry shortcake. The berries are chopped up already and we get to put them on little cakes and then squirt cream on them."

"Sounds good," he said, and of course it was better than good.

Later when Suzannah had been bathed, read to, and tucked into bed, Lucas sat on the screened porch with Mallory, sharing a glass of sparkling water she'd mixed with cranberry and orange juice.

"This is surprisingly good." He studied the beverage in his hand.

"Thanks." She dropped the mules off her feet and curled them underneath her on the sofa. "I hope I worked my way back into your good graces tonight. I can't tell you how sorry I am for what I said before."

He let her words hang in the air for a few moments before he answered. "It still bothers me you'd think I was that kind of person, Mallory."

She made a face. "My mother had a strong impact on my upbringing. She was basically distrustful and critical of people by nature and I still battle the old voices of her suspicious mind sometimes. I've had to work at learning to be more trusting, to look for the best in people rather than the worst."

"I've seen that caution in you sometimes."

"Mother always said a woman needed to depend on herself, to watch that she wasn't exploited or used. I admit I often saw Mother hurt or taken advantage of, even though she tried hard to be strong and independent." Mallory frowned. "It is still a man's world in many ways. Despite progress, women haven't attained the full equity they've yearned for—and fought for."

He lifted an eyebrow in question.

She sent him a challenging look in reply. "Does a woman pro golfer make as much as a man in the same profession? Does she get the same opportunities and sponsorship? And how many resorts hire women golf pros?"

"Point taken, I suppose," he acknowledged.

"Mother struggled hard in an era less kind to women, less open to their leadership qualities, and less willing to pay them what they deserved. I still see those struggles today. I read about them in the books I edit, too. It troubles me. Perhaps I'm overly sensitive on the subject because of what I've seen, what I've learned, and what I've watched."

He sat his drink down on the table beside his chair. "Yet in comparison to the lives of women in so many countries of the world, American women have incredible opportunities."

"I'm sure that's true. It breaks my heart to think of what women face and deal with in many countries abroad—the harsh restrictions and the lack of basic freedoms, being treated like property instead of as individuals of worth and value. But change is still needed in our country, too."

He leaned back in his chair and closed his eyes. "This is an interesting conversation, Mallory, but it doesn't make it okay that you judged me an opportunist and thought I might be the sort of person to use another individual for personal gain."

She sighed. "No, it doesn't."

He sipped on his drink again. "However, I do appreciate you taking care of Suzannah for me tonight. I appreciate the dinner and the apology, too." He paused, trying to find the right words. "I would like for us to be friends, but I think it's probably best we back away from more. You know what I mean. As we both know, you have your own life to return to soon. I have my life here."

"You're right, of course," she said, nodding. "We both have enough baggage on our own right now."

"Yes, that's true, too."

They sat in silence for a time, thinking over their words.

"It's getting late. I need to go," Mallory said at last. She slipped her feet back into her mules and reached for the purse slung over a chair beside her.

He stood to see her out.

She turned back to him. "Listen. Abby has pink eye and you need a sitter for Suzannah. Will you let me keep her for you until Abby is better? I enjoy Suzannah's company and it helps the days to pass more quickly for me. I'm used to being busy. I'm not comfortable being idle." She hesitated. "You have enough to deal with this week, resolving all the problems with the theft at the shop and with all the ongoing issues relating to it."

He considered her offer. "I think Suzannah would be pleased to enjoy your company. But I'd want to pay you to keep her."

She tried to interrupt.

"No." He cut her off. "I'll pay you what I pay Elizabeth. That's only fair, and cooking dinner every night is not part of the deal. Suzannah shouldn't get too used to you being in her life both day and night. You'll be leaving soon."

"Yes, but I'll come back to Millhouse for holidays. She can think of me as a friend, like she does Nonnie and Beau."

He nodded. "I'll bring Suzannah to you at Nonnie and Beau's every morning. She's used to sharing breakfast with them, and you can keep her there or bring her over here sometimes. I'll give you a key. You can take Suzannah to the pool at the lodge, too. She's a good swimmer already, although she usually prefers to wear her water wings. She thinks they're fun."

Mallory smiled at that. "We'll be fine, Lucas. Spending time with Suzannah will help me to know more about young children, to know better the kinds of books that most appeal to them. As I mentioned, I do acquisitions for our children's line at Whittier as well as for the romance line."

"You mentioned that," he said.

She paused as she pushed open the screen door. "I hope things work out regarding the problems with Barry. He seemed like such a nice man to me. It's so hard to believe he would steal from good people he cared about—or steal at all."

Lucas frowned. "Gambling, drugs, alcohol, and other addictions can change even nice people. Those vices get such a hold. I feel especially sorry for Wilma and for their two kids in college. This will be hard for their whole family."

"Who will work Barry's hours at the pro shop?"

"Andy Kiley will fill in to help Denise for now. He knows more about the pro shop than anyone, and we need stability after all this. A familiar face in the shop will help. Later we'll look for someone else to hire."

"That's a good idea." She smiled.

He studied her face, so calm and strong. "I'm glad you're feeling so much better now," he added. "I feel bad about my earlier misjudgments of you, too."

"Thanks," she said. "I'm glad we could talk tonight."

"Me, too." His eyes followed her down the pathway toward the gate. It wouldn't be easy to keep all the resolutions they'd made tonight. But he had to try.

# CHAPTER 13

The next days were busy and fun for Mallory, as well as exhausting. Keeping up with a five-year-old child all day was a full-time job.

"What are you girls doing today?" Nonnie asked on Friday as they sat at breakfast eating pancakes with strawberry syrup and fresh berries over the top. "You've had a busy week."

"We've had a *super fun* week." Suzannah leaned toward Nonnie, her eyes sparkling. "We went to Gatlinburg to see the aquarium on Tuesday. I liked all the fishes, especially the big tank with the pretty colored ones, and I liked the penguins and the jellies fish. "

"*Jelly* fish," Mallory corrected as Suzannah chattered on.

"Wednesday we went swimming and had a picnic in the treehouse. Yesterday we rode *real* horses at the Ramsey Stable. Mallory and I got to ride all the way up the mountain on a long trail and everything. I had *my own* horse, too. It was neat." She picked a strawberry off her pancake to pop into her mouth.

Nonnie smiled at Mallory. "You've certainly given Suzannah a week to remember. Maybe you girls should take a rest today."

"Uh-uh." Suzannah shook her head. "Mallory said we're going to the covered bridge today and to see my school."

"I promised Suzannah we would drive up see the school where she'll be going to kindergarten this fall." Mallory got up to pour herself another cup of coffee. "I learned there is a museum within the school telling the history of Pittman Center. I thought it would be interesting for us to see, and then on the way back I thought we'd drive over to see Emerts Cove Covered Bridge. It's been years since I visited it, and Suzannah has never seen a covered bridge before."

Smiling again now, Suzannah chimed in. "Mallory showed me a picture of it. We read about the bridge, about my school, and about the museum on the Internet." She sent Nonnie a knowing look. "You can look up almost anything on the Internet to learn all about it," she said. "Mallory even showed me how to look up stuff on Wickedpedia."

"That's *Wiki*pedia," Mallory corrected, trying not to smirk.

Nonnie stood up to begin clearing off the kitchen table. "Well, you young people are so good with those computers today. I do well to check my email and get on my Facebook page."

"Computers are super fun," Suzannah told her, pushing back from the table. "Can I go out in the yard until you finish cleaning up in the kitchen?"

"Yes," Mallory answered, "but stay in the back garden or on the patio inside the fence."

"Okay." She jumped down from her booster seat and snatched her doll off a nearby chair. "I'll take EdithAnn and teach her about *colors* while we walk around in the garden."

Nonnie shook her head, smiling, as Suzannah let herself out the back door. "That child has such a vivid imagination. She tells me entire stories about things her doll EdithAnn does or says."

"Yes," Mallory answered, getting up to begin clearing off the table. "And aren't her stories wonderful?"

"You're growing fond of her."

"I am. She's smart, well-mannered, and fun—even for a five-year-old."

Nonnie smiled. "I've always said a child can make you see life with new eyes." She began to load the breakfast dishes into the dishwasher. "Are you sure it hasn't been too much for you, keeping up with Suzannah all week? You're supposed to be resting."

"I'm fine," Mallory assured her. "David is even sending me editing work to do next week. I'm starting the first read-through of

Avery Briley's new book and David wants my take on a new author he's interested in. He read the initial chapters she submitted and really liked them. He wants me to read the full text she's submitted now. Her name is Sonia Butler."

Mallory opened the refrigerator to put away juice and butter. "David thinks she might be a bright new star for Whittier. Her books are set on Little St. Simon's Island, one of the least developed Georgia barrier islands. Sonia is related to the Berolzheim family, who partly own the island, so she has rare insights into the island's history and its heart."

"That sounds like it might be a pleasure to read with that setting." Nonnie paused thoughtfully. "It must be nice to help bring new authors out, to introduce them to the public—sort of like nurturing a child."

"That's a good analogy." Mallory smiled. "An editor does play a special role in an author's life, helping her voice to shine and her story to sing."

"That's a nice way to express it." Nonnie glanced at the clock. "Whoops. I need to get ready. Dottie and I are driving to Sevierville to shop today. I knew you'd be occupied with Suzannah so I hoped you wouldn't mind."

"Of course not."

She tapped her cheek with her finger. "I was wondering, since you and Suzannah will be over on Hills Creek Road at the Emerts Bridge, if you'd mind taking the gift basket I fixed to Tilly Walker. She sprained her ankle and did damage to a ligament, bless her heart, and has been basically home bound. The Monday Girls all brought some gift items for her to the luncheon on Monday. Yesterday I put them in a pretty basket after baking cookies to add. I've been meaning to take it over."

"Where does Tilly live? Can I find her place on my own?" Mallory leaned against the counter. "There isn't a GPS in your car that I've been driving this week and I don't know the back roads around here like you do."

"You won't have a problem. Tilly's place is only a short distance up the road from the bridge on a small side street. I'll draw you a little map and write down her address and phone number in case you need it." Nonnie retrieved the basket from the kitchen closet while she talked, and then sat down to draw a rough map and write down the information Mallory would need. "Tilly will enjoy seeing Suzannah, too. That child could brighten up anyone's day."

"Should I call Tilly first?"

"No, just drop by. That way in case Suzannah gets too tired or you need to head home instead, Tilly won't be disappointed. She's not going anywhere until that ankle heals. You'll find her at the house if you can get by."

Mallory studied the map, and then glanced toward the tearoom. "By the way, have you had any more thefts at the tearoom?"

"No and that's good news, isn't it? It worried Beau, and he has enough on his mind already with the car thefts and all that trouble with Barry."

"Beau said the police caught Barry. What will happen to him?"

"He'll be prosecuted. Beau said they might be lenient because he has no previous criminal record, but still, he'll probably serve time. It's about to break Wilma's heart." Nonnie pulled off her apron and draped it over a kitchen chair. "Barry's getting help with his problems, but there are trust issues that may be difficult to resolve between those two."

"I guess I can understand that." Mallory looked out the kitchen window. "I'd better go check on Suzannah and you need to get dressed to enjoy your day with Dottie. Stay as long as you want. There are plenty of leftovers from the Home Demonstration Club luncheon on Wednesday. You put a whole chicken casserole in the freezer. We can heat it tonight to make things easy."

"The Home Demonstration group is officially an FCE Group now. That stands for Family and Community Education Group, organized under the UT Extension office in Knoxville. But for years the old group here was called a Home Demonstration Club so most of the ladies who've been in the group a long time still call it that."

Mallory smiled. "It's the name I remember: Pittman Center Home Demonstration Club. They met in the tearoom even when I was a girl."

"Yes, and they were all tickled to see you again on Wednesday."

Mallory studied her grandmother. "It's not too much for you, is it, Nonnie, having a different group here in the tearoom every Wednesday and hosting the Monday Group every week?"

Nonnie turned to her. "What brought that question on? Do you think I'm getting old or something?"

"Well, no, but it's a lot of work."

"So is editing, but you love it, don't you?"

Mallory nodded.

"Well, running my tearoom and having my luncheons is the same for me. It's work for sure, but it's work I love." A faint smile played over her lips. "I'm invested in my groups that meet at the tearoom just like you're invested in your authors. I enjoy thinking about what to serve them for lunch every week, planning how to decorate the tables, visiting with the women when they come, and hearing about their lives. The Red Hat Group and The Book Club are my newest regular Wednesday groups but the Pittman Center Demonstration Club and the Emerts Cove DAR groups have lunched with me for almost twenty years now." She paused. "You haven't minded helping with my groups have you?"

"Oh, no." Mallory smiled. "It's been a joy and brought back many happy memories."

"Well, I know most of the women in my groups are not your age, but they're lovely women."

"I agree and I've learned a lot listening to their speakers. I especially enjoyed hearing the women in The Book Club discuss their book selection."

Nonnie smiled. "Yes, I noticed you hung around like a fly on the wall for that meeting. Have you read the novel they talked about?"

"No, but they made me want to."

"Well, I'll ask Dottie if she kept her copy and maybe you can borrow it." She glanced at the clock. "I'd better hustle to be ready when Dottie comes. You and Suzannah have a nice day."

Mallory and Suzannah did enjoy a nice day. Suzannah was thrilled to see her new school and enjoyed, to some degree, looking around the fine Glen Cardwell Heritage Museum. The history facts about Pittman Center and the old photos drew Mallory's interest more than Suzannah's, but the child liked the old artifacts on display.

The long, weathered, covered bridge on the Little Pigeon River, with its bright green roof, captivated Suzannah even more.

"Can we walk across it?" Suzannah asked with excitement, as Mallory parked her car beside it.

"Of course. See?" She pointed. "There's a special covered walkway on the side for people to walk over the bridge on."

Suzannah skipped over the bridge and back on the walkway and then clambered down a side path to the stream to explore. The day was sunny and bright, and it felt wonderful to be outdoors. Mallory spread a quilt under a shade tree by the stream and they ate a picnic lunch she'd packed earlier. Suzannah tossed bits of breadcrumbs down by the streamside for the birds to find.

"What is that little bird?" she asked, pointing.

"Just a brown sparrow, but he's happy to get your crumbs."

Suzannah sent her a wistful smile. "I wish you could babysit me every day."

"You'd miss Elizabeth and Abby," Mallory said matter-of-factly. "But we've had fun this week."

"Who is the lady we're going to see now?" Suzannah lifted the cloth on their small picnic basket to reach in for another cookie.

"Tilly Walker. She's one of Nonnie's friends in her Monday Group."

"One of the ladies that comes to the tearoom?"

"Yes. She hurt her ankle, so Nonnie and her friends in the Monday Group bought little gifts for her and Nonnie fixed them up in a basket."

"I looked at it in the car." Suzannah tossed cookie crumbs to the sparrow. "It has lotion, bubble bath, a book, candy and a lot of other stuff."

"Well, let's go take the basket to her, and then we'll go to your house until your father gets home." Mallory put the remains of their lunch in the basket and then folded up the quilt. "Be on your nicest behavior at Mrs. Walker's house, Suzannah. I'm sure she doesn't feel well."

"Okay. Abby doesn't feel good either, because she has pinkeye."

"That's right. No one feels well when they're sick."

The small road that led back to Tilly Walker's house proved easy to find. The house was a tidy white home with cheerful red shutters and a red door.

Tilly hobbled to the door at their knock, opening it a crack to look out at them over the door chain.

"I'm Mallory Wingate, Nonnie's granddaughter," Mallory said, smiling to reassure her. "I brought a gift basket to you from Nonnie. The Monday Girls put it together for you."

Tilly removed the chain and then opened the door. "Isn't that nice of them?" Tears filled her eyes. "I hope you'll come in for a minute. It's awful being cooped up here every day and hurting so much. I can't tell you what a trial it is."

"I can only stay a few minutes. I'm babysitting Suzannah today." Mallory glanced down at the child, to be sure the invitation extended to them both.

Tilly stared at them in an oddly unfocused way and then turned back into the living room. "Let yourselves in and shut the door for me," she said. "I need to sit back down and put my ankle up." She worked her way awkwardly across the room, using her crutches as a help to keep her booted foot off the floor and then she settled into an old recliner.

Mallory and Suzannah sat down on the sofa across from Tilly's chair.

"How come you're wearing that boot on your foot?" Suzannah asked, studying Tilly's orthopedic boot propped on the recliner. "Is that your hurted ankle?"

"Yes." Tilly winced on the word. "It's been really painful today." She launched into a lengthy reiteration of how she hurt it, explaining all the medical details of the diagnosis and the extent of her discomfort every day.

Suzannah shifted in her seat, restless. "You haven't looked at your nice basket," she said at last.

"Yes, I hope you like it." Mallory got up to put it on her lap, hoping the basket might shift the conversation.

Tilly picked through the basket, not seeming very enthusiastic over the nice gifts packed inside. "Look at this." She held up a pink bottle with irritation. "Bubble bath. What am I to do with bubble bath with this ankle wrapped the way it is? I can hardly get in the bath tub to use it."

Ignoring the querulous tone, Mallory said, "I'm sure you can save it until your ankle heals."

"That could be six weeks." She made a despairing face. "I cannot tell you how difficult this is when you're alone like I am. If Bobby Joe were still here, it would be a lot easier. I called to ask him if he would come and help me, but *no*, he wouldn't even consider it." Tears welled in her eyes. "It was wrong of him to leave me like he did. We were high school sweethearts you know. Everyone always said we were the perfect couple."

"Do you have children that can help out?" Mallory asked.

"No, we were never blessed with children. Just one more sorrow."

As Tilly launched into another lengthy story about that history, Suzannah pulled on Mallory's leg.

"I need to go to the bathroom," she whispered.

Hearing her, Tilly responded. "The bathroom is in the hallway." She pointed. "You go ahead. You'll see it."

Suzannah raised questioning eyes to Mallory's.

Mallory nodded, sending Suzannah a smile. When the child returned, she'd find an excuse for them to leave. Tilly certainly seemed depressed over her ankle. But then Nonnie told her she didn't handle even small health concerns well.

"You know I have to keep my weight off this ankle and that is so difficult. It's hard, too, to get the bandage on by myself or to get the boot off in order to get in bed at night." Tilly pushed another pillow under her ankle. "The X-ray showed a small hairline fracture in one of the bones, too. It may make the healing even longer. And, oh, the pain is so bad sometimes. You wouldn't believe how difficult a thing like this is."

Mallory wished she knew something comforting to say, but it seemed unlikely she could get a word in to say it anyway.

Shifting topics, Tilly began to talk about Bobby Joe again, telling Mallory about how they met, how happy they'd been, how she couldn't understand why he'd wanted to leave her.

Suzannah wandered back into the room a little later to sit down beside Mallory. "Look," she said, interrupting Tilly's stream of conversation. "Miss Tilly has a butterfly pin exactly like Nonnie's. See? It has a little blue stone in the middle like Nonnie's does." Suzannah held it up. "You have pretty jewelry, Miss Tilly. I like how you had it all laid out on that little table by the window."

She spread a handful of jewelry on the coffee table. "This is my favorite, this bracelet with the all the charms, especially the one with the pink rose. One of Nonnie's friends has one like it. She showed it to me." Suzannah picked up a ring circled with sapphires. "And look at this pretty ring, Mallory. It's really shiny."

Tilly had gone suddenly quiet and Mallory felt a shiver of discomfort crawl up her spine.

"You shouldn't have gotten those things out of my room!" Tilly spat out, her face growing angry. She pushed the foot of the recliner down, leaning forward to shake a finger at Suzannah. "You were only supposed to go to the bathroom, little girl, not go snooping through my house."

Suzannah's face fell and she bit her lip, leaning against Mallory. "I'm sorry. Nonnie lets me play with her jewelry. I saw yours on the table when I was looking for the bathroom."

"Well, you should have gone straight to the bathroom and come back." Tilly seemed overly upset. "You had no right to handle my things."

Mallory's eyes drifted over the pieces of jewelry on the table and her eyes moved to Tilly's. "These are the pieces missing from the tearoom," she said, without thinking.

Tilly's eyes flashed. "And what if they are? Those women still have men to buy them trinkets and gifts, to make them feel special. And what do I have? Nothing. Only memories." Her voice had risen, startling them, but now it dropped to a whine. "I only borrowed them for a little while. I planned to take them back. You do believe me, don't you?" Her eyes had taken on a glazed look that made Mallory nervous.

Suzannah curled up tighter against Mallory, obviously sensing trouble.

"Listen, I think I need to take Suzannah on home now," Mallory said in a calm, practical tone, standing up. "I hope your ankle feels better soon."

Tilly pushed herself to her feet and brandished her crutch at them. "I don't know if you can go home or not yet." She hobbled toward them, her voice taking on an odd singsong tone. "I don't like you getting into my things and knowing things you don't need to know. I think you might need to stay right here for a little while until I decide what to do. I need to think."

She put a hand to her hair restlessly, as if talking to herself now. "Maybe I need to get Bobby Joe's little gun. People who are bad and go snooping through other people's things can't always go home when they want to, you know."

Tilly scooped up the jewelry from the coffee table, putting it into the pocket of her robe. "I'm going to go put these away. You two wait right here." She shook a finger at them in warning and then continued babbling to herself as she started down the hallway. "I still have Bobby's little gun; I was looking at it just the other day. Pretty little thing."

Mallory looked down to see Suzannah's eyes wide with fright. Not wasting a minute, Mallory put a finger to her mouth in caution, scooped up the child and slipped across the room to quietly open the door and let them out. Not even shutting the door behind her, she ran for the car, pushing Suzannah in on the driver's side and starting the engine as quickly as she found her keys.

As she spun around to start down the driveway, she saw Tilly standing in the doorway and to her horror heard a gunshot sound behind them. It pinged off the back of the car, dissolving Suzannah into tears.

"Get down on the floor," Mallory told her, helping to push the child down to the floorboard.

She sped down the driveway and then onto the road, hoping desperately that Tilly, with her ankle in a boot, wouldn't get in her car to follow them. But who knew what a woman as obviously deranged as Tilly Walker might do? Good Lord, what a situation! And whatever was wrong with that woman?

Mallory drove as fast as she could down the road, back over the bridge, and then turned to head toward the main highway. She didn't know the countryside well enough to take shortcuts, so she simply headed straight to the main highway and then toward the resort.

She tried offering some comforting words to Suzannah—still crying, scared, and huddled in the floorboard. Gracious, she felt scared all the way down to her toenails and hoped desperately they weren't being followed.

*Please let me get back to the resort safely,* she prayed under her breath. *Don't let anything happen to this child.*

Remembering Nonnie was in Sevierville shopping, Mallory headed the car directly to the lodge, pulling up beside the pro shop, hoping to find Lucas there. She reached down to gather the crying child into her arms and then sprinted from the car into the shop, not wanting to waste a minute getting Suzannah to a safe place.

"Daddy!" Suzannah called out as they pushed through the door.

Mallory looked across the room to see Lucas in the shop talking to Andy Kiley behind the counter. Tears of relief swept over her at the sight of him. She passed Suzannah into his arms and then raced back across the room to lock the door.

"Tilly Walker pulled a gun on us," Mallory managed to get out, shaking now. "Suzannah and I were so scared. I don't know if she is following us or not."

Andy came out from behind the counter to gather her in his arms, helping her to a chair. Glancing at Lucas, all Mallory could see was an angry face.

"What in the world happened?" Andy asked in a soothing tone, rubbing her back.

Suzannah answered. "The lady Nonnie sent us to see turned all crazy." She sniffed loudly, pressing her face into Lucas's shoulder. "We had to run away fast and she shot at us."

"Someone shot at you?" Andy's voice sounded stunned.

"Yes." Mallory burst into a new spate of tears. "I felt terrified, especially with Suzannah with me. I don't know what came over Tilly Walker. It was awful."

The next hour passed in a blur for Mallory, but somehow Andy located Beau and Mallory managed to get the story out to him. The police were called and several officers dispatched to Tilly Walker's. Then finally, Mallory began to calm down as she went through the story one more time for the police officers.

At some point, Lucas left to take Suzannah home. Now as Mallory rode back to Wingate House, with Beau driving Nonnie's car—with a deep bullet scratch across the trunk now—it dawned on Mallory that Lucas hadn't offered her one kind word through the whole ordeal. He actually acted angry at first. Perhaps she shouldn't blame him for that. He probably saw her as responsible for Suzannah being upset before he learned what happened. Yet even when he listened to her story, Suzannah chiming in with her own details, he'd acted remote, keeping her at a distance, not offering her any comfort or kind words.

He never even offered her a thank you, either, for thinking fast and getting Suzannah out of that dangerous situation. Beau, Andy, and the officers gave her compliments for keeping her head, but not Lucas. It puzzled her. He'd even kept Suzannah from running to give her a hug before he took her home.

Too tired to analyze it now, Mallory leaned her head against the car seat in relief, glad the nightmare was past—and glad Tilly

Walker had been taken to a hospital where she could get some help. She felt relieved she didn't have to worry the woman would show up at Wingate House brandishing that gun again.

# CHAPTER 14

Lucas whisked Suzannah home as soon as he could, leaving the police lieutenant still talking to Mallory with Beau and fielding calls from the officers dispatched to Tilly Walker's home. Despite hearing the story, he still didn't fully understand why Mallory had taken Suzannah to Tilly Walker's today and how the visit escalated into an emotional fright scene.

After coming home, Suzannah settled down eventually and then shared in childish fashion what she remembered of the day's events, all innocent enough until she told of stopping by Tilly Walker's.

Suzannah began to sniffle and cry as she related this visit. "Tilly got mad at me for playing with her jewelry and started acting crazy, but Mallory got us out and we ran away." Her eyes grew big. "Then the lady came out on her porch and she shooted at us in the car. It was real scary."

"I'm sure it was." Lucas smoothed back her hair and gave her a kiss on the forehead. "But it's all over now."

He heated soup and made grilled cheese sandwiches for their dinner, wanting something simple and easy. After dinner, he popped a happy movie into the DVD player and made a point of reading Suzannah cheerful books before putting her to bed. Despite this, she woke up crying a little later.

"I dreamed a bad dream," she said, big tears dripping down her cheeks.

Lucas rocked her in the old rocking chair in her bedroom and then climbed into bed with her for a while, talking quietly, telling stories, and humming until she settled down to sleep again. The pattern felt familiar from past days when Cecily had acted erratic in her behavior, unsettling Suzannah, or when she'd skipped out on them for several days, causing Suzannah to cry for her. Emotional tension had too often visited Suzannah's early life, despite what she remembered, with emotional outbursts a constant throughout Lucas's married years to Cecily.

Now Lucas puttered in the kitchen, fixing a cup of coffee and trying to wind down. Beside him on the counter lay Suzannah's old baby monitor, a check-device he hadn't needed to use for a long time. But he wanted to be sure he heard the child if she woke in the night upset again.

Hearing a knock on the screened porch door, he rolled his eyes. *Lord, he wasn't in the mood to deal with Mallory Wingate tonight.*

He walked from the kitchen to the porch, surprised to see Beau at the back door instead.

"Is everything all right?" Lucas asked, letting the older man in.

"As right as can be after a day like this." Beau pushed a tin canister into Lucas's hands. "Nonnie sent fresh baked chocolate chip cookies. She always cooks or bakes when she gets upset."

"Thanks." Lucas started toward the kitchen. "Come on in. I was making some coffee. Want some?"

"No." Beau shook his head, following Lucas into the kitchen. "Coffee keeps me awake if I drink it this late at night. But hot chocolate would be good if you have it."

"I do. It's one of Suzannah's favorites." He put water on to heat and took down a box of cocoa packets from the shelf.

Beau leaned against the kitchen counter. "How is Suzannah? I wanted to come and check."

"Better now and sleeping at last." Lucas filled him in on their afternoon and evening. "I hope you understand why I brought her on home."

Beau nodded, stirring his chocolate into a mug of hot water.

A few minutes later, they settled at the kitchen table with their drinks, digging in to the cookies for an accompanying snack.

"What happened with the Walker woman?" Lucas asked.

Beau's mouth tightened. "The officers found her babbling half out of her mind in a chair, still playing with that dang gun. Fortunately, they talked her out of it without another incident." He scratched his chin. "The woman's always been a silly, emotional sort of female, worrying over something all the time, seeing trouble behind every door. She believes every media scare that comes down the pike and always imagines every little sickness will lead to a major health crisis. But no one every expected her to go off like this."

"What caused it?"

"According to a phone call I got from Bobby Joe tonight—he's her ex-husband—they think it might have been drug-induced. Evidently, Tilly had begun taking antianxiety drugs for depression and popping other prescription drugs to sleep over the last years. Bobby Joe told me candidly it grew too difficult living with Tilly, her worrying the life out of him every day with her whining and fears. That's why he finally moved out last year." He paused. "Of course, none of us know the intimate details that go on in a home between a husband and a wife. But Bobby Joe leaving Tilly tipped her over the edge more than before—even Nonnie noticed that— giving her too much time to focus solely on herself. Then with this injury to her ankle, the doctors prescribed pain meds, too—strong narcotics."

Beau stopped to sip on his cocoa before continuing. "Bobby Joe said Tilly always acted secretive about her drugs, used a variety of herb concoctions and such along with prescriptions. In the state she was in, and from what the doctors could tell from their examinations, they think Tilly overdosed on narcotics, herbs, and other meds." He ran a hand through his hair. "Drugs can make a person act totally wacko. One doctor at the emergency room said Tilly's tests also showed a bladder infection, compounding her problems. Believe it or not, a bad bladder infection can cause real erratic, crazy like behavior."

"What will happen to Tilly?"

"I'm not sure." Beau shrugged. "In some ways it's more a mental health issue than a criminal one, although brandishing a gun, threatening and shooting at others is criminal."

Lucas drummed his fingers on the table, thinking over Beau's words. "It's hard for me to favor too much leniency for the woman right now, knowing she shot at my child."

"I imagine so."

They sat quietly sipping their drinks and munching on Nonnie's cookies. When Lucas glanced across at Beau again, he found the older man studying him with one of those intent expressions of his that meant he had something serious weighing on his mind.

"What?" Lucas asked.

"You haven't once asked how Mallory is."

Lucas looked away. "So much has happened, I forgot. Sorry. How is she doing?"

"Better now." He kept his eyes on Lucas. "But that's not the reason I brought it up."

Lucas began to feel uncomfortable.

Beau scratched the tuft of beard on his face. "First, I think you may need a full explanation of why Mallory took Suzannah by Tilly Walker's house today," he said. "She stopped by Tilly's, at Nonnie's request, to drop off a gift basket this afternoon. Nonnie even asked if she and Suzannah would visit Tilly, to help cheer her up. With the ankle injury, all the Monday Group knew Tilly stayed stuck pretty close to the house every day." He spread his hands. "Nonnie had absolutely no idea Tilly was in such an emotional state or she would never have sent the girls by there."

Lucas offered a smile. "Thanks for explaining that. I'm not sure I ever picked up on why they stopped by Tilly's place before. That's good to know."

"You can imagine Nonnie felt absolutely awful about sending the girls over there," Beau continued. "Started blaming herself for what happened. I've dealt with her crying half the evening as well as trying to get Mallory calmed down."

"Sounds like you had a bad night, too."

Beau paused once more, running his hand slowly around the rim of his mug.

Lucas felt a twitch in his eye, waiting for Beau to go on.

"Mallory believes what kicked Tilly over the edge was Suzannah innocently hauling out a handful of jewelry she found in Tilly's bedroom. Nonnie lets the child play with her jewelry at our house, and Suzannah wandered into Tilly's bedroom on her way to the bathroom and saw a butterfly pin like Nonnie's that drew her attention."

"I think I remember Mallory telling the officer the jewelry Suzannah picked up from Tilly's bedroom looked like the pieces stolen from the tearoom."

"They *were* the stolen pieces. That's been affirmed now." He rubbed his cheek again. "Despite how innocently the situation started at Tilly's, it quickly escalated. Mallory suddenly found herself face-to-face with a thief threatened with discovery and an already unstable one to boot. Tilly began to threaten Mallory and Suzannah and then actually headed towards the back of the house to get a gun. No one could have envisioned a scenario like that happening."

Lucas felt uncomfortable at Beau's continuing gaze. *What else was on the man's mind?*

"A weaker woman than Mallory might have panicked," Beau said. "However, Mallory kept her head, grabbed the opportunity fate offered her, and fled with Suzannah, possibly saving one or both of their lives."

A flurry of thoughts flew through Lucas's mind of how scared Suzannah must have been as Mallory grabbed her and ran. It tore at his heart.

A small silence settled in the room before Beau finally spoke again.

"You never even thanked Mallory. Andy said you scowled at her, never even gave her a word of comfort." He stirred his cocoa idly. "I saw the same thing when I came. You kept your distance from Mallory as if she were as batty as Tilly, even keeping Suzannah away from her. I watched you hold the child back from running to hug Mallory before she left, keeping Suzannah from giving a hug to the woman who possibly saved her life."

Lucas felt himself growing annoyed at Beau's less than subtle implications. "I was upset and wanted to get Suzannah home as soon as possible. That's all it was."

Beau studied him. "No, I don't think so." He said the last words slowly. "Andy said he thought you were experiencing flashbacks from your past with Cecily, transferring them to the situation going on. He told me he's watched you distance yourself the same way before from other women who display excessive emotion."

"Like when?" Lucas knew his anger showed in his voice.

Beau's voice remained steady. "Like when that woman freaked out over wasps swarming out of a nest in her golf cart and when Mrs. McGinley learned her husband had been in a car wreck a few weeks ago and became distraught." His eyes met Lucas's. "I could name a few more."

"I don't like a lot of emotionalism."

"Well, here's the thing, Lucas. Women tend to get emotional over things. It's part of the way God made them, and my Pa always taught me it was a part of our job to comfort them." He stroked his chin again. "You seemed to do all right in offering comfort and support to Suzannah today, but not with Mallory."

"Listen, I don't know what Mallory said but …"

Beau interrupted. "Mallory didn't say anything. This is *strictly* what I noticed, Lucas. And what Andy and others have noticed. I think you need to schedule a talk with Robert about this."

His temper flared. "I don't need to see a doctor, and if you'll remember it's *your* granddaughter who had the emotional breakdown, not me!"

"Well." Beau nodded. "So that's a piece of the problem, is it? You equating Mallory's emotional break after her mother's death to this situation?"

"You saw her today." His voice rose. "So did Andy. She totally lost control, ran into the shop crying, shaking, and carrying on."

"You need to remember Mallory had just been shot at and was trying to get a small child to safety. She didn't even know whether Tilly might be following behind them in her own car, might shoot at them again." His steady eyes looked into Lucas's. "In that crazy woman's state of mind anything could have happened. I'd say Mallory had a very good reason to be upset."

Lucas looked away. "Well, people handle being upset in different ways."

"Yes, and some lock it up inside instead of dealing with it at all," Beau replied.

"You think I do that?" The accusation hurt.

"Andy and I both do, and I expect you to get a little counseling, either with Robert or with a medical associate of his if you prefer." He reached a hand across the table to lay it on Lucas's arm. "I care about the people in my employ when they have problems."

Lucas pulled back. "I don't think I have a problem."

"Well, I disagree, and in thinking back on it I shouldn't have been so candid with you earlier about Mallory's problems—although she's come through her issues with rest and help. I think today proved how well recovered she is emotionally, to handle the situation she met today with such good sense."

Lucas bit his tongue over lashing back.

Beau stood. "I'll be expecting a report on this from you after you visit with Robert." He picked up his mug to carry it back to the kitchen. "And when the time's right, I think you need to consider offering an apology to Mallory for showing her so little sympathy. You might even want to thank her for taking care of your child so well in a crisis situation."

"I'll think on it," Lucas said, not willing to commit further.

After Beau left, Lucas struggled to settle his anger. He cleaned up the kitchen and then went into the den, dropping into his favorite leather chair to lean his head back. He respected Beau and he hated displeasing him. *Did Beau have some valid points?* Trying to be objective, Lucas let his mind play over the scenario at the golf shop and found he didn't like all the aspects of his earlier behavior.

But seeing Mallory so out of control, racing into the shop, shoving a weeping Suzannah into his arms, and then breaking down like she did, babbling and sobbing, frightened him.

Perhaps it did remind him of times with Cecily. Was that so wrong? Was it too much to expect a woman not to act more rational? More collected and in control of her emotions?

Hearing a wail from the monitor, Lucas headed up to Suzannah's room.

"Another bad dream jumped in my sleep, Daddy," she told him, sniffling.

Lucas hugged her and then lay down on the bed beside her.

"I wish Mallory was here." Suzannah sighed, gathering her collection of stuffed toys closer around her.

"Why?" Lucas asked.

"Because she's nice and because I didn't get to tell her thank you for saving me from that lady." She turned wide blue eyes to his. "She did save me. Mallory put her finger over her mouth to tell me to be quiet, picked me up, and carried me out to the car real fast. It was a good thing, too, because the lady came out on her porch and shooted at us." Suzannah started to cry again as she remembered the events of the day once more. "What if she comes after me and Mallory again?"

"She won't," Lucas assured her. "Beau came over tonight to tell me the police took her to the hospital. She was sick in her mind, pumpkin, and she'd taken too many drugs that made her act crazy." He tried to console her. "She didn't know what she was doing, and she'll get lots of help before she ever gets to go back home again. So don't worry about her coming after you or Mallory."

Suzannah sniffed and then looked across the room at her mother's picture on the dresser. "Was my mommy sick like that? Is that why she killed herself?"

Lucas felt like someone punched him in the stomach. "Who told you that?"

"Abby said she heard her Mommy and Daddy talking about it once." Suzannah dropped her eyes. "Abby was supposed to be in bed but got up to go to the bathroom and she heard them." Her eyes flew to his. "Don't tell, okay?"

"Abby shouldn't repeat stories she hears." Lucas smoothed the covers over the small girl, tucking them around her.

After a few minutes, he searched for the right words to answer her question. "You mom was sick but not like Tilly Walker. She had a health condition that caused her emotions to go up and down like a roller coaster. Sometimes she felt really, really good and sometimes she felt really, really bad, like in the nursery rhyme we read together."

"The one about the girl with the curl in her forehead? She wasn't sick, Daddy. She acted good or horrid but she wasn't sick," Suzannah corrected.

"Well, it's the same idea." He picked up Suzannah's cat doll, Tommy, wishing the cat in his colorful striped overalls had the answers to Suzannah's questions he so desperately needed.

"I don't remember my mother," Suzannah said, looking across the room toward the picture again. "Elizabeth said it was okay that I don't because I was only two when she died. She said babies don't remember things like people do later on."

"That's right."

"But you've told me good stories and we have lots of nice photos. So I know my Mommy wasn't bad."

"No, she just got sick, and one time when she got sick she took too many drugs trying to make herself better and it killed her." There, he'd said it.

Suzannah considered this. "Sometimes we watch movies at Elizabeth's where someone takes drugs. Elizabeth says drugs are bad—unless you're sick and really need them and the doctor gives them to you."

"Elizabeth is exactly right about that." Lucas would thank his sister later for sharing these thoughts with Suzannah.

"Abby and I told her we would never, ever take bad drugs."

"That's a good resolution, pumpkin."

"Cause we don't want to be dead," she added.

Lucas winced at the matter-of-fact words.

"Do you think you can sleep now?" he asked, tucking Tommy under the covers with her.

"Yes, but I want to tell Mallory thank you tomorrow and give her a hug. I wanted to give her a hug today but you hurried me too much."

"I did," he admitted. "We'll walk over tomorrow so you can tell her, okay?"

She sent him a sunny smile. "Okay. Will you read me one more story before you turn out the light again?"

"Which book?"

"Let's read *Miss Suzy* about the little gray squirrel that got chased out of her tree by the mean red squirrels."

"Shouldn't we read a happier book?"

"Oh, but it is a happy book. The soldiers get Miss Suzy's house back for her because she's so nice. Then she takes care of them and everybody lives happily ever after."

"Okay, then that's the book we'll read."

Suzannah fell asleep before they finished the story and Lucas went downstairs to sit quietly, thinking over the day.

Perhaps he had tried too hard to keep things hidden in his life, not bringing them out in the open or talking about them candidly. Even Suzannah seemed to handle learning about her mother with a very healthy understanding for such a small child, and ready to move on.

Lucas sighed. When Beau made a request, he expected to see it carried out. So it seemed, whether he wanted to or not, he'd need to talk to Robert. Frankly Lucas didn't want the past to keep on haunting him. He hadn't realized it intruded into his life so often— or so obviously. A little talk with Robert or a counselor might help. Lucas probably should have talked with someone long ago.

# CHAPTER 15

"Honey, are you absolutely certain you're all right?" Nonnie asked Mallory the next morning after Beau headed out the door. He'd scheduled an early meeting with the resort's chef team, Josh and Rachel Kirkpatrick, and the events coordinator, Lois Milton, to go over menu plans for an upcoming event.

"I'm fine, Nonnie," Mallory reassured her grandmother. She sent her a cheeky smile. "Who could ever have imagined in a million years I'd run into such a monumental crisis in a small community like Pittman Center?"

"Well don't make light of it." Nonnie wagged a finger at her. "You and that child might both have been killed."

Mallory laid the newspaper aside. "Have you talked to anyone this morning with an update about Tilly?"

Nonnie put Beau's breakfast dishes in the sink and poured Mallory another cup of coffee before sitting down across from her. "The phone rang all last evening with calls. You know that. All our Monday Group were simply shocked over this. Tilly has always been highly strung, but this ..." Her voice drifted off and she shook her head in disbelief.

"I think even Bobby Joe feels guilty and somewhat responsible for this," she added. "Their divorce only finalized recently and Tilly hasn't let go of her dependence on Bobby Joe easily. She kept crying for the police to call him yesterday, so they did in order to help calm her down and to bring in someone reasonable and sane to offer accurate information about Tilly's situation. Bobby Joe headed straight to the hospital, too. Bless his heart. Polly Trentham said he helped a lot." Nonnie paused. "Polly is the closest to Tilly of the women in our Monday Group, which is surprising, considering Tilly left Polly and Alvin's church this year, embracing some new-fangled religious belief about God being in everyone."

"Well, isn't He?" Mallory leaned her elbows on the table.

"Yes, of course He is, but not the way Tilly got confused with. She started seeing God as some impersonal energy source everyone carries inside, with sufficiency focused on the individual and on seeking personal enlightenment and such." She waved a hand. "We've all heard her rattle on and on about it."

"It doesn't sound as if those beliefs helped her very much in this hard time."

"No, but Tilly can never see things practically when she's on one of her new tangents." Nonnie laughed. "When Tilly got into her vegetarian kick last year she gave us the very devil over eating meat at every one of our Monday Group luncheons. Gladys told her if she didn't stop pushing her views on us that she was going to bring up a vote to kick her out."

"A lot of people are vegetarians, Nonnie."

"I know that, and I accommodate it for my luncheon events, like I do other diet preferences or food allergies." Her grandmother crossed her arms. "But when people go to extremes and won't give you a minute's peace for holding an alternative view, it gets annoying. You know very well what I'm talking about."

"I do." Mallory hid a grin and sipped at her coffee.

Her grandmother studied her with thoughtful eyes. "You haven't gotten off into some weird religious beliefs or anything, have you?"

"No." Mallory glanced out the window toward the garden. "But I realized I'd fallen away from my faith when Mother came to stay with me, so ill and with so many problems. I didn't have enough reserves to draw on."

Nonnie shook her head. "It would be hard for anyone to have enough faith reserves to draw on when dealing with Delores

Wingate at her worst, God rest her soul."

Mallory smirked. "It's good to be able to laugh a little about that dreadful time. Mother was always difficult, even in the best of times."

"You proved a good and faithful daughter to her through that hard time, and you showed yesterday your strength of character in dealing with Tilly Walker as you did. Beau and I felt real proud of how you handled yourself. I'd say it shows for a fact you're healed from that breakdown."

Mallory winced over the word. "Perhaps, but I did fall apart somewhat after I got to the pro shop with Suzannah."

"And who wouldn't have?"

Mallory didn't answer, remembering Lucas's expressions and actions, hardly approving.

Nonnie got up to get a basket of lima beans from the counter and then sat down, beginning to open the pods to shell out the beans and drop them into a pretty blue bowl. Mallory reached over to grab a handful of beans to help her.

"I'm glad you're going back to church with us." Nonnie said, shifting the topic of conversation as she pulled a string from a lima bean pod with practiced ease. "I think it helps in life, having a strong faith. Not that church alone will build it, with every worship service filling only a short block of time on Sunday mornings, but it's a start. Reverend Campbell, at our church at Beech Grove Baptist, is a good man and gives a nice message most Sundays, although I do wish the man had more spiritual depth. That does seem to be missing in many churches today, but Beau and I work on growing our faith at home with our own studying."

Mallory listened to her, observing the familiar face of her grandmother. She noticed a few more wrinkles showing on Nonnie's face now, her short, neat hair more sprinkled with white, but her grandmother still looked slim and strong in appearance. *What would she have done without Nonnie all these years?*

She smiled at her grandmother. "I remember those Bible studies and story times at your house growing up," she said. "You modeled a genuine faith before me, did you know that? I needed it, too, as Mother saw church only as a social networking link, something appropriate to do for one's business and personal image. I can't recall her ever reading her Bible at home or praying as you and Beau do."

"Well, I'm glad if we could contribute to your spiritual upbringing." She pushed silver wire-rimmed glasses up from where they'd slipped down her nose, her eyes twinkling over them.

"I'm serious, Nonnie. You *were* a big help in every way with my upbringing, giving me the unconditional love I so needed. Do you remember I gave my heart to the Lord in Bible School here one summer?"

"I'd forgotten that."

"Well, I haven't." Mallory paused over a stubborn bean, forgetting how the pods could be the very dickens to split open.

Nonnie looked up, stopping in her work. "You know, I wonder if Tilly Walker and Barry Short might have handled the pressures, temptations, and problems in their lives differently if they'd had a deeper faith to draw on. The ways of the world exercise such a strong pull, and if you lean only to that and to your own mind and understandings to make your way through life, it can lead to problems when the crossroads come."

"Crossroads?"

"You know, those times when you come to a turning point in the road and there are several paths to choose from. Faith, prayer, and being able to hear from God can help you find the right direction."

Mallory frowned. "And what if you take a wrong direction?"

Nonnie smiled. "Well, I think God gives you a check there, too, even if you head the wrong way." She stopped, tapping her chin in thought. "Remember that movie we watched the other night where the man was whacking his way with a machete through a jungle path and then he suddenly stopped, realizing the rough terrain he encountered meant he'd taken the wrong path at the turning? What did he do when he realized that?"

"I see your point. He backtracked to the turning point again and took a different route."

"Exactly." She beamed on Mallory. "There's even a scripture reminding us that 'as we walk God will show us to the right or to the left.' So even if we miss it and start down a wrong pathway, having a strong relationship with God will help to show us if we miss our way and quicken us to turn around and regroup."

Before Mallory could digest this wisdom, Nonnie sent her a question. "Did that Ethan friend of yours have a strong faith?"

"I really don't know." Mallory paused over the bean she was shucking. "I don't think so. We never really talked about faith all that much."

"Hmmm," Nonnie said, giving her a thoughtful look over her glasses. "You know that's important."

Mallory rolled her eyes. "I know. I *should* have talked to Ethan about faith."

"Always ask a person you're dating about their faith and always meet their parents and family. That can tell you a lot about a person. It's best to marry another believer ... and remember you'll interact and spend time with a person's family for the rest of your life if you marry."

Mallory winced. "Maybe that's why Ethan pulled away. He got to know my mother."

Nonnie pursed her lips. "Now, now. Delores wasn't your *only* family. And you can't judge a person over one rotten apple in the family tree."

"I suppose." Mallory loved these cozy talks with her grandmother. She carried such good common sense and wisdom in how she viewed things.

Nonnie got up to dump a pile of bean shucks into the trash.

"What will happen to Tilly now?" Mallory asked, shifting the subject.

"Beau said the hospital would work to stabilize Tilly's physical health and then do a battery of mental evaluations." She sighed as she sat back down. "The police officer claims Tilly stole the items from the tearoom and our home with knowledgeable intent, knowing they weren't rightfully hers. He pointed out that her petty thieving began before the ankle injury and before the excessive narcotics and drugs kicked her into a highly distressed mental state. It's hard to imagine she didn't realize, at least in some way, she was in the wrong threatening you and Suzannah and shooting at you with a gun the way she did. Heavens! There are a lot of things to be considered. I'm not really sure what will happen to Tilly over all this."

Mallory glanced out the window. "I hope they don't release her until everything is resolved."

"Are you fearful she might come after you or Suzannah?"

"We did uncover her theft and without clear thinking, she might blame us for what happened."

"Well, I think it's doubtful Tilly will be released to return home for a long time yet. Beau says he thinks she might need time in mental care. There may be criminal charges to deal with, also." She reached across to pat Mallory's arm. "Don't you worry over this. The police won't let her go if they think she might be a threat to anyone."

"I know." Mallory glanced at her watch. "The morning is getting away. I need to put in some work time now, Nonnie."

"How's that new book coming along?"

"David was right about the new author. It's a fine work so far."

Leaving her grandmother working on lunch preparations for later, Mallory retrieved her computer from her room and went out to her favorite spot on the side porch to finish reading Sonia Butler's novel.

Lucas and Suzannah found her there later in the morning. As Mallory looked up to see them, Suzannah flew into her arms.

"We came to thank you and see if you were okay," Suzannah said.

Mallory hugged the child back. "I am fine. How are you?"

Suzannah pulled back to look at her with those big eyes of hers. "I'm okay but I had bad dreams. Daddy had to come and read to me. I was scared Tilly would come back to get us, but Daddy said she was sick and in the hospital and couldn't."

"That's right." Mallory glanced at Lucas, lounging in the doorway, frowning. When his eyes met hers, he stepped forward.

"Suzannah is right that we both owe you thanks. You thought quickly yesterday in a bad situation and got Suzannah and yourself out of harm's way before the situation grew worse."

His answer sounded a little rehearsed but Mallory still felt glad to hear it.

"Tilly seemed nice at first but then she acted all crazy later," Suzannah added, sitting down on the bench by Mallory's chair at the computer. "Why did she suddenly get so mad at us?"

Mallory saved the document she'd been reading and writing edit notes on, and shut down her laptop. "Do you remember the butterfly pin you found that looked like Nonnie's?"

Suzannah nodded.

"Well, it *was* Nonnie's and Tilly took it and the other jewelry from Nonnie and Beau's house when she came here for luncheons with the Monday Group."

Suzannah's eyes widened. "You mean she *stealed* her friends' things? Daddy and Elizabeth said it's not nice to steal things that aren't yours."

Mallory saw Lucas's lips twitch in a smile.

"It is never nice to steal," Nonnie added, letting herself into the door behind them. She carried a tray with a pitcher of lemonade on it, glasses, and a plate of cookies. Putting them on the metal table nearby, she said, "Come and have some fresh lemonade and oatmeal cookies. The cookies just came out of the oven."

Their smell wafted across the summer air, drawing them to the table.

Nonnie poured out lemonade and passed around the cookies.

"I am so sorry I sent Mallory and Suzannah to visit with Tilly." Nonnie's eyes moved to Lucas. "Believe me, if I'd had any idea Tilly was in such a distressed state mentally, I never would have sent the girls over there."

He reached across to pat her hand. "I know, Nonnie, and I don't blame you."

Nonnie leaned over to kiss Suzannah on the cheek. "You and Mallory were very brave girls in that bad situation. I'm so proud of you both."

"Did you get your pretty pin back?" Suzannah asked.

"I did, thanks to you." She smiled at Suzannah. "The other ladies in our group got their special jewelry pieces back, too. It's sad Tilly felt she needed to take our things, no matter her reasons. Like you said, it is wrong to steal."

Suzannah picked a raisin out of her cookie and popped it in her mouth. "I thought only bad people stealed things, but Tilly did and Barry did at the shop, too. He was nice and not bad. I liked him. He always gave me a golf ball sucker from the jar on the counter when I visited—the kind with chocolate inside." Her brow wrinkled. "Why do nice people do bad things?"

Lucas answered. "No matter how nice people are, they can make bad decisions and do bad things, Suzannah. Tilly and Barry had some personal problems at the root of what they did, but their actions were still wrong."

Suzannah nodded. "My Sunday school teacher Mrs. Mertz says we all get *temptions* but that we need to be strong and still do what is right."

"The word is *temptations*," Mallory corrected, trying to suppress a smile. "A temptation is when you get an urge or desire to do something you *know* is wrong. We all have those, but when those wrong urges or desires come we need to stop and think what the right thing to do is instead."

"Yes," Nonnie put in, "and we need to think about what will *happen* if we yield to those temptations and do wrong things. Wrong actions always bring bad consequences."

"Like maybe getting a spanking or having to sit in time out?" Suzannah asked, trying to find a way to bring the concept down to her own level.

"Exactly," Mallory answered.

Lucas glanced at his watch. "I need to get back to work. I brought Suzannah over on my lunch hour because she was worried about Mallory."

"And because I didn't get to say thank you before," Suzannah added.

He stood up. "I need to take her back to Elizabeth's now. They're going to the theater for a summer children's movie."

Reminded of that, Suzannah jumped up, her eyes dancing. "We're going to see *Horton Hears a Who*. It's one of Abby's and my favorite books."

Mallory smiled. "That's a wonderful Dr. Seuss story."

Nonnie followed them out, taking the lemonade tray with her. Mallory could hear Suzannah's bright chatter as they left.

"Sweet child," Mallory said to herself, turning her computer back on, ready to return to Sonia Butler's novel.

But instead of reading, she found her attention wandering, remembering Lucas's expressions and actions. He'd felt uncomfortable, uneasy in his apology, and all too eager to leave. Yet she'd felt that crackle of awareness, too, as soon as he entered the room, felt that calling toward him move through her. She knew he felt the drawing, too, but tried to tramp it down. He didn't want to be attracted to her. That was obvious, and he didn't want to become more involved with her. Still the temptation was there, the urge, the desire, the allure. Was it wrong, that attraction and appeal? Were they fighting some chemistry and magnetism that signaled they were meant to be? Mallory didn't know the answer but there were certainly strong feelings between them.

*Would she miss him when she went back to Savannah?* She wondered. *Would he miss her?* She'd only be here at Millhouse for a few more weeks now. *And what if things did progress further between them?* She didn't want to give up her job and her work in Savannah. Nothing similar existed in the mountains here for her to get involved in. She'd hate to think of Lucas leaving his position with Beau to follow her to Savannah, either, even if he could find work as a golf pro there. He and Suzannah were happy here; they had family here.

She sighed. It was all so confusing.

Pushing her conflicting thoughts to the back of her mind, she scrolled down in Sonia's novel to the last chapter she'd been reading. As she did, she remembered a line of Einstein's she'd printed and put on her bulletin board at Whittier. He'd advised that if you wanted to live a happy life you should tie it to a goal and not to people or things. All too often her work and goals at Whittier brought her more happiness than outside relationships with people. A sad fact but true. She remembered, too, that C. S. Lewis advised you shouldn't let your happiness depend on something you could lose. Her future at Whittier was solid but any future that might include Lucas James rested on very shaky ground.

# CHAPTER 16

On Sunday, Lucas saw Mallory again at church, but they didn't talk further. However, that afternoon, he met with Elizabeth's husband Robert at the clinic, as Beau asked him to, for a candid talk. He wanted to discuss his personal issues with Robert privately without his sister adding in her thoughts on the matter.

After Lucas filled him in on what had happened and why Beau thought he might need some counseling, Robert said, "I think Beau's right that you could use some help with feelings you might be harboring from the past. Elizabeth and I have both noticed you still carry unresolved issues in relation to Cecily."

Lucas nodded. Elizabeth had often made comments to him along that line, although he'd always dismissed them.

Robert crossed an ankle over his knee. "Counseling isn't really my field, as a medical doctor, and I think an objective outside party would be best in this situation—perhaps a minister."

"Like Reverend Campbell at the Beech Grove church where Suzannah and I attend with you and Elizabeth?"

Robert tapped his chin in thought. "Actually I think it might be best for you to get counseling from a younger man, nearer your own age, and not a pastor of the church where you attend. Plus there are other reasons Henry Campbell might not be the best choice." A smile tugged at the corner of Robert's mouth as he said the words. "Henry's wife, Mozella, tends to be a bit judgmental and somewhat of a gossip in the neighborhood. It might be difficult for Henry to keep counseling issues to himself, even though he knows he should. Wives have a way of getting information out of a man, even when he wants to keep certain things private. I doubt Mozella's counsel or thoughts about the matter would be a help."

Lucas nodded. "I've heard stories about Mozella's meddling."

"She does tend to be outspoken." Robert looked out across the green landscape of midsummer. "I think a good choice would be Perry Ammons, the pastor of the Highland Cumberland Presbyterian Church on Natty Road in Gatlinburg. He and his wife Tracey and their two children live not far from here, and they are patients of mine. I like them both very much. Perry and Tracey also own a wedding chapel on Highway 321 called the Creekside Chapel. I'm sure you've seen it, a pretty white building set on a hillside with a tall spire."

"I know where both the church and chapel are, and I've met Perry and a group of his old friends at the Garden Restaurant where they meet for breakfast once a week."

"The Jack Gang." Robert smiled. "I know the other three in that group, too—Tanner Cross, Bogan Kirkpatrick, and Keppler James." He paused. "I wonder if Keppler is any kin to you with the same last name?"

"We talked about that once and think there might be a distant link somewhere."

"Well, since you've met Perry, what do you think about me calling him to set an appointment for you tomorrow on Monday, if he can see you?"

"That would be okay." Lucas doubted he had a lot of options with Beau's ultimatum hanging over his head.

"If Perry thinks you need to talk to a psychologist he'll say so, but I think all you need is someone to help you talk things out so you can see the past more clearly and lay some false concepts to rest about it."

Robert made the call, and Lucas met with Perry on Monday. He met with Perry again every afternoon that week since Perry felt Lucas could move forward at an escalated pace. He found the young minister easy to talk with, and Perry had an artful way of helping Lucas to express and see his own problems. Perry called himself somewhat of a Cognitive Behavioral Therapist, believing his role an educational one, like a teacher's, to help clients see how they'd accepted irrational and illogical beliefs, causing them problems, and then to help examine how they needed to modify their thinking and develop a healthier mental philosophy, to bring about change in their lives.

"I minored in Counseling in college when I studied for the ministry," Perry told him with a smile one day. "Thought I might need it as a pastor and I felt I needed the help, too, personally. My father waltzed out on my mother and me when I was a kid and it impacted my own life negatively for many years before I got help and before God turned me around. I harbored anger toward my dad, anger toward God."

He hesitated, thinking. "I often think we, as men, are raised to think we should be able to fix everything, take care of things— especially regarding the women in our lives. I think I carried guilt that I couldn't find a way to get my father to come back to my mother. I wanted to be able to make her happy again."

Lucas thought about those words. "I know what you're saying. I always felt I should have been able to fix things for Cecily, that if I'd done the right thing, been a better husband, she might have turned around and gotten well."

"What do you know more logically?"

He frowned. "That her bipolar condition wasn't something I could heal or fix."

Perry waited. "And?"

Lucas winced. "That it wasn't my fault Cecily tried so little to manage her illness." He focused on several birds on a birdbath out the window as he tried to find words for his thoughts. "I think Cecily used her condition to justify behaviors of hers that were immature and self-centered." Lucas felt guilty saying the words but suddenly knew they were true. "She played the victim card to her advantage. She indulged in all sorts of negative behaviors she didn't need to act out, that weren't always caused by her bipolar condition. She self-sabotaged herself, too, when better opportunities presented themselves."

"How did that make you feel?"

"Angry. Frustrated." Lucas sighed. "I kept trying to help her walk in new directions, to make more positive choices, to want to get better and to manage her condition more effectively, but she never followed any of my advice or the advice of her counselors."

"You couldn't fix the situation for her."

"No." He shook his head.

"When you learned she died, that she'd overdosed in a hotel room, how did you feel?"

"I felt guilty." Lucas ran a hand through his hair. "I still remember the looks her parents gave me at the funeral, like her death was my fault. I remember the subtle comments people made, too, when they learned I'd been out of country at a golf tournament in the UK and that Cecily and I had separated, like my being gone caused Cecily to go off the deep end. Like I should have been there, put her first before my career."

"Would it have mattered if you'd been in the country or if you'd still been living in Arizona?"

"I don't know." He closed his eyes. "I don't think so. Even when I wasn't on tour and before I came here to the resort to work, Cecily ran off like that all the time. Most people didn't know that about her. They often saw only the positive, happy side of Cecily, never the dark side. They didn't really know her like I did."

"So what they thought or said, with so little information or insight, wasn't valid or accurate."

"Yes."

"But it hurt."

Lucas scowled. "It made me feel like crap. I couldn't fix her, Perry. Her parents thought I could, and often well-meaning friends of ours made suggestions to me that I needed to help her 'straighten out,' but I couldn't fix her."

"So you've let yourself become a victim to those other people's irrational beliefs."

Lucas looked across at Perry in shock. "I have."

"Do you want to keep staying in that place, chained to other people's views and irrational understandings you know are false? Do you want to stay lost in all those irrational absolutes—those false shoulds, oughts, and musts?"

Lucas shook his head. "That's what I've done, haven't I? I've let other people define my past with Cecily. Even falsely defined it myself. Blamed and hated myself for what she did, thinking I could have changed it."

"Do you think you should let others continue to define you?"

"No." He sat up straighter. "I don't think you should ever let others define you, but I've done that in this situation."

Perry waited, letting him think about the idea.

"What do you think you might do now to bring changes to your thinking, to your feelings, and to your behavior?" he asked after a space.

Lucas scowled, thinking. "Be purposed to see things more realistically, I guess."

"And forgive those who judged you incorrectly and forgive yourself?"

"Yeah, that, too." His eyes met Perry's.

Perry smiled. "We can pray about that one right now."

They did—leaving Lucas feeling easier and more peaceful inside.

Their sessions went like this all week, each time leaving Lucas feeling a little freer about things of the past.

"I really feel like I've dumped a lot of the guilt I've carried around for far too long," he told Perry toward the end of the week.

"It's a good beginning," Perry said. "Let's talk today about the fears and anxieties you experience when you find yourself in a situation where a woman becomes overly emotional."

Lucas rubbed his neck. "It's all linked, I guess."

"Do you think it is?"

"I guess it must be."

They talked about that issue then, examined situations in the past where Lucas had unexpectedly encountered women overwrought, upset, or excessively emotional. After some discussion, Lucas began to see how, just as Beau had suggested, he'd transferred his own frustrations and helplessness from past situations with Cecily into current situations that arose.

"I guess I assumed anything I tried to do wouldn't help, in the same way it never seemed to help with Cecily," he said.

"So when you need to face a woman's excessive emotion and those types of emotional frustrations again—what will you do?"

Lucas tried to think. "Different things. I shut down sometimes, pull away. Sometimes I run away."

"Do you think that's what the women need?"

He let his eyes wander out the window again, watching the birds splashing in the birdbath and pecking seeds out of a nearby feeder. He wondered if Perry placed the birdbath and feeder there just for an outside focus.

"Pull up a situation and tell me about it," he heard Perry say.

"Okay." Lucas let his mind travel back to one of the situations Beau reminded him of. "Gladys Beavers plays golf every Wednesday at Millhouse with a couple of friends. We had some boys cleaning and refurbishing some of our golf carts one day, so Dale pulled out a few older carts to use from the back shed. Gladys hadn't gotten far down the fairway before the wasps nesting under the cart seat started swarming around, mad to be disturbed. Seeing the wasps and getting a couple of stings, Gladys freaked out, jumped out of the cart, screaming and hollering and running back up the fairway waving her arms and carrying on."

"And you were there to watch?"

He nodded. "So were Andy and Dale."

"Tell me about how you felt?"

Lucas hated remembering it now, never having analyzed any of these events logically before. "I pulled back, let Andy and Dale handle the situation."

"How did they handle it?"

He tried to recall. "They stayed calm but were sweet and

understanding. Gladys had a couple of bad welts from the stings. I guess she felt pretty panicked when those wasps came swarming out. Andy and Dale helped her settle down and then took her inside to put some medicine on the stings. They kept talking to her and stuff."

"What did you do?"

Lucas closed his eyes. "Pulled away when Gladys ran at me. I guess she wanted me to hold her or something. But she was crying and screaming and carrying on." He opened his eyes to look at Perry. "It scared me. It made me think of Cecily and some of her times of getting out of control."

"You weren't thinking about what Gladys needed. You were remembering a time with Cecily instead."

He considered it. "Yeah, I guess, like Beau said, I had a sort of flashback moment."

"A flashback is often involuntary. An event in the present causes a vivid and often highly disturbing memory of a similar past experience. Soldiers often experience flashbacks, but a flashback can also be caused by food, people, places, or an event similar to one experienced in the past. Often in a flashback, the person may feel as though a past event is happening all over again."

Lucas winced. "How can a person stop that from happening?"

"The first step is to be able to realize it is happening, then to remind yourself you're in the present and that the past event is over. Often psychologists advise taking slow, deep breaths to calm down and to move out of a panic mode. Also, for many, who don't have serious emotional problems or severe post-traumatic stress, simply realizing they are experiencing a flashback sometimes is key. Then they can plan how to cope when or if they encounter a trigger event again."

Lucas thought about this. "So if I encounter an overly emotional situation with a woman, what should I do?"

"What do you think?"

"Well, obviously not regress to the past." He grinned.

"And?"

"I think I might try more consciously to pull in to the present, to separate my past memories of times with Cecily from what is happening in the now. I've already learned the effectiveness, too, of positively focusing and doing deep breathing exercises to help with anxiety. I've done that before big golf tournaments when I'm under a lot of pressure."

"What did Gladys need from you?"

The answer wasn't so tough to answer when Lucas thought about it logically. "Kindness, understanding—for me to stay calm to counteract her being upset. The way I handle upsets with Suzannah."

"Do you touch Suzannah or pull away?"

"What do you think?" He scowled at Perry. "She's a little girl. When she's upset, I pick her up, hug her, and kiss her just like you would your kids."

"Physical touch is comforting when a person is upset."

"Yeah." He nodded, seeing Perry's point. "I guess I didn't even want to touch those women because it reminded me of Cecily and those bad times."

"What might be a better response in a situation like this in the future?"

"Well obviously, I need to work on touching and comforting and being better at understanding women when they get emotional in a traumatic situation."

"Those sound like wise words."

Lucas smiled. "You do have a way of getting the client to counsel himself."

He grinned. "Would you be willing to try acting out some emotional situations to see if you can handle them in a different way now?"

"With you?" Lucas felt surprised at the idea.

"We might try a situation or two with me but then I think I'll bring Tracey in so you can try your new ideas out with her for handling an emotional situation with a woman." He wriggled his eyebrows. "Women are different creatures sometimes in how they view things and respond to things. They find the same mystery in us as to how we, as men, often respond to situations, too."

"Do we need to do this?" Lucas felt uncomfortable at the idea of playacting.

"No, but it's a lot like golf, Lucas. Practice makes perfect. Without trying a new swing, it's hard to know how it will work in a tournament later when the pressure is there."

"I get it," he said, resigned. "I guess we can give it a try."

They tried out several mock role scenes that day and a few exercises Perry called Gestalt experiments at another session. As an action man, Lucas had to admit the exercises and experiments helped.

He even ended up talking with Perry about Mallory as their sessions of the week drew to a close.

"You felt attracted to Mallory, from what you told me, Lucas, until you learned she'd experienced a recent emotional breakdown. Then you pulled back from her, not wanting to risk getting involved with another woman who might not be emotionally stable."

"Yeah, that's about it." He crossed his arms, probably a defensive gesture. "It still troubles me that Mallory broke down like that. I'd hate to become seriously involved with another woman again who has mental health issues."

"But you told me Mallory's condition is totally different from Cecily's and that she is better now, going back to work soon, already doing editing for her publishing company."

Lucas fidgeted in his seat. "But how do I know Mallory might not break down again or develop some other health issue that might be difficult for me or Suzannah to cope with? I've watched guys on the tour with anger issues break from pressure or from mistakes on the course and display fits of anger, even when they've sworn it won't happen again."

"You think this breakdown of Mallory's might be an indication she isn't emotionally stable?"

He sent an anguished look toward Perry. "How can I know?"

"How can you know anyone will always stay emotionally stable?

Life doesn't come with guarantees."

Lucas fidgeted in his seat. "Well, I know that's true, but when you see a behavior once, it makes you wonder if it might occur again. When you see a guy lose his temper and haul off and smack his girlfriend, you wonder if he might not do it again."

"Do you think Mallory's situation and that example you just gave me are the same thing?"

"Well probably not exactly," he had to admit.

"So I guess what it comes down to is—are you willing to take a risk?"

"You're saying Mallory is a risk?"

Perry smiled. "No, I'm saying *you* see Mallory as a risk."

"That doesn't sound like an answer."

"No, you'll have to find your own answer for this one. How do you think you might do that, by avoiding Mallory until she leaves or by spending time with her until it's time for her to go back to Savannah?"

Lucas drummed his fingers restlessly on the table beside him. "I really hate the way you throw everything back in my own court and make me think about it logically."

Perry leaned back in his chair. "You'll work this out, Lucas. You have a good mind and a good heart. You've known some rough times emotionally in the past, but I think you've come to terms with those in our sessions this week. You can come back and talk some more in the future when you think you need to, but I think you've confronted your problems and found peace with your past in most ways now."

He closed the folder he'd been making a few notes in. "You can tell Beau you've had your sessions and that he can expect to see you handling emotional situations with women better in future."

"Do you think I will?"

"I do. An emotional event might still start to trigger a flashback for you, but I think you'll reign yourself in. Take more control than in past, pull back into the future, respond more in the present."

"I guess I won't know until I get there, like how well a new golf swing I've practiced will perform until I'm on the course, in the heat of things."

"Yeah, that's the way it is with life. We do our best, and if we don't do well the first time out, we do better the next time."

"Spoken like a true optimist."

"Yes, I am a true optimist, like a Christian should be. You'd do well to draw on the strength of a higher power in all the situations you face, too."

"That's a truth," Lucas admitted. "I've seen that factor at work in our sessions. Thanks for your example and counsel in that area, too, Perry. I need to strengthen in my faith and I need to learn to rely more on God in my daily life. It's probably another of those guy things, thinking I can and should handle things myself."

Perry smiled. "No, that's a human thing. People try to figure out and find their way on their own every day when by leaning to God and getting His help and understanding, they could make their everyday walk so much easier and better." He paused. "Would you mind if we say a prayer together at this week's end?"

"Sure. That seems like just the right ending to our sessions."

On his drive back from Gatlinburg—heading to pick up Suzannah at Elizabeth's—Lucas thought over Perry's words about Mallory, especially his question about whether he'd learn more about his feelings for Mallory in avoiding her or in spending time with her. It was a no-brainer question to answer really, even if Perry had left the answer to him.

The more Lucas thought about it, looking back over his time with M.T. Wingate, the more he felt willing to take the risk. To find out where their relationship might go. After all, wasn't everything in life a risk when it came right down to it? And without risk there was no potential for gain.

# CHAPTER 17

**M**allory spent the week wading through a lengthy editing project David had sent her but decided to take a break on Friday to help Elizabeth with her roadside stand on the highway. With July nearly here, Elizabeth had an abundance of garden vegetables to sell and was always busy. She usually opened the stand on Fridays in fair weather so people could pick up fresh vegetables for the weekend, along with flowers, starts of herbs, or yard and garden plants.

The cute, whitewashed stand, with its wide, open window in front, sat back from the road under a small grove of shade trees. Robert and Elizabeth had also created a smaller shed behind it as a playhouse for the girls to enjoy, adding a big wooden sandbox and a colorful plastic wading pool beside it. The girls could play happily while Elizabeth worked. Abby and Suzannah sat in the shaded sandbox now, toward the end of the day, building a sandcastle for a family of plastic play figures Elizabeth had picked up at a garage sale last week.

"Whew, what a day." Elizabeth sighed as she and Mallory finished helping an older woman put a large flat of flower plants into the trunk of her car and waved her on her way.

Mallory rubbed the small of her back. "I'll get us a couple of colas from the cooler," she offered. "Let's sit down for a minute or two while we can."

Colas in hand, the girls soon settled into lawn chairs under a shady maple tree beside the stand for a break.

"Thanks so much for helping me today, Mallory." Elizabeth

propped her feet on a wooden crate they used for a footstool. "With as much traffic as we've experienced I'm really grateful for the help."

"It's been fun." Mallory smiled at her. "It's amazing to me how many of the customers you know, too."

"Oh, well." She waved a hand. "The Greenbrier and Pittman Center community is a pretty small one. You get to know the locals once you live here for a while and the others that I recognized are regulars who stop by whenever I'm open. Everybody loves fresh vegetables, but not many people like to garden anymore—or have the time for it. I didn't when I worked full-time, so I know exactly what that's like."

Mallory glanced with affection at Elizabeth's sun-browned face, sprinkled with summertime freckles. "Most people were full of questions today, too, and you were the 'answer woman' for everyone. I learned so much listening to you—telling them how to cook their green beans and corn, where to plant their herbs, or how to care for the bedding plants they bought to put out in their yards."

"It's easy to talk about what you enjoy." Elizabeth grinned at Mallory. "Like you told me with enthusiasm about the romance book you've been editing this week. What was that author's name again?"

"Cleo McDonald. The book is the first in her new series about a small bookstore owner in downtown Waynesville, North Carolina. It's a charmer, packed with local color, a loveable cast of characters, and a twist of mystery threaded into the plot. Cleo is already a popular author, with her past novels in other small town settings, so I think readers will love this new story."

"Reading is such a pleasurable escape." Elizabeth tightened the elastic band holding her hair back in a loose ponytail. "I've never understood people who don't enjoy reading."

"Me neither, and those are the kind of words Whittier Publishing and I really love to hear." Mallory giggled.

"I sure will miss you when you go back to Savannah." Elizabeth sighed. "We've started to become good friends."

"Well I'm not leaving tomorrow." Mallory sent her a smile. "And you promised to come down and bring Abby and Suzannah for a visit when the girls get their first school break this fall. We'll have fun seeing the sights around the Savannah area."

"I fully intend to take you up on that offer," Elizabeth said, crossing her ankles. "By next summer I'll have the baby and it won't be easy to travel then."

Mallory glanced toward Elizabeth's tummy. "You're not showing yet at all."

"No, but I will soon." She took a long drink of her cola. "I'm already wearing elastic waist shorts and pants. My waistline will soon be history."

Mallory laughed.

"Look, here's Lucas." Elizabeth pointed to his car pulling into the gravel drive in front of the stand. "He's early today."

Mallory watched Lucas angle his car into one of the parking spaces along the dirt side road leading in and out from Elizabeth's stand. It was the first time she'd seen him since the weekend. He'd obviously been avoiding her again.

"Hi, Daddy," Suzannah called. "Come see the *big* castle we're building."

He went over to inspect the girls' sandcastle and then wandered into the shed to get another lawn chair to set up beside theirs.

"How was your day?" Lucas asked, flashing them one of those charming smiles of his as he settled into his chair beside them.

Elizabeth leaned over to give him a quick kiss on the cheek. "It was hectic, and thankfully Mallory spent the day helping me with sales—and the girls. She was a godsend."

Lucas sent Mallory a studied and relaxed look, reminding her of the man she'd met on the airplane, comfortable and easy with himself. He wasn't edgy today as he'd been on Saturday. Seeing her watching him, he winked at her.

"Got another cola in the cooler?" he asked Elizabeth.

"Yes, and you'll find cookies in a tin under the counter in the shed. Get a couple if you want."

"What kind of cookies?"

She swatted at him. "What difference does it make? You like every kind of cookies I make."

"That I do." He laughed as he headed toward the shed once more to find the cooler and the cookies.

"You're in an awfully good mood today," Elizabeth said as he came back to join them.

"Yes, I am. Life is good, isn't it? The weekend is coming up, the weather is great, and the Fourth of July celebration in Gatlinburg is next week."

Elizabeth's eyes brightened. "Oh, I'd almost forgotten that." She turned to Mallory. "We all go down to Gatlinburg for the Fourth of July parade every year. Clyde and Mary Maples, long-time friends of Beau's and Nonnie's—and patients of Robert's, too—own the old Parkway Motel right on the main highway through town. It's the one with the big balcony over the drive-in entry. We set up chairs on the balcony with the Maples and their family every year to enjoy the parade."

Mallory smiled. "Do Beau and Nonnie still rent a room from the Maples during the parade? They used to, and we always spent the night because the parade didn't even start until midnight. I remember those times well."

"Oh, I keep forgetting you came here every summer as a girl," Elizabeth said. "When was the last time you saw the parade?"

"The summer of my junior year in high school. It's been a long time now."

"Well, I'm thrilled you'll be here to enjoy the parade with us this year. You remember it's always scheduled the night *before* the Fourth of July to kick off the celebration in high style." She stopped to think. "That's this Thursday since the Fourth is on Friday this year." Elizabeth turned toward Lucas. "You and Suzannah plan to go, too, don't you?"

"Wouldn't miss it." He grinned again, drumming his fingers on the arm of the lawn chair in his usual restless fashion.

Elizabeth chatted about their day then, telling Lucas about this and that, and Mallory noticed as Elizabeth talked how easy and comfortable Lucas seemed this afternoon—laughing, his comments witty. She also noticed his eyes often slid to catch her glance. *What was going on with him now?*

Elizabeth glanced toward the girls, now patting out sand pies and giggling. "Abby and Suzannah played in the wading pool and the sandbox today," she said. "You'll need to dunk Suzannah in the bathtub when you get her home and wash her hair, too." She sighed. "I'd invite you all for dinner, but I need to load my plants into the truck to take to the house and then pop Abby into the tub. Supper will probably be late tonight. I'm thinking of asking Robert to pick up pizza."

"I have a better idea." Lucas smiled. "I'll treat everyone to dinner at the Millhouse Restaurant tonight—Mallory, too. It's seafood buffet night. Suzannah loves the shrimp so I'd already promised to take her."

"You sweet man." Elizabeth beamed at him. "I'd love a meal out tonight and we haven't been to the Millhouse in weeks."

"I'll call and reserve a table for us," Lucas said, pulling out his phone. "What time should I say?"

Elizabeth glanced at her watch. "It's five now. Let's say six-thirty. Robert closes the clinic early on Friday; he ought to be here with the truck any minute to help me load my plants."

"I really should get back to Beau's and Nonnie's for dinner," Mallory put in before Lucas could make his call. "I'm sure they'll be watching for me."

"Oh, no." Elizabeth objected. "I want you to go with us, too."

"So do I," Lucas said, surprising her. "I'm sure Beau and Nonnie won't mind. I'll buzz them before I call the reservation in and tell them you're eating with us tonight. They can join us, too, if they want." He started punching in the phone number before Mallory could think of another reason to decline.

"Here comes Robert with the truck." Elizabeth pointed. "Right on time."

Lucas glanced toward the driveway. "I'll help him load after I finish these calls."

Mallory could hear him talking with Nonnie next. She realized quickly from the conversation on Lucas's end that Nonnie was delighted for her to go, although she and Beau wanted to eat at the house.

"We'll show her a good time," Lucas said before hanging up. "She's worked hard today helping Elizabeth and deserves a night out, too."

Resigned to the inevitable, Mallory decided to go along. She had little choice, after all.

Along with Lucas, Elizabeth, and Robert, Mallory helped shut down the road stand for the day and load the plants and vegetables into Robert's truck. When they finished, Lucas offered her a lift back to Wingate House since it was on his way home. Suzannah, delighted for more time with Mallory, filled the space with childish talk until Lucas dropped her off.

"If you'd like to walk over to the restaurant with me and Suzannah, come by our place a little before six-thirty," he said as he stopped the car. "It isn't far to walk and we'd enjoy your company."

Mallory hesitated, even though Suzannah's eyes lit up with excitement at the idea. She couldn't figure out why Lucas was being so unusually cordial today, and she could hardly express to him in front of Suzannah that she still felt wary and uncertain around him after what happened between them last week.

"I won't bite," he said in a soft voice, seeming to read her mind as she reached to open the car door. "Or at least not so it will hurt."

Mallory knew her eyes widened at his words, and she saw another of those cocky grins spread across his face as she glanced at him. *Whatever was he up to? And why was he acting so different all of a sudden?* Not sure of the answer, she simply nodded in reply as she let herself out of the car, deciding not to comment further.

About an hour later, she found Lucas and Suzannah waiting for her on the screened porch of their house. Lucas wore a dinner jacket, expected for the Millhouse Restaurant on Friday evenings, and Suzannah wore a pink satin dress with two fluffy skirt layers, embellished at the waist with a silk rose.

"It was her Easter dress," Lucas explained. "She wanted to wear it tonight even if it's a little dressy." He shrugged. "And of course it's pink, too."

Mallory tried not to laugh. "You look beautiful," she told the child, as Suzannah twirled so Mallory could see the full effect of the dress.

"So do you," Suzannah said, and Mallory saw Lucas nod in agreement.

Mallory had slipped on a simple, V-neck sundress in a deep cobalt blue, with a graceful flared skirt dropping to mid calf. On her feet she wore dressy sling-back sandals and she'd pulled her hair up to clasp it in a jeweled clip.

"That blue color brings out the blue in your eyes," Lucas said, getting up from his chair to walk closer to her.

Wary of his assessment and eager to avoid his eyes, she glanced toward the porch chair where Baby lay sprawled across it, her big belly distended.

"She's getting really fat now," Suzannah observed, seeing Mallory's eyes shift to the cat.

"Yes, she is." Mallory walked over to pet the well-rounded mother cat, who purred loudly in gratitude at the attention.

"Do you think Baby's getting close to her time?" Lucas asked.

"Yes," Mallory answered, feeling the cat's protruding stomach. "I think she could deliver any time now, but I'm not an expert about pregnant cats."

"Wonder how many babies she'll have?" Suzannah asked.

"It's hard to say—usually two to five kittens on average, though."

"Oh, boy!" Suzannah danced to the door Lucas held open for them now.

"Yeah, oh boy," Lucas repeated with a smirk as he let Mallory walk out the door in front of him.

A well-worn pathway led from the back of Ivy Cottage, across a side yard and then along the edge of the woods. The path came out by the picturesque two-storied Retreat House that Millhouse often rented to organizations and groups wanting a separate building for their accommodations and meetings. After passing the old stone house, with its green shutters and lush yard, they followed a neat, flagstone walkway directly into the resort grounds, past the tennis courts and the swimming pool and then around the side of the three-storied Millhouse Lodge to its wide front door.

As they walked under a rock archway and entered the building, they joined a stream of other well-dressed couples and families heading up the wide stairway to the restaurant. The restaurant, on the lodge's second floor, offered panoramic views of the Smoky Mountains from the long plate glass windows of the spacious dining room. Porches opened from the dining area at several points so guests could walk out to enjoy the night air, also, if desired.

Mallory had always believed there was something magical about the big rustic dining room with its oak beams overhead and its tall rock fireplace rising to the ceiling on one of its paneled walls. Muted lighting and flickering table candles gave the room a warm glow and a soft murmur of conversation filled the room. Along one side of the large dining area long buffet tables were spread, presided over by two of the restaurant's waiters dressed in crisp white shirts and black vests. At the front desk, another waiter checked the reservation listing before leading them to a table by one of the room's wide windows.

Lucas pulled out Mallory's chair as she sat down and extended the courtesy to her again as she returned from the buffet. Despite the old-world elegance of the room, guests saw themselves through the buffet line in an informal way at the Millhouse Restaurant, choosing what they wanted to eat from the spread of meats, seafood, vegetables, and salads. With fresh produce in abundance from the local farmers, the Millhouse chefs, Josh and Rachel Kirkpatrick, had glorious food to work with for the dishes they prepared.

"Our new chef team brought a great array of new recipes to

our restaurant," Lucas said, as they started to eat after filling their plates at the buffet.

"I admit I loved Percy Zollie, the old chef who worked here for so long, but this husband and wife team are fabulous, too," Elizabeth said.

"I remember Percy." Mallory smiled at the memory of the balding, overweight man—who could be a terror to the staff—but who always found a way to make a little girl feel special whenever she visited his restaurant. "I felt brokenhearted when I learned he suffered a heart attack and died."

"We created a collection of pictures in his memory in the entrance hall to the restaurant in case you missed seeing them," Lucas told her. "It wasn't easy replacing a legend like Percy."

They ate and visited congenially over dinner and then all went back to the dessert table for a sweet or two as an ending to their meal. Except for a little giggling, Abby and Suzannah behaved impeccably and even stopped to speak to guests and staff members they knew in the big dining room.

"The girls behaved beautifully tonight," Mallory commented to Elizabeth as the girls headed back to the dessert table with Robert and Lucas to get seconds.

Elizabeth smiled. "We practice," she explained. "We play restaurant at the house and practice how we should talk and act. By making it a game they learn what is expected. Plus both of them know if they do not behave appropriately they'll have a sitter the next time and won't get to come. To eat out with adults is a privilege."

"Hmmm. It seems to me that a lot of children could use lessons in how to behave in public places."

Elizabeth nodded. "That's true. We playact how to act in libraries, malls, theaters, and many other places, too—and we practice proper table manners, introductions, and other social niceties. Most of the time children who misbehave simply haven't had anyone to spend time teaching them how they should act in public."

"Maybe you should write a book about that," Mallory suggested.

"No, thank you." Elizabeth laughed. "I have enough to do. Besides, books are *your* business. Have you ever thought about writing a book?"

"Occasionally. I suppose many editors do." She shrugged. "But right now I'm content to help writers make their books the best they can be."

"I'm sure you're good at it."

"Good at what?" Lucas asked as they returned to the table.

"Good at editing. I told Mallory I felt sure she was *very* good at her job."

"I have no doubt of it," Lucas said, putting a couple of chocolate covered strawberries on Mallory's plate and then a few on Elizabeth's. "You girls need to try these. Rachel makes the chocolate from scratch and they're terrific."

As if on cue, the young chefs, Josh and Rachel Kirkpatrick, came out of the kitchen to begin their walk around the dining room to greet their guests. This had always been a custom at Millhouse Restaurant. Watching them stop to mingle and visit with the guests at each table, Mallory felt swamped with pleasant memories. She loved that so many of the old traditions continued on at the resort. Frankly, she'd forgotten how much a part of this place she truly felt, as a Wingate, and how at home and somehow right she felt whenever she spent time here.

As they walked back from the restaurant later, Lucas paused by a side trail heading out behind Retreat House. "Mallory, this trail— that we call the Rock Creek Trail—is the one that follows over to connect with the roadbed leading to the cemetery and the trail to the falls. If you continue on this trail all the way up the mountain instead of cutting off to the falls, it leads eventually to the old cabin on top of the hill."

"Chessy Bohanan's place?"

"Yes. It's a good distance up the mountain to where the trail runs into Old Settlers Trail, and then you need to swing east for about a half mile to an unmarked side path to the cabin, but it isn't hard to find." He ran his hand across the signpost. "Of course, the faster route is to wade across the creek at the falls and then climb uphill on the woods trail to the cabin. That trail is rougher but it isn't hard to follow either. I usually go that way because it cuts off over a mile's walk."

"How many miles is it to Chessy's old place?"

"Probably two and a half miles cutting across the creek on the short route and nearly four miles via the main path." He grinned at her. "When we drove up there, I told you it wasn't as far as you might think from the resort, even though it's a long drive to get to the cabin by car."

"Thanks for pointing out the trail," Mallory said, as they walked on. "I don't think I ever walked up to Chessy's old cabin with Daddy or Grandad when I was a girl. Maybe I'll take a little hike up that way some day. I really want to take some hikes in the mountains before I go back to Savannah. With July here, the rhododendrons should be blooming along the trails."

He sent a smile her way. "I'm off tomorrow if you want to take a hike together. We can do one of the trails over in the Greenbrier area, pack a lunch to carry, make a day of it. Suzannah is going to my folks' house in Knoxville with Abby for the day. Elizabeth and my mom are taking the girls to the zoo."

"I thought you were trying to avoid me," Mallory said before she thought.

"I was; I changed my mind," he said, leaning over to give her a quick kiss while Suzannah skipped ahead at a distance in front of them.

"That's somewhat indecisive of you," Mallory said, pulling away. "Are you always a wishy-washy sort of person?"

He laughed. "No, I've had a little help getting my thinking straightened out this week. I'll tell you about it tomorrow on our hike. Will you go?"

"I suppose." She considered it. "If only to learn why you've had this transformation today."

"I seem different?" He grinned at her. "I hope it's for the better."

She sent him a considering look. "Perhaps. We'll see."

"So will you go?" he asked again.

Mallory hesitated before answering, not sure she really wanted to spend more time with him, regardless of the invitation.

"Yes," she answered finally. "I do want to enjoy the mountains more before I need to return to the city and I don't think it's very safe to hike alone."

"I agree." He reached down to pick up a pinecone in the pathway, turning it in his hand to look at it. "Walk over to the house about nine tomorrow and we'll head out as I take Suzannah by Elizabeth's. Do you have boots and either a waist pack or a backpack for the trail?"

"I brought boots and I think I saw an old waist pack hanging on a peg in the utility room." She glanced at the pinecone in his hand, trying to remember what kind it was. "Will I need a hiking stick?"

"Nah, I don't think so. We can always pick one up along the trail side if we need one." He dropped the cone. "I don't like to carry extra gear if I don't have to, but you should pack a bottle of water, a sandwich, and lightweight snacks like raisins or nuts for lunch on the trail later."

She nodded. "I hope you're going to be this nice again tomorrow and not turn into a jerk again," she couldn't help adding.

"Ouch. I deserved that." He winced. "Give me a try, Mallory. I'm transitioning."

Suzannah interrupted their discussion. "Look, I see a hooty owl." She pointed at a big tree. "Come see." They walked on down the trail to catch up with Suzannah and to check out the owl, the matter settled for the moment.

Back at the house, Suzannah talked Mallory into staying to read a bedtime story and then Mallory came down to the kitchen after Suzannah fell asleep to find Lucas standing by the counter watching the cat with a scowl on his face.

"Baby keeps crying," he told her. "I thought she was trying to tell me she's hungry but that doesn't seem to be the case."

The cat meowed again, looking first at Lucas and then at Mallory before walking toward the door leading into the kitchen. She stopped there, looking back at them and crying once more.

"I think she wants us to follow her," Mallory said.

They followed Baby, who stopped to turn and meow again to be sure they followed. She headed toward the closet door in the mudroom and then walked inside the closet's partially open doorway, still meowing. As Mallory watched, Baby got into the bed they'd made for her and starting walking around it in circles, as if trying to figure out a way to get comfortable.

"Ah," Mallory said after opening the closet door further to watch her for a minute. "I think Baby's getting ready to have her kittens."

Lucas turned panicked eyes to hers. "We don't have to do anything, do we? Do I need to call our vet? I don't know anything about this kind of stuff or how to help her or anything."

Mallory smiled at his obvious unease. "Instinct will tell her what to do."

"Gosh, I hope so." He turned to start back toward the kitchen, but Baby began to cry and started to follow when he did.

"She wants you to stay with her."

"What?" He turned, wrinkling his nose at the idea. "I thought animals did this sort of thing on their own. Why do I need to stay with her?"

"House cats are sociable," Mallory answered, leaning down to pet Baby and to croon to her, urging her back into the bed. "She wants company and encouragement. These are her first kittens. Remember? She doesn't want to go through this alone."

He eyed the cat that lay on her side now, panting a little. "What do we do?"

Mallory kicked off her shoes. "We settle down here on the floor by her bed to keep her company." She sat down cross-legged by the closet door, reaching over again to pet the cat, now lying sideways in the basket.

As Lucas hesitated, Mallory looked up at him. "I'd take that nice jacket off if I were you. Throw it over there on that bench." She pointed at a wooden bench nearby under the window.

"Can't I just sit over here?" he asked, indicating the bench.

"Maybe later, but I think you should sit down here with me right now. Look how she keeps following you with her eyes. I think she'd like it if you sat near her and talked to her and encouraged her. You know."

He grunted, taking off his coat and draping it over the bench before settling down beside her on the floor. "The last thing I expected was to practice my new empathy on an emotional girl cat."

Mallory glanced at him. "What are you talking about?"

"Never mind," he said, reaching out to run a soothing hand down the cat's back, talking some sweet nonsense to her.

Baby shifted positions several times, meowing several more times, and then Mallory could see the first contraction begin. "Here we go," she said.

Surprisingly, it only took four or five contractions before the first kitten began to emerge, wrapped in its embryonic sac.

"Looks like it's inside a water balloon," Lucas said, as the kitten moved fully out, where Baby began to lick and clean it immediately. "She sure knows what to do," he added.

"Isn't this a miracle?" Mallory smiled, watching Baby take care of her new kitten and then seeing it start to root against her seeking a nipple to suckle.

Before they had time to fully examine the first tiny baby, tabby-yellow in coloring like Mr. Tom, contractions began for the next birth. Baby seemed to settle into the process then, birthing two more little kittens over the next twenty minutes, cleaning each carefully and thoroughly inbetween.

Lucas decided to get up and go to the kitchen for a glass of water after the third birth, but Baby meowed her complaints and tried to climb out of the box to follow him.

"Hey, whoa! Come back Lucas." Mallory laughed as she grabbed at his pants leg to stop him. "Baby's going to leave her bed to follow you and I don't think that's a good idea in the middle of birthing kittens."

He sat back down shaking his head. "Dang. Do you think she'll expect me to sit here with her all night?" He stroked Baby's head to assure her he was back. She settled down again, licking the new kittens once more.

"No, I think she'll be fine after she finishes birthing all the kittens. She just doesn't want to go through this by herself." She grinned at him. "Would you?"

"Shoot no, and watching all this makes me real glad I was born male instead of female. Besides I know the birth time and pain is worse for women than cats."

She turned to look at him. "Did you watch Suzannah being born?"

"No." He dropped his eyes. "I'd just finished a tournament when Agnes called to tell me she was driving Cecily to the hospital. Suzannah decided to come early. I thought I'd be home before Cecily went into labor." He ran a hand around his collar, loosening his tie and then pulling it off to toss it on the bench with his coat. "But I caught a quick flight out as soon as Agnes called and made it to the hospital as soon as I could. I didn't miss things by much."

"You couldn't know Suzannah would come early." Mallory could tell he regretted missing out on the birth. "Look," she said to distract him. "Baby has three fine kittens now. There's a tabby like Tom, a white, and a little calico."

"Looks like another's on the way, too." He reached over to pet Baby and croon some encouraging words to her as another contraction began.

Mallory smiled. "You've been really sweet with her."

He stroked Baby's head again. "Do you think we should wake Suzannah to experience this?"

"No," she answered. "Let her be surprised in the morning." Mallory laughed. "Besides this is traumatic enough for the two of us without having the additional emotional overload of trying to explain it all to a five year old."

He chuckled at her words. "You're right there, and quite frankly, the entire scene's a little graphic for a small child to watch."

Mallory agreed. "I guess we can count our blessings Baby started her labor after Suzannah went to bed."

"Here comes our next kitten," he said in answer.

About twenty minutes later, after the delivery of a small kitten that looked very much like Baby, it seemed as if no further kittens would make an appearance.

"Well, I think that's it," Mallory said, reaching out a finger to gently touch the last chocolate brown kitten, now licked and clean. "She has four little kittens—just like in the Little Golden Book story."

Lucas grinned, leaning his back against the bench and stretching out his long legs. "Suzannah loves that book. We'll need to read it again now."

Mallory rubbed her neck. "I can't remember the colors or the names of the kittens in the book but I remember Nonnie reading it to me, too."

"I guess we all grew up on Little Golden Books." He reached out to pull her into the crook of his arm. "Gosh, I'm glad you were here to go through this with me tonight."

"You'd have been all right." She settled in beside him, stretching out her legs, too, both of them cramped from the time on the floor by Baby's bed.

He glanced toward the cozy bed in the closet, where a now contented mother lay, purring and nursing her kittens. "She looks happy, doesn't she?"

"She does," Mallory agreed.

They sat quietly watching Baby with her new kittens for a little while, before Lucas pushed himself to his feet. "I need to go to the bathroom, so I hope she'll let me out of her sight now."

"I think she will," Mallory answered. "I'll stay for a few minutes more and then see if I can slip out, too. She's resting now, purring happily, and the kittens are all nursing and seem fine."

She glanced around the room. "It's warm in this mudroom, too, so I think she'll be comfortable here for the night. Her litterbox is nearby and her food and water dishes are around the corner in the kitchen if she wants either."

Mallory sat in the quiet, studying the cat and kittens after Lucas left. What a precious time it had been to watch Baby become a mother. The experience touched her deep inside, watching it all, and made her yearn for a child in an odd way, to wish for a baby of her own. She'd felt a sweet drawing toward Lucas that she hadn't felt before, too, watching him lovingly pet and encourage Baby, using crooning, soft words to her. Despite her problems with Lucas, she could see he was a kind and gentle man underneath.

"I've started heating water for some hot cocoa," Lucas called, sticking his head around the door from the kitchen. "See if Baby will be all right on her own now. We can sit in the kitchen where we can hear her if she cries."

"Okay." Mallory pushed herself up from the floor and stretched before walking into the kitchen to join Lucas. Baby seemed content as Mallory peeked at her a last time, sleeping along with the kittens, probably worn out.

She and Lucas talked about quiet things over their cocoa, both seeming somewhat lost to their own thoughts—and tired. When Mallory stood to head home, she suggested that Lucas stay behind where he could keep an eye on the new family. He agreed, giving her a casual kiss before letting her out the door, as if they were a comfortable, longtime couple.

The shared evening with Baby had brought them closer, into a new place together. A sweet and bonded place. Despite all their ups and downs—and past misunderstandings—Mallory found herself looking forward to the day hiking with Lucas tomorrow.

# CHAPTER 18

Lucas heard Mallory knock on the back door the next morning and then heard her let herself in.

"You're early," he said, leaning around the kitchen door to smile at her.

"I came early to check on the kittens." She walked from the screened porch into the mudroom where Suzannah sat on the floor watching them.

"Look. Baby had her kitties last night," Suzannah said unnecessarily.

"Yes, I was here." Mallory reminded her, sitting down on the floor beside her. "How are the little kittens doing today?"

Suzannah bit her lip. "All they do is sleep and eat and crawl around. They can't even walk and their eyes are all sealed shut."

Mallory tousled Suzannah's hair. "They're only tiny babies now but they'll grow quickly enough."

She frowned. "Daddy says I shouldn't pick them up."

"It's probably best not to until they get bigger and stronger." Mallory leaned over to stroke Baby and greet her. "You just wait. By the end of the week, their eyes will open and they'll move around more. By two weeks they'll start to walk and be more fun to watch and to play with."

"I think they need names," Suzannah said.

"Yes, they do, but I'd wait a little longer until we can tell if they are little boy or little girl kittens."

"How will you know?"

Mallory heard Lucas chuckle over that question. "We'll look at them to find out when they get a little stronger," Mallory answered, not offering any specific details. "Then you can name them."

She showed Suzannah how to gently pet the kittens and reminded her to pet and talk to Baby a lot, too.

Suzannah nodded. "We wouldn't want Baby to feel left out or think we loved her babies more than her."

"That's right." Mallory got up to head into the kitchen, leaving Suzannah with the kittens.

"I've sure had a lot of questions to answer today." He smiled at her.

"I'll bet." She handed Lucas a cookie tin decorated with butterflies and then pulled off the waist pack she wore around her waist to lay it on the counter.

"What's in the butterfly tin?"

"Chocolate chip cookies from Nonnie, fresh from the oven."

Lucas pulled off the lid and groaned at the fragrance that escaped. "Yum. My favorites."

"Nonnie thought you might like a few to take on our hike, and she wanted to send some with Elizabeth and the girls for their zoo outing today."

"I'll get down a couple of Ziploc bags," he said, popping a cookie into his mouth while he did. "Do you have everything you need for our hike? If not, I can probably rustle up anything missing from around the house." He glanced at her feet. "Nice boots and good socks. You'll be glad of those. I thought we'd hike to Ramsay Cascades off the Greenbrier Road if you think you're up for it. It's a four mile hike in, eight miles roundtrip, and a pretty strenuous walk on the upper half near the falls."

"I haven't been on that trail since high school with a group from the resort one summer." She sent him a grin. "I think I can make the mileage now, but I probably couldn't have a month ago."

"You've walked a lot while recovering." He ran a glance down her legs below her shorts. He loved those long legs of hers. "I think you'll be fine, but if you get too tired we can always turn around along the way."

Lucas picked up her waist pack from the counter to test its weight.

"Want me to tell you what's in it?" Mallory smirked at him.

"No." He grinned. "I just didn't want you to haul too much weight up the trail."

"Check inside if you want—one ham and cheese sandwich in foil, a mini box of raisins, a small bag of peanuts, and two of Nonnie's cookies in foil."

"Only two?" He feigned a shocked look her way.

She laughed. "Yes, and a bottle of water. I also put in a small hand towel, in case I wanted to wade and dry my feet off after, a tissue pack, chapstick, and a little first aid kit Nonnie gave me with Band-Aids in it."

"Sounds good. I think I have about the same, except *more* food— and I'll definitely add more cookies." He grinned at her. "I also packed a pocketknife, a small compass, and a hiking map."

Mallory glanced toward the mudroom. "Do you think we'll be able to get Suzannah away from the kittens?"

"Yes. She's really looking forward to her day at the zoo with Abby, Elizabeth, and Mom. They're going out to lunch and shopping after the zoo outing. Mom always buys the girls a treat on their shopping ventures. They love that."

Lucas finished his own packing for the hike, got Suzannah's tote bag ready to go to Elizabeth's, and then checked the cat a final time.

As they headed out through the mudroom to the screened porch, Mallory pulled the door between the porch and the mudroom shut. "Always be sure to keep this door closed for a while."

"Why?" Lucas gave her a puzzled look. "Baby can't get to her cat door on the screened porch to go outside if I shut the mudroom door."

She nodded. "I know that, but more importantly no cats or predators can slip in through the cat door to get to the kittens. Some tomcats will kill baby kittens and so will raccoons."

"Man, that would break Suzannah's heart. I'll remember to keep the door shut to the porch."

"I doubt Baby will fuss about it. She'll know instinctively it's safer for the kittens."

They started down the back walkway toward his car, parked in the old stone carport that matched the house. Clematis vines twined up a trellis by the structure, heavy with purple blooms. There was always something in bloom around Ivy Cottage and Wingate House in the warm months of the year.

"How do you know so much stuff about cats?" he asked.

"Nonnie and Beau used to have a lot of cats and one summer one of them birthed a litter of kittens." She grinned as he opened the gate. "It was memorable."

"Well, I've been glad of your knowledge during this time." He opened the car door for her and then tucked Suzannah into her car seat in the back.

"Mallory is smart about a lot of things," Suzannah added.

"That she is," Lucas agreed, settling into the driver's seat.

"Elizabeth said being smart is better than being pretty, but Mallory is pretty, too. Don't you think so, Daddy?"

"I definitely think so." He sent Mallory a wolfish grin, making her blush.

It didn't take them long to drop off Suzannah and then drive down the highway to the entrance to the Greenbrier Road. They followed the park road alongside the Little Pigeon River for a few miles through the lush green landscape of summer. Lucas rolled down the car windows so they could hear the sounds of the rushing mountain stream and smell the scents of nature on the air.

"We couldn't have picked a nicer day for our hike." Lucas slowed to angle around a rocky patch in the old road. "Even though it's early July, it's not too hot today and a little breeze is stirring."

"I've really looked forward to this day," Mallory said, leaning her head near the window and the scent of the cool mountain air.

They both wore shorts and T-shirts for their hike and Lucas gave Mallory a dark green Millhouse Resort visor like his to wear. "It's good advertisement," he said, teasing her.

After a few miles Lucas turned to drive over the river on a broad bridge and head down a narrower road to the parking area for the Ramsay Cascades Trail. They parked, locked the car, and then headed out onto the trail, which began by crossing a long bridge over the beautiful cascades of the Middle Prong.

Mallory stopped to lean on the bridge rails to look down into the stream. "I always forget how beautiful it is here in the Smoky Mountains until I come for a visit."

"Yeah, I hear you. I traveled all over the world as a golfer and I saw some incredible places, but few equaled the beauty of the Smokies."

Lucas and Mallory walked on, side by side on the first mile and a half of the trail, following an old logging road. They talked and chatted as they hiked, getting to know each other better, stopping to look at a few summer flowers, like clumps of spiky, red bee balm, and enjoying the ongoing views of the rushing mountain stream. They found rhododendrons starting to bloom along the trail and Mallory took photos of the lush white blooms.

The roadbed ended at a large clearing. "The trail narrows now in case you've forgotten and it will begin to grow gradually steeper." Lucas led the way uphill through the forest, still following along the stream.

"Oh, look." Mallory pointed toward a long, log bridge ahead. "I'd forgotten this trail had this split-log bridge to walk across."

"We'll find another a little further up the trail," he said, leading the way over the narrow, railed bridge crossing the creek. "We'll encounter some steep and rocky sections, too, after the next bridge crossing."

Mallory followed him contentedly, occasionally pointing out something that caught her interest along the trail. She seemed happy to be out of doors, enjoying the day with him, and even as the trail rose and became rocky and steep in several places she had no trouble keeping up with him. Cecily never liked to hike or do things out of doors.

"Did you and Cecily hike out in Arizona?" she asked, as if reading his mind. "I read there are some beautiful places near Scottsdale where you lived."

Lucas tried to think what to say. "Cecily didn't care much for the outdoor life. When I hiked, biked, rafted, or camped around the area, or skied at Flagstaff in the winter, I usually went with some of the other guys on the tour. A lot of PGA pros call Scottsdale home. The weather's great for golf year round and you can hang out with the other guys at the Grayhawk Golf Club."

"I've heard it's lovely in Arizona but Mother and I never lived out West, even as many times as we moved around."

"Arizona is a striking place, very different from here—more desert in appearance, with cactus, scrub brush, red hills, and rocky mountains with scanty to little vegetation in many places. But there are stunning, memorable spots to see everywhere." They climbed up a rocky stretch while Lucas talked. "When I had time off from tour, I liked hiking nearby trails in the McDowell Sonoran Preserve and in the McDowell Mountain Park nearby. The south rim of the Grand Canyon Park isn't too far either, only about three to four hours away. There are some rare, scenic wonders there."

"I've seen pictures and especially loved the ones of the rainbow hued mountains." She panted a little between words. The trail was growing steeper.

"You should take a trip out West someday." He wished he could be the one to take her. "I know some great resorts where you can stay and I still have old contacts in the area. Let me know if you decide to go sometime."

"I'll do that."

He glanced up the trail and spotted a familiar area. "Up ahead where you see the trail broadening are the 'three sisters'—three giant tulip poplars that escaped the loggers. They're five to six feet in diameter. You'll want to get your camera out to take a picture or two." Mallory had often snapped photos along their way. "We'll take a break there, as well."

"A break sounds *really* good about now."

Lucas was always amazed at the size of some of the old trees still remaining in the Smoky Mountains. He and Mallory had fun trying to wrap their arms around the vast poplars beside the trail and they took turns taking photos. Then they found a fallen log they could sit down to rest on.

"We've hiked about two and a half miles now." He pulled his water bottle out of his waist pack to take a long swig. "How are you doing?"

"I'm good, just huffing and puffing from that last steep stretch." She smiled at him. "I'll be fine, Lucas. I walk a lot at home in Savannah in the parks, around the city, down at the beach. There are a lot of nice walking trails near my townhouse downtown."

He thought of asking her if she would be glad to get back but didn't really want to hear the answer. Not today. "Our next half mile curls away from the stream and up a hillside. It's a little arduous but not as bad as the final mile."

She sighed. "That's the part that narrows and climbs in and out of rock boulders before it finally winds down to the falls."

"You have a good memory."

She laughed. "It's hard to forget that section. But once you get to the falls, it all seems worth it."

It did seem worth it as they finally climbed down to find the towering spill of cascading water tumbling over a hundred feet down a high rocky ledge. While Mallory snapped photos, Lucas found them a large, flat rock by the pool below the falls where they could spread out their picnic lunch and relax for a while.

It felt good to take a break and they'd both worked up an appetite.

After eating most of their lunch, they took off their shoes to wade in the cold water. Mallory asked one of the other visitors at the falls—a man from Virginia—to take a couple of photos of them together, and they returned the favor by snapping pictures of he and his family.

Climbing back up on the rock, Lucas and Mallory dried their feet, put their socks and shoes back on, and then dug into their waist packs to find the cookies from Nonnie they'd both packed. Starting to unwrap hers, Mallory glanced across at him. "You promised to tell me today why you've had such a transformation in your views and actions."

"That's an interesting way of putting it. I like that word transformation."

She crossed her arms. "Come on, Lucas. Even you admitted you've been acting differently."

He wolfed down a cookie, trying to think how he wanted to answer her. "I've been in counseling all week," he said at last, deciding to be totally honest.

Her eyes widened.

"Beau and Andy noticed I occasionally freeze up when faced with certain types of emotional scenes. They thought I should talk with someone about it, said it affected my work." He scowled. "I especially experience trouble with emotional scenes with women."

"Those remind you of the bad times with Cecily."

He gave a disgusted snort. "Seems like everybody could see that but me."

She wisely said nothing, leaning over to study a brown speckled salamander slipping through the water below them.

Lucas ate another cookie before speaking again. "I talked with Robert first and then drove down to Gatlinburg to counsel with Perry Ammons, the minister of a church on Natty Road. Robert knows him, likes him, and he knew Perry had counseling background. Perry helped me talk through things this week, helped me realize I experienced flashbacks when confronted with situations that made me remember my problems with Cecily."

"Problems you couldn't fix and still felt guilty about."

He rolled his eyes. "Maybe I should have come to you for counseling," he said with annoyance.

She gave him a steady look. "I'm not skilled there."

"Sorry." He picked up a rock to skip it across the water. "I'm still a little testy about admitting I had to go to counseling."

"I know the feeling." She leaned back on her elbows on the sunny rock. "I hated talking to the doctors in Savannah about my private emotions and problems, hated admitting I even had any."

"I hear you." He watched the family from Virginia start their way back up the trail. "I have to admit though that Perry helped me in several areas."

Seeing they were alone now at the falls, he leaned over to brush his lips across hers, startling her. "Perry helped me see I was avoiding you, not wanting to get involved with anyone emotionally or to risk getting hurt again."

She drew back from him, putting a hand on his chest. "You wanted to avoid me, too, because you knew I'd experienced emotional problems of my own. That made me a greater risk."

"Well, I've decided now risks are worth taking." He threaded his hand into her hair. "As Perry said, any relationship you begin and pursue is a risk. And some risks are worth exploring."

Hearing her small intake of breath and watching her eyes darken, he moved his mouth to hers. Her lips were warm from being out in the sun and he loved the taste and feel of her. She was definitely worth the risk, he decided, moving to deepen the kiss, loving the little sigh that escaped her.

"You are so beautiful," he murmured against her ear. "I thought so from the first time I saw you on the airplane, even when you hoped I wouldn't talk to you."

A little smile curled at the edge of her lips at his words.

Lucas kissed her again, wrapping his arms around her to pull her close against him, loving the way they fit together so perfectly.

"You know, when I'll admit it to myself, I'm almost crazy about you," he told her. "I find myself thinking about you far too often through my days, looking forward to seeing you, feeling my blood ramp up at the sight of you. Holding you and kissing you always feels like coming home."

She sighed, running a hand along his face. "This is a lovely moment, Lucas, but I'm still wary of how your emotions change from one day to another. You feel happy with me today, but what about tomorrow? I have to be honest and say it's really important to me to connect with someone I can count on, someone who can be a constant in my life, who can offer a love I can really rely on, like Nonnie and Beau's love for me. I've never had to question that."

He edged back at her words. "I didn't think we were talking about love."

She laughed. "There, you see? I've already scared you away with the use of a simple word."

"Love's a big word." He rubbed a hand over his neck, uncomfortable now.

Mallory regarded him with interest. "I certainly know that, reading and editing hundreds of romance novels in my work, and I don't think I said that I loved you, Lucas, or that I was looking for a declaration back. I simply explained that a constant love, a constant person to be involved with and to develop a relationship with, is what I am looking for."

"Well, isn't everyone looking for that?" He felt annoyed now that she'd made him feel uncomfortable.

"Yes, I think so, whether they will acknowledge it or not."

The voices of a new group of hikers, coming down the trail to the cascades, stopped their talk.

Lucas glanced at his watch. "I guess we should probably start back now."

Mallory slipped on her waist pack. "At least the walk back will be mostly downhill and easier than the walk in. I'm glad for that."

He gave her a hand up from the rock and kept her hand in his to help her jump from their large boulder to a smaller one in the stream and then out to the bank to start back up the trail.

She talked happily about sights along the way as they hiked back to the car, but Lucas kept thinking back to her words at the falls. Mallory had moved many times in her life, mostly at her mother's whim from what he'd learned. She'd lost her father at an early age, with her mother unable to give her the true, unselfish love she yearned for most. Because of that, she wanted someone solid and true she could count on in a relationship. Was that so wrong? Didn't he want that, too? Should he blame her for expressing it, for making that clear to him? After all, he'd certainly been candid with her from the start about what he wanted and didn't want in a relationship. What pricked his pride was the subtle suggestion that he fell short in some way of her expectations. That she didn't trust him. He could hardly blame her after the way he'd acted.

From the undertones of all Mallory's comments, Lucas got the message loud and clear that she was looking for love, no matter how she tried to deny it. Looking for a long-term relationship. He'd decided to risk getting to know her better but was he ready for more? He didn't know yet.

# CHAPTER 19

**W**eather for the big Fourth of July parade in Gatlinburg couldn't have been more perfect, Mallory thought, as she made her way through the growing crowd of people thronging the downtown sidewalks of Gatlinburg. She kept a close eye on Lucas, Robert, Elizabeth and the girls ahead of her so she wouldn't get separated from them.

"Aren't we lucky no rain is forecast for the parade tonight?" Elizabeth said, turning to grin at her as they paused at a stoplight crossing.

"Yes and I'm glad we came early and got a free spot to park at the Maples' motel," Robert added, studying the line of bumper-to-bumper traffic crawling along the Parkway through the center of town. "I feel sorry for all these folks who'll be looking for a parking space around town."

"I enjoyed seeing Clyde and Mary Maples again," Elizabeth added as they started across the road. "I'll look forward to visiting with the rest of their family later when it's time for the parade."

"Where are we going to eat, Daddy?" Suzannah asked, looking up at him. He held tight to her hand in the crowd just as Robert held fast to Abby's.

"At the Park Grill," he answered. "It's a great restaurant, and even better, the owner is a member at the golf club and locked in a reservation for us. We'd have a long wait tonight at any restaurant in Gatlinburg without one."

"The Park Grill has good food and the restaurant is pretty

inside." Elizabeth smiled at Suzannah. "You and Abby will love it. They have a nice children's menu and you two can order chicken fingers or fried shrimp. You love both."

"How come Nonnie and Beau didn't come with us?" Suzannah asked.

"They ate earlier with Clyde and Mary and they're helping to set up our spot on the porch roof for the parade now. We'll get to visit with them all later while we watch the Fourth of July parade."

"Did you bring our chairs?" Abby asked. "And our cooler and snacks?"

"Yes to both." Robert veered their route around a group of tourists blocking the sidewalk. "Elizabeth brought a big quilt you girls can lay down on, too, if you want—so you can look up and watch the fireworks better."

Suzannah grinned at Mallory. "They shoot really big fireworks," she said, her eyes brightening.

Abby frowned. "But they're loud. They hurt my ears."

"I brought your ear plugs," Elizabeth told her. "I know you're sensitive to loud noises sometimes."

They moved on down the sidewalk, trying to stay together with so many people crowding the streets, all of them talking, slowing to look in shop windows, or pushing in or out of stores.

Mallory enjoyed gawking a little herself, looking into the windows as she walked along. She liked people watching and there were certainly a great variety of people on the streets of Gatlinburg to watch tonight.

Abby put her hands over her ears as a group of cyclists roared down the street. "Are we there yet?"

"It's not that far, only about five blocks from the Parkway Motel. And look." Robert pointed ahead. "You can see our restaurant on the left."

A few minutes later, they arrived at the Park Grill, a rustic restaurant with a log cabin look. Mallory followed her group as they climbed the rock stairs and crossed the broad covered porch into the restaurant's spacious entry. Soon they were all seated at a large table, the girls enjoying the giant tree statuary in the middle of the restaurant with three carved black bears climbing on its branches.

"Those bears look real, don't they Daddy?" Suzannah asked.

Lucas winked at Mallory. "They really do, but I'm glad they're *not* real. They might come eat our food up and I'm hungry."

Suzannah and Abby giggled.

Mallory let her eyes wander to the log beams overhead, the rustic artifacts on the walls, the rock fireplace, and the chandeliers artfully created to look like antlers. She liked a restaurant with character and ambience.

While the girls chattered away about the upcoming parade, she studied the menu, deciding to order the Pecan Chicken that Elizabeth recommended, with wild rice and the restaurant's salad bar. The men ordered steak and rainbow trout, Elizabeth grilled salmon, and the girls fried shrimp from the children's menu.

"A lot of new features have been added to the parade since the last time you saw it," Elizabeth told Mallory after they filled their plates at the salad bar and returned to their table. "Especially the balloons over the last years—big patriotic hats, a statue of liberty, and an eagle."

"Plus a scary shark balloon, too," Abby added.

"Yes. The shark balloon from Ripley's Aquarium was a big hit as you can imagine." Elizabeth grinned. "So was the train float, covered in blinking lights. I hope the train will be in the parade again. The children love that train."

Lucas's eyes found Mallory's. "Mostly, this is a local parade—not like the big televised ones—just full of local bands, homemade floats, military groups, horses and riders, and picking-and-singing entertainment."

"I remember." Mallory smiled at him. "That's part of the charm of the parade, that and the fireworks."

Abby's eyes grew wide. "I like that the parade doesn't start til midnight and we get to stay up *real* late."

"That's the other charm of the evening." Robert laughed.

They talked casually through dinner, reminiscing about past parades in Gatlinburg, remembering former times and funny stories.

During dessert, Elizabeth went with the girls to the restroom but then came back to the table in a panic, dragging Abby along with her.

Seeing her strained face, Robert immediately asked, "What's the matter, Elizabeth?"

"It's Suzannah." Tears started now. "After the girls went to the bathroom, I slipped into one of the stalls for a minute. Since the bathroom was crowded, I let the girls step outside the door to wait for me in the entry. But Abby came back in to get me while I was washing my hands, all upset. She said Suzannah saw something and took off out the front door running."

"She what?" Lucas jumped to his feet. "You mean she's out in that crowd alone?"

Elizabeth grabbed his arm as he started toward the door. "I've already been out the front, looked on the porch, called and called."

"What did Suzannah see?" Robert asked Abby.

"I don't know, Daddy," the child said, tears spilling over now. "We were standing there outside the bathroom door waiting for Mommy. Suzannah looked back toward the restaurant, I think, and then she took off running out the door. She didn't say anything. She just ran away."

"I've already talked to Abby," Elizabeth said. "She has no idea what Suzannah saw that evidently frightened her. We couldn't see a thing that might have caused her to get upset and act like this. She knows better than to run off on her own."

"I'm going to look for her," Lucas said. He glanced at Robert. "You take care of my tab and I'll pay you back later."

Robert put a hand on his arm. "Let's don't panic, Lucas. We'll all go look for Suzannah. We've finished our dinner anyway." He stood, picking up the tab on the table.

Elizabeth glanced toward the door. "If Suzannah was frightened, I think she'd head back to the motel where we're staying," she said.

"Lucas, you and Mallory walk in that direction looking for her on this side of the road. Robert and I will take Abby and we'll walk down the other side of the street, in case she panicked and crossed the road."

"Should we call Nonnie and Beau?" Mallory asked.

"I hate to, but we probably need to so that they'll watch for her and call us if she comes back to the Parkway Motel," Robert said.

Lucas took Mallory's hand. "You make the calls needed, Robert. Call the front desk of the motel, too, and pay the restaurant tab. Mallory and I will start searching now. I want to find Suzannah before she gets too far."

Mallory grabbed her purse to drape it across her shoulder as Lucas headed toward the front of the restaurant, all but pulling her along. She persuaded him to let her check the restroom quickly one more time before they left but saw no sign of the child.

"Whatever could Suzannah have seen to frighten her enough to run away?" Mallory asked as they sprinted down the Park Grill's front stairs and headed into the crowds on the street.

"I have no idea," Lucas said. "It's not like Suzannah to do something like this at all."

Looking ahead, all Mallory could see were throngs of people on the street. However would they be able to spot one little girl among this crowd?

Lucas began to call Suzannah's name as they practically ran down the sidewalk.

Mallory tucked her hand into Lucas's arm as he pushed through the people. "Slow down, Lucas. We need to take time to look into the stores as we walk along. She might have ducked into one of those to hide."

"From what?" He ran a hand through his hair, looking around. "I think Robert may be right. I bet she went back to the motel."

Mallory scanned the interiors of several small shops as they passed by their windows, hoping to see a small girl dressed in a red T-shirt with a flag on the front and wearing blue-striped shorts.

"Keep an eye out for that bright red headband, with the big

patiotic bow on top, that Suzannah was wearing. That should stand out—even in this crowd."

"Good idea." She scanned ahead down the busy sidewalk.

They talked very little as they walked, both watching carefully for Suzannah, hoping any minute to spot her.

As they neared the motel, Lucas's cell phone rang. He pulled Mallory with him over against the side of a building to answer it. "Lucas here."

He listened for a few minutes before his eyes moved to Mallory's.

"Was that Robert?" she asked. "Did they find her?"

"No." He clicked off his phone. "She hasn't come back to the motel. Beau stood out front to watch for her and Nonnie watched from the window." He sighed and closed his eyes for a moment. "Robert is taking Abby and Elizabeth to the motel, and then he and Beau will continue to look on the other side of the street from us. Robert suggested we continue searching this side of the road."

He leaned his head against the building for a moment. "Lord, what will I do if we don't find her? I keep imagining how scared she must be wherever she is and my mind's going crazy thinking about what could happen to her in this crowd. She's only five."

Mallory took his arm to walk on. "Don't panic. We'll find her or someone else will. Suzannah is very smart. Once she gets past being scared, she will think smart."

"I hope so, and thanks for saying that Mallory."

They walked on down the street with darkness falling now. The people were finding spots along the road and parade route to settle into now, making it harder to weave their way along the sidewalk. Lights flashed everywhere on the silly glasses, hats, and necklaces the people wore to celebrate. Ordinarily these would make Mallory smile, but now they distracted her eyes in looking for one small girl amid so many people, so much noise, and so much festive light.

Almost an hour later, they reached the Arrowmont School of Arts and Crafts at the far end of Gatlinburg and Lucas dropped onto a bench on the sidewalk. "I can't imagine Suzannah would have come any further than this. The turn up Highway 321 toward the resort isn't far. Even if she was scared, she'd know not to go further than this from where we're staying."

"I think you're right." Mallory sat down beside him, tired and discouraged herself. "Where in the world can she be?"

Lucas shook his head. "I'm going crazy thinking of the things that might have happened to her, imagining someone frightening her or saying something to her at the restaurant, maybe even chasing after her. I don't think I can stand it if anything's happened to her."

Mallory tucked her hand into his. "We'll find her, Lucas. I've been praying and I feel somehow she's okay."

"Thanks. I hope so." He called Robert again to check to see if they'd found Suzannah and then called Elizabeth. Hanging up from both calls, Mallory could see he felt more dejected than ever.

"No one anywhere has seen her." He sighed. "Beau knows the Gatlinburg police chief Bill Magee well. He called him and some of his men are looking, too. They also alerted the shops that are still open to watch for her." He glanced around. "It's so dark now and the crowd is growing for the parade. I know she'll be even more scared."

Mallory tried to imagine what she'd have done as a little girl if she'd been alone in Gatlinburg.

"What do you always tell Suzannah to do when you get lost from each other?" she asked Lucas. "You know, like when you're in the mall or at the zoo or at Dollywood?."

"This isn't the same." He frowned.

"I know, but what do you tell her to do if you get separated when out together in a public place."

He rubbed his neck. "We always set a designated spot where we'll meet if we get lost from each other, but we didn't do that here. If we get lost from each other at other places, like hiking, I tell her not to get lost any further, to stay in the last place where we were together and that I'll find her."

Mallory considered his words, and then smiled. "I bet she went back to the restaurant then." She stood up. "Come on. We can look for her along the way, but I bet she'll be there, Lucas."

"Listen." He stood and took her hand. "Maybe you should go back to the motel. I know you must be tired."

She interrupted him with a small kiss." Don't even consider that idea. I care too much about that child, and you, to be anywhere else but here."

He tried to offer her a smile. "Thanks," he said, taking her hand as they made their way back up the street through the crowds again.

They hadn't gone a block before Lucas's phone rang. He pulled it out of his pocket to answer it and then leaned against a light pole as he listened at length.

"What?" Mallory asked as soon as he hung up.

"The sheriff has a lead." He led her a short distance away from the crowd. "Bobby Joe and Tilly Walker were in the Park Grill Restaurant tonight. Bill Magee said one of the greeters said she saw a woman start to approach Suzannah in the lobby but that the little girl ran from her out the door, acting terrified. They've figured out it was Tilly."

"Oh my gosh, Lucas." Mallory leaned against him for support, imagining how frightened Suzannah must have been to see Tilly again.

Then a sweep of anger hit her. "What is that woman doing out and around already? Does she have Suzannah?"

"No." He shook his head wearily. "Beau said Bill Magee learned Tilly is much better now; she's getting counseling and she and Bobby Joe have even reconciled. Tilly's staying at Bobby Joe's place right now and he brought her to eat tonight and to see the parade—thought it would be a treat for her."

"So now we know *why* Suzannah was afraid, panicked, and ran." Mallory said, feeling a trickle of fear herself, simply imagining it. "Did Beau say Tilly and Bobby Joe were eating in the same restaurant with us?"

"Yes. Evidently they were seated in another section of the restaurant." He winced at the thought. "Beau said Tilly went to use the restroom and saw Abby and Suzannah waiting in the entry. She started towards Suzannah, wanting to tell her how sorry she was about all that happened, but when Suzannah turned and saw her, she ran out of the restaurant. Tilly went back to her table and told Bobby Joe about it, but by the time he walked around in the restaurant to look for us, in order to explain, we'd all left. Bobby Joe said he thought Suzannah probably left with us, but he got to worrying about it later and called Beau. When he learned Suzannah was missing, he talked to Bill Magee, too."

Mallory put her hands on her hips. "What did Bill Magee do?"

Lucas slumped against the building. "He called Bobby Joe and Tilly in for questioning, but the story they're telling is the same as the greeter's. The police said Tilly and Bobby Joe were both sorry Suzannah ran off and is missing."

Mallory closed her eyes. "Bless that child's heart to see that woman coming towards her. No wonder she panicked and ran."

She crossed her arms, angry then. "Why didn't someone call to tell us Tilly was out and that we might run into her somewhere? I'd have freaked out myself to see that woman again after what she put us through. I'd imagine she escaped from a mental facility or something. I'd run, too, if she came toward me like that unexpectedly. Suzannah and I had to run before."

"It makes me mad to think about it, too." Lucas wrapped her in a small hug. "What should we do now?"

Looking into his strained face, Mallory tried to pull herself together. "I still think we should go back to the Park Grill. If Suzannah remembers your rule about going back to the last place where you were together, she might be there, and if not, perhaps we'll see her along the way." She took Lucas's arm to walk up the street. "At least we know now what happened and why she ran."

He leaned against her. "Somewhere out in this crowded, crazy city getting ready for a midnight parade is a scared little five year old girl."

"I know, but we'll find her," Mallory said again as Lucas pushed their way around a big group of tourists, dressed in patriotic colors, several wearing party hats blinking in red and blue lights.

At the Park Grill again, Lucas raced inside to look around, while

Mallory waited among the crowd of people on the porch of the restaurant, all hoping to get inside or to use the porch as a spot from which to view the parade later. As Lucas came back out, long-faced and obviously discouraged, to start down the steps toward Mallory, a small figure detached itself from the crowd.

"Daddy!" Suzannah pushed her way around a group on the porch to launch herself into her arms.

Mallory stood there for a moment, simply enjoying the scene of child and father hugging, rejoicing, both crying. Putting a hand to her cheek, she realized she had a few tears dripping down her own face, too.

As Lucas worked his way to where Mallory waited at the bottom of the steps, Suzannah spied her, holding out her arms to throw them around Mallory's neck as soon as they drew near.

"Oh, Mallory, it was that awful Tilly. She was right here in the restaurant and coming to get me." She held on to them both, drawing them into a little circle together. "I was so scared."

"It's okay, pumpkin; it's okay," Lucas soothed, wrapping an arm around Mallory, kissing her after he kissed Suzannah, so relieved and overjoyed.

"I hope she's not here anymore." Suzannah looked around anxiously. "I knew to come back here after I had to run away, but I hid on the porch so in case she came looking for me, she wouldn't find me or I could run away again."

Lucas walked them out of the stream of traffic, and then squatted down, putting Suzannah on his knee. "Tilly's not here and she won't be coming here," he assured her.

"Are you sure?" She bit her lip, still looking around.

Mallory squatted down beside them, too, putting one knee on the ground. "Tilly has been getting some help, Suzannah. She is better now and not acting crazy anymore." She stroked the child's cheek. "Tilly's husband brought her to eat at the restaurant tonight and to see the parade. When she saw you, she wanted to say she was sorry."

Suzannah's eyes grew wide. "Do you think she's really sorry?"

"Beau and the police chief Bill Magee think so from what they learned tonight, and it doesn't seem likely she meant to hurt you. Just to apologize."

She looked around and then hid her head on Lucas's shoulder. "I don't want to see her."

"Well, then we won't," Lucas told her.

"You might want to see her someday so she can say she's sorry, but you don't need to see her tonight." Mallory smiled at Suzannah. "Tonight you're safe and fine after a big scare, and there's still a parade to enjoy."

"Mallory's right. Do you think you're ready to go back to the hotel to see everyone?" Lucas asked.

"Okay," she said. "But can you carry me or let me ride piggyback. I'm tired."

"Not a problem." Lucas stood and hoisted Suzannah into his arms, obviously pleased to have an excuse to keep holding her close.

"I could use another kiss, too," Suzannah said, giving him an impish smile. "And I think Mallory could use one. We've had a scary night."

"So we have," Lucas replied, giving Suzannah a kiss and then leaning over to give Mallory one with a little more sizzle to it.

Back at the hotel, Suzannah soon relaxed, revived in part by all the attention and affection she received from everyone. With a parade soon due and excitement high, it was hard for a child's mood not to quickly change.

Mallory sat back in a lawn chair, closing her eyes for a moment to let the calm of a quiet moment steal over her.

"Penny for your thoughts," Lucas's voice came close to her ear.

She turned to find him sitting in the chair beside her.

"It's been a long night; I was just resting."

His eyes found hers. "You were wonderful tonight. Thank you. It meant everything to have you beside me through all this."

"It's what anyone would do."

"No, it wasn't. But it's what *you* did." He seemed to access her in a new way. "You're a special person M.T. Wingate, much more so than I knew when I first met you."

Uncomfortable with his praise, she looked over the rails of the high porch toward the street below. "Is it almost time for the parade?"

He glanced at his watch. "Should be starting any time now." He traced a hand up her arm. "Are you really okay? I imagine it upset you to think Tilly is already back in the area so soon, and supposedly all right."

"Beau said Bill Magee called Tilly's doctor. He said Tilly really was doing better. She's off drugs, herbs, and is receiving counseling for some of her other problems. The difference has been enough to bring Bobby Joe back into her life. Beau said Bobby Joe told him all the things that happened served as a wake-up call for Tilly, that she was acting like a new woman now—or more like the old one he fell in love with a long time ago."

"That's sweet, I guess, and I certainly should be eager to see another person get a second chance." She paused, twisting a piece of her hair.

"But?"

She turned her eyes to his. "But I'm not personally eager to see her anytime soon, despite it all. I'm with Suzannah there."

"Neither am I." He glanced up the street as sounds of the beginnings of the parade began to waft over the air.

"Daddy, it's time!" Suzannah danced over to point to the street.

They all pulled their chairs closer to the rails to enjoy the parade heading down the Parkway … marching bands playing John Philip Sousa songs, horses and riders decorated in patriotic colors, military groups, local floats lively with flags, glitter and music, picking-and-singing groups, area celebrities waving from cars.

Mallory relaxed with the pleasure of it and with the sweep of memories seeing the parade brought her. She'd watched this parade so many summers with her father as a little girl and then later with her grandparents. She looked across the porch to see Beau and Nonnie holding hands, exchanging a kiss in the dark.

Abby snuggled on Robert's lap and his hand held Elizabeth's as he pointed out things in the parade to Abby. The scenes of the Maples' family around them exuded the same sense of warmth, love, and family. She sat in her own cozy group with Lucas and Suzannah, as well, feeling a warm sense of family she struggled to keep from settling too sweetly into her consciousness. For she knew this was only an interlude for her. She'd soon be heading back to Savannah, to her own home and work where she belonged, as sweet as this time was.

As if picking up on her thoughts, Suzannah turned to hug her. "I'm glad you're here with us, Mallory, making me and Daddy a family."

Mallory watched Lucas raise his eyebrows at her remark before turning his gaze back to the street, not responding.

She smiled then. As nice as this summer interlude had been, it was only that. An interlude. She'd soon be heading home.

# CHAPTER 20

**A**s the next two weeks slipped by, Lucas couldn't help glancing at the calendar on his office wall and on his phone, counting off the remaining days to when Mallory would head back to Savannah. There were moments when he wished her gone already so he could quit agonizing and thinking about it. His other emotions weren't ones he wanted to examine.

Lucas had spent time with Mallory almost every day since the Fourth of July, sharing meals at his home, at the resort, or at Nonnie and Beau's. They'd taken more hikes together and enjoyed several side trips around the area, many with Suzannah. Every get-together they shared created another good memory—despite the subtle tension underlying their relationship. As the days moved by, Lucas knew both he and Mallory were increasingly aware of their limited time together.

"I hate to think about you leaving," he said to her one night as he kissed her goodnight, wishing for more.

She studied him with a look he couldn't interpret. "Well, don't think about it then," she replied, irritating him with her casual words. As if they could let the matter go so easily.

On his lunch hour, he drove up to the old cabin to think—and to pray a little—but the visit hadn't brought him any clear answers. He knew his feelings for Mallory were strong ones. In honest moments, he realized he'd probably fallen in love with her. How could he help it? She was smart, beautiful, and a good person— and she loved his child.

"You seem moody lately," Andy Kiley said, as Lucas walked back in the pro shop after lunch.

"Well, I've got a lot on my mind," Lucas answered, leaning on the counter. "I've got four little kittens at my house starting to take over the place, a tom cat still out of sorts from being fixed, and a group of thieves still active in the area ripping off cars at one place or another."

"We haven't had any more car thefts at the resort, though." Andy sat down on a stool behind the counter and Lucas noticed his hands shaking today.

"Why don't you go home, Andy? I can cover here in the shop for you. My afternoon lesson cancelled."

Andy scowled at him. "My hands may shake a little some days. Lucas, but my mind's still strong. I'm not ready to be turned out to pasture yet."

"I know that." Lucas fiddled with a pile of paper clips on the counter. "I simply feel guilty that you're working so many extra hours since we lost Barry. I hate that he's gone to prison for a time, too. It's still difficult to think about what he and his family are going through, but I need to start actively looking for another pro shop manager."

"There's time. You need to find the right person." His eyes met Lucas's. "It might be wise to look for someone with some golf skills that can give you relief and help when I'm not able to anymore. I'm doing all right now but the day will come."

"I don't look forward to that."

"Yeah, well life has a way of moving on. I've had a good life— sweet wife, two nice kids that have turned out all right, grandkids, my moments in the spotlight golfing on the tour and then all the years here at Millhouse. I can't complain." He sent Lucas a questioning look. "What about you and Beau's granddaughter? Seems like the two of you are getting awfully close."

Lucas tried to appear neutral. "Well, she's heading back to Savannah soon. She has work there, you know. Not much for her here in this backwoods community in the Smokies."

"If you say so."

Lucas drummed his fingers on the counter restlessly. "It's hard to know sometimes what you feel about someone, what you ought to do." He glanced toward the window, watching a golfer tee off on the first hole. "I went up to the old Bohanan cabin today with my lunch to think."

"Do any good?"

"No." He shook his head. "But I found something there I'd like you to look at. Let me go get it. I left it in the car."

Lucas came back in the shop a few minutes later carrying a small rusted tin box.

"What's this?" Andy took the box from him. "Looks like an old tobacco box from back in the day. It has some rusted lettering on it, too." He glanced up. "Where'd you find this?"

"Behind a loose rock in the fireplace. I was trying to straighten the rock and then realized why it wouldn't push back into place fully." He took the box back from Andy. "It's what's inside the box that surprised me. Looks to me like Chessy Bohanan must have been an admirer of yours."

Lucas took a couple of yellowed news clippings from inside the box. "Here's one about you winning a local tournament, another about an award you got with your picture." He handed the faded pieces to Andy.

The older man grinned. "Well, that was a long time ago. Wonder why he kept these clippings?"

"I don't know. The other clipping in the box was about Mallory's father's death." He passed the clipping to Andy. "You knew him, didn't you?"

Andy sighed. "Sure, we were good friends, even if not in the same age bracket. He and Leona Davis's boy Waylon, though, were best friends from school days. Both loved to hunt. Beau didn't care much for hunting, so I took the boys out with me a lot, even after they were grown. We went hunting together whenever Jarrett and Waylon came home. Mostly good times, those past days."

"I noticed the dates of the golf clippings and the date of the clipping about Jarrett's death were close to the same time."

"Yeah, I can see that." Andy studied the yellowed pieces. "Odd, that he'd keep old papers from that time. But he was the one who found Jarrett's body. Maybe it led him to save news clippings. Chessy wasn't much of a reader type."

Lucas dropped into a chair by the counter. "Do you think Jarrett Wingate's death was an accident, Andy? Mallory said some of the women in Nonnie's Monday Group talked like it wasn't."

Andy's voice hardened. "That's only gossipy, ugly talk. I can tell you for a fact it was an accident. I was hunting with the boy that day, looked for him with Beau and Waylon when he went missing. After Chessy Bohanan found Jarrett's body, it was Beau, Waylon, and me that went up the mountain and brought Jarrett home. We could see that no foul play occurred, just a tragic hunting accident. Don French, the primary police officer in the investigation back then, ruled it an accident, too." He pushed the clippings back into Lucas's hands. "I don't know why Chessy kept these old papers. He was a strange loner of a man. But don't go stirring up old wounds and trouble with Beau and Nonnie over this."

"I don't intend to," Lucas said, tucking the papers back into the tobacco box. "I was simply curious after finding this, that's all." He reached into the tin again. "I found something else in this old box, too. I don't know what it is, do you?" He held out a small wooden object to Andy.

"Well, look at that." Andy smiled. "It's an old wooden turkey call, probably one of Chessy's. He hunted a lot himself. A good hunter can make one of these really sing with some fine yelps and cuts, exactly like a wild tom turkey or hen." He laughed. "It looks homemade, too. Let me see it."

Lucas handed it to him.

Andy turned it over in his hands, and then grew a little quiet. "This is a real fine handmade piece. I'd like to keep it if you don't mind."

"I'd planned on showing it to Beau, to make sure it wasn't Jarrett's," he answered. "I thought Chessy might have found it when he discovered Jarrett's body and decided to keep it. If it is Jarrett's, it might hold sentimental value for Beau and Nonnie." He smiled at Andy. "If they don't recognize it, I'll tell them you'd like to have it."

"Yeah, well sure." Andy handed it over.

Later that evening, Lucas showed Beau the turkey call, the old clippings, and the tin box he found at Chessy's place. He and Suzannah had been invited to eat dinner at Wingate House with Nonnie, Beau, and Mallory. They'd moved out to the back patio to visit after dinner, when Lucas remembered to get the box out of his car for Beau to look at.

"Wonder why Chessy kept these old things?" Beau asked, studying each item. "Were these the only things in the box?"

"That's all," Lucas answered. "Just three old clippings and the turkey call."

"Well, that's odd." Beau turned the wooden call over in his hand. "Jarrett had a turkey call or two but I don't remember a fine handmade one like this. Maybe we'll get Leona to look at it. It might be Waylon's. If so, Waylon might want it back. Hunters get attached to their turkey calls."

"Keep the whole box then," Lucas said.

"I think Waylon's coming in from Asheville for a visit in the next week or two," Nonnie said. "Leona can show it to him when he comes to see if he recognizes it." She glanced at the box with a frown. "It sure is curious that Chessy kept these things, especially hidden away behind a rock in the fireplace."

"Aw, don't make something out of nothing." Beau laid the old box on the wrought iron table by his chair. "Chessy was a queer old guy, lived up there on the mountain all on his own. He probably kept money in this box, too, hidden away. A lot of old mountain men didn't trust banks much. These bits probably just got tucked in with his money."

"I'm sure you're right," Nonnie said, standing up. "I think I'll go in the house and bring out dessert now. Who wants ice cream on their apple pie?"

While Nonnie, Mallory and Suzannah went in to fix the pie, Lucas took advantage of the moment to tell Beau about finding Andy with his hands shaking earlier. "We've pushed a lot of extra work on Andy with Barry gone," he said. "I think we need to begin actively looking for a new pro shop manager. I started talking to a few people this afternoon already, and I've put out some feelers among people in the industry. I called my old golf buddy Chet Mincie, too, to see if he knew anybody looking for a job."

"Good golfer. Didn't he play with you back at the University of Tennessee, start on tour about the same time as you?"

"Yeah, he did. Nice guy. Married with four kids now." He paused. "Chet said I was lucky working here at the resort, having time with Suzannah and being away from the pressure of the tour. He's experiencing a rough time with his game lately, feels torn between the demands of the tour and the demands of his family."

"This leading somewhere?"

"Yes. Maybe. I have a sense that Chet might be open for a change. Wife's pregnant again." He tapped his fingers on the arm of his chair. "If we could expand our golf pro manager's position to include an assistant pro title Chet might be tempted to come back to Tennessee. His family and his wife Kathy's family are all still in the Knoxville area."

"Does he possess the skills to manage the shop? It's obvious he has the skills to be an assistant pro."

"We both majored in business at UT, Chet in accounting." He turned to look at Beau. "The opportunity might fall below what Chet thinks he should get in pay, but—like me—he's done well and he doesn't have to worry too much about money, even with four kids to raise and one on the way." He grinned at the thought.

"You're worried about something though."

"Yes. Andy still carries the title of assistant pro here at Millhouse. I'd hate to push him out with all he already has to deal with."

"Lucas, you know Andy doesn't work much on the course anymore. His game's gone and he knows that well." He scratched his short beard, thinking. "I tell you what. You feel out your friend a little. Put a tentative offer on the table if you want. Sweeten the salary we paid Barry." He named a figure. "I can handle Andy and find a way for him to stay useful. He likes working in the shop part-time. He can keep doing that and there are school events we host he can continue to help with. Andy wants the best for Millhouse, Lucas. You don't need to worry that he won't be on board with this if you can work it out with Chet. It would be a feather in our cap to get another pro golfer on our staff and I like the idea of hiring someone you know and have worked with to handle the books. We don't need any more trouble like we had with Barry."

"Thanks. I think Chet would be a good fit for us if he'll consider coming. He's easygoing, friendly, and generally patient. More so than I am." He laughed. "Chet's wife Kathy would be an asset to the community, too. She's a real organizer."

"A woman with a husband on the road half the time who's raising four kids on her own would need to be."

"Yes, and believe it or not, they have great kids. I always loved spending time at their house when we had off tour seasons in Arizona."

"Family is important." Beau fell silent for a few minutes. "Might be nice for you to have a little pressure off at the course, too. Give you a chance to travel if needed or to tend to other things that might take a priority." He sent a pointed look in Lucas's direction with those last words.

Lucas knew full well what Beau was talking about. "There's a lot to consider when you start thinking about changes to your life," he said with honesty. "And people's jobs and work are important to them."

Beau opened his mouth to reply, but then Suzannah came running out to join them, Nonnie and Mallory right behind, bringing their dessert. The two men wisely let the subject go.

After dessert Suzannah talked Mallory into walking home with them to see the kittens. Mallory stayed to play with them, teaching Suzannah how to pull a ribbon for them to chase.

"Jasper is the fastest," Suzannah said, giggling over the kittens scampering around the back porch after the ribbon.

Mallory and Suzannah had named the kittens now.

"What are their names again?" Lucas asked.

"Daddy, you need to remember. You wouldn't want someone to forget *your* name." She stopped her play to put her hands on her hips.

Mallory laughed. "The yellow marmalade one, that looks like Mr. Tom is Jasper, the calico is Muffin, the white female is Lily, and the Maine Coon-colored kitten, that looks like Baby—but is decidedly male—Suzannah named Buddy."

"Jasper, Muffin, Lily, and Buddy," Lucas repeated. "I'll try to remember."

Mallory smiled at him from where she sat cross-legged on the floor. "I'm glad you had Mr. Tom neutered." She glanced at the cat, sitting on the sofa watching the kittens' antics. "But you'll need to get Baby fixed, too, when she weans the kittens. I'm sure Mr. Tom isn't the only male cat in the neighborhood."

"Believe me, I'll remember to do that. It's going to be challenging enough to find homes for these four."

"Oh, can't we keep them?" Suzannah asked, sending him a beseeching look.

"Not a chance. We talked about this. Remember?" He sent her what he hoped was a stern look in return. "We have two cats already and that's enough."

Mallory traced a hand through his daughter's hair, causing Lucas a wrench to his heart with the gesture. "We already found homes for three of them nearby, so you'll get to see them sometimes. Elizabeth and Abby are taking two, Buddy and Muffin, and Nonnie says she may take Jasper. She's fond of marmalade-colored cats."

"That only leaves Lily, and she's your favorite, Mallory. You should keep her. "

Mallory stroked the small white kitten, already showing signs of having long hair like her mother. "Lily is pretty, but I live in a city townhouse and work all day. It would be lonely for Lily being by herself so much. I don't have a place where she can go outside either. I think Lily would be happier in the country with a family."

"Do you *have* to go back, Mallory?" Suzannah scrambled over to wrap her arms around Mallory's neck. "You could stay here and be a family with us—and you could keep Lily."

"You're sweet to say that." Mallory hugged Suzannah and then detached her arms from around her neck. "But remember you, Abby, and Elizabeth are coming to Savannah to see me this fall, and I'll be back for Thanksgiving and for Christmas." She smiled at the child.

Suzannah pouted. "It's not the same." She gave Lucas an accusing look. "Daddy likes you, too. He said so. I know he wants you to stay, don't you, Daddy?"

"We'll all miss Mallory," he said, not meeting Mallory's eyes with his words. "But she has work to do at Whittier. That's the publisher she works for. They are eager to get her back, too."

Suzannah sighed. "Will you read to me tonight while you can, Mallory?"

"Certainly." Mallory tweaked her nose. "Let's go start getting you ready for bed now. You can be thinking about which books you want to read."

Suzannah was already reciting book titles as Mallory followed her upstairs.

About an hour later, Lucas heard Mallory rattling around in the kitchen.

"I made coffee," he called.

"Thanks. I see it," she said.

In a few minutes, she made her way out to the screened porch carrying a cup of hot coffee and then curled up on the sofa beside Tom, tucking one foot under her in a position Lucas knew well.

She scratched the cat's head. "Pretty boy. You're about to get back to your old self now," she said to him.

Lucas laughed. "He'll never be back to his old self, if you know what I mean."

She laughed in return, that deep throaty laugh of hers that always rippled across his heartstrings. Lucas looked across at her, sipping her coffee, so relaxed and comfortable.

"I'll miss looking across the porch and seeing you here in the evenings," he said.

"I'm not here every evening," she answered.

"You've been here often enough to leave a strong memory behind."

"Well, that's nice of you to say." She pushed a strand of hair behind her ear. "Your daughter pressed her advantage tonight and talked me into three books instead of two."

"She's good at that," he said.

Mallory's cell phone rang, interrupting them.

"My purse is beside you." She pointed. "Reach in there and grab my phone and answer it. I'm sure it's Nonnie or Beau wondering why I'm staying so late."

Lucas pulled her iPhone from her purse, and answered the call. "Lucas here."

"Lucas who?" boomed a male voice. "Who are you?"

"I might ask the same of you," Lucas replied in irritation.

"This is Ethan Broussard, Mallory's fiancé, and what are you doing with her phone?"

Lucas heard Mallory groan. "I need to get that," she said, reaching for the phone.

He held it away from her. "Mr. Broussard," he said into the phone. "Mallory is no longer engaged to you and no longer interested in you. She let you know that quite clearly and also asked you to quit contacting her. I think you should keep that in mind in the future."

"We had a misunderstanding I'm trying to work out, which is certainly no business of yours," Ethan snapped back. "Now let me speak to Mallory right now."

"Why should I? You let her down when she needed you. You cheated on her if I got the story right. You don't deserve the time of day from her."

"Well, I don't know *who* you think you are," Ethan said in a calm but snotty tone. "But I can assure you I'd be surprised if you're the sort of man a cultured woman like Mallory Wingate would be interested in for long. Mallory is used to life in the city, not the backwoods of the mountains, and I have it on good authority she's leaving to come back here at the end of the month. I seriously doubt you'll be coming with her."

Mallory managed to snag the phone away from him. "Ethan, why are you calling me?" she asked, trying to reign in her annoyance. "I asked you not to call me here."

"We have a lot to talk about Mallory," he said, loudly enough for Lucas to still hear his words. "I expect to take you out to dinner as soon as you get back so we can talk. I know you've been through a difficult emotional time, but we can get past that. You know I love you, Mallory. And you know we were making plans to marry. Our relationship came under a lot of stress when your mother got ill and moved in with you, but we can move past that. I talked with Dr. Henry about it."

"My doctor?" Mallory's mouth dropped open.

"Yes, and he thinks we should try to work on and resolve our relationship."

"Look, Ethan, I really don't want to discuss this right now."

"Because that man is there?"

"For many reasons." She tried to keep her temper in check. "I'm hanging up now, and I don't want you to call me back. If there is any talking we need to do—and I doubt that—we'll do it when I get home."

"Very well. *Je volus verrai ensuite*," he answered in a sultry tone. "*Je t'aime* and *t'adore, cherie*." And he hung up.

"What the heck did he say there at the end?" Lucas demanded.

She sighed and tucked the phone into her pocket. "Just 'I will see you then' and 'I love you and adore you.'"

"He's very confident and sure of himself."

"Yes, he always has been." She closed her eyes. "Ethan is *very* sure of what he wants."

Lucas caught the subtle meaning behind her words that she didn't say.

Before he could decide how to respond, Mallory stood and walked toward the kitchen with her coffee cup. "I need to head back to the house," she said. "Beau and Nonnie will worry if I'm any later getting back."

"I'll walk you to the gate," he said as she came back to the porch and picked up her purse to drape it across her shoulder.

"You don't need to. You've had a long day."

"I want to," he said, watching her shrug at his words and head out the door.

He caught up with her as she started down the path. "Are you upset with me about something?"

"Only somewhat, because you stepped out of line to go after Ethan."

"I don't like him."

She shook her head. "I can't imagine he's thinking positive thoughts about you right now either."

"Will you see him when you go back to Savannah?"

She paused at the gate. "Why should it bother you if I do?"

"What do you mean why should it bother me?" He felt his anger rise. "You know it will bother me. He's a jerk and he hurt you. I don't want you spending time with someone like that."

She put a hand on his chest. "Lucas, you don't have any say over who I might or might not see—either here or in Savannah."

"That's an unkind thing to say." He reached for her, meaning to kiss her and make her see she was wrong.

But she kept her hand on his chest and turned her head away.

"You know I care for you," he said, his voice softening.

"Yes, but even someone like Ethan can say I love you and I adore you to someone he cares about. You can't even do that. That lets me know clearly where I stand with you. And what my future is with you."

"You know it's complicated between us, Mallory. We both have careers and work that matter to us. I have a child, and you don't really want to give up your work at Whittier, do you?"

"Why? Are you asking me to?"

Lucas hesitated, and as soon as he did Mallory opened the gate and stepped through it, starting away from him down the path toward Wingate House.

Lucas stood, miserable and confused, watching her go.

# CHAPTER 21

**O**n Monday, Mallory spent the morning working on edits for Sonia Butler's book. Whittier had signed a three-book contract with the author, with Mallory as her editor. Mallory found Sonia's work relatively clean of errors and well written, but even with a strong author, there was always a large amount of work to do with the first edit. Authors lived too close to their work to see the areas where their stories slowed or read awkwardly, even when they self-edited well.

Nonnie stuck her head out the door to where Mallory sat working on the porch. "Did you get any lunch?" she asked.

"No, but I'll stop in a minute and fix something."

"Just as I thought," Nonnie replied. "I brought you a tray." She pushed open the door, bringing out a tray with lunch, tea, and a dessert on it.

Mallory smiled at her. "You're spoiling me while I'm here."

"You deserve a little spoiling, and you know this is what I served to the Monday Group for lunch today. It was no trouble bringing you a tray." She sat down in a rocker on the porch, pushing the chair back and forth in a gentle rhythm. "I'm glad to sit down to rest for a minute."

"I should have stopped to help you clean up after the luncheon," Mallory said with regret. She glanced at the computer screen in front of her. "But I got involved in editing and forgot the time."

"Spoken like someone who loves her work." Nonnie smiled at her. "Are you looking forward to getting back to Savannah?"

"Yes in many ways." Mallory pulled Nonnie's tray toward her and cut into a wedge of homemade quiche, glad to see salad and fruit with it today. Nonnie's excellent cooking had tucked a few extra pounds on her since she came.

"I imagine you'll miss Lucas and Suzannah when you leave."

Mallory heard the careful nonchalance her grandmother tried to put into the words. "You know I will, Nonnie, and I'll miss you and Grandad—and Elizabeth, Robert, Abby, and many others I've grown fond of while here."

"Only fond of?" Nonnie asked, more directly now.

Mallory sighed. "Whatever feelings I've developed for Lucas James, which I know is what you're probing about, are still uncertain ones, and Lucas is still uncertain, too, about his feelings for me."

"Things haven't looked uncertain to Beau and me—or to Elizabeth and Robert," she replied. "Maybe you should look closer at those feelings."

Mallory ate a little more of her lunch, trying to decide what to say. "There are days when I think those feelings are more, but Lucas's own uncertainty makes me hold any of my own deeper feelings in check. He experienced an unhappy first marriage and is having difficulty deciding whether he wants to get into another serious relationship."

"I think he's already in another serious relationship and simply doesn't want to acknowledge it. Maybe you should try to help things along."

Mallory raised her eyebrows. "I'm surprised at you, Nonnie."

She waved a hand, blushing. "Oh, I didn't mean that. I only meant you might make your own feelings clearer to him."

Mallory thought back to Saturday evening when she took a chance and did exactly that. "I doubt it would make a difference," she said, not wanting to tell Nonnie she threw out a challenge comment to Lucas before they parted. She smiled at her grandmother. "Besides, I'm old-fashioned enough to believe the man should come after the woman. Perhaps it's from editing so many romance books over the years."

"Well, it is better for a girl's ego when that happens." She touched her wedding rings thoughtfully. "I still remember how Beau pursued me when we courted and it's a good memory."

"Well, you see?" She drank some of Nonnie's peach tea. "I want that, too. I want to remember being pursued—and being loved enough to be pursued."

"Hmmm." Nonnie rocked back and forth a few more times. "Well, perhaps Lucas will come around when the time for you to leave grows closer."

"Perhaps and perhaps not. Even if he does come around, I need to think and pray a lot about what to do. I love my work and moving here would mean giving it up."

"You're continuing to edit while you're here now." Nonnie gestured toward the computer.

"Yes, but it's not the same." Mallory decided to change the subject. "I heard some of the women in your Monday Group talking about Tilly when I went in the tea room to say hello to everyone. What's the story on her?"

"Well, actually the news is very good. Tilly has responded well to counseling and resolved her medical issues. She's been staying with Bobby Joe at his house in Sevierville, and it looks like the two of them will get back together. Several of the girls visited with Tilly last week and said she seems like the old Tilly we remember from our younger days."

"I know I should feel happy about that, but I'm still glad she didn't come to the lunch today."

"Old hurts and disappointments in people are hard to get past," Nonnie said. "I have to say, though, I'm glad to hear the good reports about Tilly. I'm happy if she's changing back to the woman we remember—before she became such a worrywart and got into all those strange health fetishes and weird beliefs. Polly told us Tilly started coming back to church, too. That can only help."

Mallory finished her lunch while Nonnie chatted on about Tilly and other topics of conversation from the Monday Group's luncheon.

"I let Leona take that old tin box Lucas found at the Bohanan cabin to show Waylon when he comes in this weekend," Nonnie said. "Leona didn't recognize the turkey call but she said Waylon might remember it."

"Yes, I heard her say that. I was helping you serve lunch then. Gladys said we ought to go back to the cabin to see if we can locate anything else related to Daddy's death. She said we might find something to solve the mystery of it."

Nonnie pursed her mouth in annoyance. "That Gladys is always trying to stir up something out of nothing. Jarrett's death was an accident, pure and simple. I've prayed over it many a time and never felt any unrest in my spirit about that time, despite the occasional gossip."

"Still, no one ever came forward to confess firing the shot that killed Daddy. Don't you ever wonder about it?"

"Only in an odd moment or two," she admitted. "Don French and the police always believed the hunter, who fired that haphazard shot hitting Jarrett, probably never even knew he hit a person. Those types of random hunting accidents are more common than you'd think. The hunter might have been a tourist in the area, far away in another state now. It's highly unlikely there will ever be a definitive answer about who fired that shot, Mallory."

"I know," she agreed, finishing a last bite of the lemon pie Nonnie brought her for dessert.

Nonnie glanced at her watch. "What are you going to do this afternoon while I go into town to do my grocery shopping and errands?"

"Probably finish my editing and then take a walk for some exercise."

"That sounds nice." She stood. "I'll take your tray back to the kitchen as I head that way if you'd like."

After her grandmother left, Mallory settled back into her work for a time, but her mind kept drifting to that last conversation she and her grandmother had about her father's shooting. Despite Nonnie's words, it seemed peculiar that Lucas found those news clippings hidden away in Chessy's cabin, especially the one about her father's death. It made Mallory wonder if Chessy might have been the one who accidently shot her father. He was the one who found Jarrett. Perhaps he accidently shot him, as well. If so, like Gladys said, there might be something more at the cabin to help resolve the mystery. It would be good to know what really happened.

Mallory glanced at her watch. It was only a little after two. She could walk to the cabin and be back before five to help Nonnie with dinner. Mallory closed her computer and took it into the house. She'd told Nonnie she planned to talk a walk, but she knew if she called to tell her exactly where she planned to go, Nonnie would try to talk her out of it. Lucas said it was only about two and a half miles to the cabin, crossing over Rock Creek at the falls and walking uphill after. The trail was also on resort property.

Her mind made up, Mallory put on her hiking socks and boots, tossed a water bottle and a few small items into her waist pack, and headed out the back door of Wingate House. She tacked a note on the bulletin board in the kitchen to remind Nonnie she'd gone walking, in case Nonnie returned before she did.

Mallory got to the old cabin a little after four. Just as Lucas suggested, the mileage to the cabin was about two and a half miles total, but she'd dawdled along the way—stopping at the cemetery, looking at summer wildflowers—and she had to take off her boots and socks to wade the stream at Rock Creek Falls, too.

After dropping her waistpack on an old chair on the cabin's front porch, Mallory pushed open the front door to the cabin and stood looking around for a few minutes at the rundown state inside. She really needed to talk to Beau about fixing this place up. Millhouse could rent it if some care and money were put into it. The little cabin had a rustic charm with its wide front porch, old rock chimney and wood floors. But it was nasty and dusty inside. Mallory wrinkled her nose. The windows looked filthy and a thin layer of dust and grime lay over the rickety sideboard and battered table and chairs in the main room. Spider webs festooned the corners of the walls, and Mallory imagined mice and other vermin found the cabin a nice little place to call home. *Ewww.* She wouldn't stay long.

Crossing to the fireplace, she found the loose stone after a little examination but nothing else lay in the space behind it. The rest of the rocks in the fireplace seemed secure and her exploration around the main room revealed no other place to hide anything. A peek into the even grimier kitchen with its open cabinets showed nothing but dirt, so Mallory moved on to the cabin's one bedroom.

She made her way around a broken-down chair, leaning to one side, to stop beside the old iron bedstead, with a faded soiled mattress still on it. The ends of the bedposts, rusted and broken off, looked like the tips of medieval swords. *Who'd choose a bed frame like this?* she wondered. Mallory angled around the bed toward a battered chest-of-drawers in the corner. Maybe she'd find something in one of the drawers.

Voices and the sound of the front door opening caused her to freeze in place instead. She heard two men's voices and then the sound of a dog growling.

"The dang dog's growling," one said. "Think there's somebody here?"

"Not likely. Probably a varmint or something, but we'll check."

Mallory heard steps walking around in the cabin and then toward the closed bedroom door.

"Keep your stocking over your face just in case," she heard one of the men say.

The door opened and the dog began to bark and bare its teeth, pulling against the man's hand holding its collar. Mallory pressed against the wall, wanting to scream but finding no sound came out. Both men wore women's hosiery pulled over their heads, grotesque and frightening to see.

"Dagnabbit, if it ain't a girl," the shorter man said.

Mallory curled her arms around herself, scared to see the dog growling and lunging against its restraint. "Don't let the dog hurt me," she managed to say.

"Bandit, sit down," the taller man said, jerking on the dog's collar. "It's only a girl and no need for you to act out."

Amazingly the dog quit growling and sat.

The taller man took a small gun from his pocket. "Girl, that dog ain't the worst of the trouble you've gotten yourself into. You didn't pick a good day to be here and that's a fact."

"I have nothing valuable on me and no money." Mallory tried to keep her voice from shaking as she said the words. "I hiked in."

"That explains why we didn't see no car," the other said.

"What are you doing up here?" the tall man asked, looking around in puzzlement at the dirty old bedroom. "This old cabin ain't close to anything and it sure ain't nothing worth seeing."

"A mountain man my grandfather used to know once lived here. I was curious to see the old place again," she answered. "I can go now." She started away from the wall, but the dog began to growl again when she did.

"I'd stay where you are if I was you," the tall man told her, reaching down to take the dog's collar again and speaking to it once more.

"What are we going to do about her?" the short man asked.

"I don't know. Tie her up for now. There's some rope in the truck." He looked at Mallory. "I won't use a gag if you don't decide to start hollering and carrying on. But you'd better settle your mind to the fact that you aren't going anywhere for a while. We've got some work to do and we'll need to call in and find out what we ought to do about you when we're finished."

Mallory's nightmare continued as the short man came back with rope from the truck and tied her hands behind her. Too tightly. She winced.

"Don't tie her up like you would a man." The taller man fussed at him. "Just be sure she's secure and tie a line from the rope on her wrists to that bedpost so she can't go far. I don't want her causing any trouble. Set her down on the bed there when you're done." He glanced at his watch. "We got work to do and a time schedule to do it in."

"Think she'll stay put?" the shorter man said as they left the room.

"Yeah. She ain't going nowhere. You go on and do what you need to do. I'll go out to the truck and call in to find out what we ought to do about the girl when we're finished."

Mallory heard the short man chuckle as they shut the door. She knew their voices now, even when she couldn't see them.

"She's a right pretty woman," he said. "It might not be safe to leave her alone with you."

The tall man snorted. "Don't worry about that. Rape ain't a charge I want on my record nor nothin' worse either. If they want her brought in, I guess they can do what they want with her. But we ain't gonna be doing it."

"Who do you think she is?"

"I don't know, but I reckon we could find out if we needed to."

Mallory sat on the old mattress listening to them, trying to get her heartbeat to settle down. *What in the world were these men doing here and what had she gotten herself into?*

The short man posed another question. "If I can't get the car started that we spotted earlier with our electronic device, do you want me to try another one?"

"Yeah, but I don't think you'll have a problem. We've gotten SUVs like that one before with no trouble. But try another if you hit a snag. Call me as soon as you're in the car and heading out. I don't want to hang around here too long in case someone comes looking for the girl. My guess is Hawk will want us to leave her tied up here. She won't have much to tell. I don't think they'll want us to take her to where she could see even more and be a greater problem."

"Think I'll run into anyone as I hike in?"

"I doubt it. That group of hikers from New Jersey, staying at the retreat house, plan to spend the night on the trail tonight. None of them will be coming back to use the cars they left until late tomorrow. But you'd better start on down the trail now so you can drive out of the resort with the employees and golfers around five like we planned. It will draw less attention to you."

She heard them opening the front door of the cabin.

"Are you going to stay in the cabin to watch the girl while I'm gone?" the shorter man asked.

"No. I'll stay out here on the porch with the dog or in the truck. That cabin isn't a place that makes you to want to spend more time in it than you need to. If the girl starts trying to move around the dog will know it."

The shorter man laughed. "You'd think a pretty girl like that wouldn't want to be digging around in a rundown old place like this, wouldn't you?"

"I'm sure she's regretting that decision now."

And then Mallory heard the front door shut.

She closed her eyes, trying to settle the fear that had left her shaking all over and weak in the knees. She took deep breaths to calm herself and tried to think. *What could she do?* She looked around. *Not much.* She was tied up tightly and secured to the old bed frame, and even if she could find a way to get out of the bedroom, the tall man and the dog were still there.

From their comments, it seemed obvious the men belonged to the theft ring stealing cars around the mountain area. They obviously planned to steal a car parked at Retreat House at the resort today.

Mallory sighed. She wondered if they'd hiked in from this point to steal the other cars from the resort property. It was a smart plan. A man hiking wouldn't draw much attention.

She looked toward the one grimy window in the bedroom, vines grown over it and shrubbery blocking most of the sunlight. She was in a bad situation. Furthermore, no one even knew where she was. Mallory regretted her hasty decision now to come up here by herself. But who'd have thought she'd run into thieves? It read like a scene from one of Whittier's suspense novels.

Fighting down the tears, Mallory wondered if she'd ever get back to Savannah to edit any novels again. The tall man said he'd call to find out what the higher ups wanted to do with her. *What if they took her in?* She wondered. *Or what if they decided to kill her so she wouldn't talk?*

Time crept by as she waited, every minute filled with a new fear or worry. Worn out from it finally, Mallory dropped onto the bed on her side, closed her eyes and started to pray. It's what she should have done from the first.

Sometime later—she lost track of time—Mallory heard the truck start up and heard the man whistle and call to the dog. A few minutes later, she heard the sounds of the truck leaving.

Had the other man successfully broken into and driven off in the targeted car? Was the tall man now leaving with the dog as he suggested he might? He didn't come back to speak to her, but why should he? He didn't care if she was scared and worried or about what might happen to her.

Feeling a flash of anger at the thought, Mallory pulled herself into a sitting position. Either they'd left her here, not caring what happened to her or if anyone ever found her, or they planned to send someone back to get her later. Either option was awful to consider.

Noticing the dimming light outside the window reminded Mallory, too, that dark would fall soon. She didn't even want to think about what it would be like to spend the night in this old cabin in the middle of nowhere all by herself. She tried to think. *What could she do?* Her eyes moved around the almost barren room and then back to the bedposts on the bed. Hadn't she noticed earlier that the rusted tops on the bedstead frame looked like medieval spears? Maybe she could use them to cut the rope.

She struggled to get closer to one of the bedposts, maneuvering to get the rope behind her into a position where she could saw it against one of the sharp posts. She worked for over an hour to gradually fray and shred the rope, stopping several times to weep over the difficulty of it. The sharp edge of the bedpost stabbed her arms often in the process, making her cry with the pain. Finally— and feeling like shouting to celebrate—Mallory felt the last of the rope break, freeing her wrists.

Slipping out of the bedroom quietly, she crept across the main room of the cabin to look outside. No truck, no car, and no one in sight. She opened the front door carefully, looking and listening to be sure they hadn't left the dog to guard her. Then she raced outside and behind the cabin to go to the bathroom—a major need before anything else. Returning to the cabin porch, she found her waistpack still on the old chair, slipped it on and started back down the trail.

Night was beginning to fall and Mallory didn't relish hiking back on a dark trail without a flashlight, but she had little choice. If she took the road, she might run into the thieves or some of their ring returning to get her. And she knew the road down the mountain was a long one.

By the time she got down the hill to the stream and the falls, darkness had enveloped the shadowy mountain path. Mallory glanced at her watch. It was nearly eight o'clock. She took off her shoes and socks, waded the stream, put them back on and moved on as quickly as she could.

She could barely make out the path in front of her now, and the sounds around her in the darkness made her skin crawl. Mallory fell twice, not able to see roots in the pathway. Only a trickle of moonlight now and then through the trees kept her basically on the trail.

As she walked on, she felt a sharp branch swat at her face, got her leg caught in a blackberry vine, and nearly screamed as a small animal scurried across the dark path in front of her. But she kept walking. When she finally reached the trail intersection and the broader pathway leading downhill to the resort, she felt like weeping for joy. Following this more traveled path proved easier and she soon began to see the lights of Ivy Cottage and Wingate House in the distance.

Tears of relief trickled down her face as Mallory walked the last piece of the path home. This late in the day, she knew Beau and Nonnie were probably out looking for her, worried sick, too. With this in mind, she turned toward Lucas's house. He'd been in her thoughts all day, and right now she simply wanted to throw herself in his arms and feel safe again after this awful time.

Letting herself in the back screened porch of Ivy Cottage, she followed the sound of voices into the kitchen, finding Lucas and Suzannah starting to fix their bedtime snack.

Suzannah saw her first and shrieked. "Mallory, what happened? Nobody knew where you were. Did Tilly get you again or did you get lost?"

Lucas turned toward her, his eyes wide with shock.

Thrilled with relief to see him, Mallory flew across the kitchen and into his arms, bursting into tears and holding on to his shirt. She knew she looked a fright but she didn't care. She just felt so glad to be safe again and away from those awful men. Safe against Lucas's heart.

It took Mallory a minute or two to realize Lucas wasn't cuddling and hugging her back. Suzannah was holding on to her leg, crying, but Lucas had stiffened.

He separated himself from her, his eyes almost cold. "Everyone's been worried sick about you," he said, glancing toward his daughter. "Let me take Suzannah upstairs. Then I'll come and help you clean up before I take you home to your grandparents. You're obviously very upset."

He turned and picked up his daughter.

"But Daddy," Suzannah cried. "I want to stay and help Mallory. We shouldn't leave her by herself. She's been hurted, you can tell. She's crying and upset. She needs us."

Ignoring her comments, Lucas carried her out of the room.

Standing in the kitchen alone, Mallory felt stunned. Had he really just walked out and left her here? *How could he do that?* After all she'd been through? She couldn't believe it.

Still weeping and in shock, Mallory turned and made her way through the screened porch again and out the back door of the house. She'd go to Nonnie and Beau's instead. She needed to be with someone who loved her.

# CHAPTER 22

Lucas settled Suzannah into bed, with continuing complaints and tears, and then headed back downstairs to Mallory. She wasn't in the kitchen when he got back. *Had she gone into the bathroom to start cleaning up?* Lucas glanced around in confusion. Perhaps he shouldn't have left her. He'd seen she'd been hurt, saw traces of dried blood on her arms, scratches all over her. It was obvious she was emotionally upset, but he didn't think the scene one Suzannah needed to deal with.

He began to look for Mallory, checking the den, the guest room downstairs, and the bathroom. He went out on the screened porch and, noticing the door slightly ajar, went outside to look down the pathway. *Surely she wouldn't have left again as upset as she was*, he thought. He walked down the flagstone path to the gate and then let his eyes scan down the broader path leading to Wingate House. Not a sign of her.

Worried now, Lucas headed back to the house. *Where would she have gone?* His cell phone rang as he let himself in the back door.

"Lucas here."

"It's Beau. I wanted to let you know Mallory came on here. Nonnie thought I should call."

"Is she all right? Whatever happened to her? I know people were searching all evening after she didn't come back from her walk. I searched, too, with Robert, while Elizabeth kept the girls earlier. When Mallory showed up here, in such bad shape, I ran upstairs to settle Suzannah and when I came back she was gone."

"So I heard." Beau's voice sounded hard.

Lucas caught the curt tone in his voice. "Do you think I shouldn't have left her to take Suzannah upstairs? The child's too little to see stuff like that …"

"You've done it again, Lucas," Beau interrupted. "You don't walk out on a woman who's been through what Mallory experienced…"

"Listen. I don't know what Mallory might have experienced, Beau. I assumed she got lost or something, seeing those scratches and all." Lucas knew irritation threaded into his words.

"You didn't wait around to find out, either. If you had you'd never have left that girl alone like you did."

A wail from the doorway interrupted their call. "Where's Mallory?" Suzannah cried, scrubbing at tears on her face. "I want to see Mallory. She's hurted."

Lucas heard Beau snort, hearing the child in the background. "Even that child has better sense than you. Let me speak to her."

Rattled but responding to Beau's authoritative tone, Lucas handed the phone to Suzannah, telling her, "Mallory's at Beau and Nonnie's. Beau wants you to know she's all right."

Lucas leaned against the doorway, trying to think as he heard Beau assure Suzannah that Mallory was fine.

"But I want to see her," Suzannah cried.

"You can come see her tomorrow, sweetie," he heard Beau say. "I know she would like that. Right now she's really tired. She got locked in an old cabin in the woods by some bad men and had to get away and walk home mostly in the dark. It's been a scary time for her."

"Like with Tilly." Suzannah nodded, already calming down while talking to Beau.

"A lot like that," he agreed. "She's getting a good bath now and Nonnie's fixing her something to eat and then she's going to get a good night's rest. She'll feel lots better in the morning."

Lucas signaled that Suzannah should give him the phone back. "Tell me the rest," he said.

Beau sighed. "Mallory got curious about the items you found at

Chessy Bohanan's cabin relating to her father. She hiked up there this afternoon while Nonnie was shopping to see if she might find anything else. She ran into the car thieves. They'd been hiking in from the old cabin to steal cars from the resort. They stole another car from Retreat House's parking lot this afternoon. Mallory has experienced a pretty rough time of it but she's going to be all right." He paused. "It could have been a lot worse. We're fortunate. They tied her up and left her there, but she managed to break her ropes, sawing them off on a rusted bedpost, cutting herself up in the process, and then she got away. She had to hike back in the dark and experienced some falls, too—a pretty intense day overall."

"I had no idea." Lucas felt stunned at Beau's account.

"A thing to tell yourself, Lucas, when you think this over later is that Mallory came to you first before she came to us."

A sweep of guilt hit Lucas at the words. "I let her down."

"I'll be honest. You did, and she shed tears over that after she came to us."

"Will you explain to her I was concerned about Suzannah?" he asked. "Or maybe we could come over now?"

"Tomorrow's soon enough." Beau stopped to speak to Nonnie. "I need to go. You tuck Suzannah in and assure her Mallory is all right." And he hung up.

Lucas glanced at his daughter to see a frown on her small face.

"You see? She needed us, Daddy." Suzannah obviously heard Beau's words. "We shouldn't have left her. It hurted her feelings."

"Yes, I see that now." Lucas picked Suzannah up to start back upstairs with her. "I didn't read the situation accurately."

"We need to tell Mallory we're sorry."

He kissed her cheek. "Yes, we do. We'll tell her that tomorrow when we go over to Beau and Nonnie's, okay?"

After settling Suzannah into bed again, Lucas paced the floor, thinking about Mallory, remembering her tears, the cuts and scratches he saw on her arms and face, the anguish and relief in her eyes when she ran across the room to throw herself at him. He saw something more he'd been too stupid to see before, too.

As Beau said, Mallory came to him first when hurt. What should that tell him? Why couldn't he respond to her as he should have?

Glancing at his watch, he called Perry Ammons, even though it was late, needing to talk to him about what happened. "Why didn't I see what Mallory needed most of me and respond the way I should have?" he asked after relating the situation to him.

"Let me ask you this," Perry said. "In the past, when Cecily began to act out emotionally or had difficult times when Suzannah was a baby, what did you do?"

Lucas tried to remember and then sighed. "I tried to get Suzannah out of the picture." He stopped at his own words. "I did the same thing again without thinking, didn't I? I went into flashback automatically."

"I'd say that's it. Now that you're thinking it through, you realize your response should have been a different one. Right?"

Lucas closed his eyes. "Even Suzannah knew the right thing to do and she's only five. What kind of a creep am I, Perry?"

"Emotional healing takes time. You've examined your past with Cecily very little before this. It's only now you're really dealing with what you went through during your marriage to her and examining how it affected you."

"Well, I really failed Mallory tonight because of it." He slumped into a leather chair in the den, keeping the phone to one ear.

"You said you planned going over there tomorrow. Explain to Mallory why you acted as you did," Perry advised. He chuckled a little before adding, "And like Suzannah suggested, say you're sorry, too."

Lucas couldn't enjoy the humor of the situation like Perry. He paced the floor much of the night, getting little sleep.

The next morning he called the pro shop and talked to Denise. "I'll be late coming in this morning," he told her. "You probably heard Mallory inadvertently ran into those car thieves last night and got a bad scare. I need to go by Wingate House this morning to check on her. If you wouldn't mind, could you see if Andy would take my ten o'clock lesson with Pat Mulhanney?"

"I'm sure he would ordinarily but Andy went to Wingate House himself," she said. "I can call Pat and reschedule, though. I know he won't mind. Or Dale might help him with his swing. Dale isn't the golfer you and Andy are, but he plays well enough to help Pat. I'd say Pat would be happy with that solution, too, and Dale would enjoy a round of golf with Pat. They're friends."

Before Lucas hung up, Denise added, "Don't forget you're flying out the day after tomorrow to help with the Grayhawk Golf Club's Charity Pro-Am Tournament in Arizona where you used to live. Ruth Sisson, the bookkeeper at the resort, made your reservations. She called to say she emailed you all the information and for you to look it over and check back with her if you need to."

Lucas sighed. He'd almost forgotten the Pro-Am coming up. He'd promised friends in the Scottsdale area he'd help with it over a year ago. He'd be gone for a few days, but the event was for a good cause.

Hunting up Suzannah now, Lucas headed out the back door to walk to Wingate House. After their visit with Mallory, he would take Suzannah on to Elizabeth's and then get back to the office. He and Beau had a meeting scheduled with the sheriff later today about the latest car theft. He imagined they'd want to talk to Mallory, too, to see if she saw or heard anything that might help the investigation.

Coming in the back door, he found Andy sitting at the kitchen table with Beau. It looked like the older man had been crying, surprising Lucas.

Beau gestured them on with a hand wave. "Mallory's upstairs in her room with Nonnie. Take Suzannah on up."

Lucas walked up the stairs, pausing at Mallory's door to knock. Nonnie opened the door and Suzannah flew past her to fling herself on Mallory, tucked up in the bed. "Are you okay?" she asked, patting Mallory's cheek.

Mallory gave her a hug. "Yes, I'm doing better now."

"We came to see you and to say we're sorry, didn't we, Daddy?" She turned her eyes to him.

He nodded as Mallory's eyes studied him quietly.

Suzannah looked Mallory over. "We should have taken care of you when you were hurted. Daddy thought I was too little to help, but I'm not."

"You're a sweet, kind girl," Nonnie told her, leaning over to give the child a big hug. "I know Mallory is glad you came by to check on her."

Lucas could see bruises and scratches on Mallory's arms and face and her eyes looked shadowed.

"Nonnie, do you think I might talk to Mallory for a few minutes by myself?" he asked.

Nonnie glanced at Mallory and she nodded.

The older woman reached for the child's hand. "While your daddy talks to Mallory for a minute, let's walk downstairs and get a few books for you and Mallory to look at. You'll know the best ones to pick."

"Okay," she said, scrambling off the bed. "I know Daddy wants to say he's sorry all by himself."

Lucas saw a small smile flicker on Mallory's face.

"Get the naughty Nancy books, *Naughty Nancy* and *Naughty Nancy Goes to School*," Mallory told Suzannah. "You can read both of those to me by yourself because they only have pictures in them and no words."

"Those are good books, too," Suzannah said, smiling as she and Nonnie left.

Mallory moved her eyes back to Lucas, still standing in the doorway. "It's safe to come in. I won't fall apart emotionally today."

Lucas winced at her words and then crossed the room to slump into the chair by her bed. "I was a jerk last night," he said. "I'm really sorry. I called Perry Ammons to talk once I came to myself. He said I reverted back, doing the same thing I used to do when Cecily had one of her emotional times—immediately trying to get Suzannah out of the scene. I know I wasn't there for you like I should have been."

Her serious thoughtful eyes studied him again before she answered. "Beau said he told you what I went through yesterday." She paused as if thinking out what she wanted to say next. "It's not inappropriate, Lucas, for a person to break down after an ordeal like I faced. Those men might have raped me, cut me up, killed me, or dropped me off in the mountains somewhere. They were criminals and I listened to them discuss the possibilities for handling me. When they left me, tied up in a nasty bedroom in that old cabin by myself, I didn't know if they'd come back for me or if they just intended to leave me there. You can imagine the idea of spending the night there alone was *not* a good one. I was scared."

She sighed, pausing for a minute. "But I kept my head and got away. When I finally got out of danger and walked into your kitchen, after running on pure adrenalin all those hours, I collapsed. That's totally natural and normal. But you couldn't see that. All you saw was that I was having another breakdown. That I was like Cecily, that I might upset Suzannah and your well-ordered world. You didn't offer me support and kindness when I desperately needed it. So I came here, to people that I knew loved me."

Lucas looked down at his hands gripped in his lap, hating to meet her eyes. "As soon as I came to myself, all I could do was beat myself up with regrets. I don't know what else to say, Mallory. I'm getting help and I'm trying to do better about situations like this that pull me back into the past."

She shook her head. "I think it's ironic how you've been concerned about the way my breakdown might affect your life, when the truth is that your emotional problems have caused more difficulty between us than mine."

Lucas winced, trying to decide what to say.

Suzannah put her head in the door. "Are you done with 'pologizing, Daddy?"

"Yes he's all finished," Mallory said and the tone of her words troubled him.

Nonnie followed Suzannah into the bedroom. "Lucas, you need to go downstairs to talk to Beau and Andy now. There's more news we had to deal with today. They need to talk to you about it."

"Go on downstairs," Mallory added. "I'll be fine, and Suzannah and I need to share some girl time together."

Seeing that he wouldn't get more private time with Mallory anyway now, Lucas agreed, getting up from his chair to start toward the door.

He trudged down the stairs, feeling even more like a heel after hearing Mallory's words to him.

Beau looked up from the kitchen table as he came in. "Did you make an effort to set things straight with Mallory?" he asked, direct as always.

"Yes, sir," he answered.

"How'd she take your apology?"

He shrugged, not sure how to answer.

Beau gave him a worried look. "Son, you need to get this problem of yours worked out. It's important to be there for people when they need you, even when it's messy and emotional...." His words drifted off.

"I got some more counseling last night from Perry Ammons," he answered. "He said I flashed back to times when Cecily would get overly emotional, to times when the first thing I thought of was to get Suzannah away from her and safe." He rubbed his neck. "I'm working to improve."

Lucas's eyes moved to Andy, who still had red eyes and looked distraught. "Are you okay, Andy?" Lucas asked.

Andy shook his head.

"Sit down," Beau said. "Andy's got something he needs to tell you. He's already talked to Nonnie, Mallory, and me about it, but he needs to talk to you about it, too." Beau looked toward the other man with encouragement.

Lucas came over to sit down at the table.

Andy took a deep breath. "When I heard the report about Mallory, where she'd been and what she'd been doing there, something snapped in me. She might have been killed up there, trying to learn what happened to her daddy, trying to get resolution to that old mystery." His red eyes lifted to Lucas's. "If anything had happened to her, it would have been my fault."

"How do you see that?" Lucas asked, confused.

"It was my gunshot that accidently killed her daddy."

Lucas knew his mouth dropped open with surprise.

"Tell him what happened," Beau said.

"You know I was turkey hunting with Jarrett and Waylon Davis that day. We split up to hunt after we got up on the mountain, planning to meet back at a designated spot later. You can usually hunt better by yourself. A turkey hunter wants to be as quiet as possible in the field, walking slow, being careful not to make any noise. A hunter knows if he makes a wrong move and doesn't get a shot off right away, too, that the bird will be gone. A turkey's senses are real keen."

Andy swallowed hard. "Hunters usually imitate a hen to call a gobbler into gun range. You wear camouflage so you can blend in with your surroundings. I was in an open area where I could see for about a hundred feet, when I started to draw a response from my calling. It was obvious to me later that Jarrett came to the same open area from another direction, both of us hearing and spotting the same bird."

He gave Lucas a sorrowful look. "When I got off a shot I watched the turkey take flight and realized I'd missed, even shot in the wrong direction at a false noise. Probably a critter, I thought. I didn't even go check, just moved on knowing I wouldn't get another opportunity to shoot there again."

Beau added a comment. "Andy and Jarret were both hunting not too far from Chessy Bohanan's cabin."

"When I met back up with Waylon later," Andy continued. "Jarrett wasn't there. Waylon and I waited a long time and then came on down to the house here, figuring maybe something happened and that Jarrett came back early for some reason. That was in the days before cell phones and such."

"Of course, then the search began," Beau added. "Later, near dark, I got a call from Chessy, who'd found Jarrett."

Andy uttered a sound of despair. "I went up with the sheriff, Beau, and Waylon to get Jarrett. When we found him, I didn't realize at first I'd been the shooter. But something about the location kept niggling at my remembrance. Later I went back up there, walked the area and found the spot where I'd fired off my shot and I realized what probably happened. By then, it was pretty well established that Jarrett's death was a tragic shooting accident and somehow I couldn't find it in myself to come forward." He dropped his head. "I loved that boy like one of my own; I love Beau and Nonnie. I hated to think that forever more they'd never look at me again in the same way, always seeing me as the man that shot their only son if I told what happened."

Andy rubbed his neck. "But I couldn't deal with keeping it to myself anymore after Mallory almost getting killed yesterday. What if something happened to her looking more for the answer that I held?"

"You did the right thing coming to us," Beau said. "I know it was only an accident."

Andy rubbed a shaking hand through his hair. "I admit, too, that I knew Waylon would remember the turkey call, that Lucas found at the cabin, as one of mine. An old man I knew hand-carved that thing for me. It had his initials and the date he made it carved on the back. Waylon would remember it. I was always bragging about what a great turkey call it was. I must have dropped it where Jarrett was killed when I went back looking. I sat down in that spot that day where we found him, behind the remnants of an old settlers' wall, and squalled like a baby."

Lucas considered all he'd heard Andy say. "Do you think Chessy found the turkey call later after you were there?"

"I expect so. I saw the old man as I started back down the mountain that day. He just stood there and watched me for a time. I always wondered if he knew, but he never said anything."

"Chessy might have witnessed the shooting or he might have watched the spot to see if anyone would come back," Beau said. "It explains why he kept those old clippings and the turkey call. He must have known. Perhaps he intended to tell someone someday. I guess we'll never know since he's long dead now."

"How did Mallory handle this?" Lucas asked. "She'd already been through a lot already without hearing this about her father today."

"Spoken more like the man I've come to know and love," Beau said in a quiet voice, shaking his head before Andy plowed on with his story..

"I know it was a lot to hit her with," Andy admitted. "I told Nonnie and Beau first, but they thought I should go ahead and tell Mallory, too. She was real sweet and kind about it. Nicer than I deserved, considering I'd kept all this hidden from everyone all these years." His eyes found Beau's. "I can see now you all  needed resolution. That you needed to know what happened, even if you had to learn it was my accidental shot that killed your boy."

The rest of the day flew by in a blur. Lucas and Beau still had to talk to the sheriff about the theft of the car from the resort, and Lucas had to meet with the group of guests staying at Retreat House, who'd had a car stolen, to try to explain what happened. On a good note, the group's concern for Mallory, and what she endured at the hands of the thieves, dulled the anger they'd shown earlier about one of their vehicles being stolen.

With as little sleep as Lucas got the night before, he felt exhausted by the end of the day. When he stopped by to see Mallory again the next day, Nonnie said she was taking a nap. The following morning, Lucas boarded the plane to fly to Scottsdale. He hated leaving at this particular time, but he'd committed to this Pro-Am Tournament a year ago and he knew they'd personally advertised him in their promotions. Several of his golfing friends were coming for the tournament, including many who lived in Scottsdale that he looked forward to seeing again. Lucas had also agreed to speak to the local Rotary Group on Thursday and to enjoy dinner with Chet, Kathy and the kids on Thursday night. He knew he could talk to Chet then, too, to learn if he might be open to leave the PGA Tour to come work at the resort.

Flying back from Scottsdale on Sunday afternoon, Lucas experienced a short wait on one of the airlines because of weather problems. He found himself smiling and thinking of Mallory then, remembering their interlude on the plane when they first met and remembering many other sweet memories of their time together. He was glad he had at least one more week to spend with her. Maybe she'd decide to stay on a few extra weeks in August, too. There were things he wanted to talk out, things he wanted to say. He hoped their time together could help to heal the way he'd let her down after her encounter with the car thieves.

After picking up his car at the airport, Lucas drove straight to Wingate House to see Mallory, even before going to Elizabeth's to pick up Suzannah. He needed to see her again, wanted to see her. And he itched to be alone with her.

"She's not here," Nonnie said, after he knocked and let himself in the kitchen where she worked on dinner.

"When will she be back?"

She turned to glance at him with a pitying look. "She's gone back to Savannah, Lucas. Didn't anyone tell you?"

He felt like someone punched him in the stomach. "I didn't think she was going back for at least another week."

Nonnie gave him a studied glance. "I think she decided it was time to go on back a little early."

Lucas didn't need for her to tell him why.

# CHAPTER 23

Over the next weeks, Mallory gradually began to settle back into her life and work in Savannah again. After her episode with the thieves, she decided Lucas's trip to Arizona offered her the perfect opportunity to slip away while he was gone. She knew it a little cowardly, but she wanted to avoid a parting scene with him. Saying goodbye to Suzannah, her grandparents, Elizabeth, Robert, and Abby proved hard enough.

Mallory claimed several reasons for heading back early, but she doubted she fooled Nonnie and Beau with her rationales. In truth, she really did need to get her townhouse cleaned out before she settled back into work. All her mother's things were still there. And she needed to attend a scheduled meeting relating to her mother's small estate.

Today, back at work full-time again, Mallory was lunching with Nancy Franklin, the other associate editor at Whittier. Nancy had been Mallory's friend and mentor since she first started work at the publishing company.

"I thought we'd walk down to Firefly's," Nancy said as they headed down the steps of the renovated historic building Whittier Publishing called home.

Mallory glanced across the street toward the fountain in the middle of Lafayette Square and at the gracious old oaks lining the park's brick lined pathways.

Nancy slowed to look across at the park, too. "Pretty isn't it?"

"It is. Have you ever regretted leaving New York?'

"You mean when David's father died and David decided to relocate the publishing company to Savannah?"

"Yes. You'd lived in New York for a long time and both your sons live there."

"Perhaps you don't know I grew up in Virginia, just outside of Richmond. I moved to New York with my husband Dean with a job transfer and accepted a job at Whittier as a copyeditor. I'd done editing before, plus an assortment of other tasks with my father's printing company, while raising our two small boys. Going to work at Whittier fit skills I already had experience in. As an English major, my only other job prospect at the time was to teach high school, and I wasn't really interested in that."

The two women cut across to Harris Street, passing the Cathedral of St. John's and a group of tourists taking photos.

"I forgot you came from Virginia originally." Mallory picked up the conversation again.

"My blood is more southern than it might seem, even though I lived in New York for so long. After Dean died, I found myself hungry for a change, too. Everything in our apartment and neighborhood reminded me of him. The boys were in college and I was on my own." She shrugged. "I jumped at the chance to relocate when David decided to move Whittier's main office to Savannah. He was ready for a change from the city and the move has worked out well for the company. As for the boys, I see them every time I fly to our New York branch for business meetings or when I attend a book conference or event there. It's been a good change for me."

"David said it wasn't until his father died that he could consider the move."

"Yes. His dad wasn't for it, but David and his wife Arlene already owned a vacation house here on Tybee Island and they loved the area. David had considered a move for a long time."

Nancy and Mallory slowed as they neared the café, glancing across at Troup Square, one of Savannah's smaller city parks. The two soon settled into a favorite table at the picturesque restaurant across from the park, chatting with the waiter, deciding what to order. Both settled on their usual—Firefly's house chowder with a side salad.

Mallory studied her friend as she talked about a few business matters. Nancy was a trim, attractive woman in her middle years with short, dark no-nonsense hair and thoughtful gray eyes behind silver-rimmed glasses.

"How are you getting along since coming back from your grandparents?" she asked Mallory, changing the subject.

"Fine," Mallory answered.

"I need to admit to you that one reason I invited you to lunch today is because David and I are worried about you."

Mallory's mouth dropped open in surprise. "I am fine, Nancy. I saw Dr. Henry when I got back. My checkup was perfect, and he saw no concerns. I actually recovered quickly and I could have returned to work a few weeks after I left Savannah. But as you know, David insisted on additional time off."

"I know all that." Nancy waved a hand. "But we both think you're carrying a new unhappiness related to your visit."

Mallory bit her lip. "What do you mean?"

"Quite frankly, it seems clear to us that you left Savannah with problems over one man but then came back with greater problems over another."

"Who have you been talking to?" Mallory snapped the words out before she thought. "Did Ethan say something to you?"

"I'm not even going to ask how Ethan is involved in this, but your response tells me there *was* someone. You should know by now it's not healthy to keep things in emotionally. When you have problems, you should share them with your friends."

Mallory sighed. "I hated to say anything. I'd already caused what I thought were enough concerns for everyone. I did meet someone I developed some feelings for but he wasn't ready for a more serious relationship, and I wasn't certain I wanted the changes it might require either."

She told Nancy about Lucas then, about meeting him on the

airplane, about how their relationship had grown and developed but always had problems. And she told her about Suzannah.

"Well, after listening to you, I hope you're not going to try to convince me you didn't fall in love with this man."

Mallory's eyes flew open at the words.

"You haven't even acknowledged your own feelings to yourself yet, have you?" Nancy laughed. "I would think, as a romance editor, you—of all people—would recognize all the ways you've tried to deny your own feelings to yourself."

Mallory picked at her salad, thinking over Nancy's words. "I probably haven't wanted to acknowledge those feelings since I know nothing will come of them."

"Are you sure?"

She sighed. "You haven't seen him running after me, have you?"

"Is that what you want?"

"I don't even know." She shook her head, confused.

Nancy sent her a small smile. "It's funny when we women who read about romance every day, and should know more about it than anyone, still have all the same old problems as anyone else dealing with love when it comes our way."

"I healed from Ethan. I can heal from this time with Lucas, too," Mallory said with a stubborn tone.

"Are you completely past your old feelings with Ethan? He still keeps stopping by the office and calling often enough."

Mallory wrinkled her nose. "He's had trouble accepting our relationship is over. It's not as though I haven't told him often enough, Nancy."

"Going after what he wants is one of the hallmarks that made Ethan so successful in business."

"Yes, I agree. And I do know Ethan sees me as a good potential acquisition, but that understanding troubles me. I don't really believe Ethan loves me, even though he values me."

"I see." Nancy laughed.

"Look, "Mallory said, leaning toward her friend. "I'm sorry I've acted a little distracted since getting back, working my way past this relationship with Lucas, but I don't think my work has suffered."

"No, your work is fine. David and I are simply concerned about you because we care. So do the others at Whittier. It is a small company. We're close. It's hard for one of us to hurt and go through something difficult without the others picking up on it."

Mallory pushed her finished salad plate back, thinking about this. "Should I say something about it at one of our meetings?"

"If you want to." Nancy smiled. "Sometimes talking about something keeps people from speculating about it."

Mallory frowned. "I have acted secretive about my time at my grandparents, not talking about it like people usually do after a vacation, obviously kicking up everyone's radar."

"You know we all love you, Mallory. We only want you to be happy."

The waiter stopped by, interrupting their discussion.

"Do you miss your husband Dean?" Mallory asked, shifting the subject after the waiter left them.

"Every day," Nancy answered honestly. "I felt robbed to lose him so early. He missed seeing the boys graduate from college, missed their weddings. He missed seeing our first grandchildren. At every family vacation when the boys bring their families down, and when we rent one of the beach houses nearby, I feel the void of not having him in our lives. I really loved him, Mallory. We had such a warm, comfortable relationship. We were best friends as well as sweethearts."

"I'm sorry I brought it up."

"Don't be. I carry only good memories and no regrets." Nancy paused. "You talk about Lucas and Suzannah with such warmth. Please think carefully about your choices, Mallory. Real love doesn't come along often. Don't let it slip away and have regrets."

Mallory made some mundane comments in reply and then changed the subject again. But later, back in her office, she pulled a familiar packet of photos out of her desk drawer to study them, photos of Lucas and Suzannah. They had stolen her heart more than she wanted to admit, but what could she do differently than she did? Lucas hadn't been ready to consider entering into another serious relationship, still locked in old fears and issues relating to Cecily and their unhappy marriage. He'd made it clear in many ways he wasn't ready to move on. If love had begun to develop, it was only on her part.

She tried to settle her mind later as she walked home along the quiet tree-shaded streets of the city to her townhouse on Taylor Street. She lived only a few blocks from the Whittier offices on Whitefield Square and she enjoyed her walks to and from work. As she neared her pretty brick townhouse with its hexagonal front and wrought iron balcony on the upper level, she scowled to see a familiar figure leaning against a car parked by the sidewalk.

"Ethan, what are you doing here?"

"I wanted to see you," he said, walking forward to kiss her on the cheek. "You've been home three weeks now and we still haven't had our dinner out together. I made reservations at Drayton's on Forsythe Park for this evening. I reserved the table looking out over the park in our favorite corner."

Mallory twisted the strap on her purse, trying to think what to say. "I don't think that's a good idea, Ethan."

"We've been friends a long time. Can't friends share dinner together?" He smiled at her, a polished warm smile she remembered very well.

Her eyes traveled over him. He was a handsome man, dressed impeccably in one of the dark suits he wore for work every day.

He straightened his tie, aware that she was studying him. "What do you say, Mallory? We still have a little time before our reservation. You can go in and freshen up if you like. I brought the car, but we can walk if you'd prefer."

She moved over to stand by the steps leading to her door. "Ethan, I don't want to continue in a relationship with you, even a friends only relationship. If I held strong feelings for you before, those ended when you chose to indulge in an affair while we were practically engaged."

"I tried to explain to you that woman meant nothing to me."

"Well, she meant something to me. I want someone who will be true to me. You disappointed me, not only with the affair but by not being the support I needed while my mother was ill."

"I hardly knew your mother," he interrupted crossly.

"Yes, but she *was* my mother. I needed understanding while she lay ill and dying, the kind of understanding I'd have offered to you if one of your parents became seriously ill and came to live with you." Mallory knew he valued his relationship with his parents and she watched him scowl considering her words.

"Perhaps I might have offered more caring," he suggested. "I can work on improving in that area." He smiled then, as if that resolved everything.

"Ethan, I simply don't care for you anymore the way I did."

He reached out to put a hand over hers on the wrought iron railing beside the steps, moving closer to her. "I don't believe that, *bella*. We became sweethearts; we fell in love. We planned our future together."

"That was then." She pulled her hand away and stepped back to get out of close proximity to him. "I don't feel the same way anymore."

His voice grew cross. "It's that man you met when you visited your grandparents, isn't it? Well, I don't see him here—asking to take you to dinner, talking of a future with you. Do you?"

Mallory felt a wince in her heart at his words. "There isn't someone else in my life right now, Ethan. I simply don't want to continue a relationship with you. I'm sorry. I don't mean to hurt you, but there it is."

He studied her unhappily. "Perhaps in time you will feel differently."

"No, I don't think so." She tried to lighten the moment. "But thank you for suggesting dinner tonight. I do wish you continued success and happiness in your business and in your life. I'm sure we'll see each other now and then around the city and at events we both enjoy."

He backed away, jangling his keys. "This isn't goodbye, Mallory.

I'm just giving you more time to think. You're still not fully back to yourself after all you've been through."

She turned to head into her front door, deciding it pointless to argue further. Ethan had always been a sore loser, hating to admit defeat in any conflictional situation, even when his own actions contributed to the problem. He would see in time she meant what she said.

Letting herself in her townhouse, she walked through the living room, past the dining area, also used as her office, and into the kitchen. She tucked the remains of a leftover casserole in the oven to heat before going upstairs to change. Glancing out the kitchen window, she saw a white cat sitting on the wall behind the patio, grooming. It made her think of Lily and the kittens. She knew from Elizabeth's calls and texts that the kittens were nearly ready to give away to new homes.

Shaking the thoughts away, Mallory walked upstairs to her bedroom to change. A little later she brought her dinner upstairs, moving through the second bedroom—empty now of all her mother's things—to sit on the balcony where she could look out over Whitefield Square. A small crowd had gathered around the gazebo for a wedding, a frequent occurrence in the park. As she watched, a man separated himself from the group to walk over and pick up a small, blond girl, swinging her around and laughing with her. They looked like Lucas and Suzannah. Pushing her dinner aside, Mallory closed her eyes and wept. *How could two months change her life so much?* She wondered. *And how long would it take to get back to herself?*

The next day she ate alone on her lunch break at another café near the office. While at lunch, she purposefully studied a newspaper to look for local events to attend on the upcoming weekend. Perhaps she'd call one of her friends to drive to the beach at Tybee Island or go to a movie.

Heading back into the Whittier offices, she saw that Tina was not back at her front desk spot yet—probably off to the post office while on lunch break. Moving into the large entry area, she heard

David's voice calling her from his office. Pushing open his door, she stopped, freezing in place.

"Mallory!" cried a high familiar voice as Suzannah James raced across the room to throw herself into Mallory's arms. "We've been waiting for you to get back and visiting with Mr. David while we waited."

Across the child's shoulders she saw Lucas stand up from the chair where he'd been sitting across from David's desk. She turned her attention back to Suzannah, too overcome to meet his eyes.

David spoke up then. "You had some company arrive while you were out for lunch," he said, with a twitch of a smile at the corner of his lips. "We've been getting better acquainted while we waited for you."

"We told David we need you back, Mallory," Suzannah said. "We need you to help with the kittens, and I need you to read me my books at night. It's not the same since you've been gone. We miss you. Daddy isn't as good as you to help me fix my hair or to help me decide what matches good with my clothes. I'm starting kindergarten soon and I need to look nice. You help me with my letters and my numbers, too." She began to cry. "We need you to come back and be family with us."

"That's really sweet Suzannah. I'm glad you came to visit, but I have my work here. David needs me, too."

As Mallory put Suzannah down, she ran across the room to climb onto David's lap. "We've been talking to David, too, Mallory. We've made plans so we can all be together and David says it's okay with him."

Mallory found Lucas's eyes then and raised her eyebrows over the words.

"I tell you what," David said, getting up and taking Suzannah's hand. "Why don't you and I take a minute and walk across the park to see the pretty gazebo. Would you like that, Suzannah?"

She hesitated. "Maybe Mallory and Daddy can go, too."

He leaned over to whisper to her. "I think maybe they might like to be alone for a few minutes, don't you?"

Suzannah sent a look back and forth between them. "Oh," she said in a surprisingly adult tone. "I think that's a good idea."

As soon as Mallory heard the front door close, she said, "What are you doing here, Lucas?"

"Don't you know, Mallory?" His anguished eyes met hers. "I can't get along without you. I need you."

He walked the few steps across the room and swept her into a fierce hug. "How could you have left me like you did? You didn't even say goodbye. I know I had another flashback when you came in all upset after getting away from those thieves, and again I'm sorry. I told you what happened. I've been dying since you've been gone. And Suzannah has been crying. Surely you know how I feel about you?"

She pulled back from him, shaking her head. "Actually, I don't know how you feel. You've never said."

"I love you, you wonderful girl. I love your sexy tall body, your thoughtful eyes that can see right through me. Your lips I want to kiss every time I see them. I love how you fit against me when I hold you. I love the way you smile and laugh and the way you feel when I wrap my arms around you."

"Stop, you're making me cry," she said, tears beginning to slide down her cheeks. "You know you don't like emotions like that."

"I love it when you cry," he said, brushing away her tears with his finger and then kissing another tear away. "It's my new joy. Look how beautiful you are when you do it? You are your own special, wonderful person and there will be lots of times over our life together when you can cry and it can be whenever you want to or need to. I probably will, too."

She let her eyes travel over his strong, wonderful face to see if the words he said felt true and she saw a tear now at the corner of his eye.

"Please don't say you don't love me or you might see me start to cry and get emotional, Mallory."

"Is that right?" She gave him a small, smug smile.

"That's right." He wrapped her in his arms and kissed her again, spinning her heart into a whirlwind of happy emotions. How she'd missed him. Even more than she realized.

He kissed her eyes, her cheeks, ran his hands through her hair, down her arms and over her back, pulling her snug against him until every inch touched. Then he deepened their kiss into one of rich passion.

Mallory felt her knees grow weak and she knew she uttered a soft little moan as their emotions heightened.

He cupped her face in his hands, his dark eyes gazing into hers. "I love you with all my heart M.T. Wingate. Maybe I did from that first night on the airplane. I know you got into my mind from that first interlude we shared."

She threaded a hand into his hair and then pulled him against her for another kiss, so joyously glad to hold him close again.

"You know you're killing me, making me wait to hear those words from you that you know I want to hear," he said against her ear.

"Maybe I'm waiting to hear some more words from you. You know I told you at the cascades when we hiked that I yearned for a constant love in my life, someone to develop a forever relationship with."

He paused, thinking for a moment. "Come on, I'm going to do this right." He grabbed her hand and pulled her along with him out the front door, across the street and into the park, heading toward the big white gazebo where he saw Suzannah and David.

At the tree-shaded gazebo, he pulled her inside the open building to stop beside beside Suzannah and David, sitting on the gazebo's bench, before dropping to one knee in front of her.

"Mallory Taylor Wingate," he said. "In front of these witnesses I'm declaring my love for you—for now and forever—and asking you to be my wife, to have and to hold, in sickness and in health, in sorrows and in joys, for all the days of my life. I promise you I will take tender care of you and provide for you, encourage your dreams and talents, cherish and protect you. I know Suzannah will love you, too, won't you Suzannah?"

She nodded, her eyes as big as saucers.

Mallory put a hand over her heart, a few more tears trickling down her face. "I guess I'll have to say yes after all that," she said. "Besides, I love you, too." She pulled him to his feet and kissed him, not even caring that Suzannah, David, and a small group in the park watched it all.

"Yeah!" cried Suzannah, launching herself into their hug to add herself into their joy.

Pulling away from Lucas, Mallory's eyes moved to David. "I hope you understand, David."

"Oh, I do, and I'm not letting you go just because you and Lucas are getting married. I expect to be at your wedding, and after you two enjoy a nice honeymoon, I expect you back at work."

Mallory raised her eyebrows in surprise.

Lucas pulled her over to the bench that circled around the inside of the gazebo and sat down with her. "When I talked to David earlier, I told him I'd give up the resort and move here to be with you. Suzannah and I decided we could move here if that would make you happiest."

Mallory felt herself start to cry again.

Suzannah pulled on her arm to get her attention. "But David said he thought it would be best if we shared you."

Mallory looked at David, confused.

"You've edited from the resort over the last months," David said. "It's worked out pretty well. Lucas says he can let you fly down every month or so to spend a week working with us on things we need to hammer out and talk about more fully."

Mallory's eyes moved to Lucas's.

He smiled at her. "David said you owned a nice townhouse only a few blocks away. We'll keep it. You can come down to stay in it when you need to for work, and when I can get away from work, I'll come with you."

"And me, too," said Suzannah.

Lucas laughed. "And you, too, kiddo. In summertime and at vacations, we can come down as a family. Mallory can do a little work and we'll have a good time around the area seeing Savannah together and enjoying the beasch."

Trying to take all this in, Mallory looked toward David Whittier's smiling face. "Do you think this will work?"

"Absolutely," he patted her cheek. "I talked you into staying with me when your mother moved those years ago. Don't you think for a minute I'm letting you get away from me simply because you've decided to get married now. You're one of my best editors. I need you. We'll see to it that we work something out." He grinned. "Besides Lucas agreed to help me with my golf game when he comes down."

Later in the day, Lucas and Mallory sat on the balcony of Mallory's townhouse looking out over Whitefield Square. They shared a glass of wine together from the bottle David Whittier sent home with them, after the Whittier staff shared a celebrational dinner with them at the historic Olde Pink House Restaurant on Abercorn.

"Suzannah's out like a lark," Lucas said, settling comfortably into the balcony chair. "She's had a big day. It was nice of you to say we could stay here and not go to the hotel where I made reservations." He looked across at her in the deepening darkness. "I could still go over there if you'd prefer it or if it worries you for me to stay."

"I tucked Suzannah into my bed to sleep with me." She sent him a smirk. "I think I'll be safe in my room with her as a chaperone. I have another bedroom for you."

"Yeah, and Suzannah is already talking about how she wants to redecorate it. She wants cat pictures on the walls."

"I'm not surprised." Mallory smiled. "Who's keeping those kittens while you're here?"

"Beau and Nonnie." He reached over to take her hand. "I asked their permission before I came down to propose."

"Is that right?"

"Yeah, and don't get mad, but I had to call them earlier this evening to tell them you said yes. Beau all but threatened my job if I didn't call."

She laughed. "We were so busy tonight, I forgot to think about calling earlier, but I planned to in a few minutes."

"I think your call can wait unless you just want to talk to them yourself."

"No, I'm happy simply basking in the wonder of this moment." As she turned to look at him, she felt a worry line cross her forehead. "Are you sure we can afford to keep this place? I can stay in a motel when I come down to Savannah or I can stay with Nancy. I'm sure it would be all right."

"I like this place," he said. "I expect to enjoy it when I come down, too. I think I'll pay out the mortgage, though, and maybe Nancy can help you find someone to clean it and check on it when we're not here." He leaned over to kiss her again. "This is one of those times when I'm grateful for all the pro golf money I earned. It made this situation work out better for us."

"Would you really have moved here and left the resort?"

He nodded. "Definitely. While I was in Arizona I hired one of my old golf friends Chet Mincie as the new pro shop manager and assistant golf pro. As Beau said, having Chet will free my time so I can travel more, come down here with you when we need to. It's only a day's drive from Tennessee, not far really. We can come for a long weekend every month, if you like, so you can attend the monthly planning meetings at Whittier. David already filled me in on the normal working schedule." He leaned over to kiss her. "Chet can take my place at the resort if needed in future or if you find this back and forth arrangement doesn't work for you."

"No." She leaned against him, happy to be with him again. "The resort is a part of who I am, too. I came to realize that when I stayed there after being ill. I want to raise Suzannah and our children there. It's my heritage and theirs, too."

Mallory saw him smiling.

"I didn't mean to assume anything about having more children," she said, smiling back at him. "We haven't talked about that. Do you want more children?"

"I'd love more children. Suzannah has her heart set on it, too." He let his mouth find hers again in a very sizzling kiss. "I'm looking forward to making those children, too."

She giggled, snuggling against him. "Where do you think we should get married?" she asked.

"I hope you won't get mad, but Beau and Nonnie, with my sister Elizabeth and the staff's help at the resort, are already going crazy planning a big gala wedding to be held there." He wrinkled his nose. "I kept telling them that a wedding is something you and I should decide on, but they didn't pay much attention to me."

She laughed. "I can only imagine how excited Nonnie is. You know how she loves to plan things."

"Yes, and Elizabeth and the events coordinator Lois Milton are almost as bad. They already enlisted the chef team, Josh and Rachel Kirkpatrick, to work on the reception dinner. Do you mind?"

"No." She laid her head on his shoulder again. "It's wonderful they're all so happy about it. We're blessed to have so many people in our lives to love and care about us, aren't we?"

"We are." Lucas looked out across the old oak trees into the now quiet park. "The gazebo is pretty even at night, isn't it?"

"It is." She laughed. "I'll never look at it again as long as I live without remembering that you proposed to me in that gazebo right in front of David, Suzannah, and all those people."

"Well, I needed to create a memorable moment for an editor of romance books, didn't I?"

She smiled. "Did you really think about that?"

"Well, sure. I know you read romantic stories all the time. My plan originally was to propose at a fancy, candlelit restaurant later, but when you pushed me to the moment in David's office, I had to improvise."

"Well, I like the way you improvised."

"You'll find I'm good at improvising in a lot of ways." He nuzzled her neck with his lips before finding her mouth again in a long, sweet kiss.

"I like that word improvising," she said.

"We'll think up a lot of great words together, you and I, before it's over."

"I'm counting on it," she answered with a sweet sigh.

**A Reading Group Guide**

# THE INTERLUDE

# Lin Stepp

## About This Guide

The questions on the following pages are included
to enhance your group's reading of
Lin Stepp's *The Interlude*

# DISCUSSION QUESTIONS

1.  As the book opens, Mallory Wingate has experienced a minor nervous breakdown, a collapse or meltdown from the excessive stress in her life over the last two years. What stress factors led to this collapse? What treatment was advised? Why is Mallory on her way to her grandparents' resort? Have you or anyone you've know ever experienced a breakdown?

2.  In an odd twist of fate Lucas James happened to be on the same flight to Tennessee as Mallory, returning from a pro golf event. How did they first meet? What did you learn about Lucas and Mallory and their personalities in these scenes on the airplane? How did a friendship—and perhaps a little more—develop between them on their flight home?

3. Book titles are often drawn from events or scenes in a book and can actually form running themes within the story. Where do you think the title *The Interlude* came from in this book? Did Lucas or Mallory ever expect to see each other again after their chance meeting? Where did they next meet? How did the book title, *The Interlude*, and its theme play out again in other parts of the story?

4.  Although Lucas was initially attracted to Mallory, why did he not want to pursue a relationship with her after they meet again? Do you think he was justified in his concerns? Besides the fact that Mallory was his boss's granddaughter, what past factors in Lucas' life made him wary of getting involved with anyone with mental problems? Did he equate his past problems with his wife Cecily to his concerns about Mallory correctly?

5. Friends and family members can have both good and bad influences in our lives. How did Lucas's sister Elizabeth help both Mallory and Lucas? What things did you learn about Elizabeth and Robert as the book moved along? Did you like them? Did you enjoy the book scenes involving Abby and Suzannah? How did time with Suzannah also help Mallory?

6. The setting for this book is in the Greenbrier and Pittman Center area of the Great Smoky Mountains, a lovely, scenic region about halfway between Gatlinburg and Cosby. Have you ever visited in that area of the Smokies? The Millhouse Resort in the book is fictitious but it is based on beautiful resorts of this type scattered around the mountains. Have you ever stayed on a resort like the one depicted in this novel? Many places in this book can actually be found in this area—the Emerts Cove Covered Bridge, the Glen Cardwell Heritage Museum, the Ramsay Cascades Trail, and more. Do you enjoy books that introduce you to real places you can visit—or remind you of past visits?

7. Looking at other characters in the story, what did you like about Beau and Nonnie Wingate? What was the history of their resort? What was Beau's title at the resort and what attributes made him a good leader? What types of groups did Nonnie host for luncheons at the Butterfly Tea Room? How had Beau and Nonnie become closely involved with Lucas and his little daughter Suzannah? What had happened to their only son?

8. Lucas wasn't the only one with personal problems in his background. What sort of problems had Mallory known with her mother Delores Wingate? Do you think Delores was a good mother to Mallory and a good wife to Jarrett? When you heard Mallory tell Beau and Nonnie more about Delores's early life, did it make you like Delores more or less? What advice did Delores give Mallory about men that might have caused relational issues for Mallory? What illness brought Delores to live with Mallory?

9. Mental and emotional issues are a running theme in this book, highlighting the fact that people can be unkind or lack understanding about individuals who experience emotional problems. Why do you think that is? Do you know much about the history of mental illness and how people with disorders were viewed and treated in the past? Did you learn more about mental and emotional health concerns while reading this book and how they impact not only the one suffering with them but those around them? What mental illnesses and emotional problems were depicted in this book?

10. Fun coincidences in this book, just as in real life, occur to draw Mallory and Lucas closer together, like meeting on the airplane, again at the resort, or running into each other in the cemetery later. When Lucas walks Mallory to the garden gate to say goodnight one night, he asks her about the name of the flowering shrub beside the gate, knowing her grandmother taught her the names of most of the flowers at the resort. Why did Mallory hedge to tell him the flower's name? What happened when she did? Can you recall any random coincidences in your life like these?

11. Suzannah becomes a major character in this story. What did you most enjoy about this child? How did she help to encourage a relationship between Mallory and Lucas? What scenes did you most enjoy that included Suzannah? Have you noticed in your own life how children can often honestly and guilelessly express the things adults are reluctant to put into words? How did Suzannah sometimes do this? Did you or a child you know well ever have a favorite doll like EdithAnn they insisted on taking almost everywhere?

12. Several women's groups meet regularly in Nonnie Wingate's Butterfly Tea Room. Do you remember the names of some of the clubs and civic groups that met there? The twelve women in

the little Monday Group, including Nonnie, had been friends for many years. Tilly Walker is a member of this group. What was Tilly like? Why did she and her husband Bobby Joe divorce? Was Tilly happy about that? Mallory remembers Tilly, even after many years, as "the ditz, a slightly neurotic and self-absorbed worrier." Beau called her "a silly, emotional sort of female, worrying over something all the time, seeing trouble behind every door." Are these descriptions accurate? How did these traits and other health issues escalate into real trouble for Tilly—and for Mallory and Suzannah? What factors about Tilly's personality and ways remind you of people you know?

13. Mallory has had a minor breakdown as this book begins, but as the story continues you learn Lucas is having emotional problems of his own. What problems is Lucas experiencing? As the book starts, is Lucas aware of them? How do they affect his relationships with others and especially with Mallory? What situation brings Lucas's problem to the attention of his boss? What does Beau demand Lucas do? What happens later in Lucas's sessions with Perry Ammons? Did you like Perry and how he counseled? Would you like to have a counselor like this if you had problems?

14. Three types of thefts are going on in this story and the main characters soon begin to wonder who is behind each— the same people or different ones? The first theft resolved is at the golf pro shop. What theft happened there and who was responsible? The second theft uncovered is at the tearoom. Who was behind those small thefts? Finally, an understanding of the criminals behind the car thefts is identified. Who stumbles upon those thieves accidentally? Did you guess the identity of any of these mysteries before they were revealed in the book?

15. How Jarrett Wingate—Mallory's father—died is another mystery in this book. How was Jarrett killed? What did the police

investigation at the time conclude? Gladys stirs up questions in Mallory's mind about her father's death, and later Lucas finding the tin box at Chessy Bohanan's cabin, creates more questions. What was in the box? What item in that box proved to be most condemning? What happens when Mallory later goes to the old cabin to look for more clues? How does this finally resolve the mystery of Jarrett's death as well as the mystery of the car thefts ongoing?

16. Lucas's and Mallory's relationship bounced up and down through the book. How did Lucas's response after the incident at the Bohanan cabin prove the last straw to Mallory in continuing to foster hope that their relationship would grown into more? When Lucas flies out west to play in a charity golf tournament, he comes home to immediately go to Mallory, hoping to further restore their problems. But Mallory is not there. Where has she gone?

17. Several characters in Savannah played critical roles in this book—David Whittier and Nancy Franklin at Whittier Publishing and Ethan Broussard, Mallory's former love interest. What did you think of each? How were David and Nancy a support to Mallory throughout the story? How was Ethan Broussard the opposite? What did Ethan do that convinced Mallory she wanted no further relationship with him? How did he persist in trying to win Mallory after she left Savannah and even after she returned?

18. How did this story end and how did Lucas and Mallory get together again? What part did Suzannah play in that? How did David Whittier help resolve the issue about Mallory's work with his company? Did you feel that everything resolved to your satisfaction in this story?

About the Author

# Lin Stepp

CKatie Riley

Dr. Lin Stepp is a *New York Times, USA Today,* and *Publishers Weekly* Best-Selling international author. A native Tenessean, she also works as both a businesswoman and as an educator. Although not actively teaching now, she is still on adjunct faculty at Tusculum College where she taught research and a variety of psychology and counseling courses for almost twenty years. Her business background includes over twenty-five years in marketing, sales, production art, and regional publishing.

Stepp writes engaging, heart-warming contemporary Southern fiction with a strong sense of place and has twelve published novels each set in different locations around the Smoky Mountains. Her last two novels were *Lost Inheritance* (2018) and *Daddy's Girl* (2017), with previous novels including *Welcome Back* (2016), *Saving Laurel Springs* (2015), *Makin' Miracles* (2015), and *Down by the River* (2014) published by Kensington of New York. Other earlier titles include: *Second Hand Rose* (2013), *Delia's Place* (2012), *For Six Good Reasons* (2011), *Tell Me About Orchard Hollow* (2010), and *The Foster Girls* (2009). In addition Stepp and her husband J.L. Stepp have co-authored a Smoky Mountains hiking guidebook titled *The Afternoon Hiker* (2014) and a Tennessee state parks guidebook *Discovering Tennessee State Parks* (2018). Stepp has also just released another new title *Claire at Edisto* (2019), the first in her new Edisto Trilogy.

For more about Stepp's work and to keep up with her monthly blog, ongoing appearances and signing events, see: *www.linstepp.com.*

CPSIA information can be obtained
at www.ICGtesting.com
Printed in the USA
LVHW111927280419
615887LV00001B/1/P